PRAISE FOR *THE DEVILS OF CARDONA*

"What begins as a mystery becomes an adventure, a thrilling quest for justice on more levels than Mendoza (or the reader) expects. . . . In well-structured chapters and harrowing scenes, Carr allows glimpses into the behavior and actions of other characters, ratcheting the tension as crimes are solved and the criminals get their comeuppance. . . . [A] novel that is as exciting as it is enlightening from its first pages to its satisfying end." —*The New York Times Book Review*

"Matthew Carr's *The Devils of Cardona* is a page-turner in the proper sense. . . . A violent action-packed novel, with some surprising twists . . . Mr. Carr has written a gripping and enjoyable novel, and there is surely scope for his judge Mendoza to deal with other crimes and puzzles. But, inevitably, this book has a wider application and interest, given the state of the world today and the tensions between the Muslim and Christian, or Western, worlds." —*The Wall Street Journal*

"[An] engrossing historical thriller . . . A gripping tale." —*The Seattle Times*

"Fans of rich historical intrigue like Hilary Mantel's *Wolf Hall* or the engrossing 16th-century pageantry of Álvaro Enrigue's *Sudden Death* should consider Matthew Carr's historical fiction debut. . . . Fans of the genre will find much to enjoy." —*BookPage*

"Carr certainly delivers a powerful punch in his debut. *The Devils of Cardona* is also the perfect setup for a sequel, for Mendoza and his men have plenty of life left in them still." —*New York Journal of Books*

"*The Devils of Cardona* is one of those rare historical mysteries that is as thrilling as it is thoughtful. Aside from violence and philosophy, it encompasses political machinations and sexual intrigue and seems ripe for translation to the screen. In this day and age, its message of religious and social tolerance would be well served by being further disseminated, even as it is already beautifully delivered in this intelligent, entertaining book." —*Criminal Element*

"In this new novel, *The Devils of Cardona*, the author uses his knowledge of this history to weave a meticulously detailed story of intrigue, danger, sex, and suspense in sixteenth-century Spain. This religiously charged dramatic time and place filled with complex characters parallels our own time as Christianity and Islam are ideologically at war again." —*Monsters & Critics*

"While there's a mystery at the heart of *The Devils of Cardona*, the novel's strength lies in the historical details, as well as the lessons delivered about religious, racial, and sexual intolerance. The author examines a time and place torn by these conflicts that divided a town and its people. There's definitely a message for our own times in this book, but it is delivered with a light touch and strong, engaging characters."

—*Reviewing the Evidence*

"A spine-tingling thriller . . . A masterly recreation of a fascinating era."

—*Publishers Weekly*

"A religious, political, sexual jigsaw . . . An entertaining historical mystery."

—*Kirkus Reviews*

"*The Devils of Cardona* is a remarkably well-written and entertaining novel. Matthew Carr fills his work with compelling characters and handles his material—more than a little relevant for our times—with dazzling grace."

—David Liss, author of *The Day of Atonement*

"History and atmosphere, sex and superior storytelling, *The Devils of Cardona* has it all. A page-turning thriller, full of engaging male and female characters, with a great sense of time and place. A treat."

—Kate Mosse, *New York Times*–bestselling author of *Labyrinth*

"*The Devils of Cardona* delivers a gritty, meticulously detailed story of suspense in sixteenth-century Spain. Matthew Carr re-creates for us a dramatic time and place filled with complex characters and issues that resonate powerfully with our own time."

—Matthew Pearl, author of *The Dante Club* and *The Last Bookaneer*

"In Spain in the 1500s, the church could prove a murderous playground. In Matthew Carr's new novel, *The Devils of Cardona*, we're swept along on an investigation into the murder of a priest in a small Spanish town populated by mostly former Muslims. Magistrate Bernardo de Mendoza sets out to get to the bottom of the murder, ultimately falling into a complicated world of greed and faith."

—*Everyday eBook*

For Jane. *Siempre*.

FRANCE
Pau
PYRENEES MOUNTAINS
CROWN OF
CASTILE
Ebro River
Jaca
Tarazona
Huesca
Valladolid
Soria
Zaragoza
Barcelona
Duero River
Aranda de Duero
Segovia
CROWN OF
ARAGON
Mediterranean Sea
Madrid
PORTUGAL
N
Seville
Granada
© 2016 Meighan Cavanaugh

CHAPTER ONE

N THE EARLY HOURS OF MARCH 20, 1584, Padre Juan Panalles awoke from a drunken stupor to find his servant girl Inés lying naked beside him. It was the morning after the Day of the Beast, and the skinny little body that had briefly aroused him during the previous night's festivities now took up so much room that he prodded her awake with his elbow, nearly pushing her out of the narrow bed. Inés knew what was expected of her. She crawled sleepily out from under the blankets and slipped on her dress and tied back her hair in the murky half-light before padding from the room to prepare his breakfast.

The priest rolled over and squeezed his eyes shut in a vain attempt to ignore his parched tongue and throbbing temples. Finally he abandoned the effort and hoisted his heavy body upright. He sat on the edge of the bed in his nightshirt with his large feet resting on the cold tiled floor and grimaced at the acrid smell of sex, wine and stale beer and the sight of the sagging purse on the bedside table. He could not remember how much he had lost, or whether he had lost it on cards or dice, but he knew that it had been a bad night.

He told himself that there would be other games and better nights as he went out into the privy to piss and curse the shriveled cock that had led him again to stray from the path of virtue. He rinsed it clean and sponged his face and body before eating the bread, egg and ham that Inés had left him. After washing the food down with a glass of brandy, he changed into his vestments, first the white alb, then the amice draped over his shoulders, followed by the long black cape. Even when he had acquired at least the appearance of piety, the voice of his conscience told him that he was not fit to serve God or administer the holiest of sacraments. But in all his years in these mountains, he had never failed to celebrate the Eucharist no matter what he had done the night before.

Outside, the first red slats of light were spreading above the high peaks and the towering massif that separated God's chosen people from their enemies. He heard the stream flowing down into the side of the ravine, louder than usual as a result of the melting snows, and the first morning birds that he neither could name nor cared to name. Even though it was late March, his panting breath still gave off a cloud of steam as he stepped out into the courtyard adjoining the church, his sandals squeaking on the hard, stony ground with a heavy tread that anyone in the village could have recognized and which many of them had reason to fear and detest.

Father Panalles knew that his parishioners did not love him, but he had long since ceased to feel any remorse for the fact that a man of the cloth should be the object of fear and loathing. In another place he might have felt different, but not here, in Belamar de la Sierra. Its inhabitants were people from another world and time, savages and heretics who showed more affection for the black-faced performer dressed up as a bear that they dragged through the streets on the same day every year than they would ever feel for the sufferings of Jesus Christ. Even now, in the penultimate decade of the sixteenth century, they continued to believe that this pagan superstition could expunge all the year's accumulated evil from the town. But as he had told them often enough, the evil was inside them. It was something they carried in their blood, that was passed down through their mothers' milk and handed down from one generation to the next.

Such people could never be saved, not even by the holy apostles themselves, and since they could never willingly embrace the faith, then even the fact that they feared him was a kind of achievement. On this particular morning, however, he took no satisfaction from the power he held over them, but only bitterness, resentment and self-pity at the seven years he had wasted in these mountains when so many others who were just like him, and certainly no better, had obtained high positions in cathedral chapters in Segovia and Salamanca, or rich parishes and fat benefices in Castile, Valencia, and Andalusia and other places where those who served God and his Church could receive their just reward on earth as it is in heaven.

After all the years he had spent in these dismal mountains, he deserved similar reward, and yet there was no prospect of any change in his situation despite the many letters he had written to the bishop and the archbishop, pleading for a transfer to another parish and reminding them of his selfless and unrelenting attempts to plant the seeds of the one true faith in such barren soil. No one understood or cared, and as he glanced up at the white bell tower with its horseshoe arches, the possibility of escape seemed more remote than ever, and as he stared at the dark, silent houses all around him, he began to run through the names of the congregants from whom he might extract something to compensate for his losses when the service was over. He thought he heard a noise nearby and paused to look around him, but the village was dark and silent and the population was still recovering from the previous day's revelries. The church door was unlocked, as it usually was, because the doors to God's house were always open, and whatever else you could say about these heretics, they did not steal from churches.

He pushed the heavy wooden door open and stepped inside. In the same moment, he saw the dark shape sitting on the first row of benches, wearing a cloak and a wide-brimmed hat.

"What are you doing here?" he snapped. "I'm not ready yet."

The man did not answer or even turn around, and it was only then that he realized that there were others standing in the shadows behind him, and he felt afraid. He took a step away, but one of the men now shut the heavy door, and a gloved hand grasped him over the mouth and jerked his head back. Before he was able to make a sound, the blade cut into his throat and slid across it with a swift, effortless movement, penetrating deep into his flesh and cutting the trachea just below the Adam's apple.

All this was accomplished so quickly that the priest felt no pain, but only boundless shock as the grip released him and he stumbled forward, one hand clutching at his perforated throat in a vain attempt to stem the flow of the warm blood that sluiced irresistibly through his fingers. Directly in front of him, he saw the pallid shoulders of the Prince of Peace hovering in the darkness just above the altar with his arms outstretched, his dear crowned head illuminated by shafts of light coming through the stained-glass window at the beginning of a day that the priest knew he would not see. For the first time in many years, he sincerely wanted to kiss those nailed feet and beg forgiveness, because he knew now that his soul would not be saved and that there would be no resurrection for him.

The priest reached one hand out toward the altar and was still desperately trying to suck in air when one of the dark shapes stabbed him in the lower back with a sword, driving it so deep that the point protruded through his stomach. Even then he remained standing, shuffling his feet like a heavy dancer and trying to remain upright. Now the seated man finally stood up and came toward him, and disbelief and incomprehension compounded the terror as Father Panalles saw the silver mace hanging by the man's side, with its spiked ball and the handle with the leather grip. Beyond him the Black Virgin of Belamar was looking down on him with an expression of infinite compassion, and he wished that he had done more to live up to her expectations. *In te, Domine, speravi,* he thought as the mace came swinging up and around and smashed into the side of his skull.

He was dead before he hit the floor.

THE NIGHT BEFORE THE EXECUTION, Licenciado Bernardo Mendoza dreamed about the first auto-da-fé he had ever witnessed. It was the great burning of the Lutherans on October 8, 1559, and his uncle had insisted on taking him, even though he was only nine years old, because the new king was present and it was important, he said, for the child of conversos to know from a very early age what would happen to those who defied the laws of God and his Church. He saw once again the Plaza Mayor packed with people, at least two hundred thousand, it was said, many of whom had come from all over Castile and slept out in the streets and fields in anticipation of the great event. He saw the dignitaries seated on the scaffold, the judges and *letrados*, the archbishop and priests, the tonsured friars in their white-and-black robes, the lords and ladies in their finest clothes looking down from every window and balcony.

In his dream he heard the murmur of anticipation as King Philip climbed onto the scaffolding with his family, sitting beneath Inquisitor-General Valdés, because the power of the Inquisition, his uncle said, was even greater than the power of the Crown itself. He remembered how the square fell silent as the king and his family swore to support and uphold the Inquisition. He heard the great roar of affirmation when the vast crowd was called on to do the same, as though all the people in the square had now a single body with one voice, from the king and his grandees to the lowliest beggar, all of them united against the heretic enemies of God, Spain and the Holy Inquisition. He was so moved that he wanted to weep and kiss the hands of those wise men in their scarlet robes who watched over Spain day and night.

In his dream Mendoza recalled once again the anger and fascination that he had felt as the thirty-one Lutherans were led barefoot into the square, accompanied by the Inquisition commissioners and officers bearing the silk-fringed Inquisition standard with the green cross and olive branch; the jailers, priests and monks; and the green-clad *familiares* who assisted the Holy Office in its ceaseless war against the enemies of God and the king. He flinched at the sight of the yellow-and-black sanbenitos—the tunics of shame that reached down to the bare knees of the Lutheran heretics, painted with devils, monsters, skulls and flames, some pointed upward and some down. He heard his uncle say, "Remember this, boy—this is what hell looks like," and he sensed even then that he would always remember the rage of the crowd as it jeered and screamed furiously at the prisoners, some of whom were carrying candles and wearing ropes around their necks and conical hats on their heads that were also painted with devils and beasts. Others were in chains, which jangled against the paved square and mingled with the urgent prayers and imprecations of priests and Jesuits pleading desperately with the condemned to repent and save their souls before their bodies were burned.

But what drew his attention most was the young woman in the black sanbenito that hung halfway down her calves. Her head was crowned with the conical hat known as the *coroza*, and her soft, sweet expression was so strikingly at odds with the yellow devils dancing around the ragged sackcloth tunic and the pointed hat that he could not imagine what she had done to deserve the rage, revulsion and condemnation that accompanied her passage through the packed square. He heard someone say in a tone of outrage and disgust that she had been a nun, but she looked so much like an angel or the Virgin Mary that he could not help feeling an urge to rescue her. And even though he knew that it was wrong to feel pity toward these minions of Satan, her sad face continued to haunt him as a succession of priests, bishops and Inquisition officials delivered interminable homilies and sermons and proclaimed the dreadful crimes of the penitents. Most of these offenses were incomprehensible to him, and the inquisitorial recitations were sprinkled with Latin words and phrases that he did not know. But again and again the word "heresy" was passed down from the scaffolding and back and forth through the crowd, reverberating through his mind with a sibilant, menacing hiss, conjuring up vague possibilities of unimaginable depravity, obscenity and horror that he could not even define.

In his dream he accompanied his uncle once again to the burning place in the Campo Grande and saw the stakes protruding from the pyres. He watched the prisoners ascend the platforms, accompanied by the priests who were still nagging agitatedly at the unreconciled to repent. He saw the executioner fasten them to the poles one by one, and then he witnessed what was at that point the single most shocking event in his life, as those who recanted were strangled with ropes wrapped around the stakes and attached to a small stick that the executioner slowly tightened, while the spectators variously applauded and prayed aloud, before the torches were applied to the piles of gorse and branches.

In total, thirteen men and women were burned that day, in addition to the effigy of the Lutheran who had not been caught, a vile creation of wax, straw and a skull that was briefly contorted into an even more hideous shape at the first touch of the fire, before it melted away altogether. The beautiful nun who looked like Mother Mary was also consigned to the flames, and even as the flames were rising around her feet, he saw her terrified face and could not help wanting to save her as she moved her lips in prayer and shouted, "Let each one live in his own sect!" He had no idea what these words meant, but some members of the crowd were so infuriated by them that they shouted, "Burn, witch!" and "Go back to Satan!" and began to throw blazing branches closer to her so that she burned more quickly. It was then, as the flames finally reached her, that she began screaming, a long, desolate series of shrieks that cut right through to the core of him, till he fell to the ground and passed out.

Now the Licentiate Mendoza heard himself shouting, and he woke up with relief to find himself in his own bedroom. In the darkness he could make out the familiar objects: the vihuela leaning by the window next to the music stand, the colored tapestry on one wall and his friend Antonio's copy of Titian's *Salomé* and a selection of his own drawings on another; Vasari's *Lives of the Artists* in Italian and Vesalius's *De humani corporis fabrica* on the bedside table next to the oil lamp. He got up and peered through the curtains at the *sereno*. The night watchman was sitting by the charcoal burner that provided the only light, his chin slumped on his chest with his cloak wrapped around his head and body like a mourning shroud, his helmet and sword on the ground beside him. Mendoza could not sleep now, and he returned to bed and lay awake, trying to dispel the agitation and melancholy that the dream always aroused as the daylight slowly filtered through the crack in the velvet curtains.

In the days and weeks that followed the great burning, he had had many nightmares like that one, so many that his aunt had taken him to the apothecary to find something to soothe his nerves. He could not remember what she had given him, though he did recall her arguing with his uncle and telling him that the boy was too young to have seen such things. Since then he had seen more horrors than he could count. He had seen men die in battle, on land and sea, gutted with pikes and halberds, shot with cannon or harquebus balls. Even in peacetime he had seen men and women stabbed, strangled and drowned, or beaten to death with stones and planks of wood. But in all that time, the face of the burning nun had continued to haunt his dreams, and he had never attended an auto since, not even the one in which his own uncle had also worn the sanbenito.

The boy who had fainted that day in Valladolid could never have imagined that he himself would one day be sending men and women to the Campo Grande for execution. And today another man would die on his orders in the same execution ground: a student who had killed his best friend out of jealousy over a woman. There was no doubt about his guilt. The murder had taken place in a crowded tavern, and Mendoza's case file contained identical statements from all the eyewitnesses present. The student was not a noble, and he had confessed without torture, and the law demanded the death penalty and must take its course. Mendoza's three colleagues had agreed on the sentence, and even though he had voted against it, it was his duty as the investigating judge to preside over the execution. None of this gave him any satisfaction. Some murders were premeditated and planned a long time in advance, and those who planned them had ample time to consider the morality of their actions.

Such murderers deserved to lose their lives. But this case was different. Even when pronouncing sentence, he remembered the fights from his own university days and thought how easily he could have been in the student's place. It was luck, not judgment, that had saved him, because when men were drunk and brandished daggers at each other, the outcome was never predictable. The previous evening he had visited the student in his cell according to the usual custom, together with the priest, the prosecutor and the *alguacil*—the constable—who had made the arrest, and he brought the condemned man the customary biscuit, sweets and wine. A more unlikely murderer would be hard to find. The student had been studying philosophy and law, just as Mendoza once had done, and his parents had hoped for great things from him. The young man spoke in a soft, squeaky voice, and his eyes were red from sleeplessness and tears, as he expressed his regret at having broken his parents' hearts and thrown away his friend's life and his own through a combination of hot blood and too much wine. With more money and connections or a title, he might have been able to procure a lighter punishment by going above the heads of Mendoza and his colleagues, but the student's family had not even been able to gain an appeal, and now the time for a reprieve had passed.

At seven o'clock, Gabriel brought him a bowl of maize porridge, accompanied by raisins, dates and a glass of almond milk, and drew back the curtains. "A good day for a hanging, sir," he observed, looking out at the cloudless sky.

Mendoza clicked his tongue in disapproval. "An execution isn't something to joke about, boy."

"Sorry, sir, I wasn't thinking." Gabriel laid the tray on the bed. "May I ask a question, sir?"

Mendoza drained the almond milk in a single gulp. "Go ahead."

"Have you ever sentenced someone to death and found out afterward that he was innocent?"

"I never sentenced anyone who hadn't confessed first."

"But didn't some of them confess under torture?"

"Yes. But the confession isn't valid unless they confirm it afterward. And I have never sentenced anyone who *I* didn't believe was guilty."

"But isn't it possible that a suspect could confess under torture and then ratify his confession afterward—not because he was guilty but because he didn't want to be tortured again?"

Mendoza agreed that this was a possibility.

"And it's also possible that the witnesses who testified against that person might be lying?"

"Of course. The law is an imperfect instrument."

"But if that happened and the man you arrested was executed, would that also be God's will?"

"If God allowed it to happen, it must be," Mendoza conceded warily.

"Because otherwise it would mean that God had made a mistake, wouldn't it?"

"Be careful, boy." Mendoza looked severely but affectionately at the tousled black hair and the dark, intelligent eyes. "Saying something like that in this house is one thing, but outside these walls it's quite a different matter. Some thoughts are best left inside your head. Go and get dressed now—and dress well. A man will die today."

Gabriel bowed and left the room. Mendoza finished his breakfast and dressed with special care, entirely in black apart from the white ruff and cuffs protruding from the silk-lined doublet and slashed-velvet jerkin that he wore over it, its collar left open in the Flemish style, with his sword and felt cap and long judge's robe reaching down to his buckled shoes. Outside in the hallway, Gabriel was already waiting, looking suitably somber in brown and dark green, as Magdalena emerged from the kitchen in her apron to inspect him.

"Very distinguished," she said approvingly. "Like a young judge. Señor, if I may." She reached up and straightened Mendoza's ruff. "You need a wife to do these things."

"And why would I need a wife when I already have you?"

"Ay, Don Bernardo." Magda sighed and shook her head. "A judge can't marry his maid!"

"And why not?" he teased her.

"*Por Dios*, stop. I'm old enough to be your mother. Now, go." She looked at Gabriel and shook her head. "Though why you want to see something like this . . ."

"If Gabriel wants to work as a scrivener, he needs to know what the law requires," Mendoza said firmly.

"But he's just a boy!"

"He's old enough." Mendoza took his stick from its resting place near the door and went downstairs. Outside, the *sereno* had gone and the sunlight was spreading across the fine red roofs, illuminating the white window frames and black iron balconies on the upper floors as they walked along the cobbled street, past sprawled bodies that might have been drunken revelers or dead and sleeping beggars, past carriages that emanated a fleeting whiff of perfume that mingled with the smell of horse dung and excrement from the chamber pots emptied during the night, past pedestrians in their best clothes heading for the execution ground and members of the Penitential Confraternity of Valladolid in their long gray cassocks and black hoods, already collecting alms for the student's soul.

The execution was due to take place at ten o'clock, and by the time they reached the prison, a considerable crowd had already gathered that included judges, magistrates and constables, the bishop of Valladolid, members of the clergy, relatives of the accused and the deceased and the usual morbid onlookers who were always attracted to such spectacles for reasons Mendoza had never understood.

At nine o'clock they brought out the prisoner, dressed in a white open-necked smock and black hose and the blue cap that would secure him indulgences in his passage through eternity. At ten minutes past, he was mounted on the waiting donkey and the halter was placed around his neck, while the crucifix was bound to his hands. Two members of the fraternity began to beat on their tambours, and the somber procession set off in a slow, stately rhythm toward the Campo Grande, fronted by a hooded brother hoisting a large crucifix. Mendoza's face was impassive, his stick tapping the ground as he limped along beside Gabriel and Constable Johannes Necker, the arresting officer, while the two monks accompanying the donkey urged the condemned man to accept his death with Christian courage and due penitence.

The student was clearly struggling to do this, and he began half moaning, half praying when some passersby made the sign of the cross at his approach. More spectators joined the procession as they drew closer to the park, where a large crowd was already waiting. At the sight of the scaffold and the executioner, the student's legs buckled, and he had to be dragged up onto the platform, crying and protesting, still holding the crucifix bound to his hands. At ten o'clock precisely, the executioner released the trap upon the sound of the first church bell. Mendoza saw Gabriel flinch as the student plummeted downward, twitching and jerking before hanging limply from the rope, where he would remain until the Penitential Brothers were allowed to take the body down and prepare it for burial the following day.

CHAPTER TWO

HE KING'S JUSTICE HAD BEEN DONE, AND the body dangling from the rope beneath the blue Castilian sky was there to proclaim the fact to the relatives of his victim and former friend and to anyone else who thought to defy the laws of God and man. Gabriel was staring at the gallows with a horrified expression when Mendoza turned and looked at him intently.

"Don't ever throw away your life like that, boy!" he said. "That student gave death a free gift because he didn't think about the consequences of his actions beforehand."

"Yes, sir." Gabriel looked puzzled by his urgency, but Mendoza was not willing to explain to his page that he himself had once stabbed a fellow student in a tavern brawl and nearly killed him.

"Go home," Mendoza said. "Don't bother with Mass today. We'll talk later."

Gabriel nodded and walked slowly away through the crowd, looking deep in thought. Some of the bystanders were talking animatedly about the hanging and the crime that had caused it, and Mendoza heard one man criticize the student's abject collapse on the scaffold, as though discussing an actor's performance in a *comedia*. Mendoza would have liked to have gone home with Gabriel, but Mass was also part of his obligations, and he knew that his absence would be noticed.

The Church of San Pablo was packed, and all the dignitaries and officials who had attended the execution were present to hear a Mass that was even more solemn than usual. Bishop Haro had clearly written his sermon with a view to the execution. He quoted from Exodus 21:12, that whoever strikes a man so that he dies shall be put to death, and he insisted that this obligation applied to young and old, to those who killed with prior intention and those who did so in the heat of passion. Because God's laws were immutable and weakness and youth were not sufficient justification for any exception. Mendoza was not convinced by this argument, but Haro soon worked himself into a veritable lather of emotion, his arms waving and his voice rising and falling in the familiar dramatic cadences as he told the congregation that evil was in the act and its consequences rather than in the intention, that the laws of the Crown were also God's laws and that obedience to both was the only sure path to virtue and salvation.

The sermon provoked even more histrionic sighs than usual from the female congregants, many of whom, Mendoza knew, had already strayed from the path of virtue and sighed loudest in an attempt to disguise the fact. This response seemed only to galvanize Haro to new flights of emotion. Mendoza was unimpressed. He generally preferred sermons with calmer and more reasoned arguments or theological questions to chew on to Haro's melodramatic oratory, and he was uncomfortably conscious of the presence of Elena and her husband a few rows in front of him.

He was pleased to observe that she was not sighing, because there was only one place where he liked to hear her do that, and it was not in church. He continued to glance furtively at the black mantilla as the bishop's voice droned on. Her piety was oddly exciting, and he felt a guilty but not unpleasant stirring of desire at the thought of the thick red hair and caramel skin that her prim church clothes concealed. He would have preferred not to linger when the service was over, but propriety and the dignity of his office obliged him to make his exit slowly as the congregation filed out of the church.

He and Elena had often arranged their liaisons after Mass, whether verbally or by passing notes, and to some extent it was better to speak to her when her husband was present, in order to avoid generating malicious rumors among those who fed on such things, even if these meetings demanded a talent for deception that he was not always confident he possessed. Elena, on the other hand, was not at all discomfited by such occasions, and he sensed that she rather enjoyed the element of theater and subterfuge that they required. He stood talking to two of his colleagues and watched out of the corner of his eye as she maneuvered herself and her husband inexorably through the congregants toward them, pausing briefly to pay her respects to the bishop and the grandees until she finally came alongside him.

"Good morning, Licenciado Mendoza," she said. "A stirring sermon today, I thought. Bishop Haro had fire on his tongue."

Mendoza bowed and doffed his cap graciously. "He did indeed, Doña Elena. Good day, Don César."

The *procurador* Izarra smiled his usual supercilious and condescending smile, as though he were looking down on the whole world from a great height, and Mendoza immediately felt a little less guilty. Izarra was one of the most successful attorneys in Valladolid, and there were those who predicted that he would one day become president of the Chancery and buy his way into the nobility whose interests he had served so diligently. If so, it would not be a reward for ability or integrity, and Izarra had an irritating tendency to behave as if he had already achieved his promotion.

"Justice was well served this morning, Mendoza," he said in his faintly nasal whine. "And well attended, too. You must be pleased."

Such crass observations were typical of Izarra, who often seemed to be mocking everything, including his own wife. Though he dealt with litigation and civil law suits, he was known for his fondness for the death penalty, and Mendoza had no doubt that he would have strung up as many people as necessary to assist his upward progress if he had chosen criminal law instead.

"It wasn't a particularly difficult or significant case," Mendoza said, knowing that Izarra knew this already.

"Well, they all count for something."

Mendoza nodded politely and wondered once again what Elena was doing with such a husband, who regarded the death of a man as nothing more than another career milestone and an opportunity to be noticed.

"The Fanini troupe will be giving a private performance at our house this Thursday, Licenciado, on their way back to Florence," Elena said matter-of-factly. "There will be music. Will you be able to attend and play for us?"

Her tone suggested that it was an issue of complete indifference either way, and the first-person plural was superfluous, since her husband did not share Elena's fondness for the arts. She was good at this, Mendoza thought, perhaps too good, because a woman who could deceive her own husband so effortlessly was capable of doing the same to any man.

"It would be my pleasure, Doña Elena," he replied. "Duty permitting."

"Of course." Elena gave the faintest of smiles behind her mantilla and continued her onward progress through the crowd toward her waiting carriage. Mendoza hurried quickly back to the Plaza Mayor with a feeling of relief and also anticipation at the prospect of an evening of theater, music and lovemaking—the perfect antidote to the squalid spectacle that had taken place in the Campo Grande earlier. The square had long since recovered from the great fire of 1561. That same year the king announced his decision to move the court from Valladolid to Toledo and then to Madrid, and there were those who thought that the city would die as a consequence. But the rebuilt plaza was once again pullulating with people enjoying the spring sunshine, from priests and friars, nuns, groups of students horsing around, to couples and families strolling with their children, to noble hidalgos and the occasional grandee showing off his wealth and status.

Even though he was not yet on duty, Mendoza instinctively scanned the crowd for signs of illegal activity, from purse snatchers and pickpockets to shell gamers and card tricksters, vagabonds from other towns and child beggars over the age of five to whores wearing gold or silver. He already knew many potential offenders by sight, and there was no sign of any of them this morning. On the far side of the square in the direction of the Plaza Zorrilla, he saw two women in black mantillas who were obviously soliciting, even though it was

Sunday and public women were not allowed to ply their trade in the main square.

Vice and crime were everywhere, seeping through every pore of the city, despite the veneer of virtue and respectability with which polite society surrounded itself, from the grubbiest slum to the richest palace, and it was his job as one of the four *alcaldes de crimen*—criminal judges—in the Royal Audience and Chancery of Valladolid to prevent it. But first he had arranged to meet Constable Velasco at the lockup.

He found Velasco dictating the results of the night's patrol to the scrivener, interrupting himself to give Mendoza a quick summary: two murders and five stabbings, a violation of house arrest by the son of a hidalgo who had previously breached his terms, a sword fight in which two men had been seriously wounded, a brandy-house brawl in which one man had had a broken bottle rammed into his face and lost an eye, and a burglary. Only one of the murders had a culprit. The other had taken place in the street, during either a robbery or possibly a contract killing. In the course of the night, they had made six arrests. Most of this activity had taken place in the poorer districts away from the city center, but one woman had been tied up and her house robbed only a few streets away.

"Only robbed, I hope?"

"It seems so, Your Honor," Velasco replied. "The lady in question says they were very well mannered—even when they entered her bedroom."

"So chivalry is not dead. Well, I suppose we should go and speak to her and get some more details. Have the preliminary reports delivered to my office first thing tomorrow."

"Can't we let some of the prisoners go, sir? The cells will be full if we make any more arrests today."

"Then you'll have to make room."

Just then the door opened and one of Judge Saravia's messengers appeared and announced that he wished to see Mendoza at his house immediately. Mendoza did not usually receive such requests, let alone on Sundays. The president of the Chancery was one of those judges for whom the law was useful only insofar as it made him rich, whether through the offices and favors he received from the king and his ministers or the payments and bribes that he was rumored to have extracted from his clients. The fact that there were many others like him did not make such behavior any more acceptable to Mendoza, and he knew that the antipathy was mutual.

MENDOZA'S CURIOSITY was aroused still further when he saw outside his house the splendid walnut carriage, whose corners were embossed with silver filigree. The carriage was accompanied by an escort of ten soldiers and servants, who were grandly turned out in gleaming morions, chest armor and identical pale blue smocks that attracted numerous stares from curious passersby.

The majordomo took him into the president's sumptuously furnished office, where Saravia was seated behind his desk, his bulbous, balding head protruding from a wide and over-elaborate ruff like a large egg, in front of a painting from the Flemish school showing St. Paul banishing the snakes from Malta. Directly opposite him sat a man he did not recognize, whose clothes and bearing marked him out immediately as a man of distinction, a member of the court or the aristocracy—an impression confirmed by Saravia's eager, ingratiating manner. The visitor was handsome and in his mid-fifties, immaculately groomed, with a short, well-trimmed beard and a triangular face and a small bud-shaped mouth, whose pale complexion was highlighted by a buttoned brown tunic and matching felt hat with a golden chain around it. What struck Mendoza most were his eyes. From the moment he walked into the room, they looked straight at Mendoza, or rather into him, as if they were weighing him up, as a goldsmith might hold a nugget to test its quality.

"Ah, Mendoza, there you are," Saravia said amiably. "The execution went well, I heard?"

"Everything as it should be, Your Worship."

"Splendid. May I introduce His Excellency Don Francisco de Bolea, the Marquis of Villareal, treasurer-general and secretary of the Council of Aragon. Licenciado Bernardo de Mendoza."

The marquis did not rise and held out an indolent, well-manicured hand, which Mendoza shook, accompanied by a short bow.

"Excellency. I trust His Majesty is in good health?"

"Far better health than the enemies of Spain would like him to be."

"We are all very relieved to hear it."

Saravia dispatched the majordomo for strawberry water as Mendoza sat down in front of him. "Have you ever been to Aragon, Licenciado?" he asked.

"I haven't had the pleasure, Your Worship."

"Well, I want you to go there."

"The king wants you to go there," added Villareal.

"Whatever pleases His Majesty."

"There is a village called Belamar de la Sierra in the Pyrenees,"

Saravia continued. "It seems that the local priest was murdered there last month in the most barbarous and sacrilegious manner. Slaughtered in his own church and his body laid on the altar. His church desecrated, a statue of Our Lady smashed and prayer books torn up. Vile words were written on the wall in his own blood—in Arabic."

"Arabic, Your Worship?"

"Belamar is a Morisco village," Villareal explained. "It's in the demesne of Cardona near the French border. I understand that you are originally from Granada?"

"That's correct, Excellency. My family had a house in the Albaicín."

"And you also fought in the war."

"I was a lieutenant of infantry under His Excellency Don Juan of Austria."

"And fought with great courage and distinction, I hear."

Like all men of the court, Villareal knew how to flatter, Mendoza thought, and he wondered who had told him this.

"I did what was necessary to serve my king," he said.

"And His Majesty would like you to serve him once again. Given your background in Granada, you'll be familiar with these New Christians. You'll know how stubborn and ungrateful they can be. Aragon is no exception. The Aragonese Moriscos were baptized in 1525. That's twenty-five years after the Moors of Granada were brought into the Church under their Most Catholic Majesties Fernando and Isabel. Nearly sixty years later, the Inquisition of Aragon complains that they are still living as Moors while pretending to be Christians. Not only are they not fulfilling their religious obligations, but the Holy Office believes that gunpowder and weapons are being smuggled into Cardona from France. There are reports that a

Morisco who calls himself the Redeemer is inciting these New Christians to revolt and preaching hatred against our holy faith."

"Are these rumors or facts?" Mendoza asked.

Villareal shrugged. "A useful distinction that is not always easy to establish in Aragon. But there is no doubt that something unusual is taking place in Cardona." He reached into a leather file and handed Mendoza a crumpled sheet of paper. Mendoza looked at the scrawled, untidy handwriting and read the message:

Mercader, you dog.

You and your pig Inquisition are not welcome in Cardona. We will burn you as you burned us. We will drive out all the Christians from Aragon. The sultan's flag will fly over Zaragoza and all Spain. Granada will be ours once again.

You will die.

The Redeemer.

"THE WRITER HAS SOME AMBITION, though his handwriting needs improvement," Mendoza observed. "And who is Mercader?"

"Inquisitor Mercader of the Inquisition of Aragon," replied Villareal. "This message was sent to him in Zaragoza in April. Since then both the Holy Office and the secular justices have reported incidents in which crosses and roadside shrines have been desecrated in and around Cardona. Last month a church in the village of Las Palomas was vandalized and the word 'Redeemer' was written on one of the walls—in Castilian, not Arabic. In these circumstances it is only logical to see the murder of the priest as an escalation and a declaration of intent."

"Has anyone seen this Redeemer? Is there any indication of who he might be?"

"No to both questions, Licenciado. There have been bandits and smugglers in the Pyrenees for years. Some of them have never been seen except by their victims, and they have never been caught. And the Cardona estates lie close to the French border. A man can walk back and forth across that frontier without anyone knowing his business. We don't have enough troops or customs officers to patrol such wild mountains, let alone hunt down some Morisco avenger who wants to turn Aragon into Granada."

"And is there any information to connect this Redeemer to Belamar de la Sierra?"

"The Holy Office is convinced that if such a man exists, he is most likely to come from Belamar," Villareal replied. "The village is mostly Morisco, and the Inquisition believes that its inhabitants are among the most intransigent and defiant in Cardona. But wherever this man comes from, he must be found—and quickly. Do you know how many Turks and Moors fought with the Moriscos of Granada, Licenciado?"

"The figures were never known, Excellency. Some say twenty-five thousand. Others say more."

"And they had to cross the sea to get there! Imagine what would happen if the Moriscos rebelled so close to our land border at a time like this, when His Most Catholic Majesty is under attack from so many enemies. In Béarn the Huguenot king Henry still dreams of recovering his family's territories in Navarre. In Flanders the Duke of Parma is at last beginning to turn the war in our favor, but the English Jezebel is promising to assist the rebels. Our spies tell us that the heretic Prince of Orange is even prepared to deal with infidels to attack us in Flanders and seeks to persuade the Grand Turk to take revenge for Lepanto. Our ports are constantly raided by Moors, and we have no doubt that there are many Moriscos who would like to assist them. According to the Holy Office, there are foreign spies all over Aragon: Turkish, Huguenot, even English. This must be stopped. As a veteran of Granada, you know what these Moriscos are capable of, when they receive assistance."

Mendoza nodded. It seemed impolitic to point out that the Granada War was a direct consequence of the king's official pragmatic of 1567, which ordered the Moriscos of Granada to cease speaking Arabic and abandon all the other Moorish customs that the Crown believed had prevented them from becoming faithful Christians. That decision had unleashed a cascade of violence that had taken more than two years to suppress.

"Shouldn't the Moriscos be a matter for the Inquisition?" he asked as the majordomo returned with their refreshments.

"That is correct. But there are other matters that fall outside the jurisdiction of the Holy Office. Aragon is my homeland, Don Bernardo, and it grieves me to say that parts of the kingdom are so infested with brigands that you cannot travel on the public roads without an escort, without the risk of being shot or having your throat cut. The infestation is particularly virulent in the mountains and valleys of Cardona. The Puerto de Somport is one of the main routes on the pilgrimage to Santiago, and pilgrims have frequently been robbed on the road to Jaca. Banditry is a problem that is difficult to eliminate, but rebellion is an outrage that cannot be tolerated. Next year the king will visit the Parliament of Aragon for the first time in twenty-two years. In March the infanta Catalina will be married to the Duke of Savoy in Zaragoza. The wedding is a moment of immense happiness for all the king's subjects, and His Majesty's decision to hold it in Zaragoza is a demonstration of his great affection for the Aragonese. In addition this event will be attended by many princes from outside his realms. You will understand that nothing can be allowed to overshadow or detract from this occasion—or diminish the honor and prestige of His Most Catholic Majesty."

"Who is His Majesty's corregidor in the district?"

"The magistrate in the Jaca district is Pelagio Calvo."

"Pelagio Calvo from Salamanca?"

"I believe so. You know him?"

"Of course. We were students together. He saved my life at Lepanto. I haven't seen him in thirteen years. I was wounded in the battle and sent to the hospital in Venice. I lost track of him after that. I believe he went on to serve His Majesty in Flanders."

"He did," Villareal said. "And he has been the magistrate in Jaca for the last three years. He has expressed his frustration on numerous occasions at the security situation in the Cardona *señorio*. He wants to go in like the Duke of Alva in Flanders—to hang and flog the district into submission. But Aragon isn't Flanders—yet. It requires a more careful and methodical approach, which we hope you will be able to provide."

Mendoza knew little of Aragon, but the Duke of Alva's "Council of Blood" needed no explanation. Appointed governor of the Netherlands in 1567, the duke had hanged and executed hundreds of Calvin's followers, and his methods were frequently spoken of with approval by his more hard-line colleagues as a model for dealing with ordinary criminality in Spain itself, despite the fact that the war in Flanders was still going on nearly twenty years after Alva had supposedly subdued it. Mendoza was not entirely surprised to hear that his old friend was advocating similar methods. Calvo, he recalled, had relatives in Brussels, and even as a student he had taken an uncompromising position on Flanders. Mendoza had a distant memory of a tavern argument in which Calvo had argued forcefully against any concessions to heretics in Flanders. Soon after Lepanto, Mendoza had received a letter from Genoa in which Calvo told him that he had acquired a taste for war and had decided to join Alva's Army of Flanders instead of returning to Spain. That was the last he had heard of Calvo, and he had never expected to see him again.

"The Aragonese have no desire to see the king's soldiers deployed anywhere in their territory," Villareal continued. "You are familiar with the *fueros*, I presume?"

"I'm aware of the royal charters," Mendoza replied. "But I know nothing of the *fueros* of Aragon."

"And there is no reason you should. Suffice to say that these charters were granted to the Crown of Aragon by the old kings of Castile, and they have been reaffirmed by their descendants ever since. In 1518 the king's own father was obliged to present himself in Zaragoza, where he promised to uphold the *fueros* before the lords would accept his kingship. So you see the Aragonese like to run their affairs without interference from the Crown, and they are extremely sensitive when it comes to any perceived violation of these privileges by Castile. The presence of troops would certainly be seen as such a violation, and it would require exceptional circumstances to justify such an intervention. Nor will a Castilian judge be universally popular. Many towns and lordships have their own *fueros*, and some lords believe that they alone have jurisdiction over their estates. These . . . sensibilities need to be taken into account. Nevertheless His Majesty believes that the situation in Belamar can be resolved through a more zealous policing effort, under the direction of a conscientious and energetic official of good standing who knows how to proceed with discretion. Judge Saravia has informed me that you are the best choice."

"His Worship honors me."

"He has told me of your success in eliminating the banditry near Jaén last year. Your experience of Granada will be useful in the Morisco lands. You are to go to Belamar and conduct your own investigation into the murder of the priest. You will use the opportunity to investigate the wider situation in the *señorio*. Find this 'Redeemer' if he exists and arrest him and his associates. See whether these contacts between Belamar and France amount to criminal activity, treason or heresy. You will act as a special justice and carry the king's seal and the royal baton. His Majesty must have clarity in these matters, and he wishes this to be accomplished quickly. The court will leave for Aragon in January, but this matter must be resolved before the winter. After that, many of the roads in the mountains will be closed. You will report directly to me—and only to me—on a weekly basis. The viceroy will see that messengers and anything else you require will be at your disposal. Any questions?"

"Yes. As the investigating judge, will I be expected to administer punishment?"

"An excellent question, Licenciado. This will not be like Jaén. You will be required to show flexibility, diplomacy and discretion. The Aragonese have their own courts, and so do the lords. As the king's special justice, you will have the authority to conduct your investigation and make arrests. The question of punishment will depend on the results of your investigation and whether the men you arrest are Aragonese or Castilian. I'm sure we can resolve these matters through consultation. But the Aragonese will not allow you to enter their territory with a large retinue. If you need extra men, Calvo can supply them."

"Troops are useful for repression, not investigations," Mendoza said. "But I do need to take some men with me whom I can depend on. Five will be enough. Two special constables, two soldiers, and I would like to take my page as a scrivener."

"We do have scriveners in Aragon, Licenciado Mendoza. We aren't savages."

"I need a scribe who isn't fixed to any particular place," Mendoza insisted. "Someone who can travel with me. My page's writing is already of professional standard. As a nonprofessional he will require only expenses and not a salary."

Saravia looked pleased at this, and Villareal handed him two sealed letters and a thin file of papers. "Here are your letters of introduction, a copy of the last report from the Inquisition and the latest letter we have received from the viceroy concerning the priest's murder. I have already informed him that you are coming to Zaragoza. You should report to him in the first instance. How soon can you depart?"

"I can leave in three days."

"Very good." Villareal glanced at his stick as if he were still weighing up his choice. "Your wound at Lepanto—was it serious?"

"It was, Your Excellency, but it would have been worse were it not for Pelagio Calvo. We served together on the Genoese galley *Guzmana*, on Don Juan's right. Calvo and I boarded a corsair ship from the rear in a longboat. I was shot in the hip while climbing onto the deck. An infidel was about to finish me when Calvo cut him down and lowered me back into the boat. He saved my life."

"But you *were* wounded."

"A minor inconvenience that has never interfered with my ability to perform my duties."

"Then what the army lost the law has gained," Villareal said graciously, handing him the white baton. "I look forward to your first report."

Mendoza got up and bowed, and Saravia accompanied him out into the hall.

"This is a very important assignment for you, Mendoza," he said in a low voice. "The king will be following your investigation personally. Don't fail him. Because if you fail, it means I fail, too."

"I will do my duty to the best of my ability as always, Your Worship."

"I don't doubt it." The president smiled unctuously. "Good luck, Licenciado."

Mendoza shook the other man's soft white hand. He knew that some benefits from his expedition would have already accrued to Saravia, and as he walked away, he could not help feeling that Saravia would not be entirely disappointed if he never came back.

CHAPTER THREE

At the age of thirty-four, Licenciado Bernardo Francisco Baldini de Mendoza could look back on a reasonably successful career within the Hapsburg bureaucracy for the son of an Italian mother and a Granadan silk merchant of converso descent. At the age of seven, he had seen his father accused of Judaizing and forced to spend a year in an Inquisition jail. Though the elder Mendoza was eventually acquitted, the stress provoked a heart attack that killed him, and the family business fell into difficulties. To reduce the economic burden on the family, Bernardo's mother sent him to her brother-in-law's care in Valladolid. His uncle had financed his education and paid for his studies at the University of Salamanca, where he studied for seven years, enough to add the title "Licenciado," but not "Doctor," to his name. Though he was considered by his tutors to be an excellent student, too many years of having

Latin beaten into him by his grammar-school teachers had left him with an aversion to academic study, and his early years at the university were tumultuous and disorderly.

In 1569 he left the university as a result of the tavern fight and joined the army, with his uncle's assistance, to escape criminal charges. In his five years in the king's armies, he had fought the Moors in Granada and the Turks at Lepanto, where a musket ball had shattered his left thigh and ended his military career. Had it not been for Calvo, that shot would have ended his life as well. Instead he recovered from his wound and returned to Valladolid, where his uncle persuaded the university authorities in Salamanca that he was a changed man. This was true, because unlike Calvo he had lost his appetite for war and would not have returned to the army even if he'd been able to. He went on to complete four more years of study without incident, at which point his uncle was accused by the Inquisition of secret Jewish worship.

The evidence against him was slim. A disgruntled servant claimed that he wore a white shirt on the Sabbath and refused to eat pork. His uncle denied these charges, but his brother's previous record with the Inquisition worked against him, and he confessed in order to avoid a more severe punishment. His uncle always insisted that the charges were invented by a business rival. He was punished with a large fine that left him without funds to finance the education that might have transformed his nephew into a fully qualified law graduate, or *letrado*. Having spent much of his life trying to rise from the ranks of the lower nobility, his uncle now found himself ostracized and died two years after his appearance at the auto-da-fe broken and bitter.

By that time Mendoza had received his first post as a lawyer at the Granada Audiencia, and he had now been one of the four criminal judges at the Royal Audience and Chancery of Valladolid—the second-highest court in the land after the Council of Castile—for nearly four years. This was a long time for a relatively minor position, but it was better than might have been expected, given his Jewish origins and the sanbenito bearing his uncle's name, which was still kept in the Church of San Ildefonso as a mark of the infamy that was also shared by all his descendants.

Elena, like his mother, believed that he lacked ambition, because some of his fellow students had risen much further and become high-salaried advocates, attorneys and judges in the secular judiciaries or the Inquisition, or they had gone on to become governors and judges in the Indies. Some had risen through their own ability. But too many of them were men like Izarra who had achieved promotions through bribes and family connections or who faked their degrees and called themselves "Licenciado" when they had not even been at university for three years and who had achieved their positions by bowing and scraping to their superiors or taking on cases for the sole purpose of extracting fines that would pay for their rents, their lifestyles and their mistresses.

Mendoza had nothing but contempt for such behavior. If the officials who enforced the king's laws did not obey these laws themselves or used them to their own advantage, he often argued, then there was no reason his subjects should feel obliged to obey them either, and without the law there was nothing to distinguish human society from the beasts of the forest.

Nevertheless these principles were beginning to put a strain on his finances. The cost of living was rising, there were always new taxes to be paid, and it was expensive to keep Gabriel and a housekeeper, in addition to the payments that he sent to his mother. For all these reasons, he was glad of an assignment that might bring him a promotion or a financial reward that did not require him to be corrupt. Even before leaving Saravia's house, he had begun to think about the men he needed. Most of them he could find in Valladolid, but there was one man who would be especially suitable for an assignment like this and who, depending on the weight of his purse and the presence or absence of female company, might be only too glad to accept it. Mendoza had a very good idea where he might be found, and no sooner had he returned to the Chancery than he dispatched a messenger to find him.

"BLESS ME, Your Reverence, for I have sinned." Luis de Ventura, former sergeant in the Tercio of Naples, looked expectantly at the abbot, who nodded at him to continue. Ventura began, as he usually did, with the venial sins first. "I have not been to Mass in many months. I have not observed the holy days. I have doubted the existence of God. I have coveted another man's wife. . . ." Ventura reconsidered this. "I have *lain* with another man's wife. I have slept with public women. I have taken pleasure in these things."

"Well, the devil's temptations wouldn't be tempting if they weren't pleasurable," the abbot observed.

"I have gambled." Ventura was getting into his stride now. "I have frequented taverns and brandy houses. I have killed men."

"To kill in the king's wars is not a sin, my son. The wars of Spain are God's wars."

"It wasn't only in war, Your Reverence. I have fought in taverns and duels."

"And when was the last time this happened?"

"A week ago. A man sent two assassins to kill me. They were not men of quality."

"And why did he do this?"

"He believed that I was having intimate relations with his wife."

"And were you?"

"I was, Your Reverence."

"I see." The abbot sighed wearily. "And so you decided to come here for concealment?"

"No, Your Reverence," Ventura protested. "I came here to repent! Even though the dogs deserved it."

"No doubt." The abbot gave him a skeptical look. "Do you remember when you first came here? You were just eleven. Your parents had high hopes for you, Luis."

"I know that. God rest their souls."

"But you disappointed them. And now you are carrying a weight that will only get heavier as you get older. If you want peace, you must surrender yourself to God. Give yourself to him completely and unconditionally. Open your heart, and you will find him willing to embrace you, whatever you have done—and so will we."

"I will try, Your Reverence."

"For your penance I would like you to perform some exemplary work. An act of goodness that your parents could be proud of."

"Here in the monastery?"

"No, Luis. It's easy to be virtuous when virtue is untested. The world is where you belong, not here. When you leave these walls, I want you to devote yourself to goodness and virtue for at least two months. Who knows? It might even become a habit. No drinking. No gambling or fighting. And no women—married or not. Now, go and pray to God for guidance on how to achieve this."

The abbot made the sign of the cross and blessed him. Ventura kissed his hand and went into the chapel, feeling mildly cleansed. He knelt in front of the altar and tried to pray. Apart from his shoulder-length black hair, he looked the image of piety and devotion in his white tunic and black scapular. Normally the Monastery of Santa María del Parral near Segovia was one of the few places on earth where he felt something like peace. No matter what brought him there, the sight of its ancient sand-colored walls and pink slate roofs rising up in layers above the fruit orchards and vineyards, the rows of trees and the wells and fountains, seemed to him like a vision of earthly harmony each time he saw the place.

In the daytime he liked to wander the gardens and watch the monks or their workers cultivating vegetables or picking fruit, but he rarely spoke to them. With few exceptions the monks were as thick as shit, and no more thoughtful or intelligent than many unlettered peasants he'd met who had never been anywhere near a church or a monastery. And so although he ate and occasionally prayed with them, he mostly kept his own counsel, either in his cell or walking the grounds and cloisters like a ghost in his own skin.

Now, as he sat alone in the same chapel where Isabel the Catholic had once prayed and which he had first attended when he was only ten years old, his loneliness seemed far more difficult to bear than his sinful life. There'd been a time when his parents had set their hearts on his becoming a Dominican monk and even an Inquisitor, but the spirit had proved weaker than the flesh so often that he had long ago ceased to believe that it could ever be victorious.

Yet he did not believe that he was a bad man, and he had met many men who were considerably worse. The commandments said that he should not covet another man's wife, but sometimes it was difficult to resist, especially when men's wives coveted *him*. The Bible also said that he should not kill, but most of the men who had died at his hands had been Turks, Moors and heretic rebels. And those he'd killed in peacetime had mostly been bad men or men who had tried to kill him. And at least he hadn't killed anyone for money. He had not offered himself as a sword for hire. He had not cheated anyone at dice or cards who did not deserve to be cheated, and he had not robbed anyone.

The abbot was a saintly man who walked in God's path, but he had spent most of his long life in a monastery. Luis, on the other hand, lived in a world whose temptations would have tested the resolve of even the most ardent monk. He could testify from personal experience that not all wars were God's wars. He had seen men behave like beasts, and at times he had behaved like one himself. And even as he prayed for guidance on how to do good, he was not entirely sure if he was capable of it.

By the time he returned to his cell, the brief serenity that always followed confession had worn off, and he lay down on his cot in a state of restless agitation. Outside, the blue sky was slowly turning red and pink through the grilled window, and the sound of vespers wafting up from the chapel mingled with the songs of the swallows and the deep, heavy notes of the church organ. Normally he liked this time of day, and the chanting stoked memories of the religious fervor that he had once felt when he first came to the monastery, but now he looked at his sword and his short parrying dagger and his two pistols leaning up against the wall next to his saddlebags and boots, and he knew that his refuge could only be temporary. He knew that he could not return to Madrid, at least for a while, because the husband of Ágata Fernández de la Prada was powerful and rich enough to send any number of assassins to hunt him down.

For a man in his position, there were essentially three options apart from the army. He could go to the Indies and seek his fortune, he could take to the roads and become a highway robber, or he could continue to advertise himself as a master of arms and find people rich enough to pay him to teach them to fence. But the age of heroes was over, and the days when even the poorest soldier could come back from the Indies bearing cases filled with gold and silver were gone. Now wealth was accumulated slowly, if at all, by farmers, businessmen and administrators who ground their lives away in endless, tedious work that he had neither the patience nor the aptitude for. Robbery was more suited to his abilities. With his skills it would be easy, almost effortless, for him to relieve the first traveler he came across of his possessions and even his life, but the old voice of the would-be knight-errant that he had first encountered in his grandfather's stories still insisted that it was more noble and more honorable to defend the weak and helpless than it was to prey on them.

Sooner or later he would have to get back on his horse. He tried to think of a destination, but he had never been good at plans, and he soon gave up the effort and closed his eyes. He had nearly dozed off when there was a knock on the door, and a squeaky-voiced monk who sounded like a eunuch told him that a messenger from Valladolid had come to see him.

"DID I EVER TELL YOU that you remind me of Titian's *Venus*?" Mendoza ran his fingers through Elena's thick red hair and traced the perfect curve of her back as she lay on her stomach beside him in Prosecutor Izarra's bedroom, propped up on her elbows like a sphinx.

Elena laughed. "How do you know? You've never even seen her."

"I've seen Antonio's copy."

"So you compare me to an imitation?"

"Not at all. I compare you to an image of imagined perfection by one of the greatest artists on earth."

"Very well, then," she said, kissing him lightly on the lips. "In that case I accept your compliment."

She rolled over onto her side and wrapped one leg over him and pressed her face against his neck. It had been a most agreeable evening that Mendoza was in no hurry to bring to an end. First he had attended a performance in the patio of Elena's house-cum-salon performed by the Fanini commedia dell'arte troupe on its way home from Madrid to Rome. The play was inconsequential but still enjoyable, and the subject matter was appropriate—a romantic tale of forbidden and impossible love between a Morisca noblewoman and a Christian aristocrat in Don Juan of Austria's army during the War of Granada.

As a veteran of that war, he knew better than most of Elena's guests how inauthentic the play was, but he had no desire to spoil the evening, not when Attorney Izarra was in Madrid and Elena was looking fabulous in a green bodice and a pleated farthingale skirt embroidered with gold threads and pearls. He always enjoyed the company of actors, and the Italians were lively and amusing. After the play they had danced a succession of pavanes and galliards, and he had accompanied Elena on two villancicos by Mudarra on the vihuela, which were well received.

In accordance with their usual arrangements, he left with the last of the guests and pretended to go home, waiting in the shadows near her house till she drew her curtain and closed it. Then he hurried across the street with his face half covered and entered through the servants' door that her maid had left open for him. By the time he reached her bedroom, she was already in bed with her hair unfastened, and they feasted on each other with an eagerness that was sharpened by the long wait and the element of danger that their liaisons always implied. Because both of them knew what might happen if their affair ever became public knowledge. The cuckolded prosecutor would be obliged to defend his honor regardless of what he did in his own time. He would have the right to kill his wife himself or have her executed, or confine her to a convent. The law also allowed him to have Mendoza killed or challenge him to a duel.

If it came to a duel, Mendoza knew that the odds were in his favor, but the *procurador* did not have to kill him to end his career, because a mistress was not compatible with the moral standards expected of His Majesty's judges in public, however many of them might violate these expectations in private. These were not possibilities to be relished, but Elena, more than any woman he had ever met, was a risk worth taking.

"Are you really taking the boy to Aragon?" she asked.

"Why not? Gabriel needs some experience of the world. He hasn't even been to Madrid. There are boys who join the army even younger. Saravia is happy because he won't have to pay the full court rate—and he'll have been promised something from Villareal."

"Will it be dangerous in Aragon?" she asked him.

"For you, anywhere outside Valladolid or Madrid is dangerous."

"Not merely dangerous, *cariño*. Barbarous. Just the thought of the Pyrenees makes me shudder."

"You never called me 'darling' before."

"Well, tonight you've earned it."

Mendoza grinned. "I'll wrap up warm. Anyway, Gabriel is looking forward to it. He sees it as an adventure."

"I also like adventures, Alcalde," she said, rolling over to one side, "but I don't like to travel so far in search of them."

"I'm glad you still think I'm worth exploring."

"Like the Indies, there are still parts of you waiting to be discovered. And you haven't bored me—yet." She stroked his face with the back of her hand. "Who else are you taking on this expedition?"

"Constable Johannes Necker. Not much initiative. But dogged, honest and dependable, like a bloodhound—and tough as nails."

"Who else?"

"My esteemed cousin Luis de Ventura—perhaps. I haven't heard from him yet."

"I don't know him."

"He's a sergeant in the Naples tercio. We fought together in Flanders and Granada. He's a swordsman, a gambler, a rake and a bit of a rogue. I haven't seen him in two years, but my mother mentioned to me in a letter that he was in Madrid and in some kind of trouble again—woman trouble. He usually goes to a monastery when that happens."

"He sounds exciting. But why do you need such a man?"

"Luis is one of the best fighting men I have ever met. And he is absolutely fearless. In Granada he would go off by himself behind Morisco lines. We called him 'El Invisible.' He once spent three days at the court of Aben Humeya, the Morisco king, disguised as a Morisco. No one detected him. If you ever get in a fight, it's good to have Luis de Ventura on your side."

Elena regarded him with amusement. "You're rather looking forward to this, aren't you?"

"Not exactly. These investigations aren't comfortable. No more drawing classes with Antonio. No *comedias*. Bad food. No beds. My poor vihuela must remain untouched. And most of all I won't see you."

"Thank you for putting me last."

"It wasn't listed in order of importance."

"I'm glad to hear it. And how long will you be gone?"

He shrugged. "It depends on the investigation."

"You'll forget me," she pouted.

"Far more likely that you'll forget *me*. Especially if you have any more Italian actors coming by."

"Such little faith in womankind, Your Honor! Let me prove how wrong you are."

She clasped her fingers behind his neck and pulled him toward her, and they made love once more, before he got dressed and sneaked out the way he had come. Outside, the streets were completely dark, apart from the occasional faint light from the windows and the glow of a *sereno*'s brazier. He limped down the middle of the road, eyeing the darker shadows carefully. It was only ten minutes to his house, but at this time of night there was no one he might meet who could bring him anything good at all, and even an encounter with one of his own constables on the nightly *ronda* might set the wrong tongues wagging.

As he made his way through the darkened streets, he heard the scuttling of rats and the dismal wail of a cat in heat. Above him the sky was bursting with stars and moonlight made it slightly lighter than usual, as he scanned the doorways and porticoes warily for the slightest sign of movement. He had just crossed the Plaza Mayor when he heard the sound of footsteps from behind him. He shifted suddenly to his left, swinging the stick around hard at knee level of the dark shape looming out of the darkness. His would-be assailant cursed as the blow caught him on the side of the left knee, before Mendoza jabbed the stick into his belly.

The man fell to the ground with a yelp and lay clutching his knee as Mendoza drew his sword and held the point against his throat. "You know I'm entitled to kill you in self-defense, thief?"

"I'm not a thief! I was on my way home!"

"Really? Then what's this?" Mendoza kicked the wooden club away from his hand. "Get up and crawl back into the sewer you came from. If I see you again, this will be your last night on earth."

The thief got up and hobbled quickly away, cursing under his breath. Mendoza had barely resheathed the sword when he heard the sound of hooves coming toward him. He turned and saw his cousin leading his horse, wearing his familiar wide-brimmed feathered hat with one side pinned back.

"That was well done, Bernardo," Ventura said. "I'm glad to see that the law hasn't made you soft. Sergeant Luis de Ventura reporting for duty, Capitán."

Mendoza laughed at the mock salute and embraced him. "So it was true, then. You were in the monastery. Were you seeking salvation or sanctuary, cousin?"

"Both. But I decided to see what you had to offer instead."

"A complicated mission to Aragon," Mendoza said. "Which you will be paid for. Does that tempt you?"

"Right now anything that pays is tempting. Because this horse is all I own."

"The night watchman can take care of him till the morning. We leave tomorrow. And I won't ask what made you seek refuge with the Hieronymites."

"And I won't ask you what you are doing out at this time of night."

Luis laughed the ribald, infectious laugh that Mendoza had heard so many times during the War of Granada. His cousin had never been to his apartment before, and Mendoza ushered him into the dining room and produced some bread, ham and wine from the kitchen.

"Well, well, Alcalde Mendoza," Ventura said. "I see you've gone up in the world. You earn a better living than I do."

"So you've left the tercio?"

"For now. But I was thinking of reenlisting till you gave me a reason not to. And the abbot has told me I have to go out and do good in the world for my penance."

Mendoza laughed. "Did he? Well, I'll do my best to give you that opportunity."

Until Ventura had entered the monastery, the two of them had shared the same house and been more like brothers than cousins. Instead Mendoza was the one who had been brought up in his uncle's house as if he were the man's son, except for a brief period when Ventura had abandoned the monastic life. These childhood bonds were strengthened when they fought together in the same war and the same army, and the conversation quickly turned to the War of Granada, to the battles they'd fought in and the comrades they'd known and lost, until Mendoza sensed that his mercurial cousin was becoming gloomy.

"This investigation also involves Moriscos," Mendoza said. "I assume that won't bother you?"

"Not in the slightest. And the farther I am from Madrid, the better."

Mendoza shook his head in exasperation as his cousin described his near-fatal adventure with Ágata de la Prada and the cuckolded husband whose minions were hunting for him.

"You won't change, will you, cousin?"

"No. But you certainly have. An apartment like this . . . you only need a wife to complete it."

"So Magda was telling me."

"And how is Gabriel?"

"He's fine. He asks too many questions, and he doesn't know what questions he shouldn't ask. As long they are only directed at me, it shouldn't be a problem."

"Does he ever ask about Granada?"

"No." Mendoza looked at him severely. "And I don't tell him. And I don't want anyone else to do it either."

Ventura looked as though he were about to say something and then changed his mind. It was nearly dawn now, and Mendoza offered his cousin a place on his own bed, but Ventura preferred to sleep on the floor. Mendoza brought him a blanket and pillow and retired to his own room. Lying in his own bed, he found himself thinking of Granada, and he saw once again the scene that he knew would be permanently engraved in his mind until the day he died. He saw the elderly Morisca stabbing at him with a sharpened stake in the doorway of the smoke-filled house that had been hit with cannon and musket fire, ignoring his order to surrender. He saw himself run her through with his sword, and he felt once again the same shame and disgust as he walked away. He heard the piercing cry of a child from inside the bombed house and looked in through the gaping hole in the wall where the cannonball had struck, squinting against the smoke at the broken chairs and the overturned table, at the rising flames and the blood and the bodies of five children of various ages, a young woman and a much older man. He saw the toddler, naked and crying out for his mother, sitting among the bodies with the fire coming toward him, and just before he fell asleep, he saw himself go back into the house and carry the child out on his bloodstained arm.

THE FOLLOWING MORNING Ventura was greeted with great delight by Magdalena and especially by Gabriel, who had not seen him in more than ten years and barely remembered a man whom he had come to regard as something of a legend.

"So I understand you're going to be our *escribano*," Ventura said.

"Si, señor," Gabriel said. "I can't wait."

"Do you know how to use a sword, boy?"

"He's not coming to fight," said Mendoza. "The quill will be his sword."

"You never know," Ventura said. "Aragon is a lawless place. Haven't you heard that those Morisco bandits like to eat their victims alive? They roast them over a slow fire first."

"Jesus and Mary!" Magda made the sign of the cross. "You cannot take the boy to such a place, Don Bernardo!"

"See what you've done?" Mendoza asked.

"Only joking, Magda." Ventura grinned. "I've been to Aragon many times. It's perfectly safe. And don't worry about the fighting, boy. It's probably the only thing I'm good for. And your guardian can fight, too, by the way. A judge of cape and sword."

"And a veteran of Granada and Lepanto," Gabriel said proudly. "But he never talks of it!"

"Some things are better forgotten than remembered," Mendoza replied.

He had arranged for a carriage to take the three of them to the stables to load the horses and mules, and Magda looked tearful as she came out into the hallway to say good-bye and saw their weapons, knapsacks and saddlebags, and the wooden bureau that contained Gabriel's writing materials.

"You're sure you have enough ink and paper?" Mendoza asked him.

"Yes, sir."

"Must he go with you, Don Bernardo?" Magdalena pleaded. "Suppose something happens to him?"

"Now, Magda, we're going to the Pyrenees—not Barbary."

The housekeeper embraced Gabriel and clung on to him, much to his embarrassment and Ventura's amusement. The carriage stood outside, and they rode over to the stables with their bags, with Ventura riding alongside. Necker was already waiting for them with Daniel and Martín, the two Valladolid militiamen whom Mendoza had managed to wrest from the city council to serve as special constables. Neither of them looked much older than twenty, and Necker towered over them, with his craggy, blocklike face and deep-set green eyes staring out from beneath his three-cornered *alguacil*'s hat and his slightly protruding jaw that always reminded Mendoza of the king's father.

Both of them had served as harquebusiers in the king's armies during the conquest of the Azores the previous year, and Necker assured Mendoza in his impeccable but heavily accented Castilian that they were men of ability and experience. In addition to pistols, swords and daggers, both men had brought two short matchlock carbines or escopetas, which hung in holsters from their horses' saddles.

Mendoza would have preferred flintlock carbines in the mountains, but Necker said that they were the only weapons the militia commander had been willing to part with. If Necker was pleased with the two militiamen, he looked less impressed by Ventura and cast an openly disdainful gaze at his plumed hat, his silver-handled sword and crab-hilt parrying dagger, the ornate pistols clipped to his belt and his knee-length deerskin boots. Ventura merely smiled back and looked dubiously at the enormous double-bladed two-hander that was tied to the saddle of Necker's horse.

"You don't see many of those relics nowadays," he said. "Is it for chopping wood?"

"It was my father's sword," Necker said, bristling.

"As long as you know how to use it."

"I do, sir." Necker tapped the hilt of the shorter Landsknecht sword that hung from his left side and the pistol that hung from the other. "And I also know how to use these."

Mendoza now explained the purpose of the investigation for the first time. Daniel and Martín did not look pleased to hear that they would be away from their homes for some weeks and possibly months in the Morisco lands of Aragon, but the devout Necker's face darkened when Mendoza told them that a priest had been murdered.

"So Moors did this?" he growled.

"That's what we are going to Aragon to find out." He noticed that Martín was looking at him with a perplexed expression. "You have a question, Constable?"

"Yes, sir. Where is Aragon, sir?"

"It's in the Pyrenees. Next to France."

Martín looked none the wiser. "Where is France?" he asked.

"You just keep heading north," Ventura explained, pointing in that direction. "Until you bump into some mountains. Then you cross them."

After loading their mules and horses, they rode slowly back to the Palace of the Chancery to pick up the expenses for the journey. Outside the main entrance, horses and carriages were lined up on the street, accompanied by their drivers and servants, and they followed two handcuffed prisoners who were being led to trial by their guards into the main patio, which was thronged with lawyers, judges and *oidores* in black robes and clients, plaintiffs and defendants waiting for civil and criminal cases, some of whom were already shouting and arguing with one another as notaries and scriveners hurried back and forth clutching sheaves of papers.

It was the usual bedlam, and Mendoza thought that he would not be sorry to be away from it for a while as he and Necker pushed through the crowd to the accountant's office. They returned to the waiting horses, carrying four bulging bags of coins, and Mendoza turned his back on the king's courts and led the expedition out of the city, toward the Crown of Aragon and the distant mountains where His Majesty's laws were being flouted.

CHAPTER FOUR

FROM THE GALLERY OVERLOOKING THE PATIO of Santa Isabel, Inquisitor Mercader looked down at the ornate hedges and orange trees, the bubbling water fountain and the white marble walkways with their lobed Moorish arches. As always they charmed and soothed him, and the fact that they had been built by Moors did not detract from his enjoyment. On the contrary it seemed to him a fitting outcome that the Aljafería Palace that the infidel invaders had constructed centuries ago in Zaragoza and inscribed with prayers to Allah and his false prophet had now become the headquarters of the Inquisition of Aragon. If anything this transformation only enhanced the pleasure that he took in the serrated stucco workings, the geometrical designs and gold-paneled ceilings.

Such buildings were no longer possible in Spain, not since the last conversions of the Aragonese Moors in the second decade of the century. Some of their mosques and public buildings had already been torn down or reconditioned centuries before, and those that remained had undergone the same fate. But it was no bad thing to retain some reminders of what had once been and never could be again, and the massive walls and towers and the defensive ditch provided a formidable barrier against an Aragonese population that, unlike that of Castile, had never wanted the Holy Office in the first place and still resented its presence after nearly a century.

Beyond these walls lay a kingdom infected with heresy and sedition, where Moriscos brazenly followed the law of Muhammad with the complicity of their Christian masters. And nowhere was the infection more advanced than in Cardona, in the mountains of the far north where the infidel Moor known as the Redeemer had called upon the Moriscos to rise up and make war on all the Christians. Mercader pictured him now like a wild creature—hairy, bearded and wearing a turban, with the stink of the forest and the stain of his poisonous faith on his dark skin—looking down from some mountain cave with mad, staring eyes, the image of his damned trickster Prophet. He imagined the Redeemer in the church at Belamar de la Sierra, standing over the body of the dead priest with his scimitar dripping blood, while the Moriscos laughed and looked on approvingly like the murderous savages they were.

These images filled Mercader with disgust. At the same time, he felt a sense of satisfaction and keen anticipation as he imagined the Morisco killer who had dared to threaten him by name, gazing down from his mountainous lair and dreaming of entering Zaragoza with the sultan's army. Whoever this monster was, he no doubt believed, like his fellow heretics, that he was beyond the reach of the law and the Inquisition. But he was wrong. Because all this was about to change, for now the time prophesied by Luke was coming, in which there would be "nothing covered, that shall not be revealed; neither hid, that shall not be known."

These thoughts were interrupted by the sound of footsteps, and a moment later Secretary Bleda appeared at the top of the stairs, accompanied by the tonsured commissioner of the Huesca Inquisition, Domingo Herrero, and his green-clad *familiar* Diego Pachuca.

Mercader looked at them in surprise. "Good afternoon, señores," he said. "I did not expect you to return so soon. Have you made arrests?"

"We have not, Excellency," Herrero replied nervously.

"And why is that?" Mercader's voice was calm, but his eyes were as hard as polished glass.

"We were not able to enter Belamar, Your Excellency. We were prevented from doing so."

"Prevented by whom?"

"By Sánchez!" replied Pachuca indignantly. "He said the Holy Office was not permitted to enter Cardona without the approval of the Cortes."

"Not permitted?" Mercader repeated scornfully. "So the Inquisition must ask the Aragonese parliament for permission even when a priest is murdered and a church defiled?"

"We did, Excellency," Herrero said. "We told Sánchez we had come to read out the Edict of Grace. He insisted that we had no legal authority."

"How fortunate that we have bailiffs to explain the king's laws to us. I assume he didn't stop you by himself?"

"No, Your Excellency," Pachuca replied. "He had forty men with him. And well armed, too. He said the countess had given orders that no one was to enter Belamar without her permission."

"So this Redeemer has threatened the Inquisition directly. He has killed a priest and promised to kill more Christians. Yet this Christian countess will not allow the Inquisition to enter her estates to find him." Mercader grimaced and shook his head at the absurdity of the situation he had described. "This will not stand," he said darkly. "This woman will not defy me."

"Baron Vallcarca has been more cooperative, Excellency," said Herrero. "He has asked us to carry out an investigation at a Morisco village in his *señorio*."

"What village?"

"Todos Santos, Excellency. The baron has received reports of sorcery and witchcraft there."

"And why have I not heard of this place before?"

"We have only just received information about it," Herrero replied. "We believe that these reports are sufficient to warrant a full investigation."

"Baron Vallcarca is a good and faithful Christian. Very well, you may proceed. But we will return to Belamar. These delaying tactics merely confirm the countess's complicity in the depraved practices of her vassals. You will await my orders, and the next time you return to Belamar, you will not be stopped."

Herrero bowed, and Bleda showed the two of them out. Afterward Mercader remained staring for a long time at the gardens and the wisps of cloud that drifted above the patio. The countess's latest act of defiance was frustrating. Now letters and petitions would have to be written and representations made to individuals and institutions, a process that might take weeks or months. But the Inquisition was tenacious, and its authority would prevail. Witchcraft and sorcery were of no real interest or importance to Mercader, nor was Todos Santos. What he wanted were the Moriscos of Belamar. It was only a matter of time before he got them.

And when that happened, the Moriscos and their Redeemer and the mistress who protected them would all discover that no one was immune to God's justice.

EVERY YEAR, in the first or second week of April, the Quintana brothers brought their sheep back up from their winter pasture on the plain of the Ebro to their home village above the Gállego River for the summer. Their father generally advised them to leave before the other shepherds, in order to keep their herds separate and avoid the confrontations that invariably ensued when they brought their herds up through the valleys and across the old drover routes through the Morisco lands that the shepherds had used for centuries. Every spring and autumn, there were quarrels and fights between the Old Christian mountain men and the Moriscos, and some of them were fatal.

These fights generally took place when the *montañeses* drove their cows, goats or sheep right through plowed or cultivated Morisco fields, to the fury of the farmers and peasants who worked on them. Such damage was not always easy to avoid, because the larger herds often strayed from their allotted paths, and the drover routes that shepherds had used for centuries to move their flocks back and forth between the plains and the mountains sometimes led through lands that had been placed under cultivation, where the rights of passage were still disputed by the drovers on the one hand and the lords and their Morisco vassals on the other.

There were also incidents in which the mountain men deliberately led their animals through the Morisco fields and orchards in order to show them that they alone would decide who had the right to cross them. Most of these shepherds were Old Christians whose blood was unstained by any taint of Jew or Moor, and many of them had no compunction about driving their cattle directly through Morisco lands, especially when they were traveling in large groups. The Quintana brothers avoided these confrontations, because their father always advised them to avoid trouble, and they were good Christian boys who obeyed their father, even though they saw him for only four months of the year. This spring they were late getting away, because it had been a harsh and bitter winter even down on the plains, and many lambs had died and others had been born so weak that the brothers had kept them back for extra feeding. On the morning of April 27, the feast day of Our Lady of Moreneta, the Black Virgin of Montserrat, they abandoned the stone hut where they had spent the winter and set off with two mules and fifty sheep on the *cañada* that led around Huesca and through Vallcarca and Cardona.

Their parents had a small statue of La Moreneta at home, and usually the brothers arrived in time to pay homage to her with a candle and prayers, and their mother cooked a special lamb stew in her honor. This year only the feast would still be waiting for them once they had crossed the Morisco lands. Like most drovers, the Quintanas were armed. The eldest brother, Pepe, carried a sword and also a light matchlock hunting rifle, though their father had specifically ordered them not to hunt until they had passed through the *señorio* even if an opportunity presented itself, because that was another potential source of dispute. Juanxo Quintana was also armed with a short sword, and even though Simón Quintana, the youngest, was barely fifteen years old, he carried a hunting dagger in addition to the slingshot he used to keep the herd from straying. None of the brothers had ever used these weapons against a human being, but they were glad to have them when they entered the Belamar Valley on May 5, because the news of the murder of the priest had already reached the lower plains, and there were stories circulating among the shepherds of a Moorish bandit in the mountains above Belamar who cut the throats of Christians and drank their blood.

As usual they aimed to get their flock well above the town by the end of the day and spend the night in the next valley beyond it before pushing on toward their home village the next morning. They took the usual route along the right-hand side of the valley, using stones to keep the herd bunched and moving at the same unhurried speed and preventing wayward animals from straying onto the plowed or cultivated fields, orchards and vineyards. The valley looked much the same as it had the previous year as they passed laborers chipping away in the fields and terraces and weeding with forks and hoes, in some cases helped by their wives and children. As they drew closer toward the ravine below the town, they saw men and women going about their business above them, and only the barking dogs showed any interest in their presence.

By the time they began to climb up through the woods, the three brothers had already begun to relax as the line of sheep spread out along the well-beaten path. By the early evening, they had crossed over the ridge and reached the higher valley, where they usually camped. The brothers were in a cheerful mood, knowing that they were less than a day away from their family and neighbors, whom they had not seen for nearly eight months. They ate the same supper of bread, oil and vinegar that they had eaten every day since leaving the plains, and Pepe undertook to light a fire while his brothers went to gather more firewood from the edge of the forest.

Simón was just returning from the woods with a pile of branches when the men on horseback came bursting out of the woods on the other side of the field, riding hard toward the campsite and scattering the sheep before them. From where he was standing, their faces were nothing more than misshapen white blobs, and it wasn't until they came closer that he realized they were wearing masks. He saw Pepe run for the rifle, but he did not even have time to load it before one of the riders came alongside him and shot him in the back with a long pistol.

The firewood dropped from Simón's hands as his brother toppled over, and Juanxo came running toward him, pursued by two of the horsemen. One of the riders leaned out to his side, with one hand holding the reins, and brought the curved falchion sword down into Juanxo's neck. Pepe was still trying to crawl away as the rider who had shot him walked slowly toward him and planted a foot on either side of his body. Simón watched as he drew a long pommeled dagger, squatted down and drove it into his brother's back, pushing on the round hilt with both hands. It was only then that Simón turned and ran back toward the forest. He had nearly reached the trees when he saw the flashes of white ahead of him, and the crossbow bolt struck him in the chest just above the heart. The grass seemed to turn to liquid beneath his feet as he sank down into it and the sheep ran past him, with no one left to guide them.

. . .

THE JOURNEY NORTHEAST from Valladolid to Zaragoza took twelve days, even though Mendoza followed the most direct route through Aranda de Duero, Soria and Tarazona across the Castilian plain known as the *meseta*. Gabriel had never ridden for so long and so far. After two days he could barely walk upright, and it was an effort even to get back on his mule. By the fourth day, he had begun to get used to being in the saddle, but the roads were poor and sometimes almost nonexistent. In some places they had to lead their animals knee- and even waist-deep through water, because the road had been washed away and a bridge had collapsed. On some days they traveled for hours along dusty roads through an interminable, almost treeless plain, where only the occasional farm, castle or shepherd's stone hut provided anything to relieve the emptiness. And then they would come across a beautiful town like Aranda, with its fine churches and squares, its shops and markets and its ancient stone bridge spanning the green banks and rows of poplars that lined the Duero.

On some nights they camped out on the great plain in the open air, and he preferred this to the grubby inns run by fat men who looked as if they had gone to sleep in their unwashed aprons and by wide-hipped women with sullen faces and unwashed and unbrushed hair, where they slept two to a bed on dirt-encrusted sheets red with blood from mosquito bites or sometimes on the floor, in low rooms that reeked of wine, brandy and bacon. Even though they ate the meat that they brought themselves, the inns were insalubrious and evil-smelling, with walls black from smoke and plates and cups that were as greasy as the tables.

He preferred to camp outside, despite the cold, and eat the raisins, fruits and fresh bread that they bought from markets or peasant roadside vendors. One evening Ventura used his crossbow to shoot a rabbit, which they cooked at the campfire. On another afternoon Mendoza bought a lamb from a peasant and Ventura slaughtered it on the spot before slinging it over his saddle. Most days they rode from early morning until late in the afternoon, because Don Bernardo was determined to reach Aragon as quickly as possible.

Despite the physical discomfort and the primitive conditions, Gabriel felt happy. In Valladolid he had risen early and gone to bed early. Apart from Don Bernardo and Magdalena, his companions were classmates, tutors, teachers and priests, and the boundaries of his world had consisted of the Pisuerga and Esgueva Rivers and the poorer suburbs that Magda always told him to keep away from.

Now there were no classmates to call him "Moor," "bum boy" and "slave," and he thought of the envy that his tormentors would feel if they could see him riding in the company of policemen and soldiers on a mission in the service of His Majesty the king to the land of James the Conqueror and Ferdinand the Catholic. Every day he saw a world that most of them had never seen, and the more he saw of his native land, the more impossible it seemed to him that there could be a greater country than Spain, or that the Turk or any ruler in Christendom could ever hope to conquer it.

He took an almost proprietary pride in its walled cities and strong castles, in the monasteries and convents perched on mountainsides and cliff edges. Despite Mendoza's urgency, Gabriel's guardian invariably found time to stop at churches and cathedrals or a fine palace or public building and admire the paintings, the wood and stone carvings and gilded altar panels or retablos, or point out some example of fine workmanship in the construction of a pillar or an arch or pictorial skill in the features of Jesus and Mary or the face of an apostle from a Gothic bas-relief, or examine a few rocks that he said might have belonged to the ruins of Numancia, where the Celts of Iberia had once committed suicide rather than surrender to Scipio's legions.

He cast a more critical eye at the sight of fields that should have been under cultivation and had instead been left barren for no good reason, at streams and creeks that should have been dammed up or directed into canals, at bridges that had not been maintained. Such things were bad for Spain, he said, because a hungry population was an unhappy population, and unhappiness bred lawlessness, crime and rebellion.

Gabriel knew that these observations were part of his education, but he was always more interested in the people they encountered than he was in his guardian's meditations on architecture, agriculture or road maintenance. Along the roads they encountered a wide variety of people from all trades and classes, from muleteers and merchants carrying carts piled with merchandise to priests, monks, nuns and soldiers; from sellers of real or faked indulgences to French and Italian craftsmen; from laborers and stonemasons heading for Valladolid and Madrid in search of work to nobles in gleaming black coaches with leather interiors and silk curtains to protect their passengers from the dust. Some traveled alone on foot or horseback; others had formed groups for protection as they moved along roads where the only visible signs of law and order were the constables from the Holy Brotherhood who intermittently patrolled the highways of Castile.

Many members of the Santa Hermandad looked like bandits and

highwaymen themselves. They were grim, hard-faced men who wore leather chest armor and bristled with weapons. On Mendoza's party's fifth day out, they saw a small crowd standing by the roadside just outside a village. As they drew closer, they saw three members of the Hermandad holding a young man to the ground while another stood waiting with an ax. The young man was almost naked, and he was writhing desperately in an attempt to escape. Necker paused to ask what was happening, and it was not until they had ridden past that he told Gabriel that the Holy Brothers were about to cut off the young man's right hand because he had been caught thieving in a market.

They also encountered peasants sitting outside mud houses, in rough yarn shirts and hide jackets, some of whom were barefoot or wearing tattered rope-soled sandals, and shepherds with their flocks whose dirty, unwashed faces and primitive appearance shocked him. Everywhere there were paupers and vagabonds moving from one place to another, who Mendoza said would have been arrested had he encountered them in Valladolid. Some were army veterans, missing arms and legs, who clustered around them brandishing their stumps or pointing at their mutilated faces, crying out "Lepanto! Lepanto!" and the names of other wars and battles.

Mendoza said that these experiences were sometimes invented, and Lepanto was a particular favorite of beggars because of the religious obligation it entailed. To have fought at Lepanto was to have fought in a war blessed by the pope and all the great princes of Christendom, and it was incumbent on all good Christians to treat its veterans with charity, reverence and gratitude. Ventura sometimes caught them out by inventing the names of ships and asking if they had fought on them, and Mendoza threatened to arrest those who said they had.

. . .

THE PLEASURE OF THE JOURNEY was greatly enhanced by Gabriel's traveling companions. They spoke of cities he had only read or heard about, such as Antwerp, Paris, Rome, Tunis and Naples, with the easy familiarity with which the people of Valladolid spoke about their neighborhoods or surrounding villages. Even Daniel and Martín had been to Lisbon and the Azores, despite the fact that they were only a few years older than Gabriel. In the evenings they passed stories back and forth across the campfire or the tavern table, of wars and battles in the Alpujarras and the marshes of Flanders, of wounds and narrow escapes, of bandits and criminals arrested or killed.

They were men of action who seemed afraid of nothing. They drank wine and brandy and cursed—particularly Ventura, who uttered a constant stream of profanities despite Necker's obvious disapproval. Mendoza took little part in these exchanges. Most evenings he rarely talked at all but sat reading his book or drawing faces or architectural features from memory in the leather-bound sketchbook that he had brought with him.

Of the two special constables, Gabriel liked Daniel more. Martín was taciturn and morose and gave the impression that he regarded a scribe who had never borne arms as a burden to be carried rather than an asset to the group. Daniel was more cheerful. One afternoon when they were out gathering firewood together, he explained that Martín had a wife and child in Valladolid and didn't want to spend a long time away from them.

"Me, I'm happy to be away," Daniel said. "Just as long as I get back by next summer."

"Why next summer?"

"I'm getting married, *chico*. Settling down. I'm going to work on my wife's parents' farm. I've had enough of bad food and officers screaming in my face. And I'd rather ride a good woman by night than a bad horse by day, if you know what I mean?"

Gabriel did not, but he sensed that he should. All this manly talk made him conscious of his own inexperience and bookishness and filled him with a determination to show his companions that he was more than a scribe. He saddled and unsaddled mules and horses. He gathered firewood and learned how to strike two flints and make a fire himself. He also tried out his companions' weapons. Almost every evening he persuaded one of them to give him basic instructions in fencing positions and technique. Necker's zweihänder was too heavy and unwieldy. Gabriel preferred Daniel's short cinquedea with its thick base almost as wide as a hand tapering off to a sharp point, his guardian's side sword with its bluish tempered steel or Ventura's basilard parrying dagger and swept-hilt Italian rapier with its S-shaped guard, its silver pommel and leather grip and the Latin words *Usque mors*—"Until death"—which Ventura had had engraved in the blade just above the guard.

With these weapons Gabriel learned how to position his feet, to thrust, lunge and parry and to gauge distance and anticipate his opponent's movements. He also learned about the different schools of fencing. Ventura talked about Euclid's theories of geometry, about the relative importance of obtuse and right angles in the meeting of the blades, about the exact distance of each step and the positioning of the feet for a thrust and lunge, about maintaining distance through circular movement within the same sphere and the importance of maintaining the same parallel distance between the rapier and parrying dagger.

Ventura used Italian as well as Spanish expressions to describe particular movements and strikes. He talked of the *mediotajo*—the cut from the elbow—the *stramazzone*—the flip of the point—and the *stoccata*—the thrust delivered under the opponent's sword with a turning of the wrist. Necker had learned his sword fighting in the Holy Roman emperor's mercenary Landsknecht and was not impressed by Ventura's intellectual approach. He often made disparaging remarks about the lighter blade that Ventura used and his enthusiasm for the new Italian methods, and Ventura teased him that his own sword was good for sacking Rome but not much else. One evening as they were setting up camp in an open field where Mendoza said that Numancia might once have stood, Ventura playfully insisted that the Passau wolf on Necker's two-hander was a fake and annoyed him so much that the German challenged him to a mock duel.

Mendoza agreed, on condition that there was no blood or physical contact. For more than half an hour, the two men fought in the open air, and Ventura eventually won the argument, as he effortlessly parried and evaded the big German's slashing attacks before finally dropping onto one knee to deliver what would have been a killing blow. As Gabriel watched them fight and listened to the clash of their swords, he thought of the legions at Numancia, of Roman gladiators, and imagined himself and his companions as a band of knights embarking on a great quest.

As much as he admired their skill, Gabriel could not imagine himself actually thrusting a sword into another man's body, and he could not entirely shake off his nervousness whenever a sword was pointed at him. His favorite weapons were Ventura's pair of matching flintlock pistols. Sometimes he held them simply in order to admire their lacquered finish, the mother-of-pearl inlay of hunters chasing deer and the delicate floral designs in the metal barrels. The first time he held them, he thought they were the most beautiful objects he had ever seen.

"Has anyone ever tried to steal them?" he asked.

"Sometimes," Ventura replied. "But I still have them."

That evening Ventura taught him how to load and cock a pistol, and Gabriel fired two shots at a piece of wood that he set up as a target. On both occasions he missed. That same evening Daniel demonstrated how to load, aim and fire his escopeta. The militiaman hit the target from just under eighty yards, but when Gabriel tried from a much shorter distance, the kickback knocked him backward and the weapon nearly slipped from his hands, to general hilarity. That night he lay awake for a long time as the others slept, looking up at the stars and imagining himself performing heroic deeds and wondering whether he had the courage required. It was comforting to think that he was accompanied by men who did and who would not be deterred or intimidated by the prospect of bandits or the dubious-looking characters they sometimes met on the roads who cast furtive predatory glances at their horses and possessions. It was especially reassuring to think that he'd be accompanied by such men when they arrived in the Morisco lands. He had never met a Morisco, as far as he knew, but he had heard terrible stories about them. Magda said that the Moriscos of Granada were more like devils than humans. She told him that they drowned priests in barrels of wine, that they ate the hearts of Christians and cut the throats of young babies. Lying there beneath his thin blanket, Gabriel tried to imagine what kind of men would do such things, and he felt a chill that was only partly due to the cool breeze that blew across the barren *meseta*. For a few moments, he imagined that he heard faint screams that might have been his own.

CHAPTER FIVE

ON THE TENTH DAY, THEY SAW THE BOUNDary stones that divided Castile from Aragon and passed through the customs post at the walled city of Tarazona, some eighty leagues northeast of Valladolid. The next day they traveled over a flat desert plain that was even more barren and arid than Castile, where the surface of the land seemed to have been torn away and there was barely a tree or any sign of human habitation. The following day the land became more fertile as they took the ferry across the Ebro River and followed its course eastward toward Zaragoza.

In the early evening, they saw the Aragonese capital up ahead, and Ventura pointed out the four rounded towers of the Basilica-Cathedral of Our Lady of the Pillar among the mass of churches, palaces and great buildings that dominated the plain. With its ancient stone walls, its riverbank palaces, its churches and the imposing towers of the Basilica, it was easily the most splendid and most crowded city Gabriel had ever seen. At the massive stone bridge that led to the Puerta del Ángel, they stopped at the tollbooth to pay yet another fee and rode into the crowded central thoroughfare known as the Corso. Gabriel stared in admiration and amazement at the merchants and traders milling around the grand market building, at the rows of shops and craftsmen's workshops, at the brick and stone palaces, some of them three or even four stories high, with curved wooden doors flanked by ornate pillars and statues.

He was still taking all this in when they heard a commotion coming from one of the adjoining streets, and a crowd came surging toward them. Three green-clad men on foot were accompanying a topless woman who was sitting tied to a mule with her head bowed in shame as the members of the crowd mocked her and shouted abuse. Gabriel was staring with guilty fascination at her breasts when suddenly one of the green-clad men brought a whip down across her back with such force that she sobbed.

Behind her a priest in a soutane was alternately praying in Latin and shouting out over and over again that the woman's name was Juliana Maldonado and that she was guilty of adultery as the whip crashed down repeatedly on her back. With each blow the woman let out another cry or begged her tormentors to stop, and every time she did so, the crowd jeered with a relish and satisfaction that Gabriel found revolting.

"The dogs of God," muttered Ventura contemptuously. "Aren't they the pride of Spain? If every wife who committed adultery was flogged, the country would run out of whips."

"Careful, cousin." Mendoza had forgotten his cousin's visceral loathing of the Inquisition. Ventura, unlike him, had seen his father paraded in his sanbenito in the act of faith with his penitent's candle, and he had always blamed the Holy Office for his subsequent death. Mendoza imagined Elena on the back of the mule, and he was relieved when the crowd swept past them and the sobs and swish of the whip began to fade. The viceroy's palace was located in the middle of the Corso, and they announced their presence to a servant who was waiting by the door. A few minutes later, Don Artal de Alagón, the third Count of Sástago and viceroy of Aragon, came out to meet them.

"Licenciado Mendoza! Welcome! We've been expecting you." The count barely even looked at Mendoza's companions as his servants now hurried around them to unload their animals and take them to the nearby stables. He ushered them into a wide courtyard, with pink walls and marble tiles, flanked by four floors of overlooking balconies. His servants took Necker, Gabriel and the two militiamen to their quarters on the first floor, while Mendoza and Ventura were taken to their rooms on the second, where his wife was waiting to receive them.

She was a dour and somewhat plain-looking woman, with her hair tied up in a bun above her forehead and a severe black dress in the austere Castilian style that was buttoned up to the neck and flattened out her bosom, but Ventura bowed with an elegance that would not have disgraced a courtier and kissed her outstretched hand. The count led them through an enormous reception room with a beautifully carved and painted wooden ceiling, past portraits of knights, soldiers and aristocrats, and showed them to two large and well-furnished paneled rooms that adjoined each other.

"His Majesty will be staying in these rooms during the wedding," the count said proudly.

"His Majesty does you great honor," Mendoza observed.

"He does Zaragoza great honor, Don Bernardo. For our city this will be the most momentous event since the emperor received the crown of Aragon. The entire court will be here. And princes, diplomats and other great men. You have no idea how much work and effort this requires to prepare. Hardly a day passes without some new demand or instruction from Madrid. We talk and think of nothing else. The only question is whether we can get everything done in time."

"I'm sure you will," Mendoza said reassuringly.

"We have to. But I shall let you rest. My servants will bring you hot water shortly."

Mendoza thanked him, and he bowed and shut the door. Ventura lay down heavily on the mattress with his boots on as the viceroy's footsteps echoed down the corridor.

"It's not often I've lain down in a king's bed." He grinned.

"The king may not lie on it if we fail," Mendoza said. "And I think you should take your boots off, cousin."

Shortly afterward Gabriel came upstairs to assist Mendoza as he bathed and changed. After they had rested, a servant summoned them to the dining room for supper. They found the countess seated in the Moorish style on a large cushion in the dining room, sucking on a piece of glazed pottery, as many Castilian women did, because of its sweet taste and because they believed that it made their skin whiter and more attractive. Mendoza did not know whether sucking pottery really had this effect, but he found it simultaneously unappealing and vaguely erotic. Her husband and two other men were sitting in chairs. One of them was a white-bearded prelate in a purple soutane. The other was a younger man dressed in somber dark brown, with a crisp white collar and white sleeves protruding from his tunic and a large crucifix around his neck. He might have been in his early thirties, but his gaunt cheekbones, sallow complexion, hooded dark eyes and lack of hair made him look older. The count introduced Monseñor Andrés Santos, the bishop of Zaragoza, and Inquisitor Don Felipe Silesio de Mercader. Mendoza kissed the bishop's ring and shook Mercader's bony hand.

"A pleasure to meet you, Alcalde," the inquisitor said. "We are all very curious about your mission here."

"Inquisitor Mercader, please," scolded the countess. "These poor men have been on the roads for two weeks now. Let them at least eat something before you discuss business."

Mercader's thin lips tightened in the vague approximation of a smile, a movement that clearly did not come easily to him. It soon became obvious that he had no interest in small talk, as the countess brought up the subject of the court's visit to Aragon in the coming year and the marriage of the infanta Catalina to the Duke of Savoy.

Mendoza was always bored with talk of marriages, dynastic or otherwise, but the wine and food were excellent, and the main course of shredded partridge cooked in melted cheese and laid on tostadas tasted even better after the last two weeks. Mercader showed little interest in the food or the dinner table conversation and barely spoke at all. It was not until dinner was over and the countess had discreetly left the men to talk, that the inquisitor immediately returned to the subject that was clearly uppermost on his mind.

"Count Sástago tells me that you are here to investigate the murder of Father Panalles," he said.

"That—and other matters," Mendoza replied.

"What matters?"

Mendoza suppressed his irritation at the inquisitor's sense of entitlement.

"His Majesty is concerned at the situation in the Morisco lands near the French frontier."

"You are referring to the Redeemer?"

"Among other things."

"His Majesty is right to be concerned," Mercader agreed. "But it is still not clear to me why he chose to entrust this investigation to the secular justices rather than the Inquisition. This problem would not have become so deep-rooted had it not been for the complete impunity with which the enemies of God in Belamar are allowed to flaunt their heresy and treason. Our own officers tried to go there two weeks ago to read out the Edict of Grace, and they were turned away!"

"Turned away by whom?" Mendoza asked.

"By vassals of the Countess of Cardona, acting under her authority, bearing weapons! They said the Holy Office was not allowed to execute its duties in her territory."

Mendoza had not been aware that the Inquisition had attempted to enact the Edict of Grace in Belamar. Had that taken place, its population would have been given a month to confess their crimes voluntarily or denounce their neighbors before the Inquisition began its investigation. This process inevitably resulted in arrests and denunciations, and those found guilty faced even more severe punishment because they had not come forward of their own free will. The evidence against them here, unlike that in civil courts, was always kept secret, and most of those who were arrested would not even know who had denounced them. If nothing else, such an investigation was not likely to do anything to facilitate his own, and he could not help feeling grateful to the militiamen who had turned Mercader's officials back.

"Did the Holy Office receive any specific information that prompted an Edict of Grace?" he asked.

"As you know, the Inquisition does not share its sources with the secular justices."

Mendoza did not tell Mercader that he was already familiar with many of the allegations against the Moriscos of Belamar from the documents that Villareal had given him, which included a copy of Mercader's own report to the inquisitor-general. That report was more than a year old, and most of the accusations contained within it consisted of religious offenses that were not his concern. It was not his responsibility to arrest Moriscos because they failed to pay attention at Mass or comported themselves in a disrespectful and unchristian manner during Communion, because they made insulting remarks about the Virgin or questioned the existence of the Holy Ghost. Nor was he interested in whether they went to confession during Lent.

Moriscos who possessed Arabic books and texts or performed Moorish prayers and religious ablutions fell under the jurisdiction of the Inquisition. But there were also allegations where the boundaries were less clear, whether it was the reports of sedition or of the stockpiling of weapons and gunpowder, and if Belamar really was the heretic's nest that Mercader had described, it might also explain why Father Juan Panalles had been murdered.

"How long ago was the edict prepared?" he asked.

"It was ready in February this year." Mercader looked visibly impatient. "Father Panalles had been reporting for some time that the Moriscos of Belamar were continuing to worship as Moors, and we have received similar reports from some of the other Morisco villages in Cardona for many years. Neither the countess nor her late husband ever did anything about them."

"Her late husband?" Mendoza asked.

"The count was murdered by bandits two years ago," said Bishop Santos. "The perpetrators were never found. In Cardona they rarely are."

"And was this Redeemer around then?"

"We hadn't heard of him until this year," Mercader replied. "If he was, he didn't announce himself. In any case he would have had no reason to kill the Count of Cardona, because a better friend of the Moriscos would be hard to find. Unfortunately, Licenciado, the Christian lords in Aragon don't always show the necessary zeal when it comes to dealing with these Moriscos. And the Count of Cardona was a very obliging master—like his wife. The Moriscos have more reason to love them than fear them."

Mercader paused, and Mendoza sensed that the inquisitor was gauging his reaction to see which of the two options he preferred. "I saw the message that the Redeemer wrote to you," he said. "Is there any reason he should write to you in particular?"

"These Moriscos know that I do not tolerate their heresies." Mercader's thin smile bore a hint of self-satisfaction. "They have good reason to regard me as their enemy."

"And does the Holy Office have any information regarding the possible identity or provenance of this individual?" Mendoza asked.

"We believe he comes from Belamar," Mercader said. "And have no doubt that we will discover who he is once we carry out a full investigation in the village. The Inquisition of Aragon already has more than sufficient grounds to take such action. And may I ask how you propose to enter Belamar when we could not?"

Mendoza felt irritated by the sarcasm, and by the inquisitor's general demeanor, but he replied evenly. "I shall deal with that problem when I encounter it."

"Someone needs to deal with it," said Santos. "There has been no priest in Belamar for two months now. And one of the main roads to Santiago de Compostela runs through Cardona from the Somport Pass. Soon the first pilgrims of the season will begin to cross the mountains. There are shops and inns that cannot afford to lose the trade."

"The roads will not be safe," Mercader added, "until Cardona has been cleansed of heretics as well as bandits."

THAT NIGHT MENDOZA SLEPT in a comfortable bed for the first time since leaving Valladolid. The next morning he and Ventura ate a fine breakfast of figs, raisins, bread, cheese, honey and hot chocolate with the viceroy, who apologized for the inquisitor's rudeness the previous night.

"Mercader was only assigned to Aragon last year," he said. "He just regards the post as a step toward a cardinal's cap. He has no understanding of the way things are done here. He sees heresy everywhere, and he hates the Moriscos. I believe he'd burn them all if he could."

"And you, Your Grace? Do you believe that the countess is obstructing the Inquisition?"

"Who knows?" Sástago popped a fig into his mouth. "She's certainly very fond of her Moriscos. But then so are many of the Aragonese lords, and if they aren't fond of them, they recognize their usefulness. The Moriscos work hard and they work well, and many lords are more concerned with revenue than faith. That doesn't make them heretics. I met the countess once when she came to the parliament at Monzón with her husband."

"And what was your impression of her?"

"A real beauty!" The viceroy smiled dreamily. "And a more devout Christian would be hard to find. But a woman such as that is more likely to be found in a convent than an artist's studio—unfortunately."

"Why do you say that?"

"The countess's mother died when she was a child. Her father passed away six years ago. And then her husband was murdered by bandits. These misfortunes have tempered her faith. No woman is more pious or more anxious to do good works. She is one of the richest women in Aragon, yet she travels with almost no retinue. The demesne of Cardona has about a hundred and fifty towns, villages, hamlets and castles. It has toll bridges, lead and iron mines and flour mills. Its forests send timber to the carpenters of Zaragoza and Valencia. Her neighbor the Baron of Vallcarca doesn't even have half that number."

"Does Vallcarca have bandits in his *señorio*?"

"Some. But it's worse in Cardona. Vallcarca is a very hard man. He treats his vassals like slaves and bandits like rebels. Some say that the bandits in Cardona fled his estates because they couldn't stand to be his vassals. In any case the banditry has gotten a lot worse since the count died. Some roads, you take your life and property in your hands even by day."

"Is the countess likely to marry again?"

Sástago blew on his chocolate to cool it. "In theory, yes. And a lot of men would like her to marry them. What woman wouldn't have suitors, with an annual income of ninety thousand ducats? Vallcarca wants her to marry his son—a degenerate brute like his father, but without his cunning and intelligence."

"Could that happen?"

"Who knows? It would suit Vallcarca very well if the two families could be united. He spends money too quickly and manages his estates badly. The countess doesn't. She has an excellent bailiff, Jean Sánchez. He's half French, and some say he's the man who really runs Cardona. But if Rodrigo Vallcarca married the countess, then he would become one of the richest men in Aragon, and his father would be the one in charge. But they say the countess has no interest in such a match. And really, I can't imagine her with a man like Rodrigo Vallcarca, not by choice anyway. There are stories about how he treats some of the female vassals, stories I hesitate to repeat. Of course, all these are just rumors, and every rumor in the mountains has a counter-rumor. You will have your work cut out up there, Licenciado, mark my words. Are you sure you don't want a larger escort?"

"Thank you, Your Excellency. But I prefer to travel as unobtrusively as possible. And I want to get there quickly."

"Well, I've brought you a map of Cardona and the surrounding area. It's not much good—many of the roads and paths are not even marked—but it does tell you more or less where the main roads and towns are, and the location of the frontier and customs posts. You may take whatever food you need from my kitchen. Just tell the servants what you require, and they will get it for you."

"That is most helpful."

"No need to thank me, Licenciado. If you find this Redeemer, you'll be doing all of us a favor."

Mendoza told the others to be ready in two hours and returned to his room to look at the map the count had given him. Soon afterward he heard footsteps coming rapidly down the stone corridor, and one of Sástago's servants appeared to say that the viceroy needed to see him urgently. Downstairs in the patio, Inquisitor Mercader was engaged in agitated conversation with Sástago and two other men. One of them was the Inquisition *familiar* who had been flogging the unfortunate adulteress the previous day. Mendoza had never had much respect for the Inquisition's secular helpers, but this one was a particularly unpleasant example of a bad breed. Close up he exuded cruelty and malice, from his broad shoulders and low, thick neck to his apelike hands to the sunken, narrow eyes that peered pitilessly from beneath the fringe that fell down over his forehead. His companion was a young, earnest-looking man whose mud-splattered boots and dusty cloak testified to his recent arrival from the countryside.

"Bad news, Mendoza," the viceroy said. "This is Constable Vargas, the chief constable of Jaca. It seems that three brothers have been found murdered near Belamar. All of them are Old Christians."

"One of them was nailed to a cross!" Mercader exclaimed. "With the heads of his brothers arranged next to him!"

"You saw this?" Mendoza asked.

"No, Your Mercy," replied the *alguacil*. "But some *montañeses* found him hanging on a cross by a shrine, about two leagues above the town, and they took him down. The constable at Belamar saw him and sent a messenger to Don Pelagio."

"When did this happen?"

"The bodies were found four days ago, in the afternoon."

Mercader's narrow eyes glittered, and his cadaverous features bore an expression of bitter fury as he turned toward Mendoza. "Now do you understand the kind of people we are dealing with, Alcalde?" he said.

CHAPTER SIX

THEY HEADED NORTHWARD THROUGH A treeless landscape broken by eroded, lightly cultivated fields and white hills before climbing gradually up toward Huesca and the Pyrenean foothills. After spending an uncomfortable first night in a damp and bug-infested inn near Huesca, they resumed their upward progress through the Monrepos Pass the following morning. On reaching the pass, they found themselves looking over a series of immense, wide valleys with forest-covered slopes that stretched out toward the snow-tipped peaks of the Pyrenees.

Mendoza was impressed by the scale of the mountains, by the towering slabs of rust-colored rock and the dense forests of oak, birch and pine, by the castles and fortified towers and the alpine meadows speckled with edelweiss and sweet basil, but he was also wary. He had ordered his men to load their pistols, but the only traffic they encountered on the roads consisted of peasants bringing their produce down to the markets in Huesca or Zaragoza or shepherds driving cattle, sheep and goats up toward the higher valleys. From time to time, they saw the raftsmen precariously balanced on giant rafts made from tree trunks that they were taking to Zaragoza on the fast-moving rivers, skillfully navigating their way through the surging waters with wooden rudders at the front and back.

The roads were poor, and progress was slow as they guided their animals across streams and rivers, with Necker riding ahead of the group and scanning both sides of the road while Ventura kept up the rear guard. On the second afternoon, they reached the plain of Jaca, the former capital of Aragon, and followed the flat road into the city through the former Jewish quarter, past the old Roman walls, converted synagogues, Romanesque churches, elegant three- and four-story houses with painted wooden eaves, and a large square tower that had once been the town jail.

Constable Vargas took them directly to the stone courthouse, where dozens of vagabonds, beggars and poor women were lining up to receive bowls of soup and hunks of bread. Mendoza saw a short, plump man in a cape and a soft green bonnet checking begging permits with another official who wore the red badge of an *alguacil* on his chest. It was not until they turned around that he realized that the man in the bonnet was his old friend Pelagio Calvo.

"Well, well, if it isn't Bernardo de Mendoza!" Pelagio grinned. "Should I call you 'Licenciado' or 'Your Honor'? How long has it been, my friend?"

"Too long," Mendoza replied as the corregidor enveloped him in a warm embrace. He looked at his old friend's thick walrus mustache and stubbled jowls and protruding belly. Calvo had not aged well. His hair and beard were tinged with gray, and he was barrel-shaped where he had once been firm and stocky. His clothes were of good quality but not especially rich or extravagant, and he looked like so many other provincial magistrates. Organizing soup kitchens and food distributions for the poor was as much a part of the duties of a corregidor as arresting vagrants, and Calvo exuded a mixture of quiet authority and obvious boredom as he looked over the proceedings.

"A real hornet's nest you've walked into, Bernardo," he said. "This is Constable Franquelo from Belamar. He brought in the three dead shepherds this morning."

"The Quintana brothers are here?"

"Yes, they're at the hospital. Their father is coming to collect them today."

"I'd like to see their bodies first."

"Vargas can take care of this. But it's not a pretty sight. Are these all the men you've brought with you? You'll need more than that if you're going to Cardona."

"I was told that discretion was required," Mendoza replied.

"If you want my opinion, Bernardo, His Majesty has shown a little too much discretion in these parts already. We only buried the priest last month, and now this! I don't have the manpower to deal with this level of mayhem! In theory I can call up seventy, even a hundred volunteers for the militia. But you can't do it just like that. I have to send my people all round the towns and villages to get them, and that takes time. And they can't stay out permanently. This is the Pyrenees, Mendoza, not the *meseta*. I don't think they always understand what that means in Madrid—or even in Zaragoza."

The hospital was a large, three-story building only a few minutes from the courthouse. It was staffed mostly by nuns, and in the mortuary the three bodies were lying side by side on wooden tables. Mendoza had seen many corpses in his life, but the three naked, headless shepherds were a shocking and disturbing sight. One had been shot in the chest. Another had been struck in the chest by a crossbow bolt. The third had a deep diagonal cut just above his right shoulder. The boy with the crossbow bolt bore the marks of wounds on his hands and feet and also on his chest. All the bodies had been washed, including the three heads lying neatly in a basket, and as Mendoza looked more closely at the boy's chest, he saw that the wounds were in fact letters that had been carved into it with a knife.

"IHS," he murmured. "The Holy Name of Jesus."

"That's what it says?" Franquelo made the sign of the cross. "The dirty heathen scum."

Mendoza thought of the first weeks of the Morisco rebellion in Granada, when the Moriscos had slaughtered the Christians of the Alpujarras. It was all strikingly similar, from the grotesque blasphemy and sadism to the mockery of religious symbols and rituals. And yet it seemed incredible that the Moriscos of Aragon should have dared to embark on such a provocation after the terrible punishment that had been inflicted on Granada. Gabriel was standing nearby, looking pale and distraught, and he suddenly hurried from the room with one hand over his mouth.

They found him outside in the street, leaning over a pool of vomit.

"Are you all right?" Mendoza asked.

Gabriel nodded, obviously embarrassed at being the center of attention. Just then they heard the clatter of hooves, and a mule-drawn cart pulled up outside the entrance to the hospital. In the driver's seat, a bearded old man in a frayed gray tunic and cloth cap held the reins. He was flanked by two younger men, both of whom were carrying swords and daggers. Two more men were seated in the back, one of whom was holding an escopeta across his lap.

"I've come for my boys, Franquelo," the old man said.

"They're inside, Paco. This is Alcalde Mendoza. The king has sent him from Valladolid to bring these villains to justice."

"There's only one kind of justice these devils understand."

"I promise you, Señor Quintana, that I will do everything I can to find who killed your sons," Mendoza assured him.

"Then you better go to Belamar de la Sierra, because that's where those devils came from, and everybody knows it." Quintana turned away into the hospital without waiting for a reply.

"DO YOU HAVE ANY SUSPECTS?" Mendoza asked Franquelo as they walked back to the courthouse.

"No, sir, but the killers went to a lot of trouble to crucify them. The campsite where they were killed is nearly an hour away on horseback."

"Have you searched this place?"

"Not yet. We haven't had time."

Like many rural *alguaciles* Mendoza had known, Franquelo did not seem overburdened with energy or intelligence. "And what about the priest? Do you have any suspects for that?"

Calvo laughed. "Yes—the whole town! Panalles was stuck like a pig, but no one heard him scream. Whoever did it also had time to desecrate the church, but the whole town just slept through it! No one is talking! Not to me. Not to the Inquisition. And not to Franquelo. I tell you, Bernardo, what we need to do is make a couple of arrests, bring them down here and stretch them till they talk. Then maybe the fear will open up some lines of inquiry. Especially after this."

Mendoza said nothing. Even though he himself had subjected suspects to the torment, he did not approve of torture either as a first resort or as a substitute for a full investigation, and he was disappointed to hear his old friend advocating such primitive methods.

"One thing is certain," Calvo said. "This was some kind of message. Bandits would just have robbed them. They wouldn't have carved them up like this and carried them up to the road for every pilgrim to see."

"The Redeemer?" Mendoza suggested.

"Oh, so you've heard about our Morisco avenger? Who knows? There are all kinds of wild stories going around the villages about this man. That he hides in a magic cave whose entrance opens and closes on command and rides a green horse and is armed with a scimitar. Some say he's seven feet tall and has four fingers on his right hand. There are even those who will tell you that he isn't a man at all but the ghost of Tariq ibn Ziyad, come to reconquer Spain for the Moors. Of course, when you actually ask around, you find that nobody's actually seen him—they've just heard of someone who has. These are simple people, Bernardo, people of the mountains. Some of them still believe that the high peaks are filled with dragons and monsters."

"And you? What do you believe?"

Calvo shrugged. "Well, these bodies are real. And they weren't killed for their money. Those shepherds weren't rich."

Mendoza had intended to continue to Belamar that same day, but Calvo now pressed him to stay for supper and offered to find them rooms in a local inn that was used by pilgrims. The prospect of a bed and good food swayed Mendoza, and that night they ate at the corregidor's well-appointed house. Unlike the viceroy, Calvo did not stand on ceremony, and Necker, Gabriel and the militiamen were also allowed to eat with him and his wife. Calvo had not been married when Mendoza last saw him, and his Dutch wife, Cornelia, was definitely something of a catch for a man who was not the most imposing physical specimen. She looked at least ten years younger than Calvo, with lustrous blond hair and creamy white skin and a voluptuous figure that her loose-fitting robes accentuated, to the obvious admiration of her husband's guests.

Mendoza found her less appealing. He disliked the way that she flirted with Ventura and the two militiamen as if her husband were not there. He noticed how Calvo gave her endearing looks that she did not reciprocate as he told anecdotes that were obviously designed to impress her with his manliness and boldness, about their student days in Salamanca and tavern brawls and scrapes with tutors, about his attempts to serenade the ladies accompanied by Mendoza on guitar.

These reminiscences inevitably turned to Lepanto. Calvo delivered a colorful and exciting account of the battle that reminded Mendoza of the stories he had once told in Salamanca taverns. He described the sultan's ships spread out in a crescent shape across the Gulf of Patras with their sails billowing in a great curtain, the tambours and cymbals beating out the rowers' strokes from the Turkish decks, the turbaned soldiers dancing and brandishing their weapons in anticipation of the battle as they waited on the walkways.

Calvo told his wife and guests how the Christians broke the fetters that held their galley slaves so that they could use their chains as weapons and promised freedom to those who survived, how the

Turkish arrows bounced off their boarding nets, how Don John danced a gay galliard in full view of the enemy before boarding the Turkish flagship, how the huge Venetian gunships blasted the Turkish galleys at the center of the sultan's fleet, wreaking terrible damage. Gabriel was spellbound, but Mendoza found these recollections oppressive. War stories told at suppertime might be entertaining, but Calvo's narrative did not include the thrashing of the bosun's bullwhip on the backs of the slaves as they crashed into the corsair ships, the exploding grenades and incendiaries and the screams of men jumping from burning ships with their clothes on fire into the churning red waters among the entrails of their own comrades where they were stabbed with pikes, shot dead by harquebusiers or drowned, weighed down by their armor.

When Calvo described how he had saved Mendoza's life, Mendoza remembered the awful pain as he fell to the deck and his certainty that he was about to die as the janissary raised his scimitar above his head. Once again he saw the infidel tumble over and his friend's face, splashed with blood and framed by a combed morion helmet as he reached down and pulled Mendoza upright.

"'Onward rush / The Greeks amid the ruins of the fleet / As through a shoal of fish caught in the net, / Spreading destruction,'" Mendoza quoted absently.

"'Advance, ye sons of Greece, from thraldom save / Your country, save your wives, your children save!'" cried Calvo.

Cornelia Calvo and the other guests looked at them blankly.

"Aeschylus!" Calvo yelled. "Just because I didn't finish university, that doesn't mean I can't still quote the classics, eh, Bernardo? And if I hadn't picked you off the deck that day, you wouldn't be quoting them now!"

"To friendship," Ventura said, raising his glass. "To the man who saved Licenciado Mendoza from the infidel!"

Calvo beamed proudly as they raised their glasses. His wife managed a tight-lipped smile. She asked Mendoza if he had ever been to Aragon before. Mendoza replied that he had not.

"And have you ever dealt with Moriscos before?"

"I have, señora. In Granada."

"Then you will know what to expect," she said. "The Moriscos of Aragon are just the same. Christians on the surface but Moors underneath."

"In Granada some of the Moriscos were more devout Christians than the Old Christians themselves," Mendoza said.

"Not in these mountains," Señora Calvo insisted. "Oh, they're good at pretending to be Christians, but as soon as your back's turned, they're praying to Muhammad. They'd kill us all in our beds if they got the chance. The only surprising thing about this Redeemer is that he took so long to appear."

"Does the Countess of Cardona think the same way as you do?" Mendoza asked.

"The countess is a good woman, but she isn't a woman of the world," Señora Calvo replied with undisguised condescension. "She treats her Moriscos as if they were children, and that only encourages them to believe they can do as they like."

"She needs a man!" said Calvo with a lewd expression that made his wife visibly stiffen. "The Moriscos run rings around her! What they need is discipline—like Granada."

Mendoza felt himself becoming irritated. "You were in Flanders, not Granada," he said. "The Moriscos had real grievances that were ignored. Too many Old Christians exploited and oppressed them, and when they went to the courts, there was no redress. Even the priests fleeced them, but the Church did nothing. Instead of addressing these concerns, the king issued the Royal Pragmatic. In one year the Moriscos were supposed to abandon their language, their dances, their public bathhouses and their clothes. It was unreasonable to impose these demands. Wiser government could have avoided the rebellion."

"Are you saying His Majesty is not wise?" Señora Calvo asked with a faint smile.

"I'm saying, madam, that His Majesty does not always receive accurate information. And when it comes to Moriscos, I am often skeptical about the information one does receive—and also about the sources of such information."

Señora Calvo's smile abruptly faded.

"But the Moriscos were punished," Calvo said. "And you helped administer the punishment."

"Of course!" Mendoza replied hotly. "Because they rebelled. And rebellion must always be punished."

"Well, let's hope you can nip this in the bud, Bernardo," said Calvo. "Before it gets any worse. Because we need to find these criminals before someone else dies."

This seemed so self-evident that it barely needed saying, and Mendoza merely nodded. Calvo sensed that he had displeased his old friend, and he seemed eager to make up for it as he accompanied them to the inn.

"Remember, Bernardo," Calvo said in a slurred voice as his two servants walked beside them with torches, "anytime you need help, you know you can depend on me—just like at Lepanto. You need more men and I'll call out the militia."

"I don't need the militia," Mendoza replied. "But I do need to make sure my reports get to Madrid at least within a week."

"Of course! Franquelo can bring them to me from Belamar. From here the post is very fast."

On reaching the inn, Calvo embraced Mendoza once more. "It's good to see you again. After all these years! Who'd have thought it? And who'd have thought that the man I pulled off that deck would go on to become a judge?"

"That's one man with his cojones in a vise," Ventura murmured as Calvo stumbled away, flanked by his two servants. "And someone should tell him to hold back on the wine and brandy."

"He always drank too much," Mendoza said. "But he wasn't like this when I knew him. He gave up the law for the legions because he liked to fight. I always expected him to come back."

"Well, he should have stuck to soldiering. His wife may be pretty, but a woman like that is not for marrying."

Mendoza laughed. "I didn't know you were such an expert on the subject of marriage, cousin. Now, sleep. Tomorrow we shall be in Belamar."

THE NEXT MORNING they left before sunrise. As they rode out onto the darkened plain, they heard a wolf howl from the direction of the mountains farther north, and Mendoza wondered whether he had made the right decision to reject the viceroy's offer of extra men. By the time they reached Sabiñanigo and the Valle de Tena, the sun had already risen above the mountains to the east, and they rode parallel to the Gállego River across a wide plain flanked by rows of valleys that folded back like waves.

After about two hours, they crossed the hanging bridge that Calvo had told them about, where they paid yet another exorbitant fee to the toll keeper before crossing into the *señorio* of Cardona. They followed the road eastward and upward through ravines and passes and stepped valleys dotted with farmhouses, villages and hamlets, interspersed with the occasional crumbling remnants of old defensive towers. The mountains now enclosed them so completely that at times it was not possible for them to see beyond the immediate ravine or valley they found themselves in as they ascended toward the towering massif.

Much of the road passed through woodland that offered numerous potential points of ambush, whether from bandits or a would-be Morisco avenger with even the most rudimentary grasp of military tactics. The Moriscos of Granada had staged surprise attacks against armed columns that were considerably larger, and Mendoza ordered his men to be especially vigilant. By midmorning they were climbing through a forested slope when a young man on a mule appeared on the road in front of them. He halted his animal and looked warily at their weapons, with one hand poised over the handle of the short pistol protruding from the sash around his waist. As they came closer, Mendoza saw that he also carried a long dagger in his belt. Both were weapons that would have been banned even among Christians in Valladolid, let alone Moriscos, Mendoza thought as Necker approached the man and called out imperiously, "Where are you coming from, sir?"

"Damián Alarcón from Belamar de la Sierra at your service, señores."

"Are you a New Christian?"

"I am. But what I lack in pure blood I make up for with a true Catholic heart!"

Necker scowled, and his jaw jutted out even farther. "Do you mock us, Morisco?"

"No, señor. My mother taught me to be polite to strangers."

"And why are you carrying weapons like these?"

"Because these mountains are dangerous, Your Mercy."

"Well, we are officers of the king. This is Licenciado Don Bernardo de Mendoza, alcalde of the Royal Chancery of Valladolid. Do you have reason to fear us, youth?"

"By God, no," the young man said. "But being the king's officers, you will know that it is not illegal for Moriscos to carry weapons in Aragon—especially in these evil times."

"So you think you know the law," Necker thundered, "when your people have been murdering priests and Christians?"

"I know nothing of that, señores," the Morisco protested. "I only came back two days ago to see my family. I'm a muleteer. I'm away most of the year. Castile, Andalusia, Portugal—I've been everywhere, and now I'm going back to Zaragoza to work. If I don't get there tomorrow, I'll lose my job."

Mendoza nodded at Necker to let him go, and they continued on their way until the road leveled out and they emerged onto a wide cultivated valley, where men and women were working side by side. At the far end of the plain, a cluster of white houses cascaded down a sloping promontory that gave out onto a narrow ravine, and Mendoza knew even before Franquelo told them that they had almost reached Belamar de la Sierra. The road led directly through the valley, past men, women and children working the fields and orchards with forks, hoes and scythes. Others were leading mules piled with herbs, hay and firewood. As they came closer, Mendoza saw the high cliff at the upper end of the town and the church tower farther down toward the ravine, where men and women were working on terraces cut into the hillside below the old medieval walls.

The valley did not look like a hotbed of murder, heresy and sedition. On the contrary, everything emanated a timeless rustic serenity, from the barking dogs and the birds of prey lazily hovering overhead to the tolling bells that counted out eleven o'clock.

"How do you tell the Old Christians from the Moriscos?" Gabriel whispered as they rode into the main entrance to the village.

"The Moriscos are the ones with horns and tails," replied Ventura.

The houses were built in the Aragonese style, tall and narrow with few windows and tiled roofs that sloped down on both sides in a V shape and brick or stone walls. The ones that faced out onto the road and the valley were built so close together that they made a natural defensive wall, with a single opening at the road that was barely wide enough for a carriage or a cart to pass through. The road went straight past a *lavadero*, where a group of women washing piles of clothes at a sheltered stone trough stopped to look at them warily as they rode up the narrow, winding street. Other people stopped and stared at them with expressions that might have been hostile or fearful or both. At the front Necker looked around him with a belligerent expression, while Mendoza glanced down at the even narrower streets and cul-de-sacs that once again reminded him of the Morisco towns and villages of Granada.

It was clear from the bare, unpaved streets to the narrow windows, many of which had no glass and were covered with sheets of greasy transparent paper or nothing at all, that this was not a prosperous village. Mendoza was conscious of the eyes watching them from the darkened interiors, and some women actually pulled their children back into the doorways as they rode past. It was not until they reached the Plaza Mayor that they found themselves on cobblestones as they drew up their horses in front of a nondescript two-story building painted with a faded pink, which Franquelo said was the village hall.

On the opposite side of the square, there was a bakery and a butcher shop, whose customers stood watching them with the same wary suspicion they had already encountered. They had barely dismounted when they heard voices coming toward them, and a moment later about twenty armed men came into the square carrying an assortment of swords, daggers and farming tools.

"What is this, Vicente?" Franquelo asked one of them. "Are you going to war?"

A sullen, handsome young man stepped nervously forward, holding a short sword. "We heard strangers with guns had entered the town," he said. "We thought they were bandits."

"Well, you can put your weapons away. This is Judge Mendoza from Valladolid, come to bring the king's justice to those who have murdered his subjects!"

"And we bid him welcome."

Mendoza turned as the door of the village hall opened and a tall, upright-looking man with a gray beard and a mane of white hair stepped into the square. He appeared to be in his early fifties, though his blue eyes seemed much younger than his tanned and deeply lined face.

"Good afternoon, señores," he said. "I am Dr. Pedro Segura, physician and mayor of Belamar. I've been expecting you. Someone like you anyway. What can I do for you, Your Honor?"

"I need food and lodging for myself and my men until my investigation is completed."

"Well, we have no inn in Belamar—only a tavern. Didn't Constable Franquelo tell you that? You'd be better off in Cardona."

"We're staying here," Mendoza said firmly. "Even if we have to sleep in a barn."

"That won't be necessary. I have two rooms and a storeroom at my dispensary. I'm sure they will cook for you at the tavern if you buy your food. My daughter can assist you as well."

Mendoza thanked him. "I also need a room where I can take statements and depositions and a secure place where any prisoners can be detained."

"You can use my office. There's a back room there with a solid door and a stable in the dispensary. And there's also the seigneurial prison in Cardona."

"Any prisoners will be held under my jurisdiction, not the seigneurial courts. And one more thing. I want the town crier to announce our investigation first thing tomorrow morning. My scribe will give you the exact wording for the proclamation later."

"Will that be necessary, Your Honor? This is a village. Everyone will know what you're doing by the end of the evening."

"This is a royal investigation, not a rumor."

"As you wish."

THEY FOLLOWED SEGURA to a three-story stone house on a street behind the village hall and led their animals through the wide double door and into the stable past the fireplace alcove and stairwell, next to the little kitchen. After unpacking their weapons and saddlebags, they went up the narrow stone stairs and into a large open room with two smaller rooms at the back. Mendoza was pleased to see that one of them contained a double bed as he looked around at the bag of surgical tools lying on a table near the window, the shelves bearing glass bottles and apothecary jars containing ointments, powders, crushed herbs and the skeletons and skulls of mice, rabbits and sheep, plus anatomical prints on the walls showing muscles, bones and veins.

"I see you're a student of Vesalius," he observed.

"Is there any doctor worthy of the name who isn't?" Segura said. "This used to be my parents' house. Now I use it as an apothecary and a consulting room. My hope one day is to turn this building into a small hospital for the people in the area. I assume that you and your page will stay here. Your men can sleep upstairs. My sons will clear it out for you and see if they can find some more mattresses."

Mendoza examined the titles on the shelves while Ventura, Necker and the two militiamen carried their bags and weapons upstairs. Some of them were old leather-bound copies, but the majority were folios without covers. It was an eclectic and wide-ranging collection for a country doctor in a remote mountain town. In addition to the Bible and the catechism, there were editions of Ambroise Paré's *Journeys in Diverse Places*, in addition to *Amadis of Gaul*, *El Lazarillo de Tormes* and *La Celestina*, Pedro de Medina's *Book of Cosmography*, and an assortment of medical texts that included Vesalius's *De humani corporis fabrica*, a French translation of Hippocrates and Castilian translations of Galen and Avicenna.

"Did you know that *Lazarillo* is on the Index now?"

"I didn't," Segura said. "Well, that's a pity."

"It doesn't bother me, but an inquisitor might see things differently."

Segura sighed and took the book down from the shelf. "Better burn it then," he said.

"But there must be at least twenty books here!" Gabriel exclaimed. "And some of them are in French and Latin."

"Some of them were given to me by the countess and her late husband," replied Segura. "And many of us speak French in these mountains. I studied medicine in Paris. You like books, young man? So do I. Have you read *The Abencerraje and the Beautiful Jarifa*? A noble tale!"

The third floor, as was the custom in the country, was a winter storehouse filled with fruit, grain and vegetables, and two of Segura's sons now dragged up two mattresses for Ventura, Necker and the two militiamen to share. Mendoza asked to be taken to the scene of the crime, and they followed Segura once again back into the street. The church was a solid white building with a sloping slate roof, its stained-glass windows reminding Mendoza of some of the smaller churches in Castile rather than the rounded Romanesque churches that he had seen while coming up through the mountains, but the horseshoe arches on the bell tower suggested that at least part of it was of much older construction.

"Was this a mosque?" he asked.

Segura said it had been until 1524, when the Moors of Belamar were baptized. It had remained unused since Father Panalles's murder, he said, because it had not yet been purified, but they continued to use the bells to mark the hours. Inside, they could still smell the slightly sweet and pungent combination of incense and spilled blood as they looked around at the thick stone arches, the alcoves containing headless or broken statues and the slashed sanbenitos.

"This is where we found him," Franquelo said, pointing to the bloodstained altar.

"Who found him first?"

"His maid, Inés. She's moved back to her parents' house in Villamayor since the murder. It's about an hour from here."

"I want to speak to her. Bring her to the town hall tomorrow."

"With respect, Your Honor, we already questioned her when the corregidor came here. She didn't hear anything or see anyone."

"*I* haven't questioned her," Mendoza said.

Some footprints were still visible in the dried blood, and he placed his boot alongside them and asked Necker to do the same. "One of them had boots—and large feet, too," he said. "Even larger than yours."

"Yes, sir," said Necker as Mendoza followed the dark streak where the priest's body had been dragged to the altar. There was blood all down the side of it and a thicker pool on its surface. He walked carefully around it and followed the trail of bloody footprints to the lectern, where a large leather Bible had been slashed with a knife and its pages torn. The headless statue of the Virgin also bore white marks that looked like blows or stab marks, and there were Arabic letters written in red on the wall behind it. It was impossible to compare the Arabic with the handwriting on the note that Villareal had given him, except for the fact that the message on the wall was neater and more level, and whoever had written it had clearly taken his or her time.

"Do you know what this means?" Mendoza asked.

"I don't speak Arabic," Segura replied.

"Dr. Segura, I'm not the Inquisition," Mendoza said impatiently.

"I don't speak it," Segura insisted.

Ventura peered at the wall. "'Slay the unbelievers wherever you may find them,'" he read.

"Thank you, Sergeant," Mendoza said as Segura and Franquelo

looked at his cousin in astonishment. "I assume you examined the priest's body?"

"I did, Your Honor," Segura replied. "His throat was cut, and he suffered ten separate wounds from sword and dagger. His skull was also shattered by a heavy weapon. It was some kind of pointed mace."

"How do you know that?"

"Because of the hole it made. The same weapon was used to destroy the head of the Virgin, as you can see." Segura showed him the stone head of the black Virgin and the conical hole that had cracked it.

"Does anyone from the village carry a weapon like that?"

"Absolutely not. The people here are mostly peasants and farmers. A weapon like that is a soldier's weapon."

"Peasants and farmers can be soldiers, too," Mendoza said. "Especially when they have someone to lead them. Someone who acts as their champion."

"If you mean the Redeemer, I assure you that he did not come from the village."

"How do you know that?"

"Because the existence of such a thing could not be concealed!"

"And you would reveal it if you knew?"

"Yes I would," Segura said firmly. "Because a man like this can only bring disaster to all Moriscos. I believe that the priest was killed by at least three men."

"What makes you so certain?"

"The variety of the size and depth of the wounds. The angle at which they were struck. And no one from Belamar would be capable of such a thing."

"What about from outside the village?"

Segura's face hardened. "You won't find many people around

here who mourned his death. Father Panalles was a drunkard, a lecher, a thief and a disgrace to his faith."

"You defame a man of God in his own church?" Franquelo said.

Segura did not even look at him. "The truth defames no one. Everyone knows what kind of priest he was. Especially you."

"With respect, sir," said Franquelo, "you cannot believe what these people say about anything."

"That's enough, Constable. Leave us. All of you. Wait outside," Mendoza ordered. "I wish to speak to Dr. Segura alone."

Franquelo glared at Segura and followed the others out of the church, leaving the two men standing by the bloodstained altar.

"These are serious allegations," Mendoza said.

"Everything I say is true. There is nothing that this priest didn't do to us. How many times did I sit here in this church and listen to him standing by this altar insulting and dishonoring us—even during Mass! In the middle of a sermon, he would abuse us and tell us that we were heathen swine who could not be saved. We were not worthy of his God—*his* God!" Segura grimaced. "That man could not have been further from God. Sometimes he was so drunk that he used to shout and swear at us—in church! He fined us if we missed saints' days or feast days, or for anything that came into his mind. If the people didn't have money, they had to bring him a chicken or a basket of fruit or perform some service for him. He took our women, even our wives and daughters! Some of our women, when they went to confession, were told that if they didn't sleep with him, he would report them to the Inquisition for some religious offense or denounce their husbands."

"What offenses?"

"Anything! They didn't have to be real. He could just invent them, and the Inquisition always believed him. Many people here were taken to the Aljafería because of him. Two men from the town are still serving eight years in the king's oars because Father Panalles wanted their wives. Three families have lost most of their property. Two women were flogged. I don't know how many were fined. Most of that was because of Panalles. Your Honor, this was a man who deserved to die, and there is absolutely no doubt in my mind that his soul is now burning in hell."

Mendoza leaned onto his stick to take some of the weight off his aching leg. He had chosen to linger in the church to see how Segura reacted, since it was not uncommon in his experience for criminals to reveal more than they intended at the scene of the crime, but there was nothing in the doctor's manner to indicate a guilty conscience.

"Did *you* have any reason to kill him?" Mendoza looked at him intently.

"No." Segura's face was stonily impassive. "But if I did, I have sufficient medical knowledge to kill a man without stabbing or bludgeoning him to death. And enough humanity to refrain from doing so, and so does everybody else from this village."

"Did you report these matters to the proper channels?"

"Of course. I wrote letters to the bishop, and I spoke to him when he came to visit us two years ago. I myself went to speak to the archbishop, to the bishop of Jaca, His Excellency Don Pedro de Aragon, and the corregidor Pelagio Calvo."

"And what did they say?"

"His Excellency Bishop Santos promised to look into it. Don Pedro also said he would report the matter to his superiors. The corregidor told us to take our complaints to the Church or the Inquisition, not him. Even though his own constable was one of Panalles's cronies."

"You mean Franquelo?"

Segura nodded. "They gambled and drank together. Franquelo also collected fines and threatened people who refused to pay."

"Can you give me the names of anyone who can support these claims?"

"I won't denounce my people, Your Honor."

"I'm not asking you to denounce anyone. But what you've told me raises questions that must be answered. It will be easier if you ask people to come forward voluntarily. Tell them that I will be taking depositions at the town hall all day tomorrow. Tell them no one will be harmed or arrested. But whatever kind of man Father Panalles was, I mean to find out who killed him and see that the perpetrators are punished accordingly. Is that clear?"

SEGURA AGREED AND RETURNED to the village hall while Mendoza asked Franquelo to take them to the rectory. At first glance the sparsely furnished rooms suggested the typical home of a humble country priest, but this impression was quickly dispelled by the unmade bed with its silk sheets and the crucifix on the wall above it, the faint smell of wine and brandy emanating from the kitchen and bedroom, the pack of cards on the kitchen table and the two expensive-looking women's dresses, which Ventura discovered in the chest of drawers in the bedroom.

"Did Panalles have any women living with him?" Mendoza asked.

"Only the maid. And I never saw her wearing clothes like that."

"Look at this." Ventura opened the drawer on the little unit next to the bed and held up a wheel-lock pistol and a powder bottle. "Not a bad weapon for a priest," he said, stroking the embossed cherry-colored handle. "There are about a dozen balls here. Too bad he didn't have them with him the day he died." He knelt down under the bed and pulled out a double-edged sword, followed by a small wooden casket with images of winged angels engraved in its sides. "Maybe this explains the weapons," he said. The others clustered around him and peered at the tufts of different-colored hair.

"This is women's hair," Ventura said, sniffing at it, "and not just one woman."

Mendoza turned to Franquelo. "You knew nothing about this behavior?"

"No, sir," the *alguacil* insisted. "Absolutely not."

Mendoza said that he had seen enough, and they were just about to leave when Ventura sat down on the bed, as if testing it.

"Is it all right if I stay here, Your Honor?" he asked. "I don't sleep well with vegetables and snoring constables."

Necker looked horrified. "You'd sleep in a dead man's bed?" he asked.

"Well, *he* won't need it, will he?"

Mendoza had no objections, and they returned to the dispensary, where Segura appeared to tell them that their food was ready. The tavern was not as bad as some of the places they had stayed along the way, with a single table in a dimly lit room that smelled of burned oil, meat and mutton from tallow, with rushes on the dirt floor. The widow Señora Ortega and her daughter, Beatriz, were clearly glad of the custom, and Beatriz immediately caught Ventura's eye as she served bowls of meat and garbanzos wearing a stained apron that accentuated her wide, curvaceous hips.

"Well, well," he said. "I didn't expect to find such a delicate alpine flower growing in these wild mountains."

Beatriz grinned, but Necker looked disapproving as Ventura appreciatively studied the sway of her hips as she returned to the kitchen.

"Look at that." He sighed and shook his head. "Enough to make Adam eat a whole orchard, wouldn't you say, Constable? And her mother isn't bad either for her age."

"I'm a married man!" Necker reminded him.

"Well, I don't see your wife here. And what the wife doesn't see can't hurt her."

"God sees."

"Maybe so. But you can always go to confession afterward."

The two militiamen snickered until Necker silenced them with a glare. After supper Mendoza returned to the dispensary with Gabriel and dictated the proclamation. He then recited the names and ages of the Quintana brothers and Father Panalles, the cause of death, the position of the wounds and other relevant details. It was nearly ten o'clock when Gabriel finally finished writing. Mendoza undressed for bed while Gabriel took the message for the town crier to Segura at the town hall. He returned five minutes later, holding a lantern in one hand and *The Abencerraje* in the other, and said that he had delivered it.

"Well done, boy. You should sleep now."

Gabriel nodded gravely but continued to hover. "Sir, may I ask where Don Luis learned to speak Arabic?"

"You can ask me. But it's not something you boast about in Spain unless you want to end up in front of an Inquisition tribunal. My cousin was captured in the Granada War. He spent four years in Algiers."

Gabriel looked both shocked and amazed. "Don Luis was a slave? I never knew that."

"It's not something he likes to talk about."

"But how did he get out? Did he escape?"

"I paid his ransom." Mendoza could see that his page was still trying to comprehend how his warrior cousin could have been taken prisoner by the Moors. He sensed that there were a lot more questions his page wanted to ask, but he was too tired to answer them. He blew out the candle and lay back on the narrow bed. "Good night, boy. I'm sorry about what you saw yesterday. The law can be a hard taskmaster, and it demands a great deal from us."

"Yes, sir."

Gabriel shut the door behind him. By the time he got into his own bed and began to read, the steady, rhythmic breathing from the next room told him that his guardian's first day in Belamar de la Sierra had come to an end.

CHAPTER SEVEN

ENDOZA WOKE UP TO THE SOUND OF A beating drum and the loud blare of a horn, followed by the town crier monotonously intoning the list of His Majesty King Philip II's kingdoms and possessions. Mendoza had slept well, and he lay on his side, half listening to the familiar preamble: in the name of His Majesty Philip II, king of Castile, of León, of Aragon, of the Two Sicilies, of Jerusalem, of Portugal, of Navarre, of Granada, of Toledo, of Valencia . . . of the East and Western Indies . . . Archduke of Austria, Duke of Burgundy . . . It was an impressive list that no ruler in the world could match, and yet even the few days that Mendoza had spent in Aragon suggested that the king's authority was more tenuous than the preamble suggested.

He was not surprised by the allegations against the priest. There had been many like him in Granada, and complaints from the Moriscos had generally met with the same official inertia from the Catholic clergy. But it was obvious that incompetence and indifference were not limited to the Church. There was no reason to think that Calvo was corrupt, even if some of his subordinates were, but Mendoza had already discovered more about the priest's death in a few hours than the corregidor had found out in the last month. He now knew that the priest had been killed by more than one man. He knew the weapons that had been used to kill him, and despite Segura's assurances he had discovered a whole village with sufficient motivation to have done so. Even if the Redeemer did not come from Belamar itself, the priest's reputation would have made him a suitable target for a Morisco avenger seeking to establish his reputation.

This was the man Mendoza had been sent to the mountains to find, and as he lay beneath the blanket, he felt daunted by the responsibility that his assignment entailed as the *pregonero* finally got around to informing the populace that Licenciado Bernardo de Mendoza, criminal magistrate at the Royal Chancery at Valladolid, was conducting an investigation into the murders of the priest Juan Panalles and the Quintana brothers, and that anyone with any information regarding these events should go to the town hall and present it to the alcalde and his officials.

At last the message ended and the crier and his companions moved off to another street, accompanied by the beating drum and further shrill blasts of the horn. Mendoza stood up in his nightshirt and opened the wooden shutters. The sun was just beginning to touch the slate rooftops, and light puffs of cloud drifted across the sky above the still-shaded street. Below him two women were walking back from the baker's with loaves wrapped in cloth and immediately fell silent and hurried away when they saw him standing in the window.

Gabriel came in already dressed and brought him a bowl and pitcher. Mendoza washed his face and, looking into a small mirror, carefully groomed his hair and beard with a comb and scissors while his page laid out his clothes. As a representative of the royal authority, it was important for him to look like a judge even in this far-flung corner of the realm, at least when he was not traveling, and he put on the lined green doublet, velvet black cap and short matching cape and leather shoes that he had brought for his official duties.

The others were already moving around above them, and when he and Gabriel went downstairs, they were surprised to find Segura sitting on one of the stone benches in the fireplace alcove. A pretty young woman in a white head scarf, a skirt and a shawl was tending the fire. She looked about the same age as Gabriel, with wide, lustrous dark eyes and pinkish lips that made Mendoza think of ripe apricots, and his page stood holding his portable desk in two hands, staring at her as if he'd been dazzled by a bright light.

"Good morning, señores," Segura said. "This is my daughter Juana. We thought you might like a fire. And Juana has brought you some breakfast."

Mendoza thanked them and smiled amiably at the girl as she went into the kitchen. "Your daughter does you proud," he said. "How many children do you have?"

"God has blessed me with seven, Your Grace. She and her sister Susana take after her mother, may she rest in peace. But I still haven't managed to marry either of them off yet. Juana is a healer, like her mother. She also helps me with patients. Her sister Susana is the countess's chambermaid."

Necker and the two militiamen came downstairs and leaned their swords and escopetas against the wall as Juana returned carrying a basket of bread, eggs and figs. They had just sat down when Ventura came in and smiled broadly at the sight of Juana.

"Well, good morning," he said with a bow. "Someone might have warned me that I would run into such a beauty first thing in the morning. I might have shaved at least."

Segura laughed and put his arm around his daughter's waist. "She will make someone a good wife one day. She reads, she cooks, she cures the sick. She also plays chess. She can dance, too, but she doesn't get that from me!"

"I'd like to see her dance." Ventura smiled happily.

Juana frowned, and Mendoza gave his cousin a warning look. "Gabriel plays chess," he said.

"Not very well." Gabriel was still gazing at Juana like a startled deer. His page had spent too much time with Magda, Mendoza thought, and the Morisca clearly appealed to very different emotions.

"A fine-looking girl," he observed after breakfast.

"I suppose she is," Gabriel replied.

"Watch out, boy," Ventura warned. "Women can lead even good men to madness."

"Don't listen to him," said Mendoza. "Without women, this world would be a desert. And I think she liked you."

Gabriel looked pleased. "You think so?"

The others laughed, and even Martín looked amused as Daniel gave him a pat on the back.

The village hall consisted of a large bare room with a desk, a few chairs and a stone stairway leading up to the next floor. Mendoza sat at the desk and gave his instructions while Gabriel placed the wooden *escritorio* next to him and set out his quills, his inkwell, his papers and the little bottle of cuttlefish bone to dry the ink. Ventura and Necker were to go door-to-door at all the houses near the church and find out if anyone had seen or heard anything on the morning of the murder. Martín and Daniel were to wait at the door of the village hall with their weapons, in case they were needed to go and bring people in for questioning.

THIS CONTINGENCY soon proved unnecessary, as a stream of men and women came to the office throughout the day to denounce the misdeeds of Father Panalles. Their testimonies universally supported Segura's allegations. They described a priest who had shamelessly abused his power and blackmailed and exploited his parishioners financially and sexually, whose appetite for attractive young women was not constrained by their marital status or lack of reciprocity.

Generally the threat of a denunciation to the Inquisition, of either the women themselves or their husbands, brothers and fathers, had been sufficient to get him what he wanted. In some cases Panalles had forced himself physically on his unwilling victims, who had been too frightened to denounce him. One woman claimed to have been ravished in the sacristy. Another said that the priest had forced himself upon her after administering extreme unction to her father. The daughter of a local carpenter sat silently as her father and mother described how the priest had come to the carpenter's house for more than six months to fornicate with his wife.

Some of the women had been obliged to visit the priest in the rectory and told Mendoza that he liked them to wear the dresses he kept there and that he would cut off a piece of their hair as a memento.

Gabriel performed his duties with professional detachment, but Mendoza knew that he was shocked by what he was hearing. The

Moriscos were considerably less forthcoming about the manner of the priest's death than they were about his sinful life. All the attestants denied having killed him and said they had no idea how he had been killed or who might have done it. All of them claimed to have been asleep in their homes on the morning of the murder and could cite relatives or neighbors to prove it. After three hours Ventura and Necker returned with similar results. They had spoken to almost all the residents in the houses around the church, none of whom had seen or heard anyone coming into the town or leaving it that morning.

After a break for lunch, they returned to the town hall at three, where more Moriscos were waiting to give depositions. The bells had just struck four when Franquelo appeared, bringing the servant girl with him. Of all the witnesses they had spoken to, she was the most frightened and overawed. She made Mendoza think of a beaten dog that expected to be kicked as he politely asked her to sit down.

"Your name, señorita?"

"Inés Mejía Pacheco, Your Mercy."

"Are you Morisco or Old Christian?"

"Old Christian, Your Honor! But not that it matters anymore. That pig of a priest ruined me! He made me his whore, and now no one will ever marry me. Even my own family despises me. Now I will have to go to the convent or lead a life of sin!"

"I advise you to choose the former option," Mendoza said. "I understand you were with Father Panalles on the morning the priest was killed."

"Yes, Your Honor, to my shame! But I saw nothing and heard nothing. I only found him!"

"You were in the next building when he was being murdered.

You really expect me to believe you heard nothing? Not even a cry or a shout or something being broken? I advise you to tell me the truth, woman, or you will go to prison, not a convent!"

The little maid's eyes widened in terror, and then her face hardened in an expression of bitter defiance. "Very well, sir. I heard the noises. But I didn't go to look. And I didn't call for help because I was afraid, like everyone else. Everyone wanted him dead! *Claro*, they'll say they heard nothing, but they heard, and like me they were glad."

"Did you know anyone who might have done this? Someone who threatened him?"

"No one threatened him. No one would have dared."

"Not even the Redeemer?"

"I don't know this man, and I don't know anyone who has seen him. Panalles certainly wasn't scared of him. He knew he could get away with anything, and that's why he did it."

"What about friends? Did he have any?"

"A man like that doesn't have friends—only cronies. In Belamar there was Romero the baker and Franquelo. And some of the Old Christians used to drink and play cards with him sometimes. He also went whoring and gambling in some of the other villages. I don't know who he met there."

"Was he a lucky player?"

"Not always."

"And did he pay his debts?"

"As far as I know. If he ran out of money, all he had to do was fine one of the Moriscos for not going to church. Or threaten to report them to the Inquisition if they didn't pay him. You should ask Franquelo or Romero about this, not me."

"Why Romero?"

"Because Romero works for the Inquisition. He—"

Mendoza had stopped listening now. He could hear the unmistakable sound of a large number of horses coming toward them, and he looked out the window as the first horsemen entered the square. Within a few minutes there were two dozen riders milling around in front of the town hall. At first sight they looked like a bandit horde, with their helmets, caps and head scarves, their sandaled or booted feet and the array of pistols, swords, escopetas and crossbows dangling from their belts or saddles. Only the red sashes around their waists gave them an air of quasi-official uniformity.

"Wait here," Mendoza ordered. He picked up his stick and went out to the doorway, where Daniel and Martín were standing with their unloaded weapons, and looked at the sullen, hostile faces as one of the horsemen prodded his animal forward with his heels.

"You are Licenciado Mendoza?" he asked with an unmistakably French accent.

Mendoza looked at the leather doublet, the white Gascon beret and the short, well-groomed beard and mustache. "I am. And you must be Jean Sánchez."

The bailiff's haughty expression remained unchanged. "In the name of Doña Isabel María Barruela y Ibarra del Cardona y Castillo, I must inform you that you have no right to conduct an investigation anywhere in Cardona without the permission of the countess and authorization from the justiciar of Aragon."

Mendoza was astonished at such insolence. He wondered whether Mercader and Calvo were right after all and whether the whip might in fact be required to restore some humility and obedience to these people.

"And I must inform you," he said, holding up the royal baton, "that I am here on the authority of His Most Catholic Majesty Philip II."

Sánchez looked unimpressed. "In Aragon we have our own courts and our own laws. You must leave Belamar now."

"I have no intention of doing anything of the kind. I am here in the service of the Crown, and I will not leave this place until my investigation is concluded. Tell your mistress I shall come and visit her in order to discuss this matter. And never think a bailiff can tell the King of All the Spains where his officials have jurisdiction!"

Ventura and Necker were standing on the balcony now, with their swords and pistols prominently displayed. The bailiff glanced at them with studied indifference and then without a word abruptly turned his horse and left the square. His companions immediately followed him. Within a few minutes, the square was empty again, and Mendoza went back inside, where Gabriel and Inés were standing by the window, and told his page to finish taking the witness's statement.

The maid had nothing further to reveal, and Mendoza ordered Franquelo to take her back to her village. For the rest of the afternoon, the witnesses continued to come to the village hall, and their statements became so similar that Mendoza told Gabriel to stop writing them down in order not to use up paper and merely to record their names and the name of the offense. By the time he told Gabriel that they had done enough for the day, it was clear that there were dozens of people who might have wanted to see the priest dead, but there was no information to suggest that any of them had killed him.

He had no doubt that some of them must have heard what was happening inside the church, but indifference was not the same as collusion. Gabriel packed away his writing materials, and Mendoza sat looking through his reports while Gabriel took the *escritorio* back to the dispensary. The boy had worked well. He had written quickly and neatly, with few mistakes and crossings-out, and accurately transcribed most of the salient facts from each deposition. Mendoza was still reading through them when Franquelo entered the room and asked if he had finished with him for the day.

"Not quite, Constable. I have a question. I assume that you yourself heard nothing on the morning of the murder?"

"No, sir. I was in bed with my wife, sir."

"Asleep, I suppose. Like everyone else?"

"No, sir." Franquelo smirked. "And my wife was not asleep either, sir."

Mendoza's face showed no sign of amusement. "People say you were a friend of Panalles," he said coldly. "Were you?"

"We played cards and dice sometimes, that's all."

"And did you ever make any money from Father Panalles's dealings with the Moriscos?"

"Absolutely not, sir." Franquelo looked scandalized at the thought. "As an *alguacil*, it's my duty to support the parish priest and enforce the laws of the Church when fines are not paid. But all fines are written down in the priest's book."

"I'm sure they are," Mendoza said. "But not everything is written in books, is it? Constable, let me make something clear to you. I don't care what little games you were playing before I came here. But if I find out that you are concealing anything of importance to this investigation, I will come down on you very hard indeed. Do you understand me?"

"Perfectly, Your Honor. But I must insist—"

"You may go now," Mendoza said, and returned to his papers.

. . .

THE NEXT DAY he and Gabriel continued to take depositions at the village hall while Franquelo took Ventura and Necker to some of Panalles's haunts in the surrounding villages. In the afternoon Mendoza decided to conduct some door-to-door inquiries of his own, accompanied by his page. Most of the men and many of the women were out in the fields or working at their trades, and the Moriscos he spoke to emanated the distrust of officialdom that he had often encountered among the Moriscos of Granada until he asked them about Father Panalles. All of them testified to the priest's bad character, and no one expressed any regret about his death.

The blacksmith spat on the ground at the mention of his name, and the village cooper agreed that whoever had killed him had done the village and the world a favor. An elderly Morisca silk weaver made the horned sign of the evil eye at the mention of him. Even the Old Christian shoemaker agreed that Father Panalles was not a good priest and would certainly have gone straight to hell. This opinion was not shared by all Old Christians. Mendoza spoke to the baker Romero outside his shop, where Morisca women were lining up to buy bread from his wife. He was a short, self-important man who reminded Mendoza of an overgrown rodent as he stood there in his flour-stained apron with his arms crossed.

The baker conceded that Father Panalles was not a perfect priest, but he insisted that he was not as bad as the Moriscos said. The main reason his parishioners hated him, Romero said, was not for his morals but because he knew what the Moriscos were doing in secret and tried to stop it.

"And what were they doing?" Mendoza asked.

"Worshipping the damned sect of Muhammad, Your Honor! Plotting against the king and the Holy Mother Church! Father Panalles's predecessor was less attentive to these matters. But Panalles was different, and the Moriscos wanted him removed from the moment he came here."

"I understand that you also played a part in these efforts," Mendoza said.

"That is true, Your Honor. I consider it my Christian duty to assist the Inquisition in the service of God and his Church."

"I assume you were rewarded by the Holy Office for these services?"

The baker did not notice the sarcasm. "The rewards I receive are small compared with the services I have provided and the risks I have taken, living here among these heretics. Without the eyes of people like me, the Holy Office would be blind. Inquisitor Mercader knows how valuable I am."

Mendoza had used informants himself, but he did not admire them as a breed, and Romero did not strike him as the most reliable witness. And despite his unlikely depiction of the priest as a martyr for the faith, Romero had not seen or heard anything on the day of the murder and had no idea who had killed him. In the late afternoon, Franquelo, Ventura and Necker returned to the village. They had visited a tavern, a brandy house and a brothel and spoken to men who had played cards and drunk with Panalles and whores who had slept with him. None of them had any idea why he'd been killed, and all of them had alibis for the day he was murdered.

The next day Mendoza asked Franquelo to take them to the place where the Quintana brothers had been found. They rode slowly back down the drover route the brothers had taken, past the neat and well-ordered fields of wheat, sorghum, hemp and barley, past orchards and vegetable gardens and rows of mulberry and almond trees, pausing to ask the gardeners and laborers if they had seen the brothers on the day they were murdered or whether they'd had any altercations with them. No one had seen or noticed anything unusual that day. After about an hour, they came back around the valley to the entrance to the ravine below the medieval wall, where they encountered an old man hoeing a well-tended vegetable garden with the help of his wife and children.

"Good day, señor," Mendoza called.

"Good day, Your Mercy." The old man doffed his tattered straw hat respectfully. His face and arms were burned the leathery brown that spoke of a man who had spent his life in the fields. Mendoza knew many Christians in Valladolid who regarded such work as beneath them, regardless of the fact that there would be no food on their tables if men did not work the land, but he found such men more admirable—and often more essential—than many of the lawyers and *letrados* who filled the king's administration.

"A fine garden you have here. Enough to feed two families."

"A third of what we grow goes to the countess, sir. And there are also church tithes. And the payments to the new monastery. But still we manage, with God's grace."

"Is a third the usual rate?"

"It is in Cardona, Your Grace. In Vallcarca they pay more. The countess is a good mistress, may God bless her."

"This is the king's special justice, Alcalde Mendoza," said Franquelo. "He's here to find out what happened to the Quintana brothers."

"A bad business." The old man sighed. "I saw those boys go up into the ravine. I recognized them from previous years. They used to come up here with their father when they were children. To die like that . . ."

"You didn't see anyone speak to them or follow them?" Mendoza asked.

The old man shook his head. "We don't have much to do with the *montañeses*. We're always glad to see the back of them, if you want to know the truth, and they don't like us either. The only people I saw go into the ravine were charcoal burners and woodcutters."

"I've already spoken to them," Franquelo said. "They didn't see anything either."

"Does the Redeemer mean anything to you?" Mendoza asked the old man.

"Only our Lord Jesus Christ, Your Grace."

Necker's eyes narrowed, but the old Morisco's expression was absolutely earnest and deadpan. Mendoza thanked him, and they rode down into the ravine and followed the path as it climbed up into the forest. After about ten minutes, they smelled smoke and passed a small track leading off toward the clearing where the charcoal burners worked. An hour later they emerged onto the flat plain where the brothers had made their last camp. Franquelo showed them the remains of the campfire where the recovery party had found some of their possessions and cooking utensils, which had been returned to their father. The Quintanas' sheep had not been found, he said, but some of the *montañeses* were looking for them and had promised to take them back to the father as well.

Mendoza told them to dismount and spread out in a circle from the remains of the fire to examine the surrounding ground. It was not long before Necker gave a shout and drew their attention to a scattered pile of branches near the edge of the forest.

"It looks like one of them was attacked here, sir," he said, holding up a small ax. "He must have been coming back with firewood."

"Good work, Constable. Form a line and keep looking, gentlemen."

Mendoza stood by the horses as the others advanced slowly across the field, looking down at the ground. It was a perfect spot for a camp, with a stream nearby and plenty of grass for the cattle, but it was also an excellent place for an ambush. After a few minutes, Daniel came back with a lone cloth sandal, and Franquelo said it probably belonged to the eldest brother, who had been found with one shoe missing.

"If this was the Redeemer, he must have had a lot of helpers to trap three men in a field this size," said Ventura. "Especially if they weren't even standing in the same place. They must have come at them from different directions."

Mendoza agreed, and a quick search of the nearby forest uncovered numerous broken twigs and branches and small fragments of white clothing. Afterward they rode on toward the shrine where the bodies had been found. As Franquelo had said, it was located half an hour away, where the well-beaten track that curved down to Belamar intersected with the road from Huesca to the French frontier. The shrine was a typical roadside sanctuary, consisting of a rounded stone monument large enough to house a small statue of Christ, with little bundles of crushed flowers on the floor that had been left by passing travelers. The statue was now lying headless and facedown in front of it and was covered in holes where it been stabbed and chopped.

"May God curse them," said Necker as Mendoza squatted and examined the cross on which Simón Quintana had been crucified. It had clearly been put together quickly for the purpose from spliced tree trunks, with a crossbar that had been roughly chopped in the middle to allow it to sit against a thicker supporting pole and be nailed on. Beneath it lay the bloodied ropes that had held the murdered shepherd fast. Franquelo showed them the position of the bodies and heads and explained how hard it had been to get the body down from the cross.

"Why would anyone go to such trouble to bring them up here if they'd already killed them?" Necker asked.

"So that they could be seen by as many people as possible," replied Mendoza. Just then he noticed that Ventura was staring intently toward a rock face rising up out of a clump of trees on the other side of the road about three hundred yards away.

"What is it, cousin?"

"There's someone up there," Ventura said.

"On that cliff?" Franquelo peered up dubiously at the bare rock. "There can't be. It must be a bird or a goat."

"No. There's a cave, and there's someone in it."

BEFORE ANYONE COULD SAY ANYTHING, Ventura was back on his horse and riding toward the cliff face. The others followed in his wake, and as they drew closer, Mendoza saw that the cliff was not quite as steep as it seemed from a distance and that there was indeed a shallow cave about halfway up, where a narrow ledge, barely wide enough for a man to walk on, led to an opening in the rock face. By the time they reached the base of the cliff, Ventura was already scrambling up through the opening while the others waited down below.

"You in there, come out now!" he called, stepping out onto the ledge, holding up one of his pistols.

There was a faint shuffle from the dark opening, and then, to Mendoza's astonishment, an old man appeared on the ledge and stared blinking down at them. He looked more like a ghost or a walking skeleton than a human being in his long hair shirt and filthy pantaloons, with his unkempt hair and long beard.

"It's a hermit," Franquelo said. "These mountains are full of them."

"You mean he lives up there?" Gabriel asked incredulously.

"All year round. People like him live on grass and berries and spend their whole day praying."

"Don't be afraid, old man," Ventura said, lowering his pistol. "The king's officers want to ask you some questions. Come down now."

The hermit regarded them uncertainly and then walked meekly toward Ventura, holding his palms against the rock face to steady himself. After a few minutes, the two of them came down together. Close up, the old man looked even more like a walking corpse, with his hollow cheeks, straggly white beard and wild, staring eyes, one of which was almost completely covered by a cataract. He was barefoot, and his feet and hands were black with dirt, and he emitted an animal-like stench that made Mendoza's nostrils curl as the old man stared at them with a bewildered and frightened expression.

"What's your name, *viejo*?" Mendoza asked.

"Elias the Nazarene, faithful servant of the One True God!"

"Is that your home?" Mendoza pointed toward the cave.

"In the playground of the Lord, I find my dwelling place."

"You must have a good view of it from up there. Have you seen anything unusual on these roads lately?"

"Blood!" the hermit burst out. "I've seen blood!"

"Seen it where, old man?" asked Necker.

"There!" Elias pointed directly upward at the sky. "The blood of the lamb! Dripping down the face of the moon! I saw a fiery serpent moving across the sky and devils with white faces riding out of hell!"

"What devils? Where did you see them? Was it over there?" Mendoza pointed back toward the *santuario*. The old man's eyes flickered toward the cross, and he looked even more agitated. "I have seen the Son of Man crucified on the road to Santiago! I heard him cry out. I saw the angels weep when his enemies stabbed him with a spear, because they couldn't save him."

Franquelo tapped his forefinger against his temple. "He's crazy as a goat. These hermits spend so much time up here eating grass and talking only to God that they don't even know what year it is."

"When did you see him crucified, old man?" Mendoza asked, ignoring Franquelo. "How long ago?"

"Every day." A sorrowful expression spread across the hermit's cadaverous face. "Every day the Son of Man dies for our sins."

"You saw him killed on that cross, didn't you?" Mendoza persisted. "How many devils were there? Did you see their faces? Or were they wearing masks?"

The hermit looked confused, as if he had not understood the question, and then he stared at them with an expression of ferocious intensity. "War is coming to these mountains!" he exclaimed. "The lion and the serpent must fight, because the King of All the Spains has allowed the heretic snakes to infest his realms! There will be fire in the valleys and blood on the cross! Satan is coming with his infidel legions, and none of you will ever return to your homes!"

"You see?" Franquelo said. "If this were a city, he'd be locked up."

"All of you will die!" the hermit repeated.

"You're beginning to annoy me, old man," Mendoza said. "Go back to your cave."

The hermit scrambled up the slope, still mumbling to himself. They trotted back down the road, and Gabriel and the two militiamen were noticeably somber. Even Necker looked glummer and more dour than usual.

"Cheer up, *chicos*," Ventura teased them. "Anyone would think that Satan himself was wandering through these mountains! But this Redeemer is a man, and men can always be killed."

"Or arrested," Mendoza reminded him.

Gabriel and the two militiamen tried to look amused, but their anxious expressions told a different story.

"Tomorrow I want you to go up to the frontier and look around," Mendoza told Ventura as the others went ahead of them. "See who's coming and going across the border on the road and away from it. The fewer people that see you, the better. I want you gone by dawn. If any of the others see you leave, don't tell them where you're going. I'll expect you back here in three days. And be careful, cousin. Whoever killed those boys is up there."

"You're talking to Luis de Ventura, cousin. They are the ones who need to be careful. And what will you do?"

"It's time to visit the countess."

CHAPTER EIGHT

N THE MORNING VENTURA WAS GONE, AND Mendoza told the others that he had been sent on a special assignment and that he himself would be visiting Cardona that day with Franquelo and Daniel while Gabriel, Necker and Martín remained in the village and continued to make inquiries about the priest's death. After saddling their horses, they descended through the valley and approached Cardona via a well-maintained road with stone bridges across the many streams and rivers flowing down from the high mountains that loomed over them.

As always, Mendoza was pleased to see land under cultivation. Even in the higher slopes, there were peasants working terraces cut into the mountains whose impossible heights reminded him of Granada. That was the only obvious similarity between the Morisco lands of Aragon and his birthplace. In the country towns of Granada, it had generally been possible to distinguish Moriscos from Old Christians, particularly the women, who continued to cover their faces with long head scarves and shawls even after the king's pragmatic.

Here it was impossible to tell the two apart. Both Old Christian and Morisco men wore the same red, black and Aragonese head scarves, the same waistcoats, short capes and rope-soled sandals strapped up around their calves, while the women wore the same long dark skirts and bright shawls and head scarves or wide hats. Had Franquelo not told him which villages were Old Christian or Morisco and which were mixed, he would not have known. Franquelo knew many of their inhabitants by name, and he introduced Mendoza's group to the local notary, mayor or *alguacil* so that they could ask them about the murders. Most of the local officials seemed cut from similar cloth to Franquelo himself, but all of them were concerned by the potential impact of the murders of the Quintana brothers on the districts they served. One mayor reported that a Morisco tinker returning from Huesca had been forced to eat pork by a group of Old Christian shepherds and was badly beaten up when he refused. Another said that a group of *montañeses* had fired upon Morisco charcoal burners near a village in the mountains above Cardona.

All of them agreed that the *señorio* was becoming progressively more lawless and disorderly. There were robberies of merchants, travelers and pilgrims on the roads on a weekly basis, and bandits were entering the more isolated villages and hamlets and robbing their inhabitants. Mendoza also spoke to peasants and laborers working in the fields, both Morisco and Old Christian, and many of the latter had brought their weapons with them in anticipation of attacks from the Moorish Redeemer. None of the men and women he spoke to had seen him or knew who he might be, but many of them were clearly frightened and prepared to believe in rumors and fantasies that were unhelpful at best. Some said that the Redeemer was a giant with six fingers who rode a green horse. Others claimed he had a scar in the shape of a crescent on his left cheek and fought with a gold scimitar that had a handle made of mother-of-pearl. An Old Christian blacksmith told them that a column of Turkish warriors had been seen crossing the frontier from France, armed to the teeth, but he could not say where they had crossed or who had seen them. Another woman said that the Redeemer was a Morisco from Granada who had come to Aragon on a corsair ship from Barbary to steal Christian children.

Many Old Christians were clearly as afraid of their Morisco neighbors as they were of the Redeemer himself, and some of them expressed their satisfaction that the king had sent a judge all the way from Valladolid to find him. Others looked less reassured and said that they needed soldiers as well as judges to protect them if the Moriscos rose up. These conversations produced no new or useful information, but they nevertheless slowed to nearly three hours what was in theory a forty-minute journey to Cardona.

The seat of the Cardona family was built on a high plateau and was surrounded on all sides by old fortified walls. The town was grander than anything Mendoza had seen in the *señorio* so far, with cobbled streets and tall three- to four-story houses with carved wooden eaves and painted adobe façades and ornate balconies that would not have been out of place in Zaragoza. There was a splendid Gothic church with high walls, gargoyles and spiked spires dominating the large, rectangular Plaza Mayor. Its inhabitants also looked better clothed and fed than those of the towns and villages they had passed through, men and women of obvious distinction mingling with the peasants, *labradores* and artisans sitting outside their open shops or strolling along the medieval walls of the main square to look at the lakes, rivers and valleys and the looming peaks of Monte Perdido.

Mendoza had always thought of Granada as the most beautiful city he'd ever seen, but Cardona was a perfect jewel of a town that impressed him all the more because he had not expected to find such a place in these mountains. The Cardona palace was an enormous building just off the Plaza Mayor, with sturdy walls built from smooth, rounded stones and narrow windows with wooden shutters and carved stone lintels. The main entrance was wide enough for a small carriage to pass through, and above it, carved into the stone frame, was the Cardona family coat of arms, consisting of a lion and crossed swords and the striped shield of Aragon.

They knocked on the heavy wooden doors, and Mendoza gave his name to the servant who appeared. A few minutes later, he returned with two more servants, who took their horses and escorted Daniel and Franquelo to the servants' quarters. The servant led Mendoza through a long hallway lined with suits of armor and paintings depicting religious scenes or portraits of the Cardona family and ushered him into an enclosed courtyard filled with lemon trees and potted plants, its walls covered in creeping vines, that echoed to the trilling of a nightingale.

A priest in a black soutane and a venerable-looking elderly gentleman with a white goatee were seated at a table watching a young girl who looked to be about nine years old, who was leaning over a caged mynah bird, trying to make it talk. Two women were seated on cushions while an older woman who appeared to be the girl's personal servant hovered nearby, smiling down on her benignly. One of the two women looked like Juana Segura, and Mendoza knew instantly that her companion was the Countess of Cardona.

"What kind of talking bird is this, Mamá?" the girl cried. "It won't even say hello!"

The countess laughed indulgently. "It takes time, my love. They won't always say what you want them to when you want them to say it."

"Hello," the girl repeated. "Hello."

The countess and her guests laughed as the bird remained silent, and then she saw Mendoza and got up to greet him. Mendoza regarded himself as something of a connoisseur of female beauty, and by any standards the mistress of Cardona was a masterpiece. Her fair hair was tied up in folded braids across her high forehead, offsetting her smooth, milk-white skin, her angular, tapered cheekbones, a long, almost Basque nose and the palest blue eyes he had ever seen. She looked about Elena's age, but unlike Elena she did not attract him physically, and there was an air of dreamy etherealness about her that seemed to preclude any suggestion of sensuality.

She was wearing a simple black satin overskirt with wide flowing sleeves, stretched over a hooped farthingale skirt that accentuated her slim, tapered waist and revealed the outline of her breasts—something that was becoming increasingly rare in the chaste, tight-fitting dresses worn in Castile. Unlike many Castilian women, she was not wearing a collar or a ruff, and her décolletage was low enough to expose her long, deerlike neck.

"Good afternoon, Licenciado. I'm very pleased to see you."

"The pleasure is mine, Countess." Mendoza bowed and kissed her hand.

"Come and eat with us. This is Father García, our local priest. And Don Lucas Tallada, first magistrate of Cardona."

"Licenciado." The priest stood up and shook his hand. The old man attempted with obvious difficulty to do the same, but Mendoza took his outstretched hand to save him the trouble.

"And this is my daughter, Carolina."

"The image of her mother," said Mendoza.

Carolina smiled back and curtsied sweetly, which brought another pleased smile from her mother. "And my chambermaid, Susana. I believe you have met her father?"

"Indeed I have." Mendoza smiled at Segura's daughter, who bowed slightly and stared back at him coldly.

"It's time for you to continue your lessons, Carolina," the countess said. "We have business to discuss."

"But, Mamá, I want to meet the judge!"

"And now you have met him. Mercedes, please."

The governess took the girl's hand and led her away, and one of the servants drew back a chair for Mendoza.

"Please eat, Don Bernardo," the countess said. "You must be hungry. And the tavern in Belamar won't be what you're used to."

Mendoza needed no persuading as he looked at the splendid assortment of cold meats, cheeses, fried eggplant, sliced tomatoes, marzipan and almond cake, and he pointed out to the servant what he wanted. The countess sat down on the other side of the table, and he was surprised to see that Susana Segura sat down beside her, as if she were a member of the family rather than a servant.

"I understand that you are staying at Dr. Segura's dispensary," the countess said as he sipped a glass of honeyed water.

"That is correct, my lady."

"Dr. Segura is a fine man. He tended to my mother and my father before they died. But he will see anybody, even the poorest. And if they can't pay him, then he'll treat them for free."

"And your bailiff, my lady? What kind of man is he?"

"I must apologize for what happened the other day. Jean is an able man, but sometimes his devotion to my interests leads him to overstep himself."

"Inquisitor Mercader certainly thinks so," Mendoza observed.

The countess frowned. "The inquisitor is also a little too zealous in the defense of the Church's interests. This leads him also to overstep certain boundaries that have been long established in these parts."

"You're referring to the *fueros*?"

"I'm referring to the very specific seigneurial statutes enacted by His Majesty King Sancho Ramírez of Aragon for the first Count of Cardona in 1085, which granted full legal jurisdiction over the *señorio* to the count and his descendants. These privileges were extended by King Pedro of Aragon in 1212, when the House of Cardona was granted new territories as a reward for its contribution to the defeat of the Moors at Navas de Tolosa. They were ratified by His Majesty the emperor when he came to Aragon in 1519—my grandfather was present at that meeting. They clearly state that any external authority wishing to enter the Cardona estates can do so only with the consent of the Cardona family itself. That includes both the Inquisition and His Majesty's own officials."

She gave him a meaningful look, and Susana Segura smiled faintly.

"But the Catholic monarchs also agreed with the lords of Aragon that the Inquisition would be permitted to operate freely across the kingdom," Mendoza said.

"They did," the countess agreed. "But these powers were not intended to be without limit or constraint. My late husband was more favorable to the Inquisition than I am. He was from Toledo, like his father. But I am Aragonese, Don Bernardo. When I was a girl, I remember my grandfather telling me how the inquisitors were turned away from Teruel when they first came to the city. It was a matter of pride for him."

"Times have changed, my lady."

"Not as much as some Inquisition officials think. I presume that you have heard what kind of man Father Panalles was?"

At the mention of the priest, Mendoza noticed that Susana looked away and her pretty mouth tightened with anger and contempt.

"I have heard certain allegations," he replied.

"They aren't allegations. There were Moriscos from Belamar arrested by the Inquisition on his testimony who had done nothing except to refuse to pay him or sleep with him. Neither the Church nor the Inquisition investigated that. And now Inquisitor Mercader would like to use the death of Panalles as an excuse to purge the town. But his real aim is to punish *me*."

"And why would he want to do that?"

"Mercader believes that the lords of Aragon are allowing the Moriscos to worship as Moors," the countess replied calmly. "He wants someone to punish in order to set an example. A widow is a convenient target."

"And are you? Allowing your vassals to live as Moors?"

"These accusations have no foundation," said Father García.

"The counts of Cardona are buried in the pantheon at the San Juan de la Peña Monastery, and the countess will be, too. Anyone who knows her knows what an exemplary Christian she is. There isn't a church or a convent in the whole *señorio* that hasn't received a donation from her. She has made contributions to two new religious orders since her husband's untimely death."

"Is the Inquisition not aware of this?" Mendoza asked.

"The Holy Office sometimes sees what suits its purposes," the countess replied. "There are those who believe that the Moriscos must be dragged to the faith and made to drink it rather than be allowed to acquire a taste for it. I choose to guide my Moriscos toward our Lord Jesus Christ with Christian kindness instead of herding them like cattle. That approach is not popular in certain circles."

"Well, your vassals certainly appreciate it," Mendoza said. "They have a very high opinion of you."

The countess looked pleased. "Not all my vassals are Moriscos, Licenciado, and if they respect me, it's because I respect them. Is that not so, Don Lucas?"

"Indeed it is, Countess," the old magistrate agreed. "The vassals of Cardona know that Her Excellency treats them kindly and will not allow her courts to punish them unnecessarily."

"Go to Vallcarca and you'll see the difference," the countess went on. "The baron treats his vassals like dogs. My husband and I always believed that we have duties and responsibilities toward our vassals, just as they do toward us. And we have a special duty to guide the Moriscos toward salvation. The Church also believes this, yet it sends a priest like Panalles to preach the faith—a man devoid of goodness or virtue. That is why we have this Redeemer—whoever he is."

"There are those who say he comes from Belamar," Mendoza said.

"Commissioner Mercader will always see what he wishes to see," the countess replied. "Especially in Belamar. He is convinced that the entire population are heretics."

"And is it your opinion that the Moriscos of Belamar are good and faithful Christians, my lady?"

"No more or less than many Old Christians, Don Bernardo. Some of them come every week to our church in Cardona. Others *want* to be good Christians, but they don't know how to be, because no one tells them what the Church expects from them. They don't know our prayers, the names of feast days or the meaning of the sacraments. Yet men like Panalles punish them for their ignorance. But what I would like to know, Licenciado, is why the king has sent you to Belamar."

"I came here to solve the priest's murder, and now I have to solve four."

"And do you have any idea who might be responsible for these outrages?"

"At present my information suggests that they may be the work of a Morisco avenger."

"Well, I assure you that this Redeemer does not come from Belamar or even from Cardona."

"May I ask what makes you so certain?"

"I know my Moriscos, Licenciado. And I know the Moriscos of Belamar particularly well. They are not killers."

"In any case I would very much appreciate your assurance that I can continue my investigations unimpeded."

"Of course. We are also anxious to solve these terrible crimes and the many others that have disturbed the peace in recent years. My late husband was killed by bandits, Don Bernardo, shot down like a dog on the public road."

"I'm very sorry to hear that, Countess. Then I trust you will allow my investigation to take its course. And let me assure you that I do not accept rumors and false testimony from anybody, and I have no other interest in these matters beyond the speedy resolution of these crimes."

The countess seemed satisfied by this. "Anything that contributes to improving the security of Cardona is good for all of us. I will instruct my bailiff accordingly. Will you ride with me, Licenciado? I have something I want to show you."

MENDOZA HAD NOT INTENDED to stay any longer, but from both a professional and a personal point of view he could see no reason why he should not spend more time in the countess's company. He sat talking with Tallada and the priest while she went to change into her riding clothes. Both men were at pains to impress on him what an exemplary Christian the countess was. The priest claimed that her strong religious convictions had enabled her to overcome the tragic loss of her husband and the deaths of two of her children in childbirth.

"The little girl is the countess's only child?" Mendoza asked.

"That is correct." The magistrate glanced around him with a slightly furtive expression and lowered his voice. "And it is also a problem—unless the countess marries again."

"Because of the inheritance?"

"Precisely. Both of the countess's parents are dead. One of her brothers was killed in Flanders. Another is a madman in an asylum and has not spoken a word for ten years. At present there is no male heir."

"Not even on her husband's side?"

"The Cardona *fueros* do not permit this," Tallada replied. "The late count appointed his wife as his executrix, but she can pass on the Cardona estates only to a son or a male relative from her own bloodline. That means that she must marry or wait for her daughter to do so."

"And what would happen if neither of them were to have sons?"

Tallada looked gloomy. "In that unhappy—and unlikely—event, Cardona would become the property of His Most Catholic Majesty."

The return of the countess and her maidservant brought the conversation to an end. Both of them were wearing long outdoor shawls, and the countess had changed into a less elaborate black dress and a black widow's manto that covered her hair and reached down almost to her feet. Outside in the street, a small carriage was waiting for them, and Mendoza rode alongside it, with Franquelo, Daniel and two of her servants bringing up the rear a short distance behind them. Their route took them out of the town in the opposite direction from Belamar, along the road that led toward Vallcarca, through villages and hamlets whose inhabitants invariably bowed or doffed their caps as they passed. The countess acknowledged them with a smile or a vague wave of her hand and occasionally told the driver to stop.

Mendoza was struck by her lack of pretension as she asked even the most humble-looking peasant woman or craftsman about their children or a sick relative or their difficulties in paying taxes. She knew many of her vassals by their first names and spoke to them with the same easy familiarity with which she spoke to him. He wondered if such behavior was typical of Aragon in general. If so, the Aragonese were in for a shock when the royal court descended on them the following summer.

"Will you be hosting His Majesty during the royal visit next year, my lady?" he asked.

"From what I understand, the king will not be doing us that honor. But I will be attending the wedding. By all accounts the Duke of Savoy is a fine match for the infanta, and an alliance between the House of Hapsburg and the House of Savoy will certainly strengthen His Majesty's interests in regard to the Valois."

Mendoza was impressed. A knowledge of diplomacy and high politics was not something that he had expected from a country widow living so far from the court and even from Zaragoza.

"What you have lost in honor, your kitchens and storehouses have gained . . ."

The countess laughed. "You are irreverent, Licenciado, but you are right. They say the court is a most exigent houseguest. Fortunately, these mountains are a little too rugged for the Castilians. I hear that your constitutions are rather delicate."

"Very delicate, my lady. The *meseta* suits us."

"Not all of you, it seems. Many caballeros from Castile have acquired a taste for high mountains since my husband's death. Am I not right, Susana?"

"Indeed, my lady," the maidservant replied.

The countess proceeded to describe some of the suitors who had approached her or written to her over the last three years to offer her their love or protection. One of them was an English Protestant baron, who had written to her from London promising to convert to

Catholicism if she agreed to marry him. She had had offers from the dukes of Villahermosa and Gandía; from assorted viscounts, marquises and barons; from impoverished nobles with hard-luck stories; from second and third sons who would never receive their inheritance and aspired to acquire the Cardona estates instead.

"So many men want to be the next Count of Cardona, Licenciado!" She sighed with mock exasperation. "And what can a woman do when she doesn't want to marry any of them?"

"I understand that the Baron Vallcarca would like his son to be one of them," Mendoza said.

The amusement immediately vanished from her face. "Vallcarca would marry me to his mule if he thought he could obtain my estates in that way. Instead he wants me to marry a brute whose only pleasure appears to be hunting and beating his father's vassals. And my own father-in-law is writing me letters almost every week pressing me to accept his hand!"

"I assume he is acting out of concern for your happiness?" Mendoza asked.

"The Marquis of Espinosa has never been concerned with anyone's interests except his own. He lives in Toledo on the income that I send him because he has gambled away most of his own. My husband also used to pay for his upkeep, out of filial duty. I do so in order to keep him as far away from me as possible. But my marital status makes the marquis anxious about his own future. And so he wants to marry me off as if his own son had never existed!"

Mendoza was curious to know whether she did plan to marry again, given the implications for her estates, but it was impertinent to ask. Soon they came to a small town and pulled up outside a one-story building that looked at first sight like a storehouse and which had obviously been recently built or refurbished. Inside, they found ten boys in white smocks sitting at benches with slate and chalk, who immediately got to their feet as they entered.

"Say hello to the countess, boys," the priest ordered.

"Good afternoon, Countess!" the boys chorused.

The countess smiled at them and told them to be seated. Mendoza stood by the doorway as she asked them what they had been learning that day. Apart from the benches, the larger slate board and a single glass-paned window, there was little to distinguish the bare walls and dirt floor from those of a barn. The boys were of various ages, from six to twelve, and all of them put up their hands enthusiastically as the priest asked them questions to test their knowledge. Mendoza was beginning to wonder whether he might have done better to return to Belamar when she thanked the priest and they went out to the carriage.

"Did you like our little school, Licenciado?" she asked as the driver flicked the reins and moved away.

"Very much, my lady."

"The pupils are all Morisco boys. I built this school for them. Until two years ago, it was a barn without even a roof."

Now Mendoza understood the point of this expedition. In that moment the school made him think of his own childhood in Granada, when he had played with Morisco boys from the Jesuit *colegio* in the streets of the Albaicín or in the gardens of the Alhambra palace.

"That is how the Moriscos must be instructed in our faith, Don Bernardo," she went on. "With kindness, persuasion and education, not with the whip or the auto. And that is the work that God intends me to do."

"A worthy endeavor, and I wish you every success."

"I am succeeding, Licenciado, whatever the Inquisition may say."

"Look, my lady!" cried Susana in surprise. "It's Jean!"

Mendoza looked along the road and saw the bailiff in the familiar white beret, riding toward them from the direction of Cardona accompanied by a smaller group of men than he had previously brought with him to Belamar. As he drew near, Sánchez glanced coldly at Mendoza and doffed his beret to his mistress, who smiled at him warmly.

"Good afternoon, Jean," she said. "I thought you were at market today."

"I was, my lady. But I have bad news. Commissioner Herrero is in Vallcarca."

"The baron allowed this?" the countess asked incredulously.

"It seems there has been an incident. Two nuns have been attacked. Things were done to them that I cannot repeat in your company."

"But this is awful," the countess said. "Have the perpetrators been caught?"

"Yes, my lady." The bailiff glanced once again at Mendoza. "They were three Moriscos. And all of them came from Belamar."

CHAPTER NINE

Y THE TIME THE SUN CAME UP, VENTURA HAD already reached the clearing where the Quintana brothers had been killed. By midmorning he had reached the French frontier, following the trajectory of the main road while taking care to keep a distance from it and remain concealed. Soon he saw the wooden customs house at the Puerto de Portalet. There were no travelers waiting to cross it, and apart from the two horses grazing nearby and a young boy selling fruit and vegetables who was dozing in the shade just outside the hut, the post might have been deserted. As Ventura approached, two officers wearing red tunics emerged from the hut, looking as though they, too, had been sleeping.

"Identify yourself," one of them yawned.

"Sergeant Luis de Ventura, special constable from the Chancery of Valladolid. I'm investigating the murders of the Quintana brothers."

"Sergeant López, chief officer of His Majesty's Customs and Excise at the Cardona frontier," the official said, puffing out his chest. "We heard about those poor Christians. There are some bad men in these mountains."

"Devils and villains," his colleague agreed.

"There are bandits, smugglers and *salteadores* everywhere," López continued. "And from everywhere. French, Spanish. Lutherans, Catholics and Moriscos—all of them ride back and forth across these mountains as if there were no frontier."

"To commit crimes against God and His Majesty," his colleague added.

"Where do they ride?" asked Ventura impatiently.

"If we knew that, we could arrest them," López replied.

Ventura could not imagine these clowns arresting anyone, and it was more likely that they turned a blind eye or actively colluded in the traffic across the frontier. He thanked them and rode on back down the road till he was out of sight of the customs post, before veering off into the mountains. For the next few hours, he rode westward roughly parallel to the frontier, using the sun to orient himself as he scanned the terrain for paths made by goatherds and shepherds that might be used by smugglers.

The mountains were hard going, even harder than the Alpujarras. His horse, Aisha, was a pinto jennet that he had bought with the last of his soldier's pay. She struggled with some of the steeper slopes and passes as they crossed lush alpine meadows and river valleys, where the *montañeses* had put cattle, sheep and goats out to pasture. From time to time, he heard the faint tollings of a church bell coming from a monastery or one of the mountain villages, but he made no attempt to approach them. In the early afternoon, he found his progress blocked by a fast-flowing river that Aisha refused to cross, and he was forced to descend until he came to a small encampment of bivouacs and a wooden hut at the edge of a forest, where a rope-pulled ferry was waiting on the other side of the river.

The outer edge of the forest consisted mostly of the stumps of trees, and there were fallen logs lying all around the clearing. He saw a fire burning near the wooden hut and was riding toward it when a bearded old man suddenly appeared in the door with a harquebus aimed directly at his head and the lighted match cord hanging from the serpentine.

"Stop right there, stranger," the old man said. "This gun is loaded, and even I don't miss from this range."

"I'm glad to hear it," Ventura said. "But I only want to cross the river."

"Well, you look like a scholar to me, sir. And a swordsman in these parts has only one purpose—to steal from those who work for a living."

"Not me, brother," Ventura insisted. "I'm an *alguacil* with the king's seal. And I have money to pay for whatever you're cooking."

"Do you?" The woodsman finally lowered his musket and extracted the smoldering fuse. "Well, I can't say no to one of His Majesty's officials."

He appeared to have forgotten all about the king's seal now, and he laid his weapon down and ladled a spoonful of watery meat stew into a clay bowl as Ventura got off his horse. The settlement was a *navatero* camp, the woodsman said. There were a dozen of them altogether, and they had spent all winter felling trees and dragging them to the river with mules and oxen, where they were strapped together with ropes and willow laths to form the rafts that were taken downriver to the Ebro and Zaragoza. His job was to guard the camp and the animals until his companions returned. It was not an easy task, he said, with so many thieves and murderers roaming the mountains, but he was too old to go make the river trip anymore.

"Maybe you're too old to be out in these mountains by yourself," Ventura suggested.

"I'll be too old when I'm dead," the old man said. "I'm a *navatero*. A raftsman. I couldn't live on the plains. All those damned priests and monks jumping all over me like fleas. At least up here I don't starve. If the bandits don't kill me, I'll live longer than many of my countrymen."

"I hear there are many of them in these mountains."

"There are." The old man's eyes narrowed once again. "But a man who wants to stay alive doesn't talk about them to people he doesn't know."

"A wise policy." Ventura jangled two silver coins in his hand. "But I reward strangers who talk to me. I want to know where the routes are. I know they don't travel by road."

"That is true, brother." The old man took the coins from Ventura's outstretched palm and slipped them into the pocket of his frayed leather jerkin. "And if you cross the river, head upward about two leagues and turn west, you might run into some of them."

Ventura finished his meal, and the old man pulled the little raft back so that Ventura could get Aisha onto it before hauling them across. Soon they were above the tree line, climbing through passes, gorges and ravines where birds and animals were more common than humans. Ventura saw eagles and buzzards, deer, lynx and chamois and at one point what looked like a boar or a wolf running across a mountainside in the distance. In the late afternoon, he heard the faint tinkle of bells, and shortly afterward a herd of goats came bobbing toward him, followed by a boy with a shepherd's crook and a dog. The boy looked about twelve years old. He was barefoot, with wild hair, a patched tunic and torn hose that came down just below his knees. On seeing Ventura he stopped and stared at his sword and pistols with his mouth open.

"Good afternoon, boy," Ventura said. "Where have you come from?"

The boy continued to stare at him with a witless expression.

"Tu est français?" Ventura asked, reaching back to the smattering of French he had picked up in Flanders. The boy still looked blank, and Ventura suspected that the distinction between France and Spain was not one that he recognized.

"Il y a une route à France ici?" Ventura was beginning to think he was talking to a simpleton when the boy gestured behind him with his thumb. Ventura rode on, wondering if it was true that shepherds fornicated with their animals. He continued up the path and around the next slope until he reached a fairly wide trail winding its way steeply down from north to south. He followed it down, noting with satisfaction the hoof marks in the dry mud, when Aisha suddenly reared up and tried to back up. There was just enough time to see the snake slither away from the spot where it had been sunning itself in front of them before the horse's hooves touched the ground again, missing the path so that she half fell and half scrambled down the rest of the slope before coming to a halt.

Aisha was dragging her front left hoof. Ventura cursed and led the injured animal off the path. He unbuckled his saddle and saddlebags and placed one arm tenderly around her neck.

"I'm sorry, my beauty," he whispered, and slit her throat with his dagger. The animal reared up momentarily, and then her legs buckled as he thrust the knife deep into her throat, still holding the reins with one hand, till she rolled over onto her side. Ventura gathered up his things and took up a vantage point farther down on a rocky outcrop overlooking the path. It was not turning out to be a good day, he thought as he held up the wineskin and let its contents trickle into his mouth, but he was not prepared to walk back to the road if he could help it.

THE WINE AND SUNSHINE made him drowsy, and he felt himself dozing off. He was woken by the murmur of voices, and he looked down to see a line of seven horses coming slowly up the path. Five of them were without saddles and roped to the two riders who were leading them in double file. Ventura scrambled backward and ran back and round, before slithering down onto the path up ahead. He pressed himself against the rock face and waited till they were nearly alongside him before he stepped out with a pistol in each hand.

"Good day, señores."

The two men gaped at the pistols and his bloodstained hands, and the first rider took one hand off the reins and reached for the crossbow hanging from his belt.

"Don't be an idiot," Ventura said wearily. "Is this really the day you want to go to the other neighborhood? And believe me, if I kill one of you, I'll kill both, so help me, as easily as I breathe. So drop your weapons and get down—now."

The smugglers did as they were told. The one with the crossbow was dressed like a peasant, with dirty white stockings and wooden clogs. The other wore leather riding boots and a long cloak and slouch hat. They stood sullenly as Ventura cast an admiring glance over their horses, all the time keeping the pistols pointing directly at them.

"Some noble animals indeed, gentlemen. Isn't this one Andalusian?" He paused before a black stallion that shifted skittishly away from him. "And these look like Holsteiners. So the question is, why are you transporting such fine beasts across the border by this particular route? What's wrong with the main road?"

"The road is full of bandits," said the man in the slouch hat.

"Is that so?" Ventura grinned and raised one of the pistols so that it was pointing directly at the smuggler's forehead. "Call me a cynic, but I can't help suspecting that what you're really trying to do is deny His Majesty the revenue that really ought to go to his officials in any transactions of this nature. Where have you come from?"

"From Huesca."

"You're lying again. I'm afraid I'm just going to have to kill one of you. Then perhaps the other one will tell me the truth."

"*Por Dios*, Your Mercy!" The peasant looked terrified. "We're just smuggling horses. You can't kill us for that!"

"I can kill you for anything I choose. And I will do it if you don't tell me who you're smuggling them for."

"I work for him!" the peasant said resentfully.

Slouch Hat glared at him until Ventura held the pistol only inches from his face.

"Can you imagine what your face will look like when I shoot you from this range?" he asked.

"These are Baron Vallcarca's horses!" Slouch Hat replied. "Franquelo brings them to us."

"Franquelo the *alguacil* from Belamar? Is that where you are from?"

"No. I have a farm a league and a half away. Near Pino."

"Are you Moriscos?"

"He is," the peasant said accusingly.

"And are horses the only thing you bring back and forth across this border? No pistols or gunpowder? No books the Inquisition wouldn't want good Christians to read?"

"None of that," Slouch Hat protested. "I'm just a simple farmer trying to make a living—not a heretic!"

"And your name, simple farmer?"

"Gonzalo del Río."

"And you?"

"Pedro Rapino," the peasant replied.

Ventura gave him a long, hard look. "Well, gentlemen, this is a good day and a bad day for you. You can continue your journey. But I'm taking the Andalusian."

Slouch Hat looked aghast. "And what do I tell them when I show up with only four ponies?"

"Tell them it's better than being dead. Now, untie him and leave me a piece of rope."

The peasant obeyed, and Ventura slipped the rope around the stallion's neck. "Get on your horses and go before I change my mind," he ordered. "And the first man who looks back will lose his face."

The two smugglers hurried away up the path with their remaining animals. Ventura waited till they had disappeared before leading his new acquisition back to the hill where he'd left his things. The stallion gave an agitated whinny as Ventura strapped on the saddle and fixed the bridle between the horse's teeth but did not resist, and as he mounted the animal and rode away, he decided that he would call him Andaluz.

NO SOONER HAD MENDOZA left for Cardona than Gabriel began writing out his first report to send to the Marquis of Villareal. The thought that what he wrote would soon be in the hands of one of the king's ministers and perhaps the king himself was enough to ensure that he took special care to avoid mistakes as he sat bowed over the sloping bureau on Segura's desk. He tore up two versions before he decided that the results were good enough to satisfy his guardian. He had just finished sprinkling cuttlefish powder to dry out the wet ink when Segura came in and invited him to lunch.

The invitation came as a surprise, and before arriving in Belamar he would have thought twice about accepting it. But he was curious to see what a Morisco household looked like, especially if it was a house where Juana might be present. He spent the next three hours at their house, in a little room lined with mattresses and covered with silks, cushions and colored cloths, together with Segura, Juana and Segura's youngest son and two younger daughters. The meal consisted of bread, cheese and lentil soup, which Juana and her sisters brought on trays, and they ate from clay bowls on their laps.

Gabriel liked Segura and found his children charming and amusing, but it was Juana who interested him the most. In Valladolid all his classmates had been boys, and he rarely encountered girls or women except in the street. Most women in the city wore veils or covered their faces in public, and for some time now he'd been mildly surprised and disconcerted at how often he found himself surreptitiously peering at them or gazing at the curtained carriages that passed through the street in the hope that their female passengers might briefly reveal themselves. On the journey up to Aragon, many women were not covered, and he found himself constantly staring even at the plainer ones.

Juana Segura was not plain at all. Even when she was not there, the thought of her olive skin and dark, serious eyes filled him with a secret excitement that grew even more intense when he was actually in her presence. He had never considered himself to be a boastful person, and his guardian had always frowned on any expression of vanity and self-importance, but now he found himself childishly seeking to impress her. When Segura's youngest daughter, Antona, asked him about Castile, he said that it was one of the richest and most powerful kingdoms on earth with the air of a man who had seen many kingdoms. He said that Valladolid was one of the great cities of the realm, where the king himself had once held his court, with wide streets, parks, squares and so many carriages that some days it was difficult to walk among them.

When Antona asked him to demonstrate his handwriting, he took out his pen and ink and wrote out a few sentences. All of them crowded around to admire his handwriting, except Juana, who only glanced at it indifferently. Segura complimented him on how elegant and straight it was and asked him if he was a professional scribe or notary. He told them that he was not and said that his guardian had allowed him to come with him as a special dispensation to prepare for his legal training as a notary. When Segura said he was lucky to have such a guardian, Gabriel was lavish in Mendoza's praises. The *licenciado* was the wisest and most fearless man he had ever met, he said, as gifted with the guitar, the vihuela and the drawing pen as he was with the sword, a man who thought about many things besides the law and knew the answer to almost any question on any subject.

If Juana was impressed by this, she gave no sign of it. When her awestruck younger sister Antona asked him what kind of clothes were worn by the rich ladies and lords of Castile, she merely watched him with a faintly skeptical smile that made him feel like a braggart.

"Were you born in Valladolid?" Segura asked.

"No, I'm from Granada, like Don Bernardo. I was a foundling."

"I didn't realize the *licenciado* was from Granada. And do you know who your parents were?"

"I don't. He never told me."

"Haven't you ever asked him?" Juana said, looking at him in surprise.

Gabriel reddened. "Of course. Don Bernardo found me in an orphanage."

"Is the *licenciado* married?" Segura asked.

"He is not, sir."

"Yet he took you in, even though he has no wife? That is most Christian of him."

"You might be a Morisco!" Juana looked amused at the thought.

"I don't think so," Gabriel said.

"How can you be so sure if you don't even know who your parents were? How old are you?"

"Seventeen." Gabriel felt himself becoming angry and defensive. "My guardian would have told me if my parents were Moriscos," he replied firmly.

"Well, it's easy to find out," Juana said with sudden bitterness. "Just prick yourself with a needle and see if your blood comes out black."

"That's enough, daughter," Segura said. "Let's be polite to our guest."

Gabriel was surprised and confused by her acerbity, and he was relieved when Segura asked him if he wanted a game of chess. He considered himself a good chess player, but the older man quickly unraveled his defenses and checkmated him within fifteen minutes, before he had hardly time to realize how it had happened.

"Don't worry, son, I've been playing this game a long time," Segura said graciously. "But let me give you a tip. Most players concentrate too much on trying to take the queen, and they forget about the pawns. But sometimes the pawns are the most important pieces. Haven't I always told you that, Juana? You should play with her—she's better than me."

Gabriel could not believe that a girl could be good at chess, let alone that Juana could be better than her father, and he felt under pressure to prove himself as the family sat and watched them intently. He tried to concentrate on the pieces, but it was difficult to think about anything except the solemn, dark-eyed beauty on the other side of the board, whose presence seemed to warm his blood as though it were being heated over a low flame. Checkmate was already looming once again when there was a loud knock on the door, and Segura went to answer it. Gabriel heard Necker asking for him and went to find the German waiting outside the doorway with Daniel.

"Licenciado Mendoza has been looking for you," he said, regarding Gabriel disapprovingly. "He says you must bring your things with you. And Dr. Segura must come to the village hall for questioning immediately."

Juana looked at her father in alarm, and Gabriel felt embarrassed and mystified as he followed the mayor and his escorts to the village hall, carrying his *escritorio* under his arm. Mendoza was sitting at his desk. He scowled at them as they came in and told Segura to sit down before he dismissed Necker and the militiaman.

"*Escribano*, take down Dr. Segura's deposition."

"Yes, sir."

"Is something wrong, Your Honor?" Segura asked as Gabriel hurriedly laid out his writing materials.

"Two nuns were violated on the road between Cardona and Vallcarca by three Moriscos from Belamar yesterday evening. Did you know that?"

Segura looked aghast. "Of course I didn't know it. Do you know the names of these Moriscos?"

"Not yet. I thought you would."

"Is that why you deemed it necessary to send an armed escort to bring me here?"

"Why didn't you tell me your daughter Susana was seduced by the priest?"

"She told you that?" Segura asked in dismay.

"She didn't need to say anything. It was written on her face when we spoke about him."

Segura looked out the window with a desolate expression. "He didn't seduce her. He raped her," he said. "She was fourteen. Just as he raped her mother. My wife died in childbirth having his baby. The child died, too. So no, I didn't tell you, Your Honor. Because there are some things a man doesn't want the world to know about."

"Do your children know about this?" Mendoza asked.

"No. I told them the child was mine. But the countess found out from Susana what had happened. She took Susana as her servant to get her away from that animal."

Gabriel had stopped writing. In that moment the world itself seemed a sadder, nastier place that was filled with dark possibilities he had not previously imagined.

"Continue writing, scrivener. Some people might ask why you didn't kill Panalles," Mendoza said more gently, "after what he did to your family."

"It was because of my family that I didn't kill him," Segura replied. "Do you think they would have given me a pardon—a Morisco who'd killed a priest? And who would look after my children if I died or went to prison? Sometimes neither revenge nor justice is possible, Your Honor, and a man must learn to live without either and trust in the will of God to put things right in the next world if not in this one. Now, with your permission, I would like to find out the names of these three Moriscos."

Half an hour later, Segura returned and said that several Moriscos had left the town three days before and still had not returned to their homes. Their names were Vicente Péris, a wood-carver, a carpenter named Pedro Navarro, and his apprentice, Juan Royo.

"What do you know about these men?" Mendoza asked.

"That they would never have done anything like this. Péris is a family man. He has two young children. Navarro has five. And Juan Royo is only seventeen. I don't even know why they would have gone to Vallcarca together. None of them had any business there."

"Have any of them ever been convicted by the Inquisition or the secular justices?"

"Yes. Navarro and Péris spent three years in the galleys for blasphemy. Péris was flogged and lost his house."

"So they weren't that virtuous after all."

"The evidence against them came from Panalles and the baker." Segura pronounced the last word with particular contempt.

"You're saying the charges were all false?"

"I'm saying that they might not always have been good Christians, but they aren't rapists. May I return to my family now, Your Honor?"

THE NEXT DAY Mendoza and Gabriel went to interview the families of the three men. Navarro and Royo were almost neighbors, and their families said that the two of them had gone together to the Huesca market to buy tools. Péris's wife said that her husband had gone to Teruel to work and had not said anything about going to Vallcarca. Their houses were poorer and more primitive than Segura's. Péris's house had almost no furniture except for a small table and two benches, and the dirt floor was covered with rush matting. His wife was pregnant, and an anxious-looking toddler hovered by her skirts as she tearfully insisted over and over again that her husband had no reason to be in Vallcarca, that he was a good man who cared only about his family.

"Do you believe her?" Mendoza asked Gabriel as they walked away.

"I don't know, sir. Her tears seemed real enough."

"Just because a woman cries, that doesn't mean she's telling the truth, boy. And there's something she isn't telling me. Something all of them aren't telling—something that's under the surface of this damned village. Did you notice anything about their houses?"

"They were poor?" Gabriel suggested.

"They had no religious images. No pictures of the Virgin. Not even a crucifix."

"Maybe they can't afford them."

"Or maybe they don't want them in their homes."

"Do you think one of these three men could be the Redeemer?"

"It's possible. Come. Let's speak to this baker."

They returned to the town hall and dispatched Necker to summon Romero, who appeared a few minutes later, still wearing his apron.

"You wanted to see me, Your Honor?" he asked.

"Yes. Do you know Vicente Péris or the carpenter Pedro Navarro and his apprentice?"

"Of course. Péris was arrested for blasphemy and for possession of an Arabic manuscript. The carpenter Navarro was also punished by the Inquisition."

"Did you denounce them?" Mendoza asked.

"I gave evidence to the Inquisition prosecutor, Your Honor."

"What evidence?"

"With respect, Your Honor. It is illegal for anyone who testifies to the Holy Office to share the contents of his testimony with anyone else."

"His Majesty King Philip would appreciate and will undoubtedly reward your cooperation."

Romero's eyes gleamed hungrily, and his wary arrogance was replaced by a sudden animation. He admitted that he had played a minor part in the arrests of Péris and Navarro. He had seen them grimace and look away from the host when Father Panalles offered the Holy Sacrament on various occasions. He had observed the carpenter Navarro giggling when the priest mentioned the Immaculate

Conception and had witnessed him in the forest washing his face and hands and kneeling on the ground to pay homage to the false prophet Muhammad. Both men had been punished by the Holy Office for these offenses, he said, but those were only the offenses the Inquisition had been able to prove.

"Offenses that can be proved are normally the ones that offenders are punished for," Mendoza pointed out.

"Not with Moriscos!" Romero replied. "They'd lie to their own mothers to protect their damned faith. No one who knows Péris will be surprised by what he's done now."

"I haven't said what he's done," Mendoza said. "How do you know?"

"This is a small village, Your Honor. Everybody knows what happened in Vallcarca."

"Well, we appreciate your assistance," Mendoza said. "And we may consult your expertise in the future."

The baker was clearly disappointed that he had not been offered money there and then, but Mendoza merely smiled at him and watched in disgust as he crossed the square and hurried back to the bakery.

"I would like to send that weasel to the galleys myself," he said.

"Do you think what he said was true—about the Moriscos?" Gabriel asked.

"Who knows? At this point I don't know who's lying and who's telling the truth. Come, gather your things. Today I want you to come with me."

"Where are we going?"

"To Vallcarca."

CHAPTER TEN

HERE WERE FEW THINGS THAT VENTURA enjoyed more than riding in open country on a fine horse, and the Andalusian was one of the best horses he had ever ridden. The mountains were an ideal place to put the young and headstrong stallion through his paces and impose Ventura's mastery over him. From the point of view of the investigation, however, these rides produced nothing of interest. After a cold night in a forest, he spent the next morning riding back and forth above the tree line between the Somport and Portalet passes before gradually working his way lower and circling back toward the main road in the afternoon. By five o'clock he had seen no one but shepherds, cattle herdsmen and charcoal burners, and he was beginning to think that he might have to return to Belamar when he saw the flash of movement coming out of the forest far below him.

As soon as he saw the cluster of dots moving rapidly across the landscape, he knew immediately that no one with any legitimate purpose in these mountains could be riding like that, and he felt both relief and exhilaration as he spurred the stallion and rode hard down in their direction, taking care to maintain his distance even as he closed upon them. For the best part of an hour, he continued at the same speed, digging his heels into the stallion's sweating flanks until finally they slowed as the road appeared in front of them.

Ventura reined the horse in, matching the pace of those he was following and moving cautiously forward till he was able to make out about twenty or more horsemen, some of whom were carrying an extra rider with them. All of them had sacks and bags covering their faces as they took up concealed positions on both sides of the road. He edged the stallion into the forest behind them, threading his way through the trees, muttering soothing noises. When he had come as close as he dared on horseback, he dismounted and tethered the horse, taking the cocked crossbow with him, and crept slowly forward. On hearing the shots, he crouched down and ran quickly along the edge of the forest till he had nearly reached the road.

Directly in front of him, he saw a carriage with a team of four mules, entirely surrounded by a horde of masked horsemen. The carriage driver was lolling almost sideways on the pillion and was clearly dead. One of the horsemen had seized the reins and climbed on board to subdue the panic-stricken mules. Inside the carriage a woman was screaming and a male voice was shouting and pleading for mercy.

"Come out of the carriage or die inside it!" one of the *salteadores* shouted when the tumult had subsided. A door opened, and two women stepped down, helped by two male passengers, one of whom was holding his left shoulder as if he had already been shot. All of them were wearing clothes of good quality that contrasted dramatically with the improvised white masks and motley apparel of many of their attackers. The women stared fearfully at the bandit chief, who was standing before them holding the reins of his horse in one hand and a silver mace in the other. He ordered the men to unbuckle their swords and the women to hand over their jewelry. When one of the women hesitated, the jefe yanked her necklace from her throat with a violent jerk that made her gasp.

"God curse you!" One of her male companions raised his fist in a chivalric gesture that Ventura knew was ill advised. The jefe stepped to one side and swung the mace upward. There was a noise like the cracking of a thin wooden box as the weapon struck the would-be knight in shining armor in the side of the head, and a jet of blood squirted from his temple as he dropped to the ground and lay still.

"Gos," the bandit sneered. The women and their wounded companion backed against the carriage as he turned toward them.

"You, little man, what's your profession?"

"A tailor, Your Mercy. Like m-my brother," the wounded man stammered, staring down at the prone corpse. "We are on the way to Monzón to make dresses for the royal wedding."

"Do you have silver?"

The tailor was silent, and the jefe drew back the mace. "If you want your brains to stay in your head, you better use them," he said.

"Inside the carriage!" one of the women burst out. "There's a false bottom."

"A sensible woman. You should listen to your woman, tailor. Then maybe you might live to see your grandchildren grow old."

His companions now swarmed in and over the carriage, ripping out the false bottom and tossing bags and boxes down from the roof.

Some of them held up their hands in triumph, brandishing silver plates, jewelry, bags of coins, fine cloths and velvet dresses, which they strutted around in as if testing them for size, to the amusement of their companions.

"See how the ladies of Monzón prepare for the infanta's wedding!" one of them crowed.

"Now they'll have to go naked!" shouted another.

"Enough," the jefe ordered impatiently. "Gather everything up. Bring the mules, too. As for you"—he turned to the passengers, who were backed against the carriage like prisoners waiting for a firing squad—"go and tell the world the Redeemer has come to liberate the Moors from the Christian tyrants! Tell them the sultan and the king of France are coming to Aragon with their armies to reconquer al-Andalus, and there will be no city that can stand against them!"

Within minutes the bandits had gathered up their possessions and ridden away with the laden mules, leaving the two women and their wounded passenger staring aghast at the body of their fallen companion. It was only then that Ventura emerged from his hiding place. For a moment he considered getting back to his horse and continuing his pursuit, but it would soon be dark, and it was obvious that the three survivors were clearly in no condition to go anywhere without help. The two women shrank back against the carriage as he came toward them out of the shadows, and the tailor halfheartedly put himself in front of them.

"It's all right, ladies," Ventura assured them. "I'm an officer of the king. I'm here to help you."

"You saw these devils? Then why didn't you stop them!" the tailor demanded.

"Because, señor, there were two dozen of them, and my name is

Luis de Ventura, not Achilles. If I had tried to do anything, they would have killed me and probably all of you, too, in the bargain. Let me see that."

The tailor flinched as Ventura drew his dagger and cut away the soaking velvet jacket.

"I've seen worse." Ventura reached down and peeled back the dead man's clothes, tearing and cutting a strip from his white tunic, which he wrapped around his companion's shoulder. "You might live if we can stop the bleeding. Get back in the carriage and wait for me."

"Where are you going?" one of the women asked fearfully.

"To get my horse. Do you think I'm going to pull you to the next town by myself?"

A few minutes later, he returned and attached the reluctant stallion to the wooden shafts. He dragged the heavy body of the dead tailor toward the carriage and hoisted it onto the broken floor at the feet of the passengers. He considered taking the driver's seat, but the dead coachman lay sprawled across it like a drunkard, and it seemed easier to leave him there.

"I know you weren't made to be a carthorse, my prince," he murmured apologetically as he took the horse's reins. "But it's for a good cause. Don't worry, señoras," he called back as they moved away. "We may take some time, but we will get there in the end."

AT FIRST SIGHT there was little to distinguish the drab, cheerless towns and hamlets and cultivated fields of Vallcarca from Cardona. It was not until Mendoza and his men had been riding through the *señorio* for the best part of half an hour that they came across the unmistakable shape of a gibbet on the outskirts of a village. On drawing closer they saw a body swinging gently in the morning breeze and vultures pecking at its face, open stomach and bare feet, the birds scattering as they approached. The scavengers had fed well, and there was little untouched flesh visible through the tattered clothes. Nevertheless Mendoza saw that the body had once been male and young.

He had seen such things enough not to be shocked by them. In Granada the bodies of executed rebels had also been left to rot as a lesson to anyone considering disobeying the king. But those were exceptional measures taken during a war. Here there were peasants working in the fields as though the gibbet and the corpse were part of the landscape.

"You there!" he called to two ragged young men who were laboriously picking stones from a terrace planted with barley. "Why was this boy hanged?"

"He was carrying a pointed dagger, Excellency."

"He was executed for that?"

The peasant nodded glumly. "No one is allowed to carry more than a dagger in Vallcarca without the baron's permission," he said. "And the point must be rounded. The first penalty is flogging. After that it's the rope."

Once again Mendoza was surprised. The Inquisition had been trying to get the Crown to enforce these restrictions on Moriscos in Aragon for years, but Vallcarca was the first place where they seemed to have been applied, apparently as the result of a decision by the baron himself. As they rode on, he noticed that pointed weapons were indeed absent from the *señorio*, with the exception of those carried by the ubiquitous members of the baron's personal militia in their maroon tunics. Even the peasants working in the fields were mostly unarmed, and Mendoza passed various gibbets and whipping posts in prominent positions.

Vallcarca was nearly two hours' ride from Belamar, at the foot of a rocky promontory with the baronial palace looming gloomily above it. The palace consisted of a somewhat dilapidated-looking medieval castle with a more modern building attached to it that was obviously still under construction. As they ascended the steep dirt road toward it, they saw a number of carts and wagons drawn up outside the main entrance, which was guarded by two halberdiers wearing breastplates and combed morion helmets. All around them, servants, stableboys and other maroon-clad militiamen were hurrying back and forth, bringing boxes and bags out of the palace while a better-dressed man shouted orders at them.

Mendoza asked to see the baron, but the official barely looked at him.

"His Excellency and his family are preparing to go to Huesca," the man said. "He is not receiving visitors. You!" he shouted to two sweating servants who were laboring to carry a large, heavy box. "Be careful with that, you cretins!"

Mendoza dismounted and stood, holding his horse's reins. He had no time for lackeys who aped the mannerisms of their masters.

"I'm not sure that you heard me correctly," he said. "I am Alcalde Mendoza, special justice of His Majesty the king, and I'm here to see the baron on a matter of great importance."

"And I told you the baron doesn't want to see anyone!" the official snapped.

"It's all right."

The guards stiffened to attention as a tall, barrel-chested man appeared in the doorway, his size magnified by the slashed black velvet jacket with raised shoulders and wide, open sleeves that hung down just above his knees. His neck was entirely concealed by a white ruff collar, which framed a great block of a head topped by a mass of thick black hair and a broad, pugnacious jaw that was partly concealed by a well-trimmed goatee.

"Good day, Licenciado Mendoza. I am Vallcarca. Please come in."

MENDOZA LEFT HIS MEN OUTSIDE and followed the baron into a spacious flagstoned corridor with little natural light, whose gloom was accentuated by the faded tapestries of hunting scenes and the gaping spaces in the walls where the plaster had fallen away.

"I heard you were in Cardona," Vallcarca said. "You've caught me at a bad time. My family always goes to our summerhouse near Huesca during this season."

"I won't take up much of your time, my lord."

The baron ushered Mendoza into a roomy, high-ceilinged study and sat opposite him with his legs crossed at the ankles and his hands folded on his lap. Mendoza looked around at the array of weapons on the walls and the large tapestry showing a group of aristocrats hunting a deer.

"A fine piece of work," he observed. "From the twelfth century?"

Vallcarca shrugged indifferently. "So how can I be of assistance to His Majesty?" he asked.

The baron's grim, imperious visage did not indicate a desire to assist anybody, Mendoza thought, and explained a great deal about the proliferation of gibbets and whipping posts.

"I've come about the nuns," he said. "I understand that the three suspects are from Belamar."

"They are. But they aren't suspects. There is absolutely no doubt about their guilt. Two of them have been arrested. The wood-carver Péris has escaped—for now."

"Could you tell me what happened exactly?"

The baron made no attempt to conceal his impatience as he explained that the two nuns had been accosted by the three Moriscos two days earlier on the road between the Convent of the Sacred Heart of Jesus and the village of Todos Santos. The Moriscos had taken the women into the forest to where their animals were tethered and violated them before leaving them naked to dress themselves and make their way back to the convent. The local militia had pursued the three Moriscos trying to flee back into Cardona that same evening. Two of them had been riding on one mule, but Péris had been riding a horse, and he had managed to get some distance in front of them and reached Cardona, where he abandoned his animal and disappeared into the forest on foot. The militia were allowed to pursue fugitives in Cardona only on the public road, and they had been forced to abandon their pursuit. The two prisoners had been handed over to Commissioner Herrero and taken to the seigneurial prison in Villamayor.

"Have they confessed?" Mendoza asked.

"Not yet, but the sisters have identified them," Vallcarca replied. "Their confessions will come soon enough, when they get to Zaragoza."

"May I ask why the prisoners are being tried by the Inquisition rather than your own courts?"

The baron looked at him in mild astonishment. "Do you know what one of these savages said when they violated these poor women? 'This will show you how Jesus was born.' These rapes were an attack on the faith, Licenciado. They aren't crimes for the seigneurial courts."

"What was the Inquisition doing in Todos Santa?"

"Todos Santos is a Morisco village. The Holy Office was investigating reports of witchcraft and sorcery there. Naturally, I allowed it. I also allowed Commissioner Herrero to use the seigneurial prison in Villamayor for temporary incarceration of any prisoners."

"From what I hear, the lords of Aragon are not all so willing to cooperate with the Holy Office."

Vallcarca nodded. "Do you see that cross?" He pointed toward a red cross on a small gold star that hung on the wall behind him. "That is the cross of the Order of San Salvador created by His Majesty King Alfonso I of Aragon in the twelfth century to fight the Moors. It is now the symbol of the Order of the Collar, to which every generation of Vallcarcas has belonged. That sword"—he pointed toward a broadsword hanging horizontally above the fireplace—"belonged to the second Baron of Vallcarca, who fought with Fernando and Isabel during the conquest of the Moors in Granada throughout the whole ten years of the war. My family has always fought for the one true faith, Licenciado, and I will not allow my vassals to worship the sect of Muhammad just because they are good workers, even if others do."

"You're referring to the Countess of Cardona?"

Vallcarca looked suddenly guarded. "I would not go that far. Let us say that the countess treats her vassals in a womanly way, because she believes that this will bring her Moriscos to the faith. But she is mistaken. Moriscos need a firm hand to keep them from straying. And here on my estates, they get one."

"So I've seen."

"You think me harsh? So does the countess. But what happened to these sisters is a consequence of too much benevolence, not harshness—on her estates, not mine. This must change if the peace of His Majesty's realms is to be preserved. I believe—I hope—that the countess will change once she is exposed to other influences and once the consequences of her actions become clear to her."

"Will a marriage to your son facilitate this transformation?"

"You're well informed, Licenciado. We certainly hope that such a union will take place. But that is the countess's decision to make."

"I understand that her father-in-law also has some influence in these matters."

The baron's thick black eyebrows twitched momentarily before the closed, baleful expression returned. "I fail to see what this has to do with your business in these mountains."

"You are right, Excellency. I have strayed from my purpose. I wonder if it would be possible to interview the two prisoners?"

"They are in Villamayor," Vallcarca said. "They are under the Inquisition's jurisdiction, not mine. Will that be all, as I must attend to my family?"

Mendoza thanked Vallcarca, who escorted him back outside.

"I wish you luck with your investigation, Your Honor," he said. "We all want to see Cardona pacified before the king's visit. But if you want to find this Redeemer, I suggest you look for Vicente Péris."

"What makes you say so, my lord?"

"Because that's how he introduced himself to those poor women. And if you need extra men to catch him, I shall be only too pleased to provide them."

Mendoza thanked him and asked him for directions to Villamayor. For the first time, Vallcarca seemed genuinely willing to help and called on one of his militiamen to guide them out on the road to the village. They had not been riding long when they noticed a small group of men and horses gathered in an open field near the road. Some of them were wearing maroon tunics, but others were carrying sticks and drums that indicated they were beaters at a hunting party. Nearly all of them were standing in a circle watching what appeared to be a fight in progress. On closer inspection Mendoza saw that one man was lying on the ground, his yelps mingling with the curses and grunts of satisfaction coming from his assailant, who was kicking and beating him with the flat of his sword.

"What's going on here?" Mendoza shouted.

The man stopped what he was doing and looked up in surprise, his face twisted into an expression of anger and cruelty. "I am Rodrigo Vallcarca, and who in God's name are you?"

"Why are you beating this man?"

"This idiot is my servant and my vassal. He coughed when I was about to shoot a deer so that I missed my shot!"

"Well, you've beaten him enough," Mendoza said.

"I will decide when he's had enough!" Vallcarca gave the man another savage kick in the stomach, and then Mendoza rode his horse directly into the circle, pushing Vallcarca back so quickly that he fell over. There were gasps of amazement from the spectators as Vallcarca scrambled to his feet and held up his sword.

"I'll kill you for that!" he yelled. "Get down from your horse!"

"You are raising your sword against an officer of the king," Mendoza said. "And if I get down from my horse, it will be to place you under arrest. Now, leave this man alone. A servant should not be beaten for coughing."

He rode away without waiting for a reply. Behind them he heard the sound of another blow, and he glanced around to see Vallcarca kicking the prone servant.

"Shall we go back and stop him, Don Bernardo?" Necker asked.

Mendoza shook his head. He had interfered enough already, and there were some things in these mountains that could not be put right. But whatever benefits the union of the Vallcarca and Cardona families were intended to bring to the baron, he thought, this encounter with the baron's son made it clear why the Countess of Cardona was not keen to offer him her hand.

ABOUT TWENTY MINUTES LATER, Vallcarca's militiaman pointed out Villamayor up ahead and turned back. When they reached the seigneurial jail, they were told that the Inquisition escort had left with the two prisoners half an hour previously on the road to Zaragoza. Mendoza decided to try to catch them, and they took out at a canter along the dusty road until they saw the inquisitorial cortege in front of them. The party consisted of a carriage and a cart bearing the two gagged and chained prisoners, accompanied by an escort of eight armed *familiares* on horses and mules. One of them was the same brutish creature with the squashed nose and the thick hands whom Mendoza had first seen in Zaragoza, who wheeled his horse and scowled at them.

"Stay back," he ordered. "The Holy Office is escorting prisoners to Zaragoza."

"I know," Mendoza said. "I want to talk to them."

"That is not permitted!"

Necker rode past him in front of the cortege, forcing it to come to a halt.

"Why are we stopping?" A tonsured head appeared in the carriage window as Mendoza rode alongside him.

"Commissioner Herrero?" Mendoza asked.

"Yes. And who are you?"

"Alcalde Mendoza, the king's special justice. I wish to speak to your prisoners."

"You'll do no such thing! That is forbidden."

"I'd like you to make an exception in this case."

"Absolutely not. And you are obstructing the work of the Holy Office. You should go back, or I will report you to my superiors."

Mendoza looked at the prisoners, who were sitting passively, their legs chained together and their arms tied behind their backs. Their gags were not unusual, since prisoners of the Holy Office were not permitted to talk to anyone after their arrest, but there were bruises on both their faces, and one of them looked as though he might be unconscious. Perhaps it was the heat, or the aching in his thigh, or the seemingly endless procession of people who he suspected were not telling him everything they knew, but Mendoza was not inclined to take no for an answer.

"I only want to ask them a few questions," he said.

"You will ask them nothing!"

The *familiares* were gathering around the carriage and the prisoners now, with their hands poised on their swords and pistols. They were only the usual lay volunteers and assistants, but they looked as though they knew how to use their weapons, and Mendoza gestured to Necker to move away. As he watched the cortege hurtle down the road, he could not help feeling that his journey to Vallcarca had raised as many questions as it had answered. He had indeed confirmed that the three Moriscos had come from Belamar, but nothing that he'd heard so far had shed any light on what the Moriscos were doing in Vallcarca in the first place. If they wanted to rape nuns, there was no shortage of them in Cardona. Why would they go to the neighboring *señorio* to do it, at precisely the time when the Inquisition happened to be working in the vicinity?

There was one other source of information in Vallcarca that might shed light on these questions, and he asked some *labradores* who'd been watching the scene for directions to the Convent of the Sacred Heart of Jesus. Twenty minutes later they rode through a patchwork of well-tended orchards and vegetable patches and knocked on the main door of the convent. A shutter drew back, and a pallid female face in a nun's habit appeared in the opening, her eyes widening with fear and amazement at the sight of them. Mendoza asked to see the mother superior, and she closed the shutter without a word. A few minutes later, they heard the faint sound of footsteps, and the shutter opened once again to reveal a severe-looking old lady whose crinkled face was also entirely enclosed in a black wimple.

"I am Mother Superior Margarita," she said. "What do you want?"

"Good afternoon, Reverend Mother. I am Alcalde Mendoza from the Royal Chancery in Valladolid. I'm here in connection with the attacks on your sisters."

"That has already been investigated by the Inquisition."

Mendoza suppressed his impatience. Was there anyone in this kingdom who did not think that he or she had the right to question his authority? "I understand that, but there are some questions I wish to ask the victims that relate to my own investigation. I believe others may be involved of whom the Inquisition is not aware, and I need to speak to the two sisters in order to establish this."

"Absolutely out of the question. They are in no condition to talk to anyone. I will talk to you, but not here. Men are not allowed within these walls. Please wait."

Mendoza stepped back, and a moment later the heavy door creaked open and Sister Margarita hobbled out, accompanied by the mouselike nun who had greeted them previously. Like him, Sister Margarita was carrying a stick, and she walked slowly and with obvious difficulty to a wooden bench overlooking the rows of fruit trees, where her companion stood attentively a few feet away from her.

"You may sit," she said as she looked out somberly toward the men who were working in the fields and orchards. "This has been a terrible event for all of us, Licenciado. Most of our workers are Moriscos, and we have very good relations with them. Some of them have worked on our estates since they were children, and their fathers and grandfathers worked here before them. Now some of the sisters are saying we should hire only Old Christians."

"Even though the perpetrators are from Cardona, not Vallcarca?" Mendoza asked.

"People are afraid, and fear breeds hatred. Some of the sisters are saying we should accept the baron's offer to use his militia to protect us. But until now we never needed protection. And some of the baron's methods are not in keeping with our Lord's teachings. Now, how can I help you?"

"Did your sisters identify their attackers?"

"Of course!" She looked at him in surprise. "That's why Vallcarca's men arrested them."

"And I understand that one of them said he was the Redeemer?"

"That is correct."

"So the sisters saw his face during the attack?"

"Not during it. All three men were wearing masks, as I told Commissioner Herrero."

"If they were wearing masks, then how did they know that the two men they saw were the ones who attacked them?"

Mother Superior Margarita's ancient, creased face looked suddenly confused. "Because they saw them before—on the road. And they also saw them later on."

"At the prison?"

"No. The baron's men brought the two prisoners here on the evening they were caught. Our sisters saw them through the grille. They recognized them both as the men they had seen on the road just before the attacks. They were the same men who were arrested by the militia while riding away afterward. There was no one else on the road apart from them. Who else could it have been?"

Mendoza did not know, and it seemed discourteous to say that he would have required more conclusive proof to reach a verdict. Instead he expressed his hope that the guilty would be punished and that the sisters would recover from their ordeal.

Mother Superior Margarita nodded. "Nothing happens without a reason, Licenciado Mendoza. But goodness will triumph with God's help."

Mendoza also felt that the nuns had been attacked for a reason, but he was starting to wonder whether it was the reason it seemed to be. A new suspicion was beginning to take shape in his mind. It was certainly fortuitous, given the Inquisition's priorities in Cardona, that Herrero should have been conducting an investigation in Vallcarca on the same day that three Moriscos from Belamar had come to the *señorio* to carry out a crime like this. And why would three rapists come all the way to Vallcarca, with its gibbets and militia, when there were nuns in Cardona who were more easily accessible? As he walked back to his horse, it occurred to him that goodness would need considerable assistance from the law as well as the Almighty if it was to prevail in Vallcarca.

CHAPTER ELEVEN

HEY ARRIVED BACK IN BELAMAR IN THE early evening, and Mendoza was pleased to find his cousin waiting for them in the village hall with Necker, the two militiamen, and Constable Franquelo. Gabriel was impressed by Ventura's new horse, and Franquelo shifted uncomfortably when Ventura said that he had acquired it on the open market after his mare had broken her leg. Ventura told them about the bandit attack on the road whose survivors he had escorted safely to Cardona, and Mendoza immediately gave new orders. From now on they were to patrol the town by day and also by night, in case Vicente Péris attempted to enter Belamar. From midnight to dawn, there would be two-man patrols lasting two hours, and he and Gabriel would take the first.

Gabriel was excited by this new task, but Franquelo made no attempt to disguise the fact that he regarded it as a burden.

Mendoza sent them to the tavern and remained behind with Ventura. It was not until then that his cousin told him about his encounter with the smugglers.

"I suppose a horse is a fair reward for saving lives," Mendoza said. "Otherwise I might have had to confiscate it as contraband. So Vallcarca is smuggling horses. And our little village constable is helping him."

"Are you going to question Franquelo?"

Mendoza shook his head. "Not yet. Right now I have other priorities than smuggled horses. Like Vicente Péris."

"Who's Vicente Péris?"

Mendoza told him about the attack on the nuns and his visit to Vallcarca. "The baron thinks that Péris is the Redeemer. But why would the Redeemer go to Vallcarca with two wretched Moriscos to rape two nuns when he has the band that you saw at his disposal?"

"There's something else I didn't mention," Ventura said. "Didn't the priest have his skull smashed in with a pointed weapon?"

"That's what Segura said."

"Well, the bandit who called himself the Redeemer was carrying some kind of silver mace with spikes on it. That's what he killed the tailor with."

"He's probably not the only bandit with a weapon like that."

"True, but there was something odd about the attack. After the bandit killed him, he called him a *gos*."

"What does that mean?"

"It's a Catalan word for 'dog.' And he spoke Spanish with a Catalan accent. I know because I spent some time in Barcelona when I came back from Flanders. The women, I tell you—"

"Hombre, stick to the point."

"So why is a Catalan waging holy war on Christians in the name of the Turkish sultan?"

Mendoza shrugged. "Don't they have Moriscos in Catalonia?"

"No doubt, but what would a Catalan Morisco be doing in these mountains? And if these people were the same people who wrote Arabic on the church wall in Belamar, then why didn't they speak it to one another?"

"Not all Moriscos speak Arabic. Granada was always different in that respect."

"Maybe. But his whole speech about the Redeemer—it didn't sound real. It was like something you hear at the theater."

"Rebels don't have to be great orators, cousin."

"True," Ventura agreed. "But this Catalan sounded like a bandit, not a rebel. And the men I saw today—they were just a rabble looking for plunder."

Mendoza pondered this for a moment as a new and completely unexpected possibility now entered his mind. "Well, if the Catalan is the Redeemer, then the Redeemer can't be Vicente Péris—unless there are two of them. But the priest wasn't robbed. And why would a bandit call himself the Redeemer if he wasn't?"

Ventura looked blank. "Maybe he thought it would frighten people. Some bandits like to give themselves a reputation."

Mendoza was silent as he considered these possibilities. "Do you think you can track those bandits?" he asked.

"Claro."

"Good. Because I need you to go back up into the mountains and get a closer look at those men. See what you can find out about them. Once you get a sighting of their camp, come back immediately. Only reconnaissance, is that clear?"

Ventura's face was a mask of injured innocence. "Have I ever disobeyed orders before? But I'll need to go on foot at least some of the way. A horse will be too conspicuous."

"Necker can accompany you as far as you need to go on horseback. You'll have to make your own way back. And right now, cousin, I have to tell you that I am so hungry I actually want to go to the tavern."

THE DEL RÍO FARM was only half an hour from Belamar, at the end of a steep dirt track leading off the Jaca road that most travelers who knew no better assumed did not lead anywhere. It was this inaccessibility that had made it attractive to Vallcarca, and the farm could also be reached from the lower plains through more complicated routes that avoided the main roads altogether so that horses could be brought up through lower Aragon and up through Monzón or Barbastro or farther west from Ayerbe unnoticed by the king's constables or anyone else, even by daylight.

It was a system that had worked well throughout the ten years Gonzalo del Río had been involved in the trade, and his section of the route was the easiest because the mountains were so lightly patrolled and because there were so many routes through the mountains that it would take a small army to watch over every one of them. In all those years, he had not failed to deliver a single animal and had never even been stopped crossing the frontier, by either Spanish or French customs officers. It was only now, thanks to the *alguacil*-bandit who had accosted them near the frontier three days earlier, that he had lost an animal and the delivery fee that came with it, and his reputation had been called into question for the first time.

Franquelo had also been penalized, and the *alguacil* had insisted that he and Rapino recoup his losses. Now there would be no more horses until Licenciado Mendoza's investigation was over, and that meant that he would have to rely only on the farm. Del Río could not help but interpret this reversal of fortune as a sign that Allah was displeased with him, and so he had made a special effort for the last two days to perform the salat five times daily. He had renounced taverns and brandy houses and pledged to keep himself pure. He did not include his comings and goings across the border in these pledges, because the laws that he broke were Christian laws and the income that he derived from breaking them helped him to pay his taxes and feed his wife and children, as well as his mother and father and his grandparents, who lived on the farm with him. He could not see how Allah could object to that.

Del Río was only intermittently pious, and he did not find praying easy. He often struggled to remember the words and had to make up his own, but opportunities to pray in groups were becoming rarer since the judge and his constables had installed themselves in the town, and now that the *alguacil*-bandit knew where he lived, he was reluctant to pray with his family or even wear a clean white shirt in his own home, even though it was Friday. He had still managed to pray three times that day, however, and he washed his hands and face once again and knelt down before the open window and looked out toward Mecca and the Kaaba Stone.

From around the farm, he heard the familiar domestic sounds that he had heard all his life. He heard his eldest daughter cranking the well, his wife singing to the baby, the cattle lowing in the barn, and the chickens pecking at the corn his son was throwing to them.

He had just touched his forehead to the ground when he heard the dog's agitated yelp, followed by a sudden silence. From the direction of the well, he heard his daughter scream, and then she, too, fell silent. The smuggler scrambled to his feet, reached for his sword and ran out into the courtyard toward the open doorway.

Outside, a hellish scene confronted him. Men were swarming into the yard. Some were wearing masks and white smocks with red crosses painted onto them. Others had their faces uncovered, and he recognized *montañeses* from his journeys back and forth across the mountains. All of them were armed with halberds, lances and swords, bills and spiked wooden maces. At first he thought that they had come to rob him, but then one of the masked men shouted, "Come out, Moriscos! Paradise awaits you!"

As if obeying a signal, del Río's six-year-old son came sprinting across the yard in an attempt to reach the house. The boy had run barely a few yards when one of the intruders tripped him up with his halberd and then calmly rammed its sharp point into his writhing body as though spearing a fish. All around him, del Río's family was screaming and crying as the intruders rushed toward the house, some of them shouting the name of St. James the Moorslayer. It was only then that the smuggler tried with the help of his father and his uncle to slam the door in their faces, but their collective weight pushed him back. He had not even time to raise his sword before one of the masked men thrust the lance into his abdomen and leaned forward, pushing it in deeper. Del Río gasped and dropped his own weapon, staring back at the pitiless hate-filled eyes through the slits as the masked man's companions hacked, poked and slashed at his defenseless family and pursued the women and children into the surrounding rooms. He wanted to ask God what he had done to deserve this, and he pleaded with the deity to allow them all to meet in paradise, before his killer withdrew the lance and let him fall lifeless to the floor.

OF ALL THE CRIMINALS Inquisitor Mercader encountered in the course of his holy work, there were few that he loathed more than sodomites. Even Jews and Moriscos were capable of genuine repentance, but sodomites were freaks of nature who had allowed their bodies to be used for purposes that the Heavenly Father had not intended, and their sins left a stain that could never be removed. Administering punishment to such prisoners brought its own special spiritual satisfactions. With most prisoners the Inquisitor was careful to see that his interrogators carefully calibrated the level of pain in order to extract their confessions. In the case of sodomites, the torment was not just a means to an end—it was a permanent message inscribed on the body in a language of torn muscles and broken bones that would always remind offenders of the words of Leviticus: "Thou shall not lie with a man as with a woman; that is an abomination."

On this particular morning, Mercader presided over a private punishment at the Aljafería of an elderly hidalgo who had committed the nefarious sin with his servant. The old gentleman had to be carried into the courtyard on a board, where he lay barely conscious of the sentence that was read out, while the servant had to be supported by guards as he was led out in his sanbenito and a candle, to be tied to the whipping post to receive his thirty lashes with a whip whose cords were dipped in pitch.

The inquisitor stood in his scarlet robes on the balcony overlooking the courtyard and observed these proceedings with his usual pitiless detachment. The Inquisition had been pursuing the hidalgo for many years, and right up until his arrest he had continued to believe that his social position would protect him. Now he knew better, and if he never walked again, then that was how God willed it, and the fine imposed upon him would greatly assist the Inquisition in its holy work. But the hidalgo's was ultimately a minor case that would have no bearing on his own career and merely completed an investigation that his predecessors had set in motion long before his arrival.

Cardona was a different matter. And now, against his expectations, the case had acquired renewed momentum as a result of the fortuitous investigation in Todos Santas. The prosecutor Ramírez had just issued a new indictment for the arrest of the three Moriscos from Belamar. Already he had dispatched urgent letters to the *justiciar* of Aragon, the Council of Aragon and Inquisitor-General Quiroga to report that three Moriscos from Belamar de la Sierra, two of whom had precedents with the Inquisition, had violated two nuns in the Baron of Vallcarca's estates and that he had reason to believe that one of them might be the Morisco Redeemer. In his letters he had reiterated the need for a full inquisitorial investigation into Belamar itself.

It was a hot day, with no breeze on the balcony, and as soon as the auto was over, he retired to his office to remove his inquisitorial robes and tell his servants to bring his lunch to the shaded patio overlooking the fountain in the Patio of Saint Isabel. Food was one of the few earthly pleasures that Mercader allowed himself, and he ate a full meal of meatballs and bread crumbs, accompanied by a glass of red wine, followed by a plate of assorted fruits.

The heat, wine and food had a soporific effect, and soon he was so lulled by the trickle of water from the fountain and the trilling of a nightingale from the garden that his head slumped forward and he fell asleep. Almost immediately he found himself in a strange dream, in which he was kneeling down to pray in a lush green garden when a naked male angel with white wings appeared on the patio in front of him. Normally angels were sexless, but this one was blond and exceptionally beautiful, and Mercader was shocked to see that the angel's shameful part was as solid and erect as a stallion's.

He woke to hear footsteps echoing from the darkened interior and looked up to see Herrero and his secretary coming toward him out of the gloom.

Herrero bowed deferentially. "Excellency, we have brought the prisoners."

"And the wood-carver?"

"Still no sign of him, Excellency. But we have reason to believe that he may be the Morisco dog who has been shedding Christian blood."

Mercader was silent for just long enough to let the *comisario* know that he was displeased as Herrero gazed hungrily at the uneaten fruit. "I have to report that Alcalde Mendoza stopped us on the road and demanded to talk to the prisoners."

"Did you let him?"

"Absolutely not. Even though he insisted."

"You did well. That man needs to learn his place. I will make it known to the inquisitor-general that he has attempted to interfere with our business. And if he persists in such behavior, I shall personally ensure that he is excommunicated. Now, let us see the prisoners."

Herrero cast a last disappointed glance at the array of dishes as he accompanied the *comisario* back into the building and up the winding stone steps to the Troubadour Tower. They found Pachuca and the prison warden hunched over bowls of bread and stew with two of the other *familiares*, oblivious to the rancid odor of excrement and musty straw and the sound of a woman sobbing from behind the locked door. Mercader was always careful to observe the prisoners in their cells when they were first brought in, so that he could make a preliminary assessment.

The foreknowledge that he acquired in these visits often shaped the tempo of the interrogations that followed. Some prisoners were like eggs who could be broken with only the lightest tap. They were the ones who became tearful as they protested their innocence or were so petrified with awe and terror that they could hardly speak at all. Men and women like this could be left alone for weeks or months, so that when they were finally brought to the tribunal, they were ready to pour their secrets almost as if they were in the confessional.

There were also those who required more severe forms of pressure, who refused to admit their guilt and were even openly defiant. The two Moriscos straddled these categories. Both men were sitting in a cell on the third floor of the tower, leaning on the great stone pillars beneath the old Arabic inscription proclaiming THE EMPIRE IS ALLAH—a message that always amused Mercader every time he saw it. The carpenter Navarro refused to even acknowledge their presence until Pachuca gave him a blow on the arm with his baton. The young apprentice was clearly terrified and insisted that he had done nothing wrong and pleaded to be told what he'd been accused of.

Mercader did not answer these questions. He had witnessed many similar protestations of innocence. Even the guiltiest men were able to show genuine conviction when confronted with the prospect of pain and death, but he had no doubt that the interrogation of the two Moriscos would produce the same results.

CHAPTER TWELVE

HE NEWS OF THE ATTACK ON THE FARM-house reached Belamar shortly after daybreak the following day. By the time Mendoza and his team arrived at the scene, much of the farm had been burned to the ground, and the flames were still licking at parts of the main building. Segura organized volunteers from Belamar and the surrounding villages to bring up water from the well to put them out, but it was not until midmorning that they were able to bring out the bodies. There were eleven dead altogether, including a baby, in addition to the young boy they found lying in the yard, the girl they found near the well, and the cows, goats and horses that had been gratuitously slaughtered in their corrals and stables or left scattered all around the farm. The bodies in the farmhouse had been blackened almost beyond recognition, and the smell of charred flesh mingled with smoke and the blood of slaughtered animals.

Mendoza ordered Necker, the two militiamen and some of the Moriscos to dig a mass grave for the animal carcasses as he tried to piece together what had happened. The nearest neighbor to the del Río family was a farmer who lived nearly one league away, and he said that he had heard screams coming from the farm at around nine o'clock in the evening and had immediately hidden his family in the forest. Others had watched the fire burn and said that they had heard but not seen a large group of men and horses leaving the area just after midnight.

No one had dared approach the farm until daylight, and Mendoza did not blame them for that. As far as he could tell, there'd been no attempt to rob the del Río household; the sole purpose of the raid appeared to have been killing and destruction, and the hideous tableau was completed by the crude wooden cross that had been planted in the yard in front of the household, which the family's neighbors insisted had not been there before. At midday the first relatives of the deceased began to arrive, and some of them wept at the sight of the bodies lying in a row in the courtyard.

Shortly after one o'clock, Pelagio Calvo arrived with a contingent of constables and militiamen, who immediately began to help the Moriscos digging and dragging the carcasses toward the deepening pit. There was already a faint smell of wine on the corregidor's breath as he stood supervising them with his hands on his hips, looking even more like a small, fat bird in his tightly fitting leather doublet with his bandy legs.

"I shit in my mother's milk, but this is a bad business, Bernardo!" he exclaimed.

Mendoza saw no reason to reply to this banal observation, which failed by a considerable margin to do justice to the horrific violence that had been inflicted on the Morisco del Río and his family.

"Did you know that del Río was smuggling horses?" he asked, leaning on his stick to shift his weight from his bad leg.

"We suspected it, but we never caught him. If he was, he wouldn't have been doing it on his own account."

"He wasn't. He was working for Vallcarca."

"How do you know this?"

Calvo listened grimly as Mendoza told him about Ventura's encounter with the smugglers in the mountains and the robbery of the tailors' carriage.

"Well, I can't say I'm surprised," Calvo said. "I always suspected that Vallcarca had business across the border. Do you think he killed del Río to shut him up?"

Mendoza had already considered this possibility. It could not be entirely coincidental that Gonzalo del Río was the same man his cousin had encountered in the mountains less than three days before and relieved of one of his horses. In addition to Vallcarca, the smuggler had also given up Franquelo's name, which might constitute a motive for an exemplary massacre, assuming that the *alguacil* even knew that he had done so. But Franquelo had been in Belamar when the massacre took place. And since he had not yet acted on his cousin's information, then the only person who knew what had happened in the mountains was the smuggler Rapino, and he was nowhere to be found.

"It's a harsh way to ensure silence," Mendoza said. "And what about this?" He pointed toward the cross.

"This is Spain, Bernardo. Business and religion aren't mutually exclusive."

That was true enough. In the Alpujarras even the scum of the Seville streets had believed that God had given them permission to loot and rape the Moriscos when they attacked their villages, but no one appeared to have even tried to rob the del Río household.

"If you ask me, Bernardo, it looks as though the Old Christians are taking their own revenge. You can blame the Redeemer for that. Your cousin has done good work. At last we know who he is. Now, let's go and get him."

Mendoza nodded. He did not tell Calvo his own doubts about the Catalan or Vallcarca's accusations against Vicente Péris, partly because he had not yet resolved them in his own mind and also because he no longer believed that the wine-sodden corregidor who had once been his friend had anything illuminating to say about them. Instead he glanced at Franquelo, who was standing in front of the entrance to the smoking farm to ensure that the Moriscos did not approach it, looking suitably grim and somber.

"What's your opinion of our constable?" he asked.

"Franquelo? He's lazy, and I wouldn't be surprised if he makes a little money where he shouldn't, but he does his job—more or less, as long as someone keeps an eye on him. You don't think he's involved in this?"

"Del Río told Ventura that he was the man who brought Vallcarca's horses."

"Then I'll take the son of a whore back to Jaca in chains!"

"No, don't do that. I don't want him to know he's under suspicion. Not yet."

"You know what I think, Bernardo? This is all getting out of hand. First you've got Moriscos killing Christians. Now Christians are killing Moriscos, and the only arrests so far are those two rapists in Vallcarca. If it doesn't stop, things are only going to get worse."

Mendoza marveled once again at his friend's ability to state the blindingly obvious.

"Maybe the king needs to start thinking about pacification rather than investigation," Calvo went on. "A few thousand soldiers and we can wipe out every bandit in Cardona and Vallcarca."

"We're dealing with crimes, not acts of war."

"For now," Calvo said ominously. "But the *montañeses* are getting restless. They're saying that if we can't protect them from this Redeemer, then the Old Christians will have to protect themselves. Maybe this is just the beginning of that. Maybe some of them thought del Río was the Redeemer. Or maybe they just thought they'd kill any Moriscos they could find."

Mendoza agreed that this was a possibility, especially after the murder of the tailor. But he also found it curious that vengeful Christian vigilantes should have killed the same man his cousin had encountered in the mountains only three days before. And the fact that del Río was both a smuggler and an associate of Vallcarca and possibly of Franquelo as well made it even odder still. The more he thought about these connections, the more it seemed to him that something beyond religion was at stake, and he had no intention of asking the king to send an army of occupation to Aragon on the basis of rumors, even if his friend was willing to do so.

"I'm returning to Belamar," he said. "I'll have to report back to Villareal immediately."

"Of course. I'll have a messenger standing by. Just send Franquelo up here. I assume you're still going to use him?"

"I am. Send him to pick up the letter before you leave. And I'd appreciate it if you don't tell him anything that I've told you."

Calvo leaned closer, till Mendoza could smell the wine on his breath, and patted him on the back. "You're doing a good job, Bernardo," he said.

Mendoza stiffened with irritation. In that moment he did not feel that he or anyone else was doing a good job at all, and he beckoned to Gabriel that he was ready to leave.

"I want a full report on the massacre," he said as they rode away. "Ready to give to Corregidor Calvo by the end of the day."

"Of course." Gabriel was frowning in the way that always preceded a question.

"What is it, boy?"

"Why does God allow such things to happen?"

"Haven't I told you to be careful of what you talk about in public?" he snapped.

"You have, sir," Gabriel replied calmly. "And that's why I'm asking you in private."

Gabriel's earnestness and solemn expression immediately made Mendoza feel guilty at his bad temper. His page's question was one that he had often asked himself, and he'd never been able to come up with a satisfactory answer. "The Church says that God gave us free will so that we could choose between good and evil," he said. "Each of us has to make that choice freely. If we didn't have that choice, then virtue and heaven would lose all meaning."

"And those people who were killed, will they go to heaven or hell?"

"It depends on when they made their last confession."

"But the children couldn't make confession. And they had no choice. Does that mean they'll go to hell, too?"

As always, Mendoza was impressed and slightly alarmed by his page's willingness to explore these concepts that were best left to churchmen, and he replied vaguely that there must be some special dispensation for them. To his relief Gabriel did not ask what it was, and soon Belamar appeared in front of them. For the first time since their arrival, Mendoza was surprised to see that there was no one working in the fields. As they approached the main street, they found five men sitting on the stone bench near the *lavadero*, armed with a motley assortment of weapons.

"What are you men doing?" he asked.

"Protecting our wives and children, Your Mercy," one of the Moriscos replied.

"Did Dr. Segura tell you to do this?"

"No one told us. We heard what happened. It was decided among ourselves."

"Well, you might do better to see that your families have food on the table rather than stand here spreading alarm for no purpose," said Mendoza testily. "And if you want to protect your village, perhaps you might see that your people come forward and give me information instead of concealing it!"

Gabriel and the Moriscos looked equally taken aback by this outburst, and Mendoza rode slowly through the village, past small groups of men and women whose faces emanated the same suspicion and fear. He wanted to shout at them that he had not washed properly since leaving Zaragoza, that his clothes reeked of smoke and burned flesh, that he was sick of trying to coax information from a population that seemed determined to resist all his efforts. After a brief lunch in the tavern, he began to dictate the letter to Villareal in the village hall. They had barely begun when Franquelo returned and asked if the letter was ready.

To Gabriel's surprise, Mendoza told Franquelo to sit down on the bench while he continued with the dictation. When they finished, he asked his page to read out the description of the massacre once again, glancing over at Franquelo as he did so. The *alguacil* showed no sign of emotion and sat staring grimly at the floor until Mendoza handed him the sealed letter.

"By the way," Mendoza asked casually, "did you know if del Río was ever involved in any criminal activity?"

"He was suspected of smuggling horses," Franquelo replied. "On one occasion the corregidor ordered me to keep his farm under observation for a few days. I did that, but I found no evidence of anything illegal."

The constable's face remained impassive. For the first time, Mendoza wondered if he was cleverer than he looked, because he had just lied without batting an eyelash, and if he could do it so easily to Mendoza, then he must have lied to Calvo as well, probably on more than one occasion. Mendoza was tempted to present him with the information that Ventura had brought back with him, but he did not want to draw any attention to his cousin's current assignment in the mountains. Instead he sent Franquelo away and promised himself that he would subject him to more rigorous questioning as soon as his cousin returned.

Necker and Ventura rode together to the point where the robbery had taken place, and the German then returned to Belamar with the Andalusian in tow, leaving Ventura to continue the rest of the journey on foot. He had an excellent memory for landscape and had no difficulty retracing his steps to the spot where he had seen the bandits emerge from the forest three days before. He took with him the same supplies he had once carried on similar solo reconnaissance missions in the Alpujarras: a small knapsack with a day's worth of food, a few extra balls and powder for his pistols and a cape to use as a blanket. In addition to the pistols, sword and parrying dagger, he also carried a smaller knife in his boot and a crossbow, as well as a quiver stuffed with extra arrows draped around his shoulder.

The opening through the forest was not visible from a distance, but he soon located a wide natural pathway that led into a forest of towering oak and beech trees. At first it was easy to follow the trail the bandits had taken, from the broken branches, trampled vegetation and occasional articles of clothing or strips of material that they had dropped or discarded. After a while the tracks became less frequent, but the trail remained fairly obvious as the forest opened up into rockier and more inaccessible terrain, bisected by steep canyons, high cliffs and streams and mountain lakes that he was obliged to wade or jump across.

From the sun's position, he calculated that he was moving northeast, away from Belamar toward Cardona and Vallcarca. He continued to keep himself concealed as much as possible, walking alongside or around the path that he thought the bandits had taken, but there were times when no tree or rock cover was available and he had to walk out in the open, uncomfortably conscious that he was visible to anyone who might be watching. By midday the sun was directly overhead and shade was scarce, and he was dripping sweat even after he'd discarded his leather doublet and stripped down to his shirt.

To keep himself cool, he wore a head scarf, which he periodically dipped in water, but it was hard-going in the heat without a horse, harder even than the Alpujarras had been. Whether it was because he was getting older or because he had spent too much time in Madrid taverns, his body felt heavy and stiff, and he stopped frequently to catch his breath. As always these signs of weakness irritated him and spurred him to walk even faster in an effort to overcome them. It was not until around two o'clock that he found himself walking in forest once again, and finally he decided to take advantage of the shade to eat something. He sat down with his back to a tree in a small clearing and ate some of the bread, figs and hard manchego cheese that Beatriz had given him. He smiled momentarily at the thought of her voluminous hips enveloping him as the priest's bed creaked beneath them like a ship on a rough sea, when he heard the sudden scrabbling movement coming through the undergrowth toward him.

He drew his sword and crouched down in readiness as the boar came bursting out of the trees, snorting and grunting. It was a large animal, as large as any he had hunted. He barely had time to take in the stiff mud-covered hair, the long snout and wide tusks before it leaped toward him, and he rolled sideways and thrust the blade upward into its exposed throat. The animal squealed and collided with the tree before rolling over on its side. Ventura rammed the blade repeatedly into the writhing body until it finally lay motionless. He was still getting his breath back when a voice from behind him said, "Drop your sword and unbuckle your belt."

He did as he was told, and the voice ordered him to drop the belt with the dagger and the two pistols and turn around slowly with his hands in the air. Ventura turned to find himself facing two men. The man who had spoken was sitting on a horse, holding the reins in one hand and a crossbow pointed at Ventura's chest in the other. His companion had been riding pillion and now jumped to the ground beside him to hold a short broadsword at waist height. His hair was covered in a head scarf, and he held his weapon as though he knew how to use it, with his feet at the correct distance apart and his free arm stretched out to the side for balance. They might have been bandits or smugglers or both, Ventura thought, but they were certainly not shepherds. Already he was calculating the number of steps he would have to take, because he knew that neither of them could leave the forest alive and that everything would be decided within the next few minutes.

"Good day, gentlemen," he said, slowing down his breathing to keep his mind clear.

"What are you doing here?" demanded the man with the crossbow.

"Hunting." Ventura nodded at the bloody carcass.

"With pistols like these?" His companion bent and picked up one of the guns while keeping his own trained at a point just above Ventura's groin. "These are gentlemen's pistols," he said. "Flintlocks, too."

He held one of the pistols toward the man on the horse. In a single swift movement, Ventura reached down and drew the short dagger from his boot and pulled the swordsman toward him by his shirt, plunging the blade into his solar plexus. The swordsman barely let out a cry before he went limp, but Ventura continued to hold him upright, shielding himself from the dead man's companion, who was circling around them trying to get off a shot with the crossbow. As soon as the arrow thwacked into the ground behind Ventura, he pushed the body away and stabbed the rider in his right thigh.

The horseman cried out in pain and tried to wheel the horse away, but Ventura was all over him now, pulling him down and stabbing him repeatedly. Even after the man was on the ground, Ventura continued to stab him until he, too, lay motionless. When Ventura looked up, the horse had bolted, and he heard it crashing through the forest. He had no idea if there were any other men in the vicinity who might come looking for their companions, and he quickly dragged the two bodies out of sight and gathered up his weapons before hurrying away from the scene, half running and half walking till he came to a stream, where the horse had stopped to drink.

He removed its saddle and slapped its flank with the blade of his sword to send it back in the direction he had come from, then paused to wash his face and hands before continuing to follow the trail.

IN THE MIDAFTERNOON he saw the thin trail of smoke rising in the distance, and he took special care to avoid unwanted scrutiny, climbing and scrambling up rocks to avoid the obvious paths or crawling on all fours through more exposed areas. The smoke was coming from another forested slope on the other side of a wide valley, and he scanned the trees and rocks for pickets and sentries as he continued to walk parallel to a distinct and clearly well-used path till he heard the sound of cattle and human voices up ahead. He waited until it was nearly dark before continuing forward, weaving through the trees and crawling on his belly for the last few yards until he was looking out across a large clearing overlooking a stream.

Dozens of men were moving around in the dusk or sitting around campfires and primitive bivouacs made from branches, with pyramid-shaped stacks of weapons protruding outside them. He estimated that there were fifty or sixty of them altogether, including some women, in addition to horses, mules and grazing cattle. They did not seem to be concerned about being discovered, and there were no sentries that he could see. The only concessions to security were the large Pyrenean mountain dogs, which seemed more interested in the cattle than in any potential intruders.

At this point his mission had been accomplished. He had found the camp where the men who'd attacked the tailors' carriage had come from, he knew how large it was, and all he had to do was retreat into the forest, retrace his steps the following day and make his way back to Belamar to pass this information on to his cousin. But as in Granada and many other places, success filled him with the same desire to go further and find out even more, the same desire that had led him to enter Purchena and the Morisco villages disguised as a Morisco and cross the picket lines of rebel camps in Flanders.

He waited until it was completely dark and then left his pack behind a tree to walk casually out into the clearing, with the crossbow tucked under his cloak. He moved without haste, adjusting his pace to the slow rhythm of the camp, keeping back from the campfires so that his face could not easily be seen.

Some of the men were sharpening knives and swords, others playing cards and dice. Many of them were drinking wine or brandy, and a few were clearly the worse for wear. Such behavior might equally have been found among bandits or rebels. Even the Moriscos of Granada sometimes drank alcohol, despite Aben Humeya's strict orders, but unlike in Granada, here he heard no Arabic, only Spanish and a similar language that he guessed must be Aragonese. And the Moriscos of Granada had had officers and men who looked and acted like soldiers. He had just recognized some faces from the attack on the tailors, sitting by a fire a few yards away from him, when a stout little man crashed against him in the dark and would have fallen over had he not caught him.

"Thank you, brother!" The man giggled foolishly and offered him the open bottle. "Baltasar Plata is indebted to you, sir! Let's drink to the Moriscos! May every last one of them burn in hell!"

"Hombre, you said it." Ventura took a swig and handed it back to him. "The sooner the better."

"God willing! I didn't leave my flock for nothing."

"You're a shepherd, friend?" Ventura asked.

"I am. And there are more of us coming! We're going to exterminate these infidels. And if we fuck some of their women first, who's to say we didn't deserve it!"

"Well, it's one way to baptize them!" Ventura said.

The shepherd laughed so much he nearly fell over backward. Just then a tall bearded man in a black cap and wearing a pistol in his belt came toward them and shouted in an authoritative voice that the jefe wanted to speak to them all. Baltasar Plata lurched unsteadily toward the biggest campfire, and Ventura followed cautiously behind him. All around the campsite, men were converging on the same spot, until they were gathered in a large, unruly group in front of the fire, where a tall and better-dressed man in a broad hat, folded on one side, was standing on a log in front of the fire. Ventura saw the silver mace hanging from his belt and recognized the man who had led the attack on the tailors' carriage as he raised his arms for silence.

"Has anyone seen Paco or El Mozo?" he asked. "They went out hunting this morning, and they haven't come back to camp."

"Probably too drunk to stay on their horses!" called one of the bandits.

"Gone whoring in Vallcarca!" shouted another.

The jefe raised his hand again, and the laughter abruptly ceased. "This isn't a joke. Some of you are new to these mountains, but let me tell you that anyone who leaves camp or stays away without permission can expect punishment! If you ride with us, you carry out my orders! Is that understood?"

The Catalan nodded with satisfaction as his listeners murmured their assent. "Now, I know that some of you *montañeses* have been wondering why you left your flocks," he went on. "You came here to fight Moriscos, and you haven't been doing it. Well, tomorrow some of you will get your chance. Tomorrow, like the Cid's, your blades will drink infidel blood! For Spain and Saint James!"

All around him Ventura heard whoops and cheers of approval, and some members of the camp raised swords and fists and echoed back the Moorslayer's name. The Catalan was just explaining that only half the camp would be required and that he would be selecting them first thing the next morning when Ventura noticed a man standing in the entrance to a large bivouac observing the proceedings. The bivouac was set so far back that his face could not be seen, and it was only because one of the bandits behind the Catalan raised his torch to cheer that Ventura even made him out at all. Ventura was about to move around the group to get a better look at him when he was dazzled by a torch directly in front of his face.

"Son of a whore, I thought it was you!"

Ventura recognized the triumphant face of the smuggler Rapino, whose horse he had taken only three days before, and he knew he was in trouble.

"This *cabrón* is an *alguacil*!" Rapino shouted. "Hold him!"

Ventura drew one of his pistols and shot the smuggler in the stomach, then lashed out with the barrel as one of Rapino's companions tried to grasp his sleeve. All around the camp, men were swarming like angry bees as he ran as fast as he could from the shouts and barking dogs and into the forest.

CHAPTER THIRTEEN

BARON VALLCARCA NORMALLY ENJOYED spending the summer at his father-in-law's country house outside Huesca. The house and its gardens were large enough for him to keep the necessary distance from his wife and children and close enough to Huesca and Jaca for him to see the women he preferred to see. His father-in-law also owned a hunting lodge, where he was able to receive them at a discreet distance from the house itself. Some summers he spent half the week hunting while his servants passed messages and letters back and forth and made the necessary arrangements. If his wife had any idea who came and went, she never gave any indication of it, and in any case she knew better than to visit him there without permission or to ask him questions about how he spent his time.

Her father had long since ceased to ask anyone questions about anything. He was almost senile and spent his days sitting on the terrace gazing out at his orchards or taking baby steps around the garden with the help of one of his servants. Every time the baron saw him, he hoped that it would be the last, and each summer he was always mildly surprised and disappointed to find the old man still sitting on the patio with the blanket on his legs, still smiling the same half-witted smile.

The old man sat beside him now, gazing out across the fountain and the lemon trees toward the setting sun with an expression of blissful serenity that might have been admirable in a saint but in Vallcarca's father-in-law's case merely confirmed his disintegration into a simpleton. Vallcarca did not feel serene himself as he looked beyond the lemon and orange trees toward the spreading sunset that lit up the horizon like a forest fire. He watched the carriage and its escort approach the entrance beyond the rows of eucalyptus trees, and his jaw tightened with anger at the sight of his eldest son riding among them.

As the carriage and horsemen came closer, the baron saw that his son was accompanied by his servants, and long before he saw the wide mouth and fleshy lips, he could hear him braying like a donkey.

"Matilde!" he called. "They're here! Tell the servants."

Vallcarca's father-in-law looked at him with vague curiosity as the baron's wife obediently came out of the house, accompanied by three servants, and adjusted the blanket on his lap. Vallcarca took her arm, and they went down the stairs to await their guests. A few moments later, the carriage came to a halt and one of the riders dismounted and opened the door for the Marquis of Espinosa.

Vallcarca considered himself to be a keen judge of human nature, even though his view of humanity was essentially predatory and concerned with whom he might be able to dominate and who might be a threat to him. He had recognized immediately that Licenciado Mendoza belonged to the latter category. The father of the late Count of Cardona was another matter. Even his letters carried the faint whiff of perfume and talcum powder, and it was much stronger in the flesh. A man who smelled like a woman would always bend to the will of a stronger man. Even his soft hands conveyed the malleability of an aristocrat who had spent too much time gambling in the Houses of Conversation in Toledo and Madrid and was too weak to recognize when his vice had become a sickness that was destroying him. And it was precisely his sickness that made him useful, Vallcarca thought as he gripped the older man's boneless white hand and smiled at him.

"Marquis. How good of you to come. It's been a long time."

"It has indeed, Baron. And what a pleasant surprise to find my future son-in-law on the same road."

Vallcarca bowed slightly and ignored his son's complicit smirk as Espinosa kissed his wife's hand.

"You must be tired, Don Alfonso. My servants will show you to your room. When you've refreshed yourself, come down to the drawing room and we can discuss the happy matter that most concerns us."

"It will be a pleasure, sir."

Vallcarca waited until his wife and servants had disappeared with Espinosa and his entourage. It was only then that he looked at his son.

"Come inside," he ordered.

Rodrigo's smile immediately vanished, and he looked wary now as he followed Vallcarca past his father-in-law into the drawing room.

"Well?" Vallcarca demanded.

"It was done as you asked, sir. But there was one minor difficulty."

Vallcarca looked at him.

"One of the alcalde's men was in the camp."

"Did they catch him?"

"No. But they will. In any case he didn't see me."

"What makes you so sure?" Vallcarca had his back to his son now and casually picked up a leather whip from a table and began winding it around his hand so that the handle was protruding like a club.

Rodrigo's smirk returned. "Because I didn't reveal myself. He couldn't—"

Vallcarca swung around and struck his son a vicious blow across the face with the leather handle. Rodrigo yelped and held up his hands to protect himself, but his father now began to flail at his head and shoulders till he dropped to his knees and covered his head with both hands. Finally Vallcarca stopped and stood panting over his son, who looked at him with an expression of pain and fury.

"I didn't know he was going to be there!" Rodrigo wailed.

"Why didn't you tell me you tried to fight Mendoza?"

"I didn't think it was important!"

"You didn't think it was important," Vallcarca repeated disgustedly. "You threatened one of the king's judges! He could have arrested you, and that would have drawn attention to me, which I don't want! But you didn't think of that, did you? Were you at the farm, too?"

"Of course. To see that the work was done well."

"I don't need you to do that, boy. What if you'd been seen there? From now on you don't go anywhere without my orders and you do not exceed them. Is that clear?"

"Yes, sir." A red weal was beginning to appear on Rodrigo's face.

"Good," Vallcarca said. "Now, get out of my sight."

. . .

THE DAY AFTER THE MASSACRE, the town crier informed the population of Belamar that Her Excellency the Countess of Cardona had invited anyone who wished to pray for the souls of the murdered family to attend a special Mass at her own church the following Sunday. Mendoza had already resolved to go to church in one of the villages, but he decided to go to Cardona instead. That morning Segura's two sons unexpectedly brought a wooden tub into the kitchen and boiled a pot of water on the fire so that he and Gabriel were finally able to bathe. Afterward Juana came and took away their dirty clothes, and later that afternoon they came back from another visit to the del Río farm to find those clothes dried and neatly folded.

On Sunday morning, he woke feeling clean and surprisingly rested. Gabriel polished his shoes and brushed off the ruff that he'd brought with him, which had just about retained its shape. Necker had also managed to brush himself down till he looked almost presentable, and they left the two militiamen to maintain an official presence and made their way toward Cardona. On the road they passed dozens of Moriscos, including Segura and all his children. Most were on foot and had set out early to get there in time. Others rode mules and horses or sat in carts dressed in their best clothes.

By the time they arrived, a large crowd was already gathered around the entrance to the church, and they left their animals with one of the hostlers and went inside. Like its exterior, the inside of the church was considerably grander than the church in Belamar, with an elaborate gilt retablo depicting scenes from the Passion, and carved wooden benches for the choir, and thick stone pillars and high walls lined with statues, shrines and chapels, decorated with gold and silver and fine bas-reliefs of martyred saints. Most of the benches were already filled, and extra chairs had been brought in, but soon these were also taken, and many of the congregants were forced to stand. The front bench had been left empty, and a murmur spread through the congregation when the countess appeared in the doorway, accompanied by her daughter, Carolina, together with the bailiff Sánchez, Susana and two other servants.

Mendoza turned to watch as she dipped her hand in the baptismal font and made the sign of the cross. She was wearing a long hooded cloak that reached from head to toe, and she pushed the hood back to reveal a black widow's manto that left only her mouth exposed. As she entered the church, the poorer Moriscos crowded around her with expressions of devotion and supplication, and some of the older women kissed the hem of her cloak before the countess continued to walk down the aisle with her gaze fixed firmly on the altar and the cross.

This was the first Mass that Mendoza had been to since leaving Valladolid and the first that he had attended since Granada in which so many congregants were Moriscos. Most of them seemed attentive and joined in the prayers and responses as if they knew them. Others looked more uncertain and seemed to be merely mouthing the words or copying what others were saying. It was impossible to tell from their outward appearance whether they really believed in what they were hearing or whether they were only pretending to, but the same could be said of many Old Christians or of the criminals he had arrested and punished in Valladolid who went to Mass every Sunday and confessed to their most recent sins before committing new ones.

Piety, like virtue, was not always detectable from the outside, he thought, and even its visible manifestations could not always be taken at face value. In Valladolid there were women who went to church and sighed as if they were fit to swoon in order to impress their neighbors; there were shady lawyers who ostentatiously went to receive Communion and seemed to assume that merely being seen to receive the sacrament was enough to cleanse their reputations as well as their souls. Mendoza had no doubt that the countess was sincere, however, as he watched her lips moving beneath the manto and the rapt attention that she brought to every part of the service.

The theme of Father García's sermon was reconciliation and forgiveness. He quoted from 1 John 2:11: "for he that hateth his brother is in darkness, and walketh in darkness, and knoweth not whither he goeth, because that darkness hath blinded his eyes" and exhorted Old and New Christians in the congregation to come together in the love of Jesus Christ and reject the hatred that had now manifested itself in such a terrible form at the del Río farm.

Mendoza doubted that the message would have any impact on those responsible for the massacre, but the countess's fervent attention suggested that she genuinely believed it might. She exuded the same humility, sincerity and innocence when she walked toward the altar and knelt down to take Communion with her head bowed. After the service he came out onto the steps to find her dispensing coins to the beggars who hovered around the entrance. In Valladolid pious ladies of high degree generally avoided contact with the humbler inhabitants of the city even during Holy Week, but the countess appeared to treat both the poorest and the better-off congregants with equal consideration.

She seemed particularly keen to speak to the relatives of victims of the massacre, and he watched her take the hand of an elderly Morisca whose daughter had been married to Gonzalo del Río and been killed at the farm and murmur words of comfort and condolence in her ear. Mendoza wanted to pay his respects, but so many people clustered around her that it was difficult to find the right moment. She also spent some time in conversation with Segura, who seemed to be doing most of the talking. At one point she glanced in Mendoza's direction, and he was just about to approach her when she turned away and walked back toward the palace with her retinue. Even though he did not generally stand on the dignity of his office, he felt put out by her indifference and told Gabriel to give a coin to the hostler as he prepared to leave. He was just about to mount his horse when Sánchez came walking briskly across the square toward them and announced that his mistress wished to see him at the palace in half an hour.

MENDOZA DECIDED to take Gabriel with him. They left Necker in the square and walked over to the palace, where a servant ushered them into the salon. The countess was seated on a sofa, with the bailiff sitting opposite her and another servant standing by the door. She had dispensed with the cloak and the manto, and she was wearing a severe black dress with a high-button collar topped by a white lace frill that completely covered her neck up to her chin. Her hair was drawn back over her forehead and piled high into a crown, which was held in place by a tortoiseshell *peineta*.

Close up she looked paler than when he had last spoken to her, and there were shadows around her eyes. Gabriel was instantly in awe of her, but he managed a surprisingly accomplished and almost courtly bow. One of the servants pulled up two chairs, and the countess dispatched his companion to bring them cakes and chocolate.

"Thank you for coming to Mass today, Licenciado," she said. "Your presence was much appreciated."

"As was yours, my lady. The Mass was well attended."

"That is cause for hope. As Father García said, we must all work together to see that these horrors are not repeated."

"Indeed."

"And are you any closer to making any arrests?"

Both the countess and the bailiff were watching him intently. Mendoza did not generally discuss the progress of investigations with outsiders, and he was even less inclined to do so when the investigation was not going well. It was only two days since he had received a letter from Villareal asking him the same question. The counselor's impatience was obvious even in a dictated letter, and news of the massacre was not likely to placate him.

"My men and I have been somewhat caught up in the events of the last two days," he said, "but we are pursuing certain lines of inquiry."

These were the identical words he had written to Villareal. It was a useful expression to use at a time when the investigation was effectively stalled and dependent on the random or unexpected event that could take it forward, but the countess did not seem impressed by it, and the pale blue eyes continued to look at him expectantly until he found himself saying, "It's possible that the massacre was carried out by *montañeses* in revenge for the murders of the Quintana brothers. My officers will be visiting some of their villages next week."

"I understand that you went to Vallcarca," she said. "It was good of you to do that. Less diligent officials would not have made the effort. They would simply have accepted what they were told."

"Are you suggesting that the three Moriscos are not guilty?" he asked.

"I don't believe they are."

"The baron thinks otherwise. He believes that Vicente Péris may be the Redeemer."

"Well, of course he does," she said scornfully. "And what was your impression of the master of Vallcarca?"

Once again Mendoza did not think his opinion of the baron was any of the countess's business. But it seemed impossible to refuse the intense blue eyes without seeming churlish.

"His reputation for severity is clearly justified."

The countess let out a humorless laugh. "The baron is indeed severe! Vallcarca does not know the meaning of pity or mercy. I understand you met his son, too. Do you think that Rodrigo Vallcarca would make a suitable lord of Cardona?"

"First impressions would suggest that he would not, my lady. And now I would like to ask you a question: What makes you so certain that the three Moriscos would not have attacked those women?"

"I've told you I know my Moriscos," she said. "And I knew all three men. Navarro and his apprentice did work here on the palace. And Vicente Péris is one of the finest wood-carvers in these mountains. He has worked on churches all over Cardona and in France. He spent two months living with us after he returned from the galleys, because I commissioned work from him to help his family. Did you see the angels in our choir gallery? They were carved by him. Vicente Péris is a pious man who fears and loves God. Is that not so, Jean?"

"Indeed, my lady," replied the bailiff. "He often spoke to Father García about matters of faith when he worked at the church. I remember he was very curious about the Trinity and the Resurrection."

"Yet he was punished by the Inquisition for insulting the Virgin and denying the Immaculate Conception," Mendoza pointed out.

"The evidence against him came from Panalles," said the bailiff. "The priest wanted his wife, and Péris punched him and knocked him down when he tried to take her. So Panalles took revenge. Péris was in prison for nine months during the trial and interrogation. He has walked with a limp ever since."

"Which might give him a very strong motive to seek revenge against any members of the Church, including Panalles," Mendoza suggested.

"I promise you that Péris did not kill Panalles, and he did not attack those nuns," the countess insisted. "Someone else is behind this. Did you know that Vallcarca has gone to Huesca?"

"Yes. He told me he goes every year to see his father."

"Did he also tell you that he invited my father-in-law to meet him there?"

"He didn't. Is there any reason he should?"

"The Marquis of Espinosa has no business with the baron unless it has to do with me."

"Can I ask how you knew that your father-in-law was in Huesca, my lady?"

"Just because I am a woman, I am not entirely without resources," she said. "I am not as powerless as either my father-in-law or the baron believes."

"Assuming that what you say is true, what would Vallcarca gain through the crimes that we have witnessed?"

"He wants to terrify me into accepting Rodrigo Vallcarca as a husband! To show that I am incapable of running my estates."

Mendoza sipped his chocolate as she described the deteriorating situation in the *señorio*. There had been three murders in the past week in various parts of the *señorio*, in addition to those he already knew about. In the last two days, she had received reports from the bailiff and other officials of violent altercations between Moriscos and Old Christians in which both the rapes in Vallcarca and the murders of the del Río family had been mentioned. Only that morning some of her Moriscos had asked her to use the militia to protect them. Some Old Christians had appealed to Vallcarca to become his vassals, and others had written to the king asking to become vassals of the Crown in order to receive royal protection.

"Do you have any evidence that the baron or your father-in-law is behind these events?" Mendoza asked.

"Of course not. These are powerful men. They would never do anything that could incriminate themselves directly."

Mendoza was not indisposed to be sympathetic toward her. Vallcarca was clearly a brute, and the mistress of Cardona was infinitely more appealing, both physically and morally. There were already enough anomalies in the investigation to suggest that the countess's accusations against Vallcarca and her father-in-law were superficially plausible. But without proof her allegations were nothing more than opinion and speculation, and it was also possible that she herself might be trying to use him for purposes that were not yet obvious.

"Well, my lady, I shall certainly give due consideration to what you've told me in the course of my investigation," he said finally.

"Thank you, Licenciado. By the way, I thought you should know that Dr. Segura and I have arranged for the bodies of the del Río family to be buried in the village of Las Palomas. It's about halfway between Belamar and Cardona. Segura says there isn't enough wood for the coffins in Belamar, and now that Navarro has been arrested, there's only one carpenter. Father García will conduct the funeral service the day after tomorrow. You are welcome to attend."

This news surprised Mendoza. He had left the burial of the bodies to the Moriscos themselves and assumed that they would be buried in the town cemetery. It was only now he realized that he had not observed any signs of preparation for burial or even heard a carpenter's hammer in Belamar itself. He said that he would do his best to attend, and the two of them finished their chocolate and got up to leave. Necker had brought the horses up to the palace, and they rode slowly toward Belamar, past the Moriscos who were still making their way on foot.

"So what did you think of our countess?" Mendoza asked Gabriel.

"She has a face like an angel," his awestruck page replied.

"Indeed she does."

Mendoza listened with amusement to Gabriel's extravagant praise of the countess's beauty and saintliness. He was not inclined to disagree, but he couldn't shake off the suspicion that she was concealing something from him and that it had something to do with the conversation she'd had with Segura earlier.

It was not until Belamar appeared ahead of them that he realized that she might inadvertently have given him a way to find out what it was.

AT NINE O'CLOCK the prisoner was brought before the tribunal in chains for the preliminary hearing. He was escorted by Pachuca and the prison warden, who was wearing a long robe and the leather slippers that were often worn by jailers who spent so much of their lives indoors. As Mercader watched them from the long table, he felt conscious of the immense power at his disposal. Like his fellow judge, Orellana, the inquisitor was dressed in a white robe and black hood and gloves. Apart from the silk-fringed Inquisition banner behind them proclaiming EXSURGE DOMINE ET JUDICA CAUSAM TUAM—Arise, O Lord, and Judge Thine Own Cause—there was no other decoration in the room.

The carpenter Navarro was wearing only a plain white shirt, tight breeches, hose and no shoes, and his spindly legs gave him the appearance of a plucked chicken, Mercader thought as the accused sat on the bench in front of him. On a smaller table to Mercader's left, the notary waited at the writing stand with his quill in hand as Mercader opened the proceedings, his imperious nasal voice echoing around the paneled gallery.

"What is your name?"

"Pedro Navarro, Excellency," the Morisco replied sullenly, without looking up.

"'Lord Inquisitor' to you. Look up at me and speak louder. Your place of residence?"

"Belamar de la Sierra, in the *señorio* of Cardona, Lord Inquisitor."

"And your occupation?"

"Carpenter."

Mercader already knew all this information, but legality demanded that he follow the procedures established more than a century earlier by His Excellency Tomás de Torquemada, first Grand Inquisitor of the Holy Office for the Propagation of the Faith. And so he continued to question the carpenter about his parentage and grandparents, his wife and children, the places he had visited in the course of his work, his knowledge of the catechism, the date of his last confession, and his antecedents with the Inquisition. The Morisco was also familiar with the questions, having already been through the process before, and he answered them with the resigned air of a man submitting to a ritual whose outcome was already decided. Finally Mercader came to the admonition, which all inquisitors were obliged to present to those brought before them.

"Do you know why you were arrested?"

It was only then that the Morisco showed signs of animation. "No, Lord Inquisitor, I do not," he replied emphatically. "We were told some nuns had been attacked, but I don't know anything about that."

The admonition had been intended by His Excellency Fray Tomás de Torquemada in his infinite wisdom and mercy in order to give the accused an opportunity to confess of their own volition, but Mercader felt more satisfaction than disappointment as he ordered Pachuca and the warden to take Navarro away. Soon afterward the carpenter's apprentice was ushered into the gallery, and the same procedure was repeated. As a minor, Juan Royo was accompanied by a guardian—a Zaragoza lawyer whom Mercader had carefully chosen for the purpose. Unlike his predecessor, Royo was terrified and overawed by the tribunal, and he trembled uncontrollably throughout the questioning. When asked if he knew the reason for his arrest, he also replied in the negative, and he, too, was returned to his cell.

In keeping with the regulations, the admonition was repeated twice more on consecutive days. Each time the prisoners were brought before the tribunal, and each time they gave the same answers. On the fourth day, the Inquisition prosecutor Ramírez attended the tribunals for the first time and formally accused the two

Moriscos of an *asalto en despoblado*—an assault on the open road—as an expression of their depraved lust and their hatred of the Holy Mother Church. The *fiscal* then submitted his formal request for torture, and the following day Mercader informed the carpenter that because he had vacillated in his replies even though there was much evidence against him, he was to be subjected to torture and torment so that the truth could be extracted from his own mouth, and that his interrogation was to begin the following day, contingent on medical inspection by a doctor.

Navarro said nothing as he was led back to the tower, but his apprentice was considerably less composed. At first he buried his face in his hands as the charges were read out, and then he shook his head and began to protest his innocence till Mercader commanded him to be silent. As the weaker of the two prisoners, Royo was taken directly to the place of torture. The young Morisco was dumbstruck with horror at the sight of the dank, cavernous room, with its arched roof and windowless walls, as Mercader explained the purpose of the hooks, pulleys and racks in a kindly, almost avuncular voice and told the young apprentice that the quilts on the walls were there to muffle the inevitable screams of all prisoners who were brought here. All this could be avoided, the inquisitor concluded, if Royo would only confess to the crimes he had been accused of.

"But how can I confess to something that I didn't do?" the Morisco pleaded.

Mercader neither showed nor felt any sympathy. Many people had asked him the same question, and the young Morisco would have to find out as they had done that the truth was always available somewhere inside him, even if he thought otherwise. That afternoon the two prisoners were examined by the Inquisition doctor and declared fit for torture. And the next morning the interrogation of Navarro began in the presence of Pachuca and another jailer, the doctor, the notary and Mercader himself.

After stripping Navarro naked and covering his shameful parts with a loincloth, the torturers fastened him to the sloping ladder and tilted it back on its wooden axis till his head was lower than his heels. Pachuca forced his mouth open with metal pincers and stuffed cork plugs into his nostrils with his thick, hairy fingers before spreading the linen *toca* over his mouth.

The other jailer slowly began to pour the first jug of water. Within seconds Navarro was choking and gasping for air and his eyes were bulging in his red face as he wriggled and writhed in a futile attempt to escape his bonds. There was a brief pause after the first jug, and Mercader asked him if he was ready to confess his crimes. When he refused, the procedure was repeated, and once again Navarro insisted that he had nothing to confess. After eight jugs the answer was still the same, and Mercader ordered him to be hung from the ceiling, beginning with the second weights. Using a long rope suspended from a pulley in the ceiling, the torturers tied Navarro's arms behind his back and attached a metal weight to each foot.

The Morisco howled as the two men yanked the rope over the pulley and hoisted his arms up behind him till he was dangling some six feet off the floor before attaching it to a hoop on the wall and looping it over a hook about two feet above it. They left him there for more than half an hour, sobbing and pleading with God to spare him, before Mercader gave Pachuca a nod and the torturers slipped the rope off the hook and let him fall. The Morisco shrieked uncontrollably as his body jerked to a halt at the end of the rope, perhaps a yard from the floor, with the weights swinging from his feet. It was a sound that Mercader knew well, an irresistible primal cry that sooner or later emanated from everyone who ever came here, rising up from some deep well of pain that no one, not even the strongest, could repress or control, because the spirit might be willing but in Pachuca's hands the flesh was always weak.

"Merciful God, you've broken my back!" the Morisco howled.

"God is merciful to those who tell the truth," Mercader reminded him. "The sooner you speak it, the better it will be for you."

"Damn you, Mercader!" Navarro cried. "I'm innocent, and you know it!"

Mercader did not tolerate profanities, even in the torture chamber, and he ordered Pachuca to increase the weights. Once again the procedure was repeated until the Morisco was finally lowered sobbing to the floor. Pachuca sat him upright for the medical examination, and the doctor said that his right arm had nearly been pulled out of its socket and recommended a night's rest before continuing with the interrogation.

Mercader reluctantly agreed. After a short break for lunch, it was the apprentice's turn. This time they began with the *potro*, binding him to the rack and tightening the ropes around his arms and legs with sticks till he was already crying out even before they began to crank the wheel and stretch him lengthways. Within a few minutes, Royo was begging them to stop and proclaiming his innocence, shouting out "God's Holy Sacraments!" over and over again like some kind of incantation as the sticks were tightened and the ropes bit deeper. His guardian urged him to admit to his crimes and bring the torment to an end, but the Morisco tearfully insisted that he could not confess to something he had not done.

This was not the right answer, and Mercader ordered the torturers to continue. Soon the apprentice was no longer able to curse or even speak, and he lay stretched out on the rack and twitching under the ropes, screaming at the top of his voice as the tears poured down his face. Within an hour he shouted that he was ready to confess. Mercader nodded at Pachuca to loosen the ropes and untie him. As he watched them sit the sobbing young apprentice upright, it was clear to him that the boy had arrived at that special state of genuine penitence in which he was willing to admit to anything.

"I don't want to die," Royo sobbed.

"Death is nothing to be afraid of, boy, as long as your soul is pure," Mercader said in the same calm, soothing voice. "Those who confess will live forever."

"But I don't know what I've done!" the boy sobbed.

"But you know what others have done," Mercader reminded him. "And if you didn't rape those women, then you know who did. Tell me the identity of this Redeemer. Tell me the names of the other men from Belamar who have influenced you to commit these crimes. Tell me their names and the pain will stop. And your sentence will certainly be reduced."

"I don't know anything, Lord Inquisitor!"

Mercader sighed impatiently. The boy had clearly not fully understood what was expected of him, and the inquisitor nodded at Pachuca to take him to the pulley.

CHAPTER FOURTEEN

VENTURA COULD ONLY BARELY MAKE OUT THE trees around him as he sprinted through the darkness, crouching down and holding up his hands to protect his face from low-lying branches. He ran till his lungs were burning, and every time he tripped or snagged his foot on a root or hummock, he picked himself up to continue his headlong flight away from the shouts and the barking dogs. He continued to run even though he had lost all sense of direction, until the rain began to come down in a torrent, filling the forest with a liquid roar that muffled all other sounds. Within minutes he was drenched but exultant, because he knew that the shower would not help the dogs or the men with torches.

By the time the rain let up, the lights had disappeared, and even the dogs sounded as though they were moving away from him. It was only then that he finally allowed himself to stop and catch his breath. He had lost the crossbow during his escape and left his powder and ammunition in his knapsack, but he still had his pistols and his sword and daggers. He had no doubt that they would resume the search and try to prevent him from getting back down to Belamar, and he knew that his survival depended on putting as much distance between himself and the camp as possible, even if he had no idea where he was going.

He continued half running and half walking until the trees began to thin out, and eventually he emerged cautiously onto an open slope that fell away sharply toward the darker outline of a canyon a short distance away. The rain had saved him, but the cloudy sky also meant that there were no stars to guide him. He was walking carefully around the edge of the forest, looking for a way down, when he heard the sound of men and horses. He ducked back into the trees and crouched, releasing the safety catch on his loaded pistol as he saw the two riders coming through the path toward him. They rode slowly past his hiding place to the edge of the forest and then back again, and he continued scrambling and sliding across the muddy ground, keeping the forest to the left of him and the canyon to his right.

Again and again he was forced to retrace his steps as the slope suddenly gave way to even slipperier rocks or a precipitous drop. Even going slowly, there was a good chance of breaking a leg or even his neck, and he decided to look for shelter. He soon found a dip in the ground beneath an overhanging rock, and after poking around with his sword to see that there were no snakes, he lay down inside it as the rain began to fall again.

As he lay shivering in his wet clothes, curled up beneath a rock like a hunted animal, hiding from men who wanted to kill him, he remembered an old tapestry he'd seen in a French church during his first campaign in Flanders. It depicted a group of aristocratic hunters surprised by the skeletal figure of death riding a pale white horse. He could still see the dumbfounded expressions on their faces, as if those rich gentlemen had believed that they were somehow protected from the plague by their wealth and status.

Ventura had no such illusions. There were men who died in their beds in their old age, surrounded by their loving wives, their children and grandchildren, with time to make their last confession and receive the last sacrament. But that would not be his fate. In many ways he considered it astonishing to have lasted so long. Time and again he had felt himself close to death and abandoned himself to it, and death had not taken him. There'd been moments in the slave pens of Algiers when he had not only expected to die but had actually wanted it. Death had not been ready to receive him then, but he had no doubt that it would come for him one day, in a time and place of its choosing, in some wild place like this, leaving his body unmourned and even unburied, to be eaten by animals—in a tavern brawl or a Madrid backstreet at some assassin's hand among strangers or on a battlefield in one of the king's wars in Flanders, France or Africa. And whatever form death took, he did not expect to die in his bed with his children or grandchildren around him.

For some men the fear of death was inseparable from the fear of hell, but the afterlife was not his concern. Years ago, at the monastery in Salamanca, he had learned that Thomas Aquinas believed that the soul was independent of the body and could therefore survive without it after death, but he could not understand how this could be true. Where did the soul go? What form did it take if it had no body?

These questions passed through his mind as he lay there on the stony ground listening to the wolves calling back and forth to one another in the distance and watching the clouds slowly part to reveal a pale half-moon and a sky thick with stars. He picked out the constellations that he recognized and conjured others from his imagination in the shapes of dragons, ships, animals and scimitars.

Perhaps that was where the soul went after death. Perhaps all the souls of all the people who had ever existed were floating up there in a stream of dust among those fields of stars. But it was also possible that Aquinas was wrong, that the only world that really mattered was the one he saw with his own eyes and felt in his own flesh. Whatever the truth, he considered himself fortunate to have survived in it for so long when he should have died many times over and to have seen and done things that men who lived to twice his age would never experience, and he fell into a surprisingly restful sleep.

He woke just after dawn, to find himself facing a lynx only a few yards off, staring at him with its yellow eyes. The animal had clearly been investigating whether he was dead and ready to be eaten, and as soon as he reached for his sword, it leaped away from him and was gone. The sky was just beginning to lighten, so that he was able to see his way more easily, but his clothes were wet and torn, there were bruises on his arms and legs, and his knee was stiff and throbbed painfully. It was nevertheless essential to make progress before the bandits began looking for him, and he left his hiding place and continued to work his way downhill, till the sun was high enough to dry out his clothes and he was able to estimate his approximate direction as southeast. Even by daylight he could not avoid retracing his steps or seek out a more gradual and circuitous route to avoid a gorge or rock face.

· · ·

ALL THESE DIVERSIONS made it impossible to follow a direct route down from the mountains, so that by midday he did not feel as if he had made any progress at all. In the early afternoon, he saw a large column of horsemen heading downward from what he believed was the direction of the bandit camp. At first he thought they might be looking for him, but the column was moving too quickly and the speed of their progress suggested they had found an easier route down than the one he had taken.

It took him nearly an hour to reach their line of descent. When he did, he found himself on a well-worn path that led into more open country. Soon the first signs of human habitation became visible on the distant slopes and valleys around, and he was able to make out the occasional fortified tower, what looked like a monastery and the distant specks of grazing sheep and cattle. He had been walking on the path for nearly an hour when he saw an earthen hut up ahead, with a thin stream of smoke rising out of it and a tethered donkey sheltering from the sun beneath a tree alongside a handful of cows and goats grazing in a nearby field. Its single glassless window emanated a smell of cooked meat that reminded him that he had not eaten in nearly a day, and he knocked on the wooden door.

"Who is it?" a male voice called warily.

"A stranger who means no harm. And who needs your help."

A moment later the door opened and a haggard, dirty little man peered out at him warily. The *montañés* was wearing homemade shoes made from animal hide, and his ragged, patched tunic was as filthy as his face and smelled as if he had been wearing it all his life. Behind him Ventura glimpsed an equally ragged woman and various children, who were staring at him out of the gloom like creatures from some forgotten subterranean world.

"My horse broke its leg," Ventura said. "Can you give me something to eat, brother?"

"You have money?" the man asked.

"I have nothing to give you but the grace of God, my friend, and the gratitude of one Christian to another."

The man's eyes flickered across Ventura's leather jerkin and the two pistols, and he stepped back to let him in.

"God bless you," Ventura said. The doorway was so low that he could not stand fully upright, and he had to bend his head as he stepped across the dirt floor. The only furniture in the hut consisted of a stool and a mattress. Crumpled blankets lay on piles of straw where a little boy appeared to be sleeping. The fireplace had no real chimney except for a hole in the roof, and there was so much smoke that it was an effort for Ventura to stop himself from coughing. Nevertheless, he was hungry enough to eat whatever was in the blackened copper pot, and he was about to sit down on the floor when the *montañés* pointed toward the stool and shooed his three dirty and sickly-looking children outside as though he were scattering flies.

He murmured something to one of them and shut the door behind him. Ventura unbuckled his sword frog and laid his weapons on the ground. He perched on the little stool and looked at the little wooden cross on the wall above the fireplace, where the woman was spooning stew into a bowl. It was a good thing that this couple believed in salvation, he thought, because their lives on earth had clearly not gone well. The woman had no more flesh on her than her husband did, and poverty had stripped her face of whatever womanly features it might once have had. She served him a plate of chickpeas flavored with flecks of meat, which he spooned down greedily despite the fetid smell, the smoke, and the occasional agitated groan emanating from the child on the bed.

"Is he sick?" Ventura asked.

The woman nodded and went over to the mattress to dab at the boy's forehead with a damp cloth. So far she had not said a word, and Ventura sensed that they were not used to talking to strangers and probably not even to each other. He was still staring at the sick child when he felt the sharp blade pressing against his throat.

"One move and I'll gut you like a fish," the man said. "Leanor, take his pistols."

The woman gaped at him uncomprehendingly. "Andrés, what are you doing?"

"This is the *alguacil* the boys in the forest are after. Whoever hands him over gets a reward. Move, woman!"

"You're making a mistake, Andrés," Ventura warned. "Now, let me go and I'll forget this happened."

"*You're* the one who made a mistake!" Andrés pressed the knife a little deeper, till Ventura felt a trickle of blood down his throat. Leanor approached him from the bed and nervously unclipped his two pistols. As she did so, Ventura kicked out with one foot, catching her in the belly, and propelled himself backward with the other. Leanor fell onto the child, who let out a cry as Andrés tumbled toward the door behind Ventura and dropped the knife. He had no time to pick it up before Ventura was straddling him, holding the parrying dagger against his throat.

"Now, that is no way to treat a guest, is it?" he said.

"God's mercy! Don't kill me!" Andrés pleaded.

Ventura had forgotten about the woman behind him, but she now struck him a fearful blow across the head with one of the pistols and sent him reeling to the floor. Leanor stood watching with her hands over her mouth as Andrés retrieved his knife and stabbed Ventura in the shoulder. Ventura grunted and jammed the poniard down into one of his bare feet, pinning him to the floor. Andrés let out a howl and lay clutching his bleeding foot as the door burst open and the three children ran toward their father shouting and crying. Ventura extracted the blade and wiped it on the shepherd's patchwork tunic as Leanor crouched by the fire and pointed the pistol at his chest with both hands.

"You need to take the safety catch off first," he said with a sigh. "And I wouldn't bother, because that one's not loaded. Now, give it to me. It's only because of your children that I'm not going to kill your husband—if that's what this creature is. But you'd better find something to stop this bleeding before I lose patience with the pair of you."

For a few moments, Leanor's face had been illuminated with a fervid mixture of desperation and hope, as if she had briefly glimpsed the possibility that some good fortune had finally come her way, but now she handed over the pistol and became once again the resigned mountain woman that she'd been only a few minutes before. Had it not been for the pain in his head and shoulder, Ventura might have felt sorry for her, but even after she had tied a rough bandage around his shoulder with a piece of torn shirt, he continued to bleed, and he dabbed the back of his head and realized that he was also bleeding where she'd hit him.

It was turning out to be another very bad day, and there was now a real possibility that after all the battles he'd fought in, death might finally overtake him in this Pyrenean hovel. Andrés was still writhing and cursing on the floor, and Leanor bent down to tend his bleeding foot, telling him that he was an idiot and it served him right. Ventura stumbled out into the daylight and staggered past the children, who were staring fearfully at his pistols and sword and his soaking shoulder. He felt dizzy and sick, but he noticed that the oldest boy was missing. He knew that the boy had gone to alert the bandits, and he stumbled over to the donkey and climbed onto its bony back.

It was not much of a beast, but a donkey had carried Jesus into Jerusalem, and this one might just be enough to get him back to Belamar.

IT TOOK SLIGHTLY OVER TWENTY MINUTES to reach the turnoff toward Las Palomas and another half an hour before Mendoza saw the church tower protruding out of the cluster of houses up ahead. The village was situated in a shallow river valley, and surrounded by woods, which made it possible to get close without being seen by the peasants working in the fields nearby. Mendoza and Necker walked their horses into the woods and made their way around the edge of the valley toward the village, until they found a vantage point overlooking the church. The cemetery was small, like the village itself, and they could see the three empty carts that had left Belamar with the bodies earlier that morning drawn up alongside a single-story annex to the church. At least ten men were digging graves among the uneven rows of tombstones that protruded up like broken teeth from behind a low stone wall, and even from a distance Segura's mane of white hair was visible.

For the rest of the afternoon, they watched the workers climbing in and out of graves with picks and shovels, and the sound of saws and hammers from the annex mingled with the sound of birdsong all around them. From time to time, Segura emerged to inspect the graves, and his sons emerged from the annex and walked to the nearby river carrying wooden buckets, which they filled with water and carried back to the church. It was nearly dusk when they finally stopped, and Segura came out of the building and walked around the cemetery once again. The work had clearly been completed to his satisfaction, and the gravediggers gathered their tools and left the cemetery on two of the carts. Soon afterward Segura and his sons left the annex and rode on the remaining cart back toward the main road, past the laborers returning from the fields.

Mendoza waited until it was completely dark before picking up the unlit torch he had brought with him.

"Wait here," he said. "I'll be back shortly."

"May I ask what we're looking for, sir?"

Mendoza suppressed a smile. There were not many *alguaciles* who would have waited for nearly eight hours before asking that question, but Johannes Necker was a man whose patience was matched by a boundless trust in Mendoza's judgment.

"I'm not even sure myself," he replied as he set off toward the cemetery with the torch in his hand. It was a moonless night, and despite the faint glow from some of the houses in the village, there was no possibility of being seen as he stepped over the cemetery wall and carefully made his way through the rows of tombstones and little crosses and the open graves with mounds of earth piled beside them.

The door to the annex was unlocked, and he stepped inside and closed it behind him. It was pitch-dark inside the room, and he could smell burned flesh, wood and a scent of almonds as he crouched down and rubbed the flint and steel together till the char cloth ignited, before touching the little flame against the tip of the torch. The fat immediately caught fire, and in the wavering light he saw eleven coffins laid out on the floor, one of which was little more than a large wooden box, and the table against the wall that was covered in wood shavings.

He balanced the torch against the wall and drew his sword, kneeling over one of the coffins. It was easy to pry open the few nails that held the lid down, and he lifted it back and held the torch over it to reveal the body, wrapped in a white shroud lying on a bed of stones with the glass of water and the two bowls filled with raisins, figs and nuts that had been placed alongside it. The smell of almonds was much stronger now, and he realized that it was coming from the sheet. There was no need to look in the other coffins, because he knew what they contained, and he shut the lid again and gently tapped the nails down with the hilt of his sword before putting out the torch.

He left the annex, closed the door behind him and walked quickly back to the copse where Necker was waiting with the horses.

"Did you find anything, sir?" he asked.

Mendoza shook his head. "Nothing of interest. Just bodies and coffins."

Necker looked even more mystified now. The *alguacil* had not fought in Granada and was not familiar with Moorish burial practices. He did not know that the food was to provide the soul of the deceased with sustenance until the two angels arrived to take it to paradise; that the body had been washed with scented water and its fingers and toenails cut before being turned on its side to face toward Mecca; that the stones had been laid on the floor of the coffin in order to separate the body of the deceased from the Christian soil in which he was to be buried the next day.

Mendoza did not tell him any of these things, because there were things that it was better for the devout constable not to know in case they offended his Christian conscience and prompted him to ask why they did not report them to the Inquisition. Mendoza's priorities were very different from those of the Holy Office, but he now knew that both the countess and Segura had attempted to deceive him, and if they had lied to him about that, then it was also possible that they had deceived him about many other things as well.

THE NEXT DAY he returned to the village with Necker and Gabriel to attend the funerals. By the time they arrived, a small crowd had already gathered around the church, a crowd that included Segura and his family, the friends and neighbors of the del Río family and Moriscos from Las Palomas itself. The countess's carriage was also drawn up outside the church, and Mendoza saw her talking to Father García along with her daughter and Susana while the bailiff and a handful of servants and militiamen hovered nearby. She nodded in acknowledgment of his arrival, but Mendoza sensed that she was surprised to see him there.

For the second time in three days, the priest celebrated a requiem Mass, and afterward the coffins were carried out and laid alongside the graves, where the gravediggers who'd been there the previous day were already waiting with their shovels. Father García commended the eleven slain Moriscos to the everlasting protection of our Lord Jesus Christ and his Blessed Mother Mary, and the countess stood beside him in her black veil with Carolina and Susana on either side of her, intoning the prayers with the same somber intensity that Mendoza had observed in Cardona.

Behind her, Segura was also praying with such sincerity that even the most observant Inquisition official would have had no reason to doubt his faith. Some of the Moriscos wept as the gravediggers began to fill the graves with earth, and the countess's daughter, Carolina, began to weep, too. The countess held Carolina's hand, and it was obvious that she was making a considerable effort not to cry herself. She left when the service was over, and he knew that she was avoiding him as she walked back toward her carriage still holding her daughter's hand, followed by Susana, Sánchez and her servants. One of her servants helped Carolina into the carriage, and the countess was just about to follow her when she saw Mendoza heading toward them.

"Don Bernardo," she said. "So you found time to come after all."

"I did, my lady," Mendoza replied. "And I would very much like a word with you."

"Can you come to Cardona in the afternoon?" she asked. "Carolina is not feeling well."

"I need to speak to you now," Mendoza insisted. "On a very urgent matter."

Both Sánchez and Susana were visibly taken aback by his rudeness, and the bailiff looked as though he were about to intervene, but the countess nodded, and the two of them walked together in silence along the road leading from the village, with Susana trailing a short distance behind them.

Mendoza waited until they were out of earshot before asking, "How long have you known that Dr. Segura is an *alfaquí*?"

Her lips parted slightly. "I have no idea what you're talking about."

"With respect, Countess. I think you do. I think you know very well that Dr. Segura is a Moorish preacher. I also think you know what's inside those coffins. The del Río family were not buried as Christians."

There was a faint pinkish tinge on her porcelain cheeks now as she stared at the gravediggers filling in the graves on the other side of the cemetery wall. "Dr. Segura is a good man," she said finally. "One of the most honorable men I have ever met. He cares deeply about his family and his community. And he also happens to believe the same thing that I do."

"Which is?"

"That each of us must be saved in our own sect."

Mendoza was momentarily taken aback on hearing the same words he had once heard shouted from the stake more than twenty-five years before by the Lutheran nun during the great auto of Valladolid.

"Even if it requires a gross deception like this?" he asked.

"The Church has left the Moriscos no other choice."

"But this is heresy, Countess."

"Indeed." She let out a despairing sigh. "That is what it is called. And now I suppose you will report me to the Inquisition—and Dr. Segura, too?"

"I have told you I am not an inquisitor, my lady. If you can help me with my investigation, then perhaps it will not be necessary to mention matters that are not strictly pertinent to it."

"I have no information to give you. If I had, I would have told you."

"Then I advise you to talk to Dr. Segura. Tell him that if I don't get some very significant assistance by midday tomorrow I shall send a letter to Inquisitor Mercader to report what he and his sons have been doing here."

"But if Dr. Segura is arrested, he will be burned," she protested.

"Then I advise you to persuade him to cooperate."

She looked at him reproachfully. "Is this how you enforce the king's justice, Licenciado?"

"Those who try to deceive me have no right to question my methods, Countess."

She remained silent as they walked back to the carriage. Sánchez looked at Mendoza with suspicion and undisguised hostility, and Susana was staring at her mistress with an anxious expression. From across the churchyard, Susana's father was also watching him curiously. Mendoza did not acknowledge any of them. The countess's servants and vassals certainly took a great deal of interest in their mistress's welfare, he thought, or else they themselves had reason to be concerned about what she might have told him. He did not take pleasure from using the Inquisition as an instrument of pressure, but he could not help feeling mildly pleased with himself. Because whatever came of this strategy, at least he was beginning to make things happen instead of drifting along at the mercy of events. His sense of satisfaction lasted almost until they reached Belamar, when Daniel came riding toward them and announced that Sergeant Ventura had returned from the mountains and urgently needed a doctor.

CHAPTER FIFTEEN

N THE EARLY HOURS OF THE MORNING, THE most powerful man in the world awoke in pain in his darkened chamber at San Lorenzo de El Escorial. This morning the gout was particularly bad, spreading through his bones and joints till it seemed that every part of him was on fire. He tried to relieve it by turning from one side to the other, but by the time the clock struck five, the pain was so awful and so overwhelming that it was only through an effort of willpower that he could prevent himself from moaning or crying out loud. As he lay there alone in the darkness in the canopied bed, he imagined his body in the same way that he imagined his country, as a fortress under siege by cruel and barbaric foes intent on its subjugation and destruction, and the thought of the satisfaction that his enemies would take in his agony steeled him to resist and endure the onslaught.

He drew strength also from the pictures of saints on his walls and the metal crucifix in his hands, whose cross of thorns, ribs and nailed feet he caressed to remind himself of an agony that was infinitely worse than anything he had suffered or would suffer. He thought of San Lorenzo, roasted alive on a gridiron, and all the other Christian martyrs who had suffered torments on behalf of the faith, and the bones of the saints in the reliquary in the monastery. He told himself that the suffering God had chosen to inflict on his earthly body was a punishment for his sins, that the body was merely the carriage that would bear his soul during its brief passage through the world as his wives and so many of his children had already been borne, and that he would be reunited with all of them someday.

He knew that that happy day might not be far off. At the age of sixty-two, he had already lived four years longer than his father, whose body had been so racked by gout and piles and so exhausted by his years in the saddle and the wars he'd fought on behalf of the faith that he'd been forced to abdicate. Long before his death, his father had lost his teeth, so that he was forced to suck and slurp his food, but his father had never complained, and nor would he. At six o'clock his manservants drew back the wooden doors to his bedchamber. A wan gray light filtered in from the study while they entered the room as silently as ghosts to empty his chamber pot and dress him. The Hammer of Heretics sat on the edge of the bed and listened to the swifts shrieking outside the window before forcing his stiff body upright so that they could put on his slippers and dressing gown. Soon afterward Secretary Vázquez brought the morning's first papers to his desk, and the king spent the next two hours working his way through them, scratching or dictating messages with his arthritic hand before signing them off with the signature "I the

King" that messengers would take by land and sea to the most remote corners of the empire, from Antwerp and Lisbon to Lima and New Spain to Naples and Sicily.

At eight o'clock the chamberlain returned with his servants to dress him for Mass, but he was still in too much pain to attend, and he told them to open the door on the other side of the bed so that he could listen to the service. Once again they shut him in the semidarkness, and he lay on his side looking up at the marble stairs and pillars and listening to the monks and congregants entering the church. From this position he was able to follow the whole service, murmuring the prayers and responses aloud till the army of pain gradually began to withdraw its forces. By the time the doors opened once again and his servants drifted noiselessly back into the room, he was already sitting up in bed. The King of All the Spains got to his feet and stood passively with his arms raised as they swarmed around him in silence, dressing him entirely in black except for his white collar, first the hose and shirt, then the black tunic with gold threads, the leather shoes with the black bow ties, lastly the medallion of the Order of the Golden Fleece, which they hung around his neck. Afterward they brushed his hair and his white beard and wiped the sleep from his eyes and dabbed him with the scent of lavender.

As was his custom, he ate no breakfast, but the infanta Catalina came to sit with him briefly, as she had done almost every day since the queen and the children had come to join him for the summer. As always, the girlish chatter of his younger daughter softened and delighted him, but now it was impossible to look upon her shining dark eyes and jet-black hair without a sense of imminent loss at the prospect of the wedding next spring. That was not such a bad way to lose a child after the many that death had taken from him, but it was no less conclusive and complete because once she left Spain with Savoy, there was very little possibility that he would ever see her again.

He knew that Catalina was conscious of this, too, and that she, too, was keen to share the precious moments that remained to them, whether helping him with state papers or simply sitting with him to pass on the latest gossip. Her dark beauty never failed to lift his spirits, and even though her elder sister, Isabella, would remain at court until a husband could finally be found for her, every meeting with Catalina was a painful reminder that he would soon be forced to say good-bye to her for the last time. This morning she made him laugh by describing the latest temper tantrum of Magdalena, their favorite dwarf, and the laughter revived and revitalized him.

At 10:25 precisely, Vázquez came to take him to the reception room, and Catalina kissed him on the cheek and promised to see him later. The king took up his position behind the ornate German console table with its carved panels of leaves and animals, directly in front of the doorway, with his hand resting on the silver statuette of Jesus on the cross at Golgotha that resided on the lower desk. Once again he resisted the urge to sit and forced himself to stand tall and present an appropriate image of power and magnificence to his visitors and petitioners.

AT 10:30 VÁZQUEZ USHERED IN the mayor of Madrid. As always, Philip said nothing and waited for him to speak first, but the mayor was so unnerved at being in the royal presence that he tried to shut the door—an unpardonable breach of etiquette that obliged the king to remind him curtly that it must be kept open. The mayor was sweating now and looked as though he might faint as he apologized profusely and launched into a tedious and repetitive description of the hunger and misery and the shortage of bread in the capital. Finally Philip put him out of his own misery by informing him that the previous day he had authorized a grain shipment from Sicily.

The mayor thanked him and apologized again, then bowed and apologized once more before finally leaving the room with obvious relief. He was followed by the Marquis of Villareal, who was experienced enough to leave the door open. Unlike the mayor, the marquis was a grandee who was not obliged to take off his hat in the royal presence, and the counselor for Aragon had attended too many meetings with the king and his ministers to be overawed by being in the royal presence. He bowed and got straight to the point.

"Your Majesty, I have received the second report from Licenciado Mendoza in Cardona. The news is not good."

The king's gray eyes were expressionless as he listened to the counselor's summary. In the month since Mendoza's departure, three Christian boys had been crucified, two nuns had been violated, two tailors bringing cloth from Paris to Monzón to make dresses for the royal wedding had been robbed, and one of them had been killed. Now a family of eleven Moriscos had been massacred. Mendoza had not identified the perpetrators, and the only arrests had been those made by the Inquisition, who were preparing to put two of the Morisco rapists on trial.

"And may I ask why you thought it necessary to bring this matter to me in person?" Philip inquired.

"Your Majesty, there are reports that Moriscos and Old Christians in Cardona are arming themselves for war. If this disorder should spread, then it may have consequences for the happy event that we all anticipate next spring."

"And where do these reports come from?"

"From the corregidor at Jaca, Majesty. And also from the Holy Office."

Philip nodded gloomily. He was already tired of the Moriscos. They had caused him enough problems in Granada, and now Archbishop Ribera of Valencia and other clerics were badgering him to expel them all from Spain. It was only two years since he had agreed to do this in principle, though how he was supposed to accomplish it in practice no one seemed able to explain.

Aragon had also been a problem for the Crown for some time. His father had been obliged to promise the Aragonese in person that he would recognize their precious *fueros* before they agreed to recognize his authority. That was nearly seventy-five years ago, and still the lords of Aragon seemed to forget that they owed the king obedience, so that he was obliged to go there next year to remind them and undertake a journey that he knew would be both painful and injurious to his health. And even though he did not agree with his more pessimistic ministers that Aragon might one day become another Flanders, Moriscos and the Aragonese were a bad combination from which no one could draw any comfort.

"Assuming that these reports are correct," he said, "what action do you propose we take?"

"It seems to me that there are three options at this stage, Majesty. We can allow Judge Mendoza's investigation to run its course and wait to hear his conclusions and recommendations. Or we can suspend the investigation and send troops to pacify Cardona immediately, including troops from Castile if necessary."

"Has Judge Mendoza asked for this?"

Villareal admitted that he had not.

"And the third possibility?" asked Philip.

"That the Crown take formal possession of Cardona and incorporate it into the royal domain."

The king's sphinxlike inscrutability momentarily gave way to an expression of mild surprise. "On what grounds?"

"That Cardona has become a danger to the realm."

"And you expect the parliament of Aragon to accept this?"

"There is a legal basis for the Crown's claims, Majesty. Your father the emperor ratified the seigneurial rights of Cardona on condition that the estates be passed down through the male line. The Countess of Cardona is a widow. Her parents are dead, and her only child is a girl."

Villareal paused to allow this to sink in before proceeding to list the number of towns, vassals and villages in Cardona and the annual income that would accrue to the Crown at a time when the king's regiments in Flanders had not received their wages for months, when there was grain in Sicily to be paid for, and the treasure fleet from the Indies was under threat from English ships.

Philip still did not look convinced. "Even if what you say is true, I fail to see how provoking conflict with the Aragonese the year before the infanta's wedding can serve our interests."

"I believe that if we act quickly and firmly, then this affair can be resolved and concluded long before then. His Majesty now has a real opportunity to demonstrate his power and authority in a way that the Aragonese will have no choice but to accept."

"And the countess? She is still young. She can marry again."

"She can. But the Zaragoza Inquisition intends to bring charges of heresy and sedition against a number of prominent individuals from the town of Belamar de la Sierra shortly, Your Majesty. These charges will directly implicate the countess herself. If—when—that happens, there will be no master or mistress of Cardona."

At the mention of the word "heresy," the king's full, sensual lips tightened, as if he had just experienced a sharp jab of physical pain, before his face resumed its expression of frosty magnificence. As always, the number of conflicting options oppressed him, and he glanced toward the window at the thick cluster of low-lying black clouds drifting beyond the forested plain and remembered the advice that his father had written to him in his abdication testament: "Support the Inquisition and never do anything to harm it."

"This judge of yours is a capable man, is he not?" he said finally.

"He comes highly recommended."

"Well, we agreed to your suggestion to carry out an investigation in Cardona in order to make ourselves acquainted with all the facts. That objective has not yet been achieved, and I think it best if we wait for his reports, as well as the Inquisition's. For now you must impress upon this alcalde the urgent need for this matter to be resolved quickly. Should the situation continue to deteriorate, then we may reconsider our options. But on no account will we ourselves undertake any precipitous action."

"As you wish, Majesty."

The king looked down at his desk to signify that the audience was over, and Villareal bowed once more and left the room to make way for the next visitor.

"So, Doctor, am I going to die?"

Ventura sat up shirtless on the priest's bed as Segura tightened the bandage around his shoulder while Mendoza and Gabriel watched from the other side of the room.

"Not this time, Sergeant," Segura said, "but you've lost a lot of blood. And your wound could become infected despite the poultice. That donkey did you a great favor."

"I thought a little bleeding was supposed to be good for you. And believe me, Doctor, I've lost more blood than this. Isn't that true, Bernardo?"

Mendoza nodded. He did not speak to Segura, and the doctor did not look at him as Juana gathered up Ventura's bloodstained shirt and the cloths and the bowl of water that he had used to clean the wound.

"Well, cousin," he said when they had left the room, "first you come back on a stolen horse, then you come with a stolen donkey. What animal will you bring back next?"

Ventura laughed weakly. "Those inbreds nearly took my life. The least they could do was get me to a doctor."

"I can send Necker to arrest them."

"Don't bother. You couldn't make things much worse for them than they already are. And Luis de Ventura is not going to have it said that he was nearly killed by two damned goatherds. Besides, you have more important things to worry about."

In his usual deadpan manner, Ventura described his fight in the forest, his entry into the camp and his subsequent escape. Gabriel looked awestruck with admiration, but Mendoza shook his head in exasperation.

"Didn't I tell you not to take any unnecessary risks?" he said wearily.

"They were necessary!" Ventura indignantly insisted. "If I hadn't gone to the camp, you wouldn't have known what kind of people you're dealing with. And it isn't rebels or Moriscos. Those were Old Christians up there. Shepherds and bandits looking for Morisco blood."

Mendoza listened with growing incredulity and amazement as Ventura described the Catalan's call to exterminate the Moriscos, and his cousin looked equally astonished when Mendoza told him about the massacre at the del Río farm.

"I shit on my hands!" Ventura exclaimed. "*That's* where those villains were headed. So one day this Catalan is preaching holy war against Christians and the next he's sending his army of shepherds to wage holy war on the Moriscos? It makes no sense."

"It doesn't," Mendoza agreed. "But there is nothing holy about any of this. And whether he is Morisco or Christian, this Catalan is not avenging anybody. This Redeemer has other purposes."

"There was a man up there in the camp," Ventura said. "He seemed to be watching when the Catalan was speaking. I didn't get a chance to see his face. Maybe we should get Calvo to call out the militia and go up into the mountains?"

Mendoza shook his head. "Even if we sent an army up there, they'd be gone before we reached the camp. These bandits are only part of the problem."

He told his cousin what he'd seen in Las Palomas the previous night and about his conversation with the countess that morning. Gabriel had not heard this before and looked increasingly dismayed when he told them what he expected of Segura.

"Sir, you're not going to report Dr. Segura to the Inquisition, are you?" he asked anxiously.

Mendoza knew that his page's concern was not unconnected to the mayor's daughter. "That depends on Segura," he replied.

"What about Franquelo?" Ventura asked. "Isn't it time to bring him in?"

"He hasn't been in the village all day. Necker will arrest him when he returns. Come, Gabriel, we must eat and allow my cousin some rest." Mendoza paused in the doorway. "I'm glad you made it back alive, Luis," he said. "Next time please obey my orders. You won't always be so lucky."

Ventura gave a mock salute with his unbandaged arm. They shut the door behind them and returned to the village hall, where they found Segura waiting outside with the resigned and gloomy expression of a condemned man.

"Go back to the dispensary, boy," Mendoza said grimly.

Gabriel smiled reassuringly at Segura, but the mayor's expression did not change as Mendoza ushered him into his office and sat down behind his desk.

"The countess said you wanted to see me," Segura said, sitting down in front of him.

"I did," Mendoza said, "but first I have a question for you. What do you think Inquisitor Mercader would do if he knew that you were burying your dead as Moors while pretending to bury them as Christians? I tell you what I think he would do," he went on without waiting for an answer. "I think that he or Commissioner Herrero would go to Las Palomas and dig those bodies up. And then they would take you and your sons to the Aljafería. And then your sons would denounce you, and you would denounce the countess and all the heretics in Belamar. Am I not correct?"

Segura said nothing.

"So let me tell you something else. I don't care how you bury your dead or whether you worship Jesus or Muhammad, but you better have something to tell me, or so help me God I will tell Mercader what I know."

Segura seemed to be weighing his options as Mendoza's fierce, dark eyes bored into him. Mendoza felt a twinge of remorse at the sight of his white hair and beard and the thought of what had already happened to his family, but he repressed it, because the law was the law and justice was not always compatible with kindness.

Finally Segura let out a sigh that expressed both surrender and resignation.

"I can tell you where you can find Vicente Péris," he said.

PEPE FRANQUELO was afraid of many things. He was afraid of the murdered men and women whom he now saw in his dreams almost every night. He was afraid of the magistrate Mendoza. He was afraid of being tortured. But most of all he was afraid of the Catalan and Vallcarca. There had been a time, not very long ago, when there'd been no reason to be afraid of anything, when he, Panalles and Romero had milked the Moriscos without fuss, when all he had to do was collect his percentages from the fines or the horses and the payments from La Moraga's brothel.

These were little ways of making small amounts of money, not enough to make a man rich but enough to supplement the salary of an *alguacil* that even a single man would struggle to live on, let alone a man with a wife and children. But now that life was gone forever, and the fear and dread had become a permanent part of him, lodged in his stomach like bad meat, dampening his clothes and twisting his guts till he was obliged to head for the privy or into the bushes to relieve himself.

And it was all his own fault, because the Catalan had promised him more money than a man such as Franquelo had any right to expect, and he had reached out like a fool and taken it, without noticing that he was sinking deeper and deeper into shit. It had been fine in the beginning, when all they wanted was information about travelers on the roads who were worth robbing. Whenever they profited from the information he gave them, he got paid something for it, and if people sometimes were killed in the course of these robberies, it was usually because they had resisted and was nothing to do with him.

But now people were dying all around him, and he did not even know why they were being killed, and he knew that Mendoza suspected him. That was why he had stayed away from the del Ríos' funeral, because he could not stand to think of those black eyes staring at him, and because he could not stand to attend the funeral of eleven people whose deaths he had helped to bring about. Instead he spent the afternoon at La Moraga's place, drinking, whoring and playing *naipe* and dice, trying to pretend that everything was the way it used to be.

He sat La Moraga's daughters on his lap and drank wine, then brandy, then more wine, and brought drinks for anyone who came by. He stayed there till the evening, and then he ate some supper and drank some more and rolled on the little bed with La Moraga's elder daughter, the one they called La Sirena—the Mermaid. For a few seconds, he really did forget everything else except the young woman who lay dutifully beneath him as he spent himself inside her, but as soon as it was over, the fear and guilt returned and the images of charred bodies passed through his mind once again in a dismal procession.

He went downstairs and tried to drink it away, until his companions drifted off and finally La Moraga told him that he should leave, too. Now the church bell pealed ten times before it stopped as he lurched out into the street and untethered his horse. The surrounding houses were dark and silent, because the people of San Antonio were for the most part simple, God-fearing folk who went to bed early so that they could rise early to work in the fields the next day. He hoisted himself up onto the saddle, nearly falling over the other side before he was able to sit himself upright and steer the horse out along the road to Belamar.

He had made this journey so many times that the horse could almost do it without him, and no matter how dark it was or how much he'd had to drink, he always managed to remain in the saddle and never got lost. He heard an owl hoot as he left the last house behind him, and then he saw the horseman in the middle of the road in front of him, his face obscured by the wide-brimmed hat and the upturned cloak collar.

"Hello, Pepe," he said. "We've been looking for you."

Franquelo heard the snort of a horse behind him and knew without turning around that his route back was blocked.

"I've been busy with Alcalde Mendoza," he said, "I couldn't get away."

"But still you managed to find your way to the whorehouse. And you didn't even go to your friend's funeral."

Franquelo tried to swallow back his fear as the Catalan came closer.

"The boss was offended, Pepe. Didn't we take care of your del Río problem for you?"

"You didn't have to kill his whole family!"

"You know we don't like to leave things to chance. But the jefe was worried about you. He thought you might be avoiding us."

Franquelo was almost sober now and conscious of the sweat trickling down his neck. Ahead of him, just behind the Catalan, he saw the outline of the road that could take him to Belamar, to his sleeping wife and children, and he felt an overwhelming desire to be in a warm, secure place with stone walls around him, away from these savage creatures whose motives he had never understood.

"Ventura discovered our camp," the Catalan went on. "He got away, and now we've had to move."

"I didn't know anything about that. I haven't been back to Belamar today."

"Well, you can't go back there now."

"Why not?" Franquelo replied in a high-pitched, almost girlish voice.

"Because Mendoza will want to talk to you about del Río. And then he'll want to talk to you about other things. And the boss is worried that he might be able to make you say things you don't want to say."

"Not a chance. Not even if he burned me with hot irons."

The Catalan chuckled. "You're a brave man, Pepe. I don't know if I could be that strong."

"So let me join you. I'll come to the mountains."

"The boss has decided on a different solution."

"Hombre, please. I've got children."

"Sorry, Pepe, but these are difficult times."

Franquelo took one last despairing look at the open road behind the Catalan and thought once more of his wife and children before the noose dropped around his neck and unseen hands pulled it taut, dragging the *alguacil* backward from his horse and down toward the darkness and the hard, cold ground.

CHAPTER SIXTEEN

HAT NIGHT MENDOZA LAY AWAKE FOR A LONG time thinking about the wood-carver Vicente Péris. The information that Segura had given him was difficult to reconcile with the pious, serious man described by the countess and the bailiff, who lovingly carved angels in the choir gallery and questioned Father García about the Trinity and the Resurrection. Segura described a Morisco who had been a Moor and a Christian at various times in his life, without ever fully belonging to either religion, and had only recently come to embrace the faith of his ancestors with a fervor that was almost entirely due to Panalles and the Inquisition. Before his punishment, Segura said, Péris had been only sporadically devout and had sometimes confided in the mayor of his fear that he would not be saved in either faith. He returned from the galleys a very different person. He no longer came to the mayor for spiritual advice. He had begun to

associate with some of the more hotheaded elements from Belamar and the surrounding villages, who liked to talk about the old days that they had never known, long before the Catholic monarchs had conquered Granada, when the Moors had ruled the whole of Spain.

Some of these malcontents had dreamed of bringing those days back and begun to talk of rebellion, Segura said, and Péris had approached him to try to get his support. Segura insisted that he had refused. He told Péris that it was still possible to be a Moor even in a Christian state and that if the Moriscos rebelled, they would be killed or banished like the Moriscos of Granada. Péris said he was a traitor and that people like him had polluted the faith of their fathers by submitting to the Christians. Despite these conversations, Segura doubted whether such discussions would have had any practical consequences, and he remained convinced that neither Péris nor his companions were capable of rape, murder or sedition. Yet the mayor also said that Péris had often traveled to Béarn to work and that he had fled there from Vallcarca.

The more Mendoza pondered what Segura had told him, the more it seemed to him that the wood-carver was not just a person eminently worthy of suspicion but that he was also crucial to the investigation. Were Péris and his companions members of the Catalan's band? If so, why had they gone to Vallcarca by themselves to carry out such an attack? And why was Vallcarca so convinced that Péris was the Redeemer when Ventura had made it clear that he could not be? By the time Mendoza fell asleep, he still had not decided how he might act on the information the mayor had given him, but he felt pleased that the investigation had at least produced another potential line of inquiry. In the morning he came downstairs to find his page sitting in the alcove in front of the unlit fire, reading *The Abencerraje*.

"Are you enjoying that?" he asked.

"Well, it is a love story," Gabriel said disdainfully.

"And a very beautiful one. But it's also a tale of honor and friendship. I read it when I was a student, shortly before I went to Granada to fight the Moors."

"And was the war like the book?"

"You mean did the Moors and Christians become friends and respect one another even as they fought one another? Would a Christian knight release his Moorish captive to allow him to marry his beloved princess on condition that he return to prison? No, boy, it wasn't like that. There was no respect and very little honor. The book is much prettier. Books always are."

Gabriel nodded. "Sir, the Moriscos you fought in Granada, were they like the Moriscos here?"

"No. They were more like Moors. Some of them anyway. Many of them spoke Arabic and wrote in it, too. They used to have public baths, and many of the women covered their faces with the white head scarf. During the rebellion they went back to being Moors. They prayed and worshipped like Moors."

"Magda says they were like devils."

"Some of them certainly behaved like devils," he said. "Some terrible things were done in the early days of the rebellion. The Moriscos murdered priests and nuns. But they were provoked. Had they been treated with justice, they would not have rebelled—and I doubt they would have behaved so cruelly."

Gabriel was listening with intense interest, and Mendoza could not help thinking that the boy's curiosity was not entirely concerned with the Moriscos themselves. Until now he had never shown any interest in Granada or in the fact that he came from there, not even when they'd returned to visit his mother five years earlier. The conversation made Mendoza feel uncomfortable and he felt a sense of relief at the sound of Necker and Martín returning from patrol. He looked up hopefully as they entered the room, but Necker said that Franquelo still had not come home and that his wife was worried about him. Mendoza was concerned, too. He was looking forward to making his first arrest, and he now felt grimly certain that Franquelo would not be seen alive again.

These suspicions were confirmed a few hours later, when the *alguacil* from San Antonio came riding into town with a mule bearing Franquelo's body. The corpse had been found lying in the main street by peasants leaving for work that morning, the *alguacil* said, before adding almost as an afterthought that the dead man's heart had been cut out.

"And where is the heart?" Mendoza asked.

"We haven't found it, Your Honor. But San Antonio is an Old Christian village, and some of the people are saying that Pepe was killed by Moriscos in revenge for the del Río family. Now they're talking about taking revenge themselves."

"What was Constable Franquelo doing in San Antonio?"

The *alguacil* looked embarrassed and reticent. "I believe he was at La Moraga's tavern, sir."

"A tavern, you say?"

"A brothel, sir. Pepe often went there."

"Thank you, Constable. And please make it known in your village that this crime was not carried out by Moriscos and that I will not tolerate acts of vengeance."

"Yes, sir."

The *alguacil* took the body to the mortuary shed and went to inform Franquelo's wife, and Mendoza ordered Necker to return with him to San Antonio afterward to make his own inquiries. The day was not beginning well, and already the brief optimism that Mendoza had felt the previous evening was beginning to recede.

Shortly after midday two members of the Cardona militia came to Belamar to report that a group of Dutch and German pilgrims had found what appeared to be a human heart nailed to a roadside cross with a wooden carving of Jesus on the road to France. Mendoza, together with Martín and the two militiamen, went out to visit the scene. The pilgrims had gone, but they found two members of the militia guarding the cross, where the organ was still obscenely nailed to Christ's chest.

"May God curse these devils and their damned Redeemer," Martín said, and made the sign of the cross. Mendoza ordered the militiamen to retrieve the heart. He watched as one of them reached up from his horse and pulled the heart down, using a sack to cover his hands.

Mendoza had no doubt that it was Franquelo's. He felt sorry for the constable, and also for his wife and children, and he wondered if he should have arrested him sooner, because he knew that he could have made him crack, if only to save his own skin. It had seemed a logical strategy to let him sweat and see what he might do or reveal, but in the end the *alguacil* had revealed nothing at all, and whatever he had been involved in, this latest outrage had effectively closed the last remaining door that the investigation had to offer in Belamar itself.

There seemed little doubt now that the Catalan was responsible for the murder of the smuggler del Río and his family. The gruesome mutilations of Franquelo and the Quintana brothers suggested that he had probably carried out those murders as well. And it was more than likely that the mace that had killed the tailor had cracked open Panalles's skull. But a Morisco avenger could not simultaneously avenge Old Christians, too. The two things canceled each other out. There was now only one conclusion that could be drawn from these events: *that the Catalan was not the Redeemer but a man pretending to be one*.

As he rode back to Belamar with Martín and the militiamen, Mendoza pondered everything he knew and thought he knew about the investigation. From the moment he was sent to Cardona, everything had pointed toward religion as a motivation for the unfolding mayhem in the demesne. He'd been sent to Aragon to prevent another Granada, and had Ventura not found his way to the Catalan, Mendoza still would have believed that was what he was trying to do.

Now, as he looked over at the bloodied sack dangling from the militiaman's saddlebag, it seemed to him that Franquelo's heart was little more than a prop in a Fanini troupe *comedia*, along with the letter to the Inquisition that Villareal had shown him, the sacrilegious mutilations of the Quintana brothers, the Arabic on the church wall in Belamar, the mutilations of Christian statues and the cross in the yard at the del Río farm. Unless the Catalan was a maniac who took pleasure in such things for their own sake, there had to be some explanation as to why he had gone to these lengths and adopted these pretenses, and there were too many people in this affair who seemed to know one another for Mendoza to believe that the Catalan was acting on his own. But with Franquelo dead, another line of inquiry had closed, and there was no one who could tell him what this so-called Redeemer was doing except the Catalan and his army, and there was no way of catching him without an army of Mendoza's own.

By the time he returned to the village, there no longer seemed any other option beyond the plan that he had considered the previous night. He went first to Segura's house to speak to the mayor and then continued on to the rectory. The curtains were drawn, and he and Gabriel heard the faint sound of female giggling as he knocked loudly on the door. A moment later a disheveled Beatriz appeared in the bedroom doorway and hurried past them, carrying a tray with an empty bowl and cup, while Ventura appeared behind her.

"I'm glad to see that you're getting better, cousin," Mendoza said.

"She is an angel of mercy." Ventura sighed. "I hear that our *alguacil* can no longer be arrested."

"No, he can't."

Mendoza told him about the heart, and Ventura pulled a face and shook his head. "These people never seem to want to just kill someone, do they?" he said wonderingly. "They always have to make a show of it."

"They do," Mendoza said. "And I think I might have thought of a way to find out why. You don't play chess, do you, cousin? You know what my favorite piece is? The knight. It's the only piece that doesn't move in a straight line, the only one that can step over others. It threatens a square by coming at it from the side."

"Bernardo, please. I'm not good at riddles."

"Vicente Péris isn't in Aragon. He's in France. He's gone to Béarn to seek sanctuary with his Huguenot friends. Segura told me. He got it from Péris's wife. I've checked it with her."

"So?"

"So I'm going to find him."

Ventura stared at him. "You're going to France?"

Mendoza nodded and told him about his conversation with Segura the previous day.

"All this makes Segura appear rather virtuous, doesn't it?" Ventura asked. "How do you know he's telling the truth?"

"He has no reason to lie. He's more or less admitted that he himself is an *alfaquí*. With the evidence I have, I could denounce him to the Inquisition and he would go straight to the fire."

"But you're not going to."

"Not if his information is correct."

"And you're prepared to go all the way to France to find this out?"

"We have no choice. You're in no state to go anywhere, or I would have sent you. With Franquelo dead we're blocked here. But Péris knows things. He went to Vallcarca for a reason—a reason that turned out to be different from what he thought—because someone persuaded him to go there. I need to know who that person was. If we find that out, we'll find the key to unlock this Redeemer business. He's my knight, and I intend to play him."

"Why don't you just go directly to Vallcarca himself? He's only in Huesca. Go and arrest him."

"On what basis? Speculation and supposition? If he does have anything to do with the Catalan, he has no reason to tell me. and I haven't enough evidence to arrest him for anything. I need witnesses, and Péris is the only one left."

Ventura still looked unconvinced. "Béarn is a big place."

"Péris's wife says there's an address in Pau where he usually stays. I'll be back in a week. I'll take Daniel as an escort. The rest of you can stay here. I need you to recover, cousin, so that I can send you back out into the field. I shall leave first thing tomorrow morning."

"But you don't speak French. And the roads are dangerous."

Mendoza smiled. "I know that, cousin. But I have an excellent guide."

. . .

At first light the next day, Gabriel saddled Ventura's Andalusian stallion, which his cousin had persuaded him to take with him. It was difficult even to make the fretting animal stand still, but Ventura insisted that Andaluz was more suited for a journey into the mountains than was Mendoza's own horse. Gabriel, Necker and Martín also watched them go, and Segura's entire family came to say good-bye to their father. Mendoza watched Segura embrace his children one by one and ignored the angry looks from Juana and the oldest sons. It was not pleasant to deprive a family of their father, but Mendoza needed to speak to Vicente Péris and Segura was the best man to help find him. Not only did he speak French, but he had also been to Béarn himself and knew the mountains well.

Segura had agreed that there was no other way to find out what had happened in Vallcarca and that a journey to Béarn might be the only thing that could save Belamar from an inquisitorial investigation, but Mendoza knew that one or all of them might not come back. It was also possible that they might not find Péris and that the entire journey might turn into a futile diversion. He had spent much of the night turning over these possibilities in his mind, and he dismissed them now as they trotted slowly down the road, past the trickle of peasants heading into the fields and out through the ravine toward the looming peaks and cliffs that separated them from France.

They followed the same route through the forest that the drovers had taken before bearing off into the more inaccessible mountain paths with which Segura was surprisingly familiar. Mendoza was armed with a sword and pistol, and Daniel carried his escopeta in a saddle holster and wore a bandolier carrying powder bottles and pouches of ammunition. Even Segura had brought a sword and a pistol with him. But such weaponry would be of only limited use against a surprise attack, and Mendoza felt tense and vigilant as they climbed up through the folding valleys and steep slopes behind Sallent de Gállego toward the higher peaks.

By midmorning they were above the tree line, climbing paths that were so steep and precipitous that they were sometimes obliged to dismount and walk the horses to coax them forward. The Andalusian handled these climbs well, as Ventura had predicted, but he needed a strong hand and constant pressure, which soon made Mendoza's thigh ache once again. The sun was nearly overhead when Segura pointed out the twin peaks of the Pic du Midi in the distance and said that they would be in France by late afternoon. Soon the path began to even out, and they were able to look down at the cascading peaks and valleys behind and in front of them as they made their way across a wide plateau where the going was easier. Eventually they reached a small mountain lake.

Segura suggested that they stop to allow the horses to graze, and Mendoza did not object. He hadn't eaten all morning, and his leg was throbbing painfully. He hauled it over the saddle and stood rubbing his thigh while Daniel took off his leather jerkin and morion and knelt by the tarn, splashing water over his face.

"Something wrong, Alcalde?" asked Segura.

"An old wound. It doesn't like long rides."

"I can give you something that might help." Segura reached into his bag and produced a small bottle of dark liquid.

"What is it?" asked Mendoza, looking dubiously at the vial.

"Laudanum. Opium and alcohol. I've only recently started giving it to patients as a painkiller. Try it. I promise not to poison you."

"You heard that, Constable?" Mendoza said as Segura measured out a teaspoon. "If I drop dead, I want you to arrest Dr. Segura immediately."

"I will, sir," Daniel replied.

"If the Turks couldn't kill you, I don't suppose there's any point in my trying," Segura said.

"Well, it certainly tastes like death," Mendoza grumbled as he drank it down. "On second thought, Constable, you have my permission to shoot him."

"Yes, sir." The militiaman forced a smile.

Daniel was normally the more sanguine of the two special constables, not difficult considering how permanently gloomy Martín seemed, but he, too, had looked downcast ever since Mendoza had given him the order to accompany them to France. Mendoza cupped his hands and drank from the lake to wash away the bittersweet taste of the laudanum, and they ate a lunch of figs and almond fritters with sugar and cinnamon that Juana had prepared for them.

"Gabriel tells me you are going to be married next year," he said to the militiaman. "Is she pretty?"

"Pretty enough for me, sir."

"And will she bear you many children?" Segura grinned.

"God willing."

"Don't worry, son," Mendoza assured him. "You will find your way to the marriage bed and have a houseful of children. And coming out here will get you back sooner."

Daniel looked pleased, and Segura also smiled at him reassuringly.

"How is it that you know these paths so well?" Mendoza asked Segura.

"When I was a boy, my father used to take me on these paths when he went to France," Segura said. "It's not what you think, Don Bernardo. Not everyone who crosses the frontier away from the main roads is a *contrabandista*. In 1513 His Majesty Fernando the Catholic himself signed a treaty with the king of France that allowed free passage across the frontier to those who live closest to the roads—on both sides. My father was a stonemason, and a good one. The king of Navarre's mother, the late Queen Jeanne d'Albret, was among his clients, so he often came to Béarn to work, and sometimes I came with him."

"Did you ever meet her?"

"I did. A most devout and saintly woman."

"And a Lutheran, and an enemy of Spain who murdered Catholics and never accepted our annexation of her father's kingdom," Mendoza said playfully.

"It is not for a country doctor to know the thoughts of queens and great princes, Licenciado. But many people dream of their lost kingdoms. It doesn't mean they have plans to recover them."

"Do you ever dream of recovering yours, Doctor?" Mendoza asked.

"All of us have dreams, Don Bernardo. But I never spoke to the queen or her son about politics, nor did my father. He went to Béarn to work, not conspire."

"Just like Péris. You Belamar Moriscos are well traveled."

Segura did not look amused. "Indeed, Licenciado, but we always come back, because Spain is our home. Your page tells me you are from Granada."

"My parents' house looked over the Alhambra. I played there as a child."

"With Old Christians?"

"With Old Christians and Moriscos. Some of them I later fought against in the War of Granada."

"And now you must prevent one here in Aragon," Segura said.

"And I will. With your help."

BY THE TIME MENDOZA remounted his horse, the pain was already beginning to recede. Soon they found themselves once again on level ground, and they made their way across a broad, windswept pass until Segura told them that they were now in France. Below them the mountains stretched back as far as they could see, like a rolling green ocean broken by splashes of gray rocks and patches of snow, and Mendoza saw an eagle flying above them. Segura pointed out the Pic du Midi, its twin peaks looming in front of them, gnawing at the sky like a large, gaping mouth. Apart from Lepanto, Mendoza had never been outside Spain, and he felt light-headed and curiously indifferent to danger as they rounded the Pic du Midi and descended the thickly wooded slopes of the Valle d'Ossau, through a succession of narrow valleys and grassy meadows dotted with sheep and grazing cattle.

Soon they reached a long, winding path that ran roughly parallel to the Gave d'Ossau and led downward past stone shepherds' cabins and austere mountain villages that seemed even poorer than their counterparts on the other side of the frontier. As they descended, they encountered men and women carrying tools, piles of wood or wooden butter churns down from the high pastures or leading donkeys and mules laden with cheeses. The women were paler and more insipid-looking than their Aragonese counterparts, Mendoza thought, and they dressed differently, with handkerchiefs tied around their heads, their four corners pointed upward, and red capelets and peaked hoods. Many of the men were wearing blue shirts and berets, which they doffed respectfully when they saw Mendoza approaching on horseback.

Segura recommended that they spend the night in a village where he had stayed before, and they were approaching it when they saw a couple walking toward them accompanied by two barefoot children wearing little more than rags. The man was carrying a wooden toolbox, and as they moved deferentially to the edge of the road, Mendoza noticed that he had a large lump on the side of his neck and that all of them had the same identical badges that appeared to be a duck's foot sewn onto their tattered, patched-up clothes.

"What kind of people are those?" he asked.

"The people here call them Cagots," Segura said. "Outcasts. They have their own villages, and they're allowed out of them only during the day. You saw the lump on his neck? That's a goiter. Many of them suffer from it. Their ancestors were lepers—at least that's what the locals in these parts believe. So they hate and persecute them. Of course, it's nonsense—these are inoffensive people. But then it seems that every country has its Cagots, wouldn't you agree, Licenciado?"

Mendoza merely grunted as they proceeded along a narrow dirt road that reeked of offal where chickens and enormous black pigs mingled with the human population, past drab houses with mostly glassless windows. The innkeeper greeted Segura warmly, but Mendoza was not at all surprised when the mayor announced that there was only straw to sleep on.

Supper was equally primitive, consisting of a bowl of millet porridge flavored with a greasy vegetable soup. Mendoza was dabbing at it without enthusiasm when an unshaven little man in a stained brown tunic and a red sash came into the room and greeted Segura in French. Segura explained that he was the village constable and that he'd come to ask for their names and the purpose of their visit.

"Ask him if he knows Vicente Péris," Mendoza said.

To his surprise, the constable recognized the name and said that the wood-carver Péris had often come through the village. Only three days earlier, he had passed through once again and told everyone that he was on his way to Pau to ask the king of Navarre to grant him sanctuary from the Spanish tyrant Philip II. Mendoza ignored the ironic smile on Segura's face, but the straw bed seemed suddenly more bearable now that they had news of his quarry. He was about to retire when there was a knock on the door and a sallow young woman appeared with an equally unhealthy-looking child, whose left eye was swollen and completely closed.

Mendoza noticed the disapproval on the innkeeper's face and the duck's-foot badge on her dirty dress that marked her as a Cagot while Segura spoke to her and knelt to examine the boy. He reached into his bag for another of his jars and applied some ointment to the boy's eye. The mother thanked him and kissed his hands, but no sooner had she left than there was another knock on the door. Within a few minutes, a line of patients of all ages stretched out into the street, and the innkeeper poured Segura a bowl of water as he pulled up a stool in front of the fire.

"You knew this was going to happen?" Mendoza asked.

Segura nodded. "There's no doctor up here, and most of these people can't afford one. So I always come prepared. I make only one condition: that I treat Cagots as well as villagers."

Mendoza knew physicians in Valladolid who would never dream of treating anybody who could not afford to pay their fees, some of whom attended only wealthy patients, and he could not help admire the heretic doctor as he watched him working his way through the line of sickly patients. He was too tired to watch for long, however, and he and Daniel retired to their communal bed. On closing his eyes, he saw an extraordinarily vivid and strange procession of images passing through his mind like a series of frescoes. He saw Romanesque paintings of the apostles with almond-shaped eyes and beautifully folded cloaks and the Virgin Mary holding in her arms a pale, staring baby Jesus who already looked like a wise man.

He saw armies of Christians and Moors fighting on an open plain and heard the clash of swords and scimitars and the cries of the dying and the wounded. He saw an impossibly beautiful Salome who looked like Elena performing a sinuous dance to the music of lutes and vihuelas. At one point he opened his eyes, and he seemed to hear the music as if it were coming from outside the inn, and he was no longer sure whether he was awake or dreaming or whether the rats scuttling around in the darkness were real or imagined as he floated just above the world, in a very warm and pleasant place where he had never been before.

IN HIS BEDCHAMBERS IN THE ALJAFERÍA, the inquisitor Mercader lowered his nightshirt to his waist, knelt at the foot of the bed and flicked the birch rod sharply across his naked back. From the bedside table, the lantern illuminated his bony arms and chest as he whipped himself till his whole body was running with sweat and the image of the apprentice Juan Royo's nearly naked body stretched out on the rack like a beautiful Christ began to fade.

Only when he was satisfied that mastery had been achieved did he pull his shirt on again across his raw back and bow his head to say his prayers. He told God that he was a paltry and disgusting thing and promised him that he would administer the same punishment to himself whenever it was necessary. But he also asked for forgiveness and reminded the Heavenly Father how well he had served him this last week. For the two Moriscos had finally revealed their secrets. The apprentice had confessed and ratified his statement without further torment. The carpenter had required more severe treatment, but he, too, had confessed and ratified his confession.

Both Moriscos had denounced each other and given up other names in an attempt to save themselves, and new charges were already being prepared. Everything had been carried out in accordance with the law, more or less, and if some corners had been cut, that was only because even divine justice was sometimes obliged to travel by a more direct route than time or the law allowed. Rarely in the history of the Zaragoza Inquisition had an investigation been brought to such a swift conclusion, and Mercader had no doubt that the information he'd acquired would now make it possible to impose the necessary discipline that would finally bring the whole kingdom to the path of virtue. As he knelt by the bed with his hands clasped and his eyes pressed tightly shut, the inquisitor was sure that God loved and forgave him and that the creator of all things would give him the strength to resist the vile images and temptations through which Satan had tried so often to undermine his most faithful servant.

The next morning he awoke feeling rested and convinced that his prayers had been heard. His servant brought him almond-scented water to wash his face and draped him in his black robes. After a light breakfast in his room, he went downstairs to the tribunal chamber, where Fiscal Ramírez, Inquisitor Orellana and the notary were already waiting with the lawyer Montes, whom the Inquisition had appointed to represent the two Moriscos. At eight o'clock the prisoners were brought in together in chains. Royo was accompanied by his guardian and walked with a limp, and the carpenter Navarro had to be carried in on a chair by Pachuca and another jailer.

It took Mercader the best part of an hour to read out the charges, with all their related details pertaining to the crimes to which the Moriscos had confessed. Navarro stared at the floor throughout with an expression of resignation and despair, while the young apprentice buried his head in his hands and occasionally let out a whimper. When Mercader had finished, Inquisitor Orellana asked their attorney if he was cognizant of any facts or information to contradict these charges or whether he wished to call on any witnesses to refute them. This was purely a formality, since Montes had already rejected these options.

"The defendants plead guilty to all charges, Excellency," he declared. "And they now await the judgment of the most holy tribunal."

Mercader proceeded to pronounce sentence on the two Moriscos and on their accomplice Vicente Péris in absentia. The three Moriscos, he said, had committed the most grievous offenses against the laws of His Majesty King Philip II and the Holy Catholic Church. Both Péris and Navarro had previous convictions and had made abjurations *de vehementi*. Yet both of them had continued to worship the sect of Muhammad and plotted to bring about the downfall of Spain. They had consorted with Huguenot heretics and Turkish spies and the infidel bandit Vicente Péris, who called himself the Redeemer. They had confessed to the murders of the priest Father Juan Panalles and the Quintana brothers. As a consequence the carpenter Pedro Navarro was to be handed over to the secular authorities for execution and the Morisco Vicente Péris would be burned in effigy until he, too, was caught and executed. Their property was to be confiscated by the Holy Office, and their two sanbenito tunics would remain in the church at Belamar as an eternal reminder of the abominable crimes they had committed against the Holy Mother Church.

In view of his youth and his cooperation with the tribunal, the Morisco Juan Royo would spend eight years on the king's oars, and a sanbenito would also be kept in the church at Belamar as a permanent testament to his infamy. On hearing his sentence, Royo burst into tears.

"I'm sorry, Pedro," he sobbed. "I couldn't—"

"The prisoner will be silent!" Mercader ordered.

Navarro stared back defiantly at the inquisitor with an oddly triumphant smile on his face. "I will burn just once, Mercader," he said. "But you will burn forever."

Mercader made the sign of the cross and declared the tribunal over.

CHAPTER SEVENTEEN

THE COUNTESS OF CARDONA WAS MODEST about her own birthday celebrations and generally felt more embarrassment than pride at the honors and blessings that her vassals bestowed upon her each year. But her daughter was another matter. For Carolina's eighth birthday, she had arranged a number of treats and surprises to ensure that it was an unforgettable day, just as she did every year. In the morning she took her daughter to the chapel to thank God for another year of life together. Afterward they ate breakfast with Susana and Mercedes in the courtyard, where the servants came to wish Carolina happy birthday and served her a breakfast of almond cake, jellies, marzipan and chocolate.

The three women then accompanied Carolina to the stables, where the countess showed her the foal that she had asked the stable hands to set aside for her. Carolina was delighted with the animal and immediately demanded to be allowed to feed it and lead it around the corral. When they were finally able to tear the child away, they stopped off at the house of a Morisco family whose father had recently died, so that Carolina could distribute alms, because, the countess told her, it was important to know that the good fortune bestowed on her was not shared by everyone.

They arrived back at the palace to find a collection of flowers, homemade sweets and cakes, fruits, handmade straw dolls and wooden animal carvings brought by the countess's vassals and other well-wishers. The highlight of the day came after lunch, when they retired to the drawing room to listen to the musicians who had been brought secretly into the palace without Carolina's knowledge. They played pavanes, galliards and old folk dances from the countess's childhood, and the women danced and took turns playing the parts of lady and gentleman, until Carolina persuaded Federico and Tomás to join in, too.

Everybody was gay and cheerful, and even Susana seemed to put aside her anxieties regarding her father's journey to France. The countess's enjoyment came to an abrupt end, however, when a servant announced that the Marquis of Espinosa was waiting in the reception room. She had half expected a visit from her father-in-law, but she had even less desire to see him now than she usually did. She found him in the guest room, perched on the edge of the sofa with his long neck and balding head protruding from the white ruff, one claw-like hand agitatedly tapping a bony knee with its long nails, like a vulture waiting for carrion.

"Isabel, how nice to see you!" He smiled.

She offered her cheeks and sat down opposite him with her hands resting on the black satin dress like pale sea creatures resting on a seabed and looked at him warily. As always, her father-in-law's deep-set brown eyes reminded her of her late husband, but unlike his son's, the count's eyes always had a faintly predatory glint that inevitably undermined his attempts to be charming.

"I assume you've come for money, sir?" she asked.

The count's smile immediately faded. "Is this how you greet your father-in-law on his granddaughter's birthday?"

"I wasn't aware that you planned to visit her."

"Well, here I am."

"Then please let us come directly to the matter, as I wish to be with my daughter."

"Very well." Espinosa sighed. "The answer to your question is no. I haven't come to ask you for money. I have come to give you advice."

"I wasn't aware that I needed anyone's advice, sir, particularly yours."

"Believe me, you do. In three days' time, Vallcarca will be here with his son. Rodrigo will once again ask for your hand in marriage. The baron has asked me to intercede on his behalf."

"That is very noble of you, sir. I am fortunate to have a father-in-law who pays such close attention to my interests."

"My dear, I have your interests at heart far more than you realize, and I urge you to accept this offer."

"And how is the baron?" she asked. "I understand he has been quite busy lately, arranging for three of my Moriscos to be handed over to the Inquisition."

"The crimes they committed were carried out on his estates, not yours, and the baron is perfectly within his rights to do whatever he sees fit. Vallcarca is not a man with a great deal of patience. And I fear that you are close to exhausting his limited reserves."

"Do you threaten me, sir?"

"Come now, Isabel," Espinosa said calmly. "I'm warning you, not threatening you. Accept this offer or—" The green eyes flashed momentarily before he left the sentence unfinished and sat back, as if he had said too much.

"Or what?" the countess persisted.

"Isabel." Espinosa lowered his voice and leaned toward her, and for the first time since she had known him, the countess thought she detected a trace of genuine concern in his face. "These are powerful men. No one can oppose them. Let alone a woman on her own. I know how much Miguel cared for you, even though you did not reciprocate—"

"You know nothing of my feelings for your son!"

"Come now, my dear. The marriage was arranged before you were old enough to know anything about it. We both understand that. It was arranged by your father for your family's sake. And I implore you to do this for the sake of your family now. It doesn't matter what kind of man Rodrigo Vallcarca is. It wouldn't even matter if he were a Jew. This is just the way the world works. Marry him and you will preserve your family's estates. Refuse and you will lose everything."

"I would not marry Rodrigo Vallcarca if he were the last man in Aragon," the countess replied. "And I will not hand over the House of Cardona to the Vallcarca family. I am scandalized, sir, that you, Miguel's own father, would come to the home he once shared with me to try to persuade me to do something that is so completely contrary to his wishes or my own."

"Your concern for my son's wishes is touching," Espinosa sneered. "A pity you didn't show a little more passion in the marriage bed. With a few more children, you wouldn't be in the situation in which you now find yourself."

"You disgust me, sir! I did not choose to marry Miguel. That does not mean that I did not care for him in the way that a woman should."

"Perhaps." Espinosa looked at her pityingly. "But if you don't accept Vallcarca's offer, then you're more foolish than I took you for. I need to be back at court, Isabel. I can't live buried alive in Toledo."

"Then you should have spent less time in gambling houses and paid your debts. You couldn't even repay my dowry when Miguel died, yet now you expect to sacrifice my future and the good name of my family in order to pay for your weaknesses? I will not, sir."

Espinosa glared at her, and then his face immediately relaxed into a smile as Susana appeared in the door, holding Carolina by the hand.

"Carolina!" he exclaimed, opening his arms. "Happy birthday! Come here, petal, and say hello to your grandfather! I've brought you something!"

Carolina had never been especially fond of her grandfather, but she did as she was told and stood with her arms stiffly by her sides as Espinosa embraced her.

"Now, close your eyes!" He pulled the girl closer toward him and placed a doll of a Moorish princess in her hands. As he did so, he looked over her head at the countess with a cynical, lopsided smile that only intensified the anger and disgust she felt toward him.

"Thank you, *abuelo*!" Carolina said. "Mamá, will you dance with us?"

"You go, darling, I'll come in a minute. I assume you are leaving, sir?" she asked coldly when the child had gone.

"Well, it is a long way to Huesca. I was planning to return in the morning."

The countess reluctantly agreed, and Espinosa went up to his room to change. She ordered Tomás to summon the bailiff Sánchez before returning to the dancing. An hour later the servant came back with a message from the bailiff's wife saying that his father was seriously ill and that he had gone to Lérida for a few days.

"Why didn't he tell me he was going?" she asked irritably.

"Señora Sánchez said he left in a hurry, my lady."

The countess felt sorry for the bailiff, but she was also annoyed that he was not available, because of all her servants and officials, Jean Sánchez was the one she depended on most in a crisis. In addition, Jean was also able to talk to her father-in-law and might have taken him hunting so that she would have less to do with him.

For the rest of the day, she managed to maintain a façade of civility, thanks to the presence of Carolina and Susana. By the early evening, she could not stand the old man's presence any longer. After putting Carolina to bed, she told Susana to tell the marquis that she had a headache and was retiring early. She let out a sigh of relief, sat down in front of the mirror and loosened her hair until her maidservant returned and knelt to unbutton her shoes.

"Are you all right, my lady?" Susana asked as she began to unbutton the countess's dress. "Did he say something to upset you?"

"Nothing for you to worry about."

Susana stood behind her and took out the comb from her hair and began to unravel her braids. "If you're worried, then I'm worried, too," she said.

"You have enough to worry about. Though your father is probably safer in France than he is here."

"You're stiff as a board."

The countess closed her eyes as Susana began to massage her

neck and shoulders and work her fingers skillfully into her muscles, until she felt her maidservant's lips brush lightly against her neck.

"Not now," she murmured. "Not with that creature in the house."

"He won't hear us."

The countess felt her resistance melting away as Susana sucked one of her earlobes and licked the inside of her ear. She reached back and pulled her maidservant toward her, holding her fast in a long, deep kiss as Susana's hand slid down under the nightdress and gently molded her breasts.

"Come to bed, my love," Susana whispered. "Come."

The countess stood up obediently and let the dress fall to the floor as her maidservant took her hand and led her toward the canopy bed. She lay under the sheets, watching Susana unbutton her bodice and dress and let down her long, dark hair before extinguishing the lantern. The room was now so dark that the countess could barely see her maidservant draw the curtain around the bed. And then she no longer needed to see her and was no longer worried about the nameless threat that her father-in-law had brought into her house as she ran her fingers through her lover's hair and responded to her kisses and caresses.

Espinosa, Vallcarca, Mendoza and all her other would-be tormentors seemed to fade away into the warm summer night as the Countess of Cardona surrendered everything—propriety, morality and rank—to the perfect beauty she held in her arms, in the darkness that hid and protected them both.

In the early afternoon on the second day, Mendoza and Segura descended from the high mountains and reached the fertile floor of the Ossau Valley. Here the going was easier, and they rode across a flat plain, past vineyards and cultivated fields of wheat, millet and rye splashed with red poppies and open meadows bursting with wildflowers where sheep, goats and cattle grazed. Everywhere they saw signs of the power and wealth of the heretic kingdom of Béarn, from the cleared streams, well-maintained stone bridges and tollgates to the coned châteaus and castle towers protruding up through the thick forests of chestnut and tall pines that tumbled down from the steep, rocky heights on both sides of the valley and the stone or half-timbered farmhouses with barns large enough for entire families to live in.

The towns and villages also impressed Mendoza. Even the more humble houses were better constructed than the ones they had seen on the higher slopes, with tile or thatched roofs instead of rushes and branches held down with stones. Their inhabitants also seemed less abject. In addition to the ubiquitous peasants and laborers in their clogs, bonnets, capelets and berets, and the barefoot boys and girls in identical soiled smocks, they passed fine carriages with curtained windows and busy markets stocked with bread, dried meats, fruits and vegetables, leather goods and metal tools.

As they drew closer to Pau, the traffic on the road began to thicken and their progress was slowed by the flow of carts, wagons, soldiers and merchants, by peasants carrying bundles on their backs and families with their children, many of whom were in a boisterous and exuberant mood. When Segura asked where they were going, he was told that the Whitsun celebrations in Pau were now in their third day and that the king of Navarre and his court had come from his residence in Nérac to attend the jousting tournament.

By the time they reached the capital, the road was so crowded that they had to slow the horses to walking pace as they crossed the great stone bridge that spanned the Gave and headed toward the enormous gray château that loomed out of the trees and buildings on the opposite bank. They eased their way through the holidaying crowds along an unpaved road overlooking a narrow ravine, past elegant stone houses with sloping tiled roofs and balconies draped with banners bearing the Navarre coat of arms and an assortment of silks and colored cloths and streamers.

All around them revelers were tottering away from stalls and overcrowded taverns selling crepes, pies and pastries, sausages, meats and cooked fish or wine and cider, or gathered in rowdy groups to watch the bear baiters, cockfighters and chicken races, the clowns, jesters, jugglers and storytellers, and the hawkers selling ointments and fluids with miraculous healing powers. Many of the spectators were in an advanced state of inebriation. Some were singing and dancing lewd dances to the music of drums, flutes and horns. Others were throwing up, or lying facedown by the side of the road, or stuffing themselves with food at crowded tables where beggars and vagabonds mingled with the dogs circulating around them waiting for scraps and bones.

Even a cursory inspection of the crowd revealed numerous offenses that Mendoza would have considered worthy of a warning or an arrest had he come across them in Valladolid, from the cardsharps and shell gamers to what appeared to be a couple openly copulating in an alleyway. But there was no evidence of any authority or control, and many of the soldiers and officers of the peace mingling with the crowd seemed no less inebriated than those around them. In the main square in front of the château, a jousting tourney was in progress, and Segura pointed out the grandstand just below the medieval wall, where the king and his guests were looking down on the proceedings. Below them spectators and combatants swarmed around the gaily colored round tents and ornate cloth-covered tilts, and armored knights charged each other with wooden lances or clashed with swords while others waited with their horses and squires for their turn.

Normally Mendoza enjoyed such events, but he was impatient to find Péris. Finally they rounded the château and entered a warren-like neighborhood that was noticeably humbler and quieter than the rest of the city. They dismounted and led their horses through the narrow, evil-smelling streets and lanes whose houses were so close together that it was almost possible to step from one roof to the other. Most of their occupants appeared to be at the festivities, and Segura asked the few people they encountered for the address that Péris's wife had given him, until they reached a dank, unpaved street flanked by overhanging houses that reeked of the powerful stench of urine.

Mendoza left Daniel on the corner to look after the horses and accompanied Segura to a door about halfway along the street. The mayor knocked discreetly, and a small, grizzled old man half opened the door and stared at them without a word. When Segura asked in French for Vicente Péris, he looked blank and shook his head. Mendoza was tired and hungry. The pain in his leg was returning now that Segura's medicine had worn off, and he had not crossed the Pyrenees only to be told that he'd gotten the wrong address. Before the old man could shut the door, Mendoza drew his pistol and pointed it directly at his face.

"Tell him I want to see for myself."

The old man did not require a translation, and he raised his arms and stepped backward as Mendoza followed him into the little room.

"Vicente Péris!" Mendoza called out. "Vicente Péris from Aragon! Come out now!"

There was the sound of footsteps from a back room, and then the young man whose handsome, angry face he had first seen in Belamar on the day of their arrival appeared in the doorway.

"You're not in Spain now, Alcalde Mendoza," he said. "You can't arrest me here."

Mendoza put the pistol back in his belt. "Is there something I ought to be arresting you for, Señor Péris?"

"In Spain you don't need a reason—not when it comes to Moriscos. Here you do." Péris looked disgustedly at Segura. "So you brought him here, old man. I didn't think even you would sink this low."

"He just wants the truth about what happened in Vallcarca, Vicente."

"There are those who say you are the man they call the Redeemer," Mendoza said.

Péris looked both angry and surprised. "Who says so?"

"Baron Vallcarca."

"And of course you believe him."

"I never said I did."

"I had nothing to do with those nuns!" Péris burst out. "We never even saw them."

"What were the three of you doing in Vallcarca?" Mendoza asked.

Péris looked suddenly guarded. "I can't tell you that."

"Why not?" Mendoza sat down on one of the chairs and stretched out his aching leg. "You yourself said I can't arrest you."

"I may be safe. But my family isn't. Or the families of the others."

"I swear to you that nothing will happen to any of them as a result of anything you say to me here."

"You swear!" Péris gave a bitter half smile. "Like Queen Isabel and King Fernando swore to our great-grandfathers in Granada that they could continue to practice their faith in peace and then forced them to become Christians? Like the lords of Aragon swore that we would be protected from the Inquisition? No, Licenciado, here I don't have to obey any Spanish officials, and I don't have to tell you anything."

Mendoza patted his thigh with the pistol. "Then I will have to take you back to Spain and make you talk."

"You'll have to shoot me first."

"No one is going to shoot anybody," said Segura nervously. "Your Honor, may I have a word?"

Mendoza was reluctant to leave Péris alone, but his defiance made it clear that he was not planning to go anywhere. He followed the mayor out into the street and stood facing the doorway, still holding his pistol in his hand.

"If I may be so bold, Don Bernardo, you aren't thinking with your usual clarity," Segura said. "You can't just come here and wave a pistol around. This isn't some pagan kingdom. They have laws here."

"The old man was lying."

"That may be so, but I know Péris, and I'm telling you he won't respond to threats from you or anyone else. I know a place where we might be able to stay. Let's go there, and I'll come back and talk to him alone. I'm sure if I explain the situation to him calmly, then I can get him to speak to you."

"And suppose he tries to escape?"

"He's already escaped," Segura reminded him.

Mendoza did not like the idea of Segura and Péris talking in private, but forcing the wood-carver to come to Spain at gunpoint was not practical. He grudgingly agreed, and Segura went back inside to explain the situation to Péris. The mayor emerged a few minutes later saying that Péris had agreed to talk and that he would return when they had found somewhere to stay. It was getting dark as they threaded their way on foot back through the teeming crowds and crossed the bridge again. Mendoza had expected to spend the night in a field, and he was pleasantly surprised when Segura knocked on the door of a private house. The Christian householder, Monsieur Marcel, cheerfully greeted the mayor like a long-lost brother and offered the dust-covered and disheveled travelers an attic room.

One of his sons took their horses to a stable while they carried their weapons and saddlebags upstairs, and a servant girl brought them a bowl of warm water to wash in. Afterward they went downstairs, where Monsieur Marcel's wife served them a supper of warmed-up mutton stew and a jug of red wine, which only Mendoza and Daniel drank. The two of them retired to the narrow single bed that they were obliged to share, while Segura left to speak to Péris. Within minutes the militiaman's snoring merged with the cacophony of horns, drums, shouting and laughter from the ongoing bacchanal outside, and it was not long before Mendoza was asleep himself.

HE WOKE to find Daniel's feet next to his face and felt immediately agitated. The room was dark, apart from a small square of wan gray light coming through the little skylight, and there was no sign of Segura.

"Wake up," he said urgently.

Before Daniel could get out of bed, Mendoza was already getting dressed, and the two of them went downstairs. The house was silent, and Mendoza had a sudden overwhelming suspicion that Segura had betrayed him, until he saw the mane of white hair protruding from under a blanket on the drawing-room sofa.

"Let's go," he said.

Segura sat up and looked around the darkened room. "It's a little early, isn't it?" he asked. "He said he'd talk to you. He's not going anywhere."

"I want to speak to him now."

Segura shrugged and got dressed. Monsieur Marcel had heard them and came down to offer them breakfast, but Mendoza politely declined the invitation. Outside, the crowds had gone and the streets were littered with bodies that might have been dead, drunk or sleeping. The stallholders were already busy packing away awnings and tables while beggars and municipal carts picked their way through the streets, sweeping up the mess of broken glass and clay pots or combing through the rubbish in search of something edible or salable.

Mendoza hurried grimly past them, like a blackbird of ill omen, his cloak flapping and his head hunched forward, tapping the ground with his stick and walking with such speed that Daniel and Segura struggled to keep up with him. As soon as they turned in to the street and saw the small crowd gathered around the entrance to the old man's house, he knew that his urgency had been justified. He pushed his way through them and into the darkened room, where he saw the old man lying barefoot in his nightshirt in a pool of blood with a candle by his outstretched left hand. On the stairwell an old woman was half sitting, half lying, with her nightdress pulled up above her knees and a dark stain across her chest and stomach from the wound in her throat. In the back room, Péris lay on his stomach in a shirt and leggings, facedown on the bed, with one arm dangling over the bloodstained mattress.

Mendoza looked at the bloodied hair on the base of his skull and the stab wounds in his back as he stepped carefully into the room, taking pains to avoid the blood, and stared down at the body of the man who would no longer tell anyone anything.

"Let me take a look at him," Segura said.

"A little late for that, isn't it?" Mendoza replied angrily. "Or maybe you knew that already?"

"You don't think I did this?" asked Segura.

Mendoza did not reply. On the floorboard next to Péris's outstretched finger, he noticed an unusual shape, and kneeling down he saw the distinct outline of an *S* that appeared to have been written in his own blood.

"Have you seen this?" he asked. "It looks like he was trying to tell us something. *S* for 'Segura' maybe?"

"No, Licenciado," Segura replied. "It's not me. It's Sánchez."

"The bailiff?" Mendoza looked at him in astonishment. "What are you talking about, man?"

Before Segura had a chance to answer, there was a sudden commotion from the next room, and a Frenchman in a wide-brimmed felt hat appeared in the doorway and began shouting at them and gesturing toward the front door. Everything about him exuded officialdom, from his gleaming leather belt and boots to the blue badge in the shape of a shield stitched onto his chest. Mendoza did not need to be told that they were being ordered out of the house, and as they went outside, Segura informed him that the man was the chief constable of Pau.

They found Daniel standing against a wall guarded by four armed constables wearing identical red tunics, helmets and breastplates and carrying pikes and halberds. The chief constable told them to line up alongside him and stood frowning as an old woman pointed angrily toward Mendoza and began to speak to the chief constable in urgent, agitated French.

"This is bad," Segura muttered. "She's telling him that we were here yesterday evening. She says that you're Spanish and that she saw you point a pistol at the old man."

The crowd was getting larger now and becoming turbulent and aggressive as the words *espagnols* and *assassins catholiques* were passed back and forth. The chief constable waved his arm at the three of them and barked out another order.

"He's arresting us on suspicion of murder," Segura said. "He wants your sword and pistol."

"This is ridiculous," Mendoza protested. "Tell him who I am. Tell him the people who did this are getting away even as he speaks!"

Segura's remonstrations had no effect. For the first time in his life, Mendoza was obliged to hand over his sword and pistol to an arresting officer, though the chief constable allowed him to keep his stick.

THE THREE OF THEM were marched through the streets to a large, two-story stone building with barred windows bearing the Béarn coat of arms of two bulls and a shield. A bored-looking clerk took their names, and Mendoza asked Segura to explain to the chief constable who he was. Once again the man showed no interest, and the three of them were ushered into a large cell packed with semiconscious revelers and assorted lowlifes, some of whom were still bloodied from fights.

Mendoza pushed Segura forward to a space near the barred window above them and stood leaning on his stick, trying to ignore the stench of sweat, wine and vomit, while Daniel squatted on the floor nearby. "I want to know what Péris told you," he muttered. "In every detail."

"Is this really the right time, Your Honor?"

"It's as good a time as any other."

"I have your word that nothing I say will have repercussions for the families of these men, just as you promised last night?"

"I thought I'd already made that clear to Péris."

Segura nodded. "You remember I told you that Péris was not capable of rebellion?" he said. "Well, it turns out I was wrong."

Mendoza listened carefully and ignored the background of French and the occasional intrusive questioning from the other prisoners as Segura told him Péris had now admitted to him that he and his companions had sought to launch a Morisco rebellion in Cardona and that they had been encouraged in these efforts by the countess's bailiff, Jean Sánchez. Sánchez had revealed that he was a Lutheran while Péris was working on the church at Cardona. He had told the wood-carver that Lutherans, Turks and Moriscos should unite to overthrow the Catholic tyrant and boasted of his connections with the Protestant nobility in Béarn.

Péris, Segura said, was not a learned or intelligent man, and the bailiff would not have found it difficult to convince him and his friends that King Henry of Navarre and the Turkish sultan were planning to invade Aragon during the royal wedding the following year. While the Béarnese attacked Spain across the Pyrenees, Sánchez promised, the sultan would land a large fleet on the Aragonese coast. At the same time, the Moriscos of Aragon would rise in rebellion under the leadership of the Redeemer.

"Did Péris say anything about who this Redeemer was?" Mendoza asked.

Segura shook his head. "He never met him. Sánchez told Péris that the Redeemer was descended from the Umayyad caliph, like Aben Humeya. He said that he had returned from Barbary to fight jihad in al-Andalus and free all the Moriscos. He said the Redeemer was as great a general as Khalid ibn al-Walid."

"Who?"

"A companion of the Prophet Muhammad and a great warrior. He commanded the Muslim forces at Medina."

"Why am I not surprised that you would know that?" Mendoza said.

Segura shrugged. "Moriscos remember their history," he said. "Just as Christians do."

"Go on."

Sánchez had promised Péris and his companions that the Redeemer would shortly give a demonstration of his power in Belamar itself. Three weeks later, on the date he had given, Father Panalles was murdered. Péris and his friends were so impressed that they agreed to join the rebellion. At Sánchez's instigation the three of them went to Vallcarca, where they expected the bailiff to take them to meet the Redeemer so that they could swear an oath of fealty to him. Instead they were arrested by Vallcarca's men at the prearranged meeting place. Péris had escaped arrest only because he had gone into the forest to answer the call of nature just before the baron's militiamen arrived and had seen his companions being arrested.

"So he wasn't chased on horseback?"

"No." Segura looked at him in surprise. "He arrived on a horse, but he escaped on foot. He walked back to Belamar, thinking that the arrest was just bad luck. It wasn't until his wife told him about the nuns and Herrero that he realized Sánchez had betrayed him. That's when he decided to come to France."

"How do I know whether a word of this is true?" Mendoza asked. "The two of you could have made the whole thing up. You could have killed him yourself."

"For what purpose? You heard what Péris said last night. He regarded me as a traitor and a collaborator. He still did even when I left him."

"Presumably he knew that you also broke the king's laws and continued to follow the sect of Muhammad?"

"I never advocated rebellion! Doesn't Jesus say that we can worship God *and* Caesar?"

"So now you quote the Bible, yet you bury your dead like Moors."

"I'm only trying to point out—"

"Never mind. Thank you."

The jangling of keys brought the conversation to an end, and one of the jailers appeared in the doorway and called out the names of some of the prisoners. To Mendoza's relief the men filed out of the room and some space began to open up around him. He'd been inside many jails, but he had never spent so much time in a cell, let alone in such close proximity to men he himself would normally have arrested, and the stench made him feel faintly nauseous as he pondered what Segura had told him.

If Péris's declarations were true, then Sánchez had murdered the priest on Vallcarca's orders and the baron and the Inquisition had colluded to frame the three Moriscos. Mendoza knew that Mercader was determined to carry out his purge in Belamar, and it was certainly possible, as the countess had suggested, that Vallcarca and her father-in-law were using the Inquisition to frighten her into marrying Rodrigo Vallcarca. But was the implacable inquisitor whom Mendoza met in Zaragoza really willing to collude in a criminal act in order to bring about such an outcome?

And why would the loyal bailiff who refused to allow Mercader's officials to enter the village be simultaneously acting against his mistress's wishes behind her back? Whatever the answers, it was clear to him that from now on these questions should be directed at Christians, not Moriscos.

And it was also obvious that whoever had killed Péris had no reason to allow Mendoza to return to Spain to ask them.

CHAPTER EIGHTEEN

OVER THE NEXT TWO HOURS, THE CELL continued to empty out to the point where the three of them were finally able to sit on a bench. They remained there for some time until the jailers returned, accompanied by the chief constable and his officers and another official whom Mendoza had not seen before. Segura introduced Monsieur LaFranc, the chief magistrate of the city of Pau, and Mendoza told Segura to ask if he could fetch the royal seal from his saddlebags. LaFranc's demeanor did not change as he ordered them to accompany him. Once again they were escorted back into the street and across the bridge toward the château and up the steps leading beyond the old medieval wall to the royal palace, where two well-turned-out halberdiers in armored breastplates and striped breeches stood by the main entrance.

Monsieur LaFranc led them down the spacious corridor,

where Mendoza heard what sounded like someone being kicked or beaten, accompanied by laughter, cheers and applause.

"Are they going to torture us, sir?" asked Daniel anxiously.

Mendoza was beginning to wonder the same thing when LaFranc halted before one of the dozens of doorways and ushered them into an enormous rectangular room with paneled walls and wooden galleries, where a handful of male and female spectators were watching four men in pantaloons, shirts and stockings hitting a ball across a fringed rope with leather gloves. Mendoza had heard of the Game of the Palm, but he had never seen it played before. He immediately recognized King Henry of Navarre from the previous afternoon. He was a stocky, robust-looking man in his early thirties with a ruddy, healthy complexion, a full, well-groomed beard and a shock of brown hair combed back high across his forehead that shook when he jumped about.

His Majesty was clearly enjoying himself and let out enthusiastic exclamations of triumph or dismay when he won or lost a point, or shouted "Bravo!" when his opponents did well and called on the spectators to applaud them. He had noticed their entrance, and as soon as the game ended, he came toward Segura with a broad smile, wiping the sweat from his forehead with one hand and shaking Segura's hand with the other.

Mendoza was struck by the stains on Henry's tunic and the pungent smell of garlic on his breath and clothes as the king of Navarre turned to him with a curious but not unfriendly expression.

"So you are the Spanish judge," he said in Latin. "Some of my officials were concerned you might be a spy or an assassin. They thought the Guises might have sent you to kill me or that you might be agents of the Catholic League."

"Absolutely not, Your Majesty," Mendoza replied in the language that he had not spoken since university. "I've come to solve a murder."

"And now you have left us with three. Strange, it seems that whenever Spaniards come to our country, they leave corpses behind them."

"That was not my intention, sire. And I have a letter from the king with the royal seal to prove it, if I can be allowed to get it."

"No need for that, Maître Mendoza. My officers have already inspected your credentials—otherwise you wouldn't be here. And Dr. Segura's father is an old friend of my mother's, God bless her soul. Come, let us eat something. Prison makes men hungry, and so does tennis."

Henry draped a towel over his shoulders, and they followed him out into the corridor, accompanied by Monsieur LaFranc and some of the male courtiers, to another room, where a long table was laden with wine and an array of cut meats, pies and cheeses.

"So, Maître Mendoza," Henry said, gnawing on a chicken leg with one hand and holding a cup of wine with the other. "Perhaps you can tell us why His Most Catholic Majesty has sent a judge all the way from Valladolid to our humble little kingdom?"

In his student Latin, Mendoza did his best to explain the investigation in Belamar, and Segura added other details in French. The king listened attentively while continuing to pick at random from the assortment of dishes with his hands, much like some of the revelers Mendoza had seen the previous day.

"So your wood-carver came to us for sanctuary, only to be murdered," Henry said. "It's curious. Three hundred years ago, the Cathars crossed these mountains into Spain to escape the Inquisition.

Now Moriscos are coming across the same mountains to seek our help for the same reason."

"And does Your Majesty help them?"

Henry laughed, and his courtiers laughed with him. "It's a good thing that you took up the law rather than diplomacy, Maître Mendoza. As a matter of fact, we Huguenots have had quite enough wars lately without giving His Most Catholic Majesty further reason to attack us. My ministers tell me that Monsieur Péris asked us for weapons and gunpowder to help the Moriscos, but we refused—politely, of course, because master wood-carvers are always in high demand. In Spain, His Most Catholic Majesty drives his Morisco subjects to rebellion when they could be an asset to him. Take Dr. Segura here—he could have worked in any hospital in Paris. We ourselves have asked him to work for us here in Pau, but he prefers to work in the land of his birth. Such men are worth holding on to, Maître Mendoza, and yet your king persecutes these people, and perhaps one day he will drive them away, just as his predecessors once expelled the Jews."

"I very much doubt that His Majesty would do such a foolish thing."

"Wouldn't he? He expelled them from Granada after the Morisco rebellion."

"To ensure the security of his realms and punish rebels—as any king would do in the same circumstances."

"Not always, *maître*. Sometimes even rebels have good cause." Henry picked a clove of garlic from a plate and chomped on it with gusto. "Here we also accept the principle that each prince must decide the faith—even in Pamplona."

Once again the courtiers laughed, and Mendoza smiled at the

mischievous reference to southern Navarre, which the king's father had annexed to Castile more than sixty years earlier. "But that doesn't mean that princes must persecute their subjects," Henry went on. "Here in France, Catholics kill Huguenots and Huguenots kill Catholics, even though all of us are Frenchmen. We've seen our cities burned, our women and children slaughtered, our fields laid barren by people who profess to worship the same God. When—if—I become king of France, I will do things differently, if His Most Catholic Majesty and the pope allow me to."

"Was His Majesty ever approached by Jean Sánchez, the bailiff of Cardona, to seek assistance for a rebellion in Aragon?" Mendoza asked.

Henry spoke in French to Monsieur LaFranc, who shook his head.

"We don't know that name. But we have heard a great deal of the Countess of Cardona. A remarkable woman by all accounts. Have you met her?"

"I have, Your Majesty."

"And is she as beautiful as they say?"

"Very much so. And very sought-after."

Henry smiled with rueful pleasure. "I would also like to seek after her, because a beautiful woman should never be a widow. But my wife and the interests of the state would not stand for it. In any case I wish her well, and I hope that you find a solution to these difficulties. But you cannot do it here. Tomorrow morning you must leave our kingdom. An escort will take you to the frontier to make sure there is no further unpleasantness. After that you must make your own way."

"We are most grateful to Your Majesty," Mendoza said, "and very sorry that we have brought these troubles into your kingdom."

"And I am very sorry for you, Licenciado. Because from what you say, your troubles may only just be beginning."

WITHIN TWENTY-FOUR HOURS of his guardian's departure, Gabriel had completed copies of the investigation reports and sent letters to the Marquis of Villareal and Corregidor Calvo. Even though there were no more depositions to be taken down, he continued to spend hours at the village hall with his writing materials, in order to maintain an official presence or to record any new information that might materialize.

On the same day that Mendoza and Segura left for France, Martín returned from Cardona to bring new supplies of paper and ink, just as Gabriel was preparing a report for Villareal. He still found the militiaman as frosty and unapproachable as he had during the journey up from Valladolid, and he was surprised when he came over to the desk and stood silently watching with a fascinated and almost reverential expression as Gabriel wrote out his report.

"How long did it take you to learn to write like that?" he asked.

Gabriel shrugged. "I learned to read and write at the *colegio*. When I was twelve my guardian bought me Juan de Icíar's *The Most Delicate Art of Writing a Perfect Hand*. I used to copy the letters every day. My guardian also taught me how to write reports. There's a special way of writing them and certain phrases you have to use. And you have to learn to keep your letters small, straight and even, so that you don't waste paper."

"I would love to learn to read and write," Martín said. "If I could, I might not have had to join the army. I could have worked in my father-in-law's shop."

"I can teach you."

For the first time since Gabriel had known him, Martín's face softened, and he looked at the younger man uncertainly. "You could do that?"

"Of course. We could start, anyway. And I can continue in Valladolid."

"Not me, *chico*." Martín rapped his helmet with his knuckles. "There's nothing inside this helmet. That's why I'm in the army."

"How do you know if you've never tried? All we need is a chalkboard. Segura has one in his dispensary. We can start today."

That afternoon Gabriel wrote out the first three letters of the alphabet and helped Martín copy them. Afterward the militiaman was glowing with pride, and Gabriel knew that the ice was finally broken. These classes gave him something else to do, in addition to patrolling the village with Necker, Martín and Ventura, who had gotten out of bed the day after Mendoza's departure in spite of Segura's instructions. After nearly a month in Belamar, Gabriel now knew each of its streets and recognized many of its six hundred–odd inhabitants enough to nod or say hello to them. Each day he passed the women washing their clothes in the river or pounding and wringing them at the stone trough in the communal *lavadero*, sitting outside their homes sewing patches on clothes, spinning wool or grinding corn with a pestle and mortar; the shepherds leaving their homes with their animals and their small flocks of sheep and goats; the peasants and laborers departing for the fields in the early morning with their hoes, picks and shovels.

He saw the Moriscos on the terraces or in the valley digging, scratching and picking at the hard soil, dragging wooden plows by hand or oxen, opening or closing the irrigation channels that led down from the water deposit higher up or carrying water from the wells, bent over the little plots or gardens outside the town where they grew their own vegetables, pulling up weeds from rows of grapes or pruning olive and almond trees. Each day he said good morning to the old men and women who sat outside their homes drowsing in the sun. He passed Carlos, the mad orphan with one eye who called him "Jesus," whom various families fed and looked after among them. In the early evenings, he saw the woodcutters bringing back piles of branches from the forest on the other side of the ravine, the children playing blindman's buff or fighting one another with wooden swords.

In Valladolid he was used to the daily clatter of carriages, carters and horses, to the cries of water carriers and street vendors calling out their wares. Here the day began with the sound of the cockerel crowing before dawn and ended with high-pitched shrieks of swifts wheeling above the village in the early evening. He realized that he had gotten used to Belamar and the valley below, to the point where it was Castile that now seemed like a foreign country, and he was able to tell what time of day it was from the shadow cast by the sun against the surrounding mountains, and he had grown to look forward with pleasure each day to the warm purple glow that bathed the town at sunset as the darkness slowly flowed into the ravine below like water.

All this had become his world, and so, too, was the pervasive fear and anxiety that percolated through the village. It was evident in the strained faces of the Morisco laborers and their families working in the fields, in the sentries who continued to guard the lower entrance to the village despite Mendoza's advice to leave the protection of the village to his men, in the rumors that coursed constantly through the town of bandit attacks on the road or in the next valley, in the reports that journeymen and peasants and tinkers brought back with them from Jaca and Huesca of fights and quarrels between Moriscos and *montañeses*, of impending inquisitorial investigations, of another pilgrim or merchant attacked on the roads.

Many of these stories were impossible to confirm or disprove, and they only added to the collective unease. Perhaps it was because these threats emanated from outside the village, but the Moriscos no longer seemed to hold Mendoza and his men in suspicion, and many of them seemed glad to have armed constables patrolling the streets. The most notable exception, from Gabriel's point of view, was Segura's family. Since their father's departure, Juana and her brothers no longer brought him breakfast or invited him next door to eat with them, and they ignored him when they passed him in the street. Gabriel knew that they were angry with Mendoza, not him, but Juana's hostility was particularly difficult to endure, because of all Belamar's inhabitants there was no one whose goodwill he was more keen to maintain and no one he thought of more frequently or more fondly.

IT WAS PARTLY in hope of seeing her that he kept his lonely vigils at the village hall. On the third day after Mendoza's departure, Gabriel was sitting by the window in Segura's office in the late afternoon, waiting for Martín to come for his class, when he glanced out and saw her crossing the square. She was wearing the same long loose skirt, shawl and sandals that she always wore, plus a white head scarf that covered most of her dark hair, and she was carrying a basket. He hurriedly put away his book and picked up his pen and stared intently down at the blank paper until she entered the room and stood looking at him dubiously.

"I want to see Constable Necker," she said.

"He's out on patrol. Can I help?"

"I think I've seen a bandit. I was up in the woods picking herbs. I saw a man on a horse near the charcoal burners' camp. He was staring down on the village as if he was spying on it."

"You shouldn't be out in the woods alone."

Juana regarded him pityingly. "I'm not afraid, scrivener, even if you are. I was only on the other side of the ravine. I saw the horseman looking down from the ridge."

"Well, then." Gabriel got to his feet and picked up his borrowed sword from the table. "You'd better show me where you saw him."

"Don't you have to ask for permission first?" she said mockingly.

Gabriel reddened. He heard his guardian's voice telling him that she was right, but in that moment he was filled with a sudden desire to prove to her and to himself that he was not just a scrivener who wrote down the things that other people told him.

"There's no need for that. Just show me what you saw."

A faint smile briefly flitted across her face before she resumed the same expression of frosty disdain. He followed her down to the old village wall, and they descended the steep footpath past the stream till they reached the floor of the ravine where he had watched his guardian disappear only three days before. Within a few minutes, the village was out of sight, and for the first time in his life he was alone with a girl, and with a sword hanging from his belt. The experience was so unusual and so pleasant that it left him tongue-tied as the two of them walked side by side along the ravine.

"My father's too old to go to France," she said suddenly. "It was wrong of Licenciado Mendoza to make him go."

"He didn't make him. And he wouldn't have gone if he didn't think it was necessary."

"Well, if anything happens to him, I'll hold Mendoza responsible—and you as well."

"Nothing's going to happen to him. My guardian will make sure of it."

She did not look convinced, but she seemed less hostile now that they were away from the village. He asked her what she had in her basket, and she explained the names and properties of the flowers and herbs she had collected: chamomile for settling stomachs, yarrow for treating wounds, mint for toothaches and resin for improving the flow of blood. He barely paid any attention to the names, and as he glanced at her jet-black hair under the head scarf and listened to the sound of her voice, he remembered what his guardian had told him about women and realized that Mendoza was right about that, as he was about most things. Her company was so enjoyable and so sweetly intoxicating that Gabriel felt disappointed when she pointed to the hill above the woods where she had seen the horseman and he saw that there was no one there. Once again he heard Mendoza's voice telling him to go back, but he found himself saying that he was going to take a closer look.

Once again she smiled, but this time there was no mockery in it. "If you're going, then I'm going, scrivener," she said.

He smiled back at her as they walked toward the path leading up into the woods. They had just reached it when he saw the dark shape running down the path toward them. At first he thought it was an animal, but as it drew closer, he saw that it had two legs and that its face was entirely black. It was not until the creature was nearly upon them that he realized that it was a young girl. She looked about ten years old, though it was difficult to tell from the smoke that covered her matted hair, her face, legs and arms and her hessian smock.

"It's the charcoal burner's daughter!" Juana said as the girl gesticulated back toward the woods.

"Why doesn't she say anything?" Gabriel asked.

"She doesn't speak or hear."

Even without words the girl was obviously terrified. Gabriel's first instinct was to return to the village. But then he thought once again of all the times he had taken the long way around to the *colegio* to avoid the boys who would be waiting to attack him, or had run away when he saw them coming. He thought of Ventura and Necker and knew that they would not turn from danger, and he was filled with a sudden surge of bravado.

"How far is the charcoal burners' camp?"

"It's about ten minutes from here," Juana replied.

"Take her back to the village and send Constable Necker and Sergeant Ventura," he said. "I'm going to take a look."

HIS VOICE SOUNDED strange and new to him. It was a man's voice—bold, fearless and decisive—and he sensed that even Juana was impressed by it. She took the girl's hand, and the two of them hurried off. As soon as they were gone, he felt his courage begin to falter. He heard a bird fly out of the trees and a sudden breath of wind that made the leaves tremble all around him. Fragments of old myths and stories flitted through his mind, of dragons and witches and brave knights on quests. He thought of stories he had read about Amadis of Gaul, the perfect knight, slayer of giants and dragons. He thought of Theseus in the labyrinth, Jason and the Golden Fleece, Perseus and Medusa, as the forest swallowed him up till he could no longer see the ravine.

Even though he was walking slowly and cautiously, his footsteps seemed to echo, and he stopped frequently and looked around at the silent forest to ensure that no one was following him. He'd been walking for nearly ten minutes when he heard the strange wail from somewhere ahead of him. It was midway between a moan and a scream, and he was not sure whether it came from a man or a woman or whether it was even human at all. Once again he wanted to turn back and run, but he told himself that if he did, he would be abandoning whoever had screamed, and no man who wanted to be a hero would ever do that. He could smell smoke now, and he saw a clearing up ahead through the dim light as he continued to inch forward, holding the sword in both hands.

At the edge of the clearing, he stopped, lowered the weapon and stared in disbelief at the scene of horror that confronted him. Directly before him a dead dog was lying in the still-smoldering fire pit. To the left of it, on the other side of the clearing, a man and a woman were dangling side by side from the tree where they'd been hanged. Both of them were barefoot, and their blackened faces and clothes gave them an inhuman, ghoulish appearance.

On the right of the clearing, a man in a brown tunic and a cloth hat folded down over his ears was sitting on a bench outside a wooden hut, nonchalantly gnawing on a piece of bread. He had his back turned, and a short broadsword was thrust into his belt behind him. He was looking into the dark doorway, where Gabriel heard the sound of violent movement and the unmistakable moans of a woman.

"God's blood. Aren't you whoremongers finished with her yet?" The man yawned.

The moans abruptly stopped, and a moment later a tall, bearded man emerged from the doorway.

"We have now." He bent down to wipe his knife on the grass. As he did so, he looked up and saw Gabriel standing by the clearing.

"Well, well. We have company."

Gabriel felt his bravado draining out of him now as he turned sideways and raised the sword horizontally in front of him with his palm turned upward, holding the other hand out for balance as Ventura had taught him. But the weapon no longer felt the same as it had when he'd practiced with it or cut elegant shapes in the air in the solitude of his own room. It seemed to have gotten heavier, or else he'd become weaker. The man in the cloth hat had turned around and reached for his own sword, and now another man emerged from the hut. The two of them moved away from their bearded companion, who crouched down slightly, moving the knife back and forth in slow, almost playful movements.

"So you want to fight, boy?" he sneered. "Let's see, shall we?"

It was only then, as the three bandits spread out and slowly advanced toward him, that Gabriel gave in to panic and turned to run. But his movements were too clumsy and too sudden, and he tripped and let go of the sword. Before he could retrieve it, the bearded man had grabbed him by the hair and pulled him upright till Gabriel was kneeling on the ground in front of him. All thoughts of great deeds had evaporated into the chill dark forest now, and his whole body flinched at the awful realization that he was about to be slaughtered like an animal and that it was all his own fault.

"Please don't kill me," he whimpered.

"The Morisco says we shouldn't kill him!"

"*Por Dios*, stop playing with him and get it over with, Manu," said the man with the cloth hat. "We haven't got all night."

"I'll finish him, all right. But the boss said he wanted a show. Let's string him up with the others."

"Hombre. There's not enough rope."

"There's some in the shed. Go and get it."

The bandit gripped Gabriel's neck with one powerful hand and dragged him to his feet while his companion rummaged around in the shed. It was nearly dark now, and Gabriel looked up at the purple sky and tried to pray, but he could not remember the words to any prayers. Instead he found himself saying, "I'm not Morisco."

"Well, isn't that your bad luck!" the bearded man exclaimed.

"I can't find it, Manu," the bandit called nervously. "And I don't like being in here with her."

"Believe me, she won't get up."

"Her eyes are still open."

The bearded man chuckled. "They can't see you!"

"But I can."

The two bandits turned around and stared at the dark figure standing in the path from which Gabriel had emerged only a few minutes before. It was impossible to see his face, but Gabriel recognized Ventura's voice even before the pistol shot rang out. The bearded man relaxed his grip and fell back across the dead dog and the burning coals. The other bandit ran toward the two hanging bodies, but Ventura calmly aimed the other pistol and shot him in the back before he reached the shelter of the trees.

"Come here, boy! Quickly!" Ventura shouted. "Are there any more?"

"In the hut!"

No sooner had he spoken than the third bandit came bursting out of the doorway and ran toward them with his sword raised. But now Necker emerged from the trees beside Ventura and brought his two-hander down on the top of the man's head, splitting his skull like a large nut. Behind him, armed Moriscos now appeared at the edge of the clearing, some of whom were carrying torches, and Gabriel saw Juana standing with her hand over her mouth and looking at the hanging bodies. Necker ordered the Moriscos to cut them down and held up a torch in front of the shed.

"There's a woman in here," he said. "She's dead, too."

"Well, bring her out, then," Ventura ordered.

"She shouldn't come out," replied Necker. "Not as she is."

Ventura peered into the doorway. "By the Holy Cross, they don't do things by halves, do they? Cover her up and put the other bodies in the shed. We'll come and get them in the morning. The animals can have these bastards. Did they bring horses?"

"I don't know," Gabriel said. "I didn't see any."

"Never mind. We'd better get back. There might be more of them."

Necker and the Moriscos cut the two bodies down and carried them to the shed, and the German pushed the bench against the door to keep it shut. Gabriel retrieved his sword and sheathed it once again. He did not look at Juana, but he was glad that it was too dark for her to see his face.

Ventura patted him on his shoulder. "Are you all right, boy?"

"Yes, sir. Thank you, sir. And Constable Necker, too."

"You should thank Juana. If she hadn't gotten back so quickly, we wouldn't have made it here in time. She was very concerned about you." He lowered his voice. "And when we get back, maybe you can tell me what in all the devils in hell made you think you could come up here by yourself without telling anyone."

Gabriel nodded. As they followed the dwindling torches back down through the forest, he thought the air smelled fresher and thinner than it ever had before. He did not speak to Juana or anyone else, and when they emerged from the forest and back into the ravine, he took special care to keep away from the light, so that no one could see his tears.

CHAPTER NINETEEN

N THE LITTLE HOUSE CHAPEL, THE COUNTESS knelt down and prayed for the strength and vision to withstand the storms that were gathering around her. As was often the case, her entreaties were interrupted by the stern, accusing voice that insisted that she was a *bujarrona*—a female sodomite—who had no right to speak to God about anything except repentance. As on previous occasions, a softer and equally insistent voice told God that she loved Susana with the same love that Ruth the Moabite had once felt for her mother-in-law, Naomi, the widow of Elimelech of Bethlehem, when they found themselves without husbands and without sons and Ruth begged to return with Naomi to Judah rather than remain alone in Moab.

That was how the countess felt about her maidservant, and she told herself that a love that brought her such happiness and pleasure could not be sinful. Once again the voice of her education rejected this defense and told her that she loved her servant more than she loved God and reminded her that a woman could never lie with another woman and that she had betrayed the memory of her husband and dishonored her parents. She responded with the same arguments she had so often prepared in her head but which she had never dared speak to anyone: that she had not chosen to be this way, that she had tried to love her husband as a woman should even though the marriage had not been her choice, that she had honored and respected him as the Bible commanded.

This had not been difficult, because Miguel was a good man and a man worthy of honor and respect, who had loved her and treated her well. But no matter how many times she had lain with him, she had never warmed to his touch, even though she'd tried to pretend otherwise out of concern for him and because she knew that it was her duty to conceive. Once, she had asked Father García for guidance, and the priest told her that copulation was an obligation incumbent on every Christian wife and that it was not meant to be pleasurable as long as it produced results. She had hoped that over time she might have felt for Miguel what he so obviously felt for her. Perhaps that might have happened had he lived. But then Susana had come to her household, and her initial desire to offer Christian comfort to one of Panalles's victims had turned into something quite different, something so overwhelming and irresistible that she had no choice but to surrender herself to it.

Even then, she reminded God, she had not betrayed Miguel while he was alive. She had not broken her vows. It was not until after his death that she and Susana had known each other carnally. And now she felt that she and her chambermaid were as closely bound to each other as any married couple could be, and she could not imagine living without the happiness Susana brought her. And as she knelt in the chapel before the altar and the stained-glass window, she pleaded with God to forgive her and to remember the many good things that she had done to serve him, to consider the great harm that would be done to so many people if her estates fell into the hands of the Baron of Vallcarca. Still the voice in her head replied that she loved Susana more than she loved God, more than her own child or the good name of her family, and it warned her that she would lose all these things if she did not stop.

She left the chapel feeling no better than when she had entered it, and she went to the salon to await the baron's arrival. It was a meeting she did not want but one she could not avoid, and she had sent Susana out into town with Carolina for the morning, so that the two people she loved most in the world would not be present. She sat alone now on a cushioned seat by the window, looking through the Latin bestiary that her father had given to her as a child and which she had passed on to her daughter. Once, she had believed that the mountains were inhabited by the strange and marvelous creatures it depicted. Now she found it comforting to look again at the winged flying fish, the griffins and dragons and lions with human heads, the wide-eyed crocodiles and serpents with human legs protruding from their mouths.

She was still sitting there when her servant announced that Vallcarca and his son had arrived. She took a deep breath and rose to greet them as Rodrigo Vallcarca's braying voice echoed down the corridor and the baron swept in through the doorway like a cold winter wind, followed by his son. He doffed his green velvet cap and bowed to kiss her outstretched hand while his son looked on with the pouting smirk that she imagined he'd been born with, before he, too, pressed his lips against her limp hand, holding it in his hot palm just slightly longer than propriety allowed. It was not until they sat down that she noticed the faint red weal on the side of his face, which he had obviously tried to cover with makeup.

"Why, Don Rodrigo," she said. "Whatever has happened to your face?"

Rodrigo replied that he had ridden into a branch while hunting, but the countess sensed that he was lying. It was more likely that Vallcarca had beaten him for some vile indiscretion. She had no desire to know what it was. She expressed her regret with as much sympathy as she was able to muster before turning back to his father.

"My father-in-law told me that I might expect the honor of your visit," she said.

"Then you'll know what I've come for, madam," replied Vallcarca.

Rodrigo's smirk grew even wider, and his watery eyes looked up and down the high-collared black dress that she had worn for the occasion.

"And my father-in-law will have told you my answer."

"Indeed. But he led me to understand that you might have second thoughts."

"I can't imagine how he could have reached such a conclusion," she replied calmly, "because I made my intentions very clear."

Rodrigo was not smirking now, but Vallcarca merely smiled patiently, as though he were talking to a child or an idiot, and asked the countess to hear him out. It was true, he admitted, that his son was not the most handsome or intelligent man in Aragon and that his manners were not as refined as those of the men of Zaragoza, but he was loyal, honest and true, and he felt only the warmest feelings toward her and the sincerest desire for her happiness. Rodrigo tried to look warm and tender, but the effort was beyond him, and his cold, fishlike stare only made her more anxious for the conversation to end.

Vallcarca insisted that the strength of his son's devotion would surely lead her to reciprocate it in time, as would the many children that would result from the marriage and ensure the survival of the House of Cardona in perpetuity. He spoke of the financial benefits and security that this marriage would bring to Cardona and reminded her that he would also become her father-in-law and that he would treat her like his own daughter. The countess had heard much of this from Espinosa and she wondered which of the two of them had composed the speech.

"I thank you for the honor you have shown me," she said when he finished. "But as I told the Marquis of Espinosa, I cannot marry your son."

"Cannot, my lady?"

"Oh, let's not waste our time, Father!" Rodrigo exclaimed. "She's obviously not interested, and I'm not going to beg her!"

"Get out, you imbecile," Vallcarca snapped without looking at him. "Go and wait in the carriage."

"But—"

"You heard me. I want to talk to Doña Isabel alone. Close the door behind you."

This was not what the countess wanted at all, but Rodrigo slunk out of the room while Vallcarca sat watching her with an odd, bitter smile and flicked back his cloak to rest his hand on the pommel of his sword.

"How's your little Morisca whore?" he asked suddenly.

"I beg your pardon? How dare you use such language in my house, sir!"

"The audacity is not on my part, Countess," Vallcarca replied. "I know what goes on within these walls. There's nothing you won't do for your Moriscos, and it seems there's nothing they won't do for you. Am I not right, my lady?"

The countess was too stunned to reply as Vallcarca abandoned all pretense at tact and diplomacy. "In the next week, Inquisitor Mercader will come to Belamar," he said, "and my militia will ensure that he is not turned back. Segura and most of his family will be arrested, and they will talk and give him names. One of those names will be yours, my lady. Another will be your maidservant's. The two of you will then be taken to Zaragoza, and you will reveal your secrets. Your little *criada* will denounce you, and you will denounce her. Maybe you'll burn. Maybe you'll go to prison. Either way you will lose your estates."

Vallcarca paused to allow this to sink in. "Your father-in-law will then become the guardian of your daughter," he went on. "As any loving grandfather would. Then she, not you, will be betrothed to Rodrigo. Oh, he won't actually marry her till she comes of age, but Espinosa will ensure that no one else does. Long before my son consummates the marriage, however, I will already be helping the marquis in the management of your estates."

"My father-in-law has no rights over the Cardona estates," the countess protested. "The *fueros* prohibit it."

"Oh, the *fueros*!" Vallcarca waved his hand disdainfully. "They weren't designed for situations like this. Espinosa may not be able to take over your estates, but as Carolina's legal guardian he decides whom she marries. Even if the Crown takes interim possession, the Cortes of Aragon will never allow the king to claim permanent jurisdiction as long as there is the possibility that your daughter will produce an heir. You know how sensitive we Aragonese can be regarding such matters. In any case all this must go through the courts, and that will take years. In that time Carolina will be married. And if there's one thing Rodrigo has a talent for, it's producing children. Why, he's left so many of the brats around Vallcarca that he doesn't even know their names. That's good Vallcarca seed, my lady, perfect for continuing the Cardona line."

"You revolt me, sir."

"Perhaps. But there is only one thing you can do to prevent this from happening, and that is to marry my son."

"This is the most villainous blackmail!" the countess said weakly.

Vallcarca looked unperturbed. "Indeed. But your stubbornness and stupidity have left me no option. My son proposed to you a year ago. Did you think that you could defy me after what happened to your husband? You can always report this conversation to Licenciado Mendoza when he gets back from France. But if you do, I'll deny it. And you have no proof. And what will you tell him—that the pious widow who guards her husband's memory is a sodomite? No, Countess, you wouldn't be so foolish. If you want to save your estates—and your daughter—you know what you have to do. So do I have an answer?"

"You do, sir. Please leave my house. And never come back to it again."

Vallcarca shrugged and stood up, holding his hat in his hand.

"Very well. But it will be as I said, however long I have to wait. And if you do change your mind, you know where I am. I suggest you think it over and act accordingly, for your daughter if not yourself."

She did not get up to show him out and doubted whether her legs would have allowed her do it. It was only after he had shut the door behind him and she listened to his fading footsteps that she felt an urge to cry. She immediately repressed it, because this was not a time for tears or weakness. The threat was too real, and it was not limited to Vallcarca. Someone had given away her secret, and she could not think who it might be. But as she glanced at the bestiary beside her, she felt menaced by monsters that were far more ferocious than any of those the artist had taken from Herodotus, and she realized with a crushing mixture of betrayal and incomprehension that one of them must be a member of her own household.

MENDOZA KNEW THAT THERE was a very good chance that he and his companions would be attacked on their way back to Belamar. As a precaution he wrote letters describing the events in Pau to Calvo in Jaca and obtained King Henry's permission to use the Béarnese royal post to take it to him. He also asked the corregidor to send an armed escort to the customs post at the Puerto de Somport to take them to Jaca and persuaded the king to let them remain in Pau for an extra two days to give Calvo time to raise the militia.

Throughout the ride out of the Ossau Valley and up into the high mountains, Mendoza felt reasonably confident that no one would want to ambush an escort of ten well-armed Béarnese cavalry in a country where reinforcements were easily available. Aragon was a different matter. From the moment their escort left them on the French side of the Somport Pass and he saw that there was no escort waiting for them, he knew that their prospects of survival had suddenly receded.

When Mendoza was a child, his father had sometimes entertained and frightened him by making the shapes of animals and monsters with his fingers in the candlelight, casting shadows across the walls that sometimes seemed much bigger than his hands. Now he knew that the Redeemer was like these shadows—a reflection cast by someone else's hand, a hollow man like the carnival giants of kings, queens and warriors, their papier-mâché faces propped up on costumed wooden frames carried by men whose own faces could not be seen.

None of this was reassuring, because Péris's murder made it clear that the Catalan was not the only one carrying the Redeemer's frame. And if Sánchez was responsible, then he could not take the risk that Péris had told them what he knew, and that meant that they could not be allowed to return to Cardona. The realization that he felt safer in the heretic lands of the Huguenot king than he did in his own country filled him with a sense of irony that he did not enjoy. He felt angry at Calvo's inability to perform even this simple task, until the Spanish customs officers told them that a French post rider had been killed farther down the Jaca road early the previous morning.

With no prospect of an escort, they could either stay where they were and send a customs officer to get help or make their way back themselves. But Sánchez's men were almost certainly watching the road, and an isolated customs post was no defense against the assault that would most likely follow if they remained there. Their best course of action was to leave the road that crossed the mountains by a route of Segura's choosing. Segura had already reached the same conclusion, and they set off at an unhurried pace down the winding road that descended from the pass. It was an overcast and windy day, and puffs of low-lying gray clouds drifted through the upper valleys, obscuring the higher peaks. As soon as the customs post was out of sight, Segura wheeled his horse away from the road. They followed him at speed down a steep slope and then climbed upward once again toward a long ridge, where they paused to catch their breath.

On the opposite side of the valley from the road, they saw the seven black shapes coming down the slope behind them. Segura dismounted and led his horse downward, below the level of the ridge, so that they could not be seen. Despite his age, the mayor moved surprisingly quickly through the mountains even on foot, and it was an effort for Mendoza and Daniel to keep themselves and their horses upright as they followed him.

On reaching the bottom, they rode rapidly along rough but reasonably flat ground before ascending once again. The next two hours followed the same remorseless and exhausting pattern as they climbed and descended only to ascend once again, sometimes on foot and sometimes on horseback, in an attempt to increase or at least maintain the distance between themselves and their pursuers, but whenever they reached a high vantage point, they could see the cluster of horsemen coming toward them.

In the midafternnoon the weather came to their rescue when a thick mist enveloped the mountains, so that they were barely able to see more than a few yards in front of them. Segura insisted that they keep going on foot, and they continued to follow the seemingly haphazard trajectory in and out of gorges and valleys, leading their horses by the reins. All this was more physically demanding than anything Mendoza had done in years, and the pain in his leg was excruciating, but Segura no longer had any laudanum to give him.

After an hour the mist cleared, and they got back on their horses and continued to press on, pausing only to refresh themselves and their animals at the occasional stream or river before threading their way downward through thick forests and ravines where they would not be visible from a distance.

NOT SINCE THE ALPUJARRA MOUNTAINS had Mendoza felt so far from safety, law and civilization. But in Granada he had fought as a soldier in the royal army to suppress a Morisco rebellion against the Crown. Now his survival depended on the ability of a Morisco doctor to lead them through a wilderness infested by unknown enemies who were trying to kill him for reasons he did not even understand. And Segura was not infallible. He had lost his original route in the mist, and the continual cloud cover made it difficult to reorient themselves as they zigzagged back and forth in an attempt to find their way down through the mountains.

It was nearly dark when they finally stopped in a small clearing at the edge of a forest of beech and sycamore trees, where they allowed the horses to graze. Segura said that it was pointless to go on in the dark when he was not sure where he was. Besides, it was unlikely that anyone else would look for them at night, and so they set up camp just inside the forest in a spot where they could see anyone who approached it without being seen themselves. They ate some bread and hard French cheese that they had brought with them from Pau and took turns keeping watch throughout the night.

Mendoza was unable to manage more than a brief doze even when he lay on the hard ground beneath his blanket. Most of the time he sat against a tree with his weapons by his side, listening to the whirring insects and the countless inexplicable sounds issuing from the dark forest as the hours passed interminably. Daniel was also restless, looking up repeatedly at the fluttering of wings or the sound of a snapping twig even when it was not his watch.

Only Segura managed to catch some sleep, and he looked almost rested when they continued their progress at first light. The sky was clear, and when the sun came up, he quickly established that they had drifted too far east. By midmorning they had reached the Somport-Jaca road again, and Mendoza decided to go directly to Jaca and seek help from the corregidor rather than attempt to cross the countryside to Belamar. The road was almost flat now, and they'd been riding for about half an hour when a group of mounted men blocked the road in front of them.

Once again they jabbed their heels into their sweating horses and drove them off the road and onto the nearby trail that led up through the low foothills toward the Gállego River. The pursuit continued for more than thirty minutes up the hill and down into another shallow valley, which funneled out into a steep gorge before them.

"Stop when you reach the entrance!" Mendoza shouted as he passed Daniel. On reaching the gorge, he reined in the stallion and waited for the others to catch up.

"Constable, dismount and load your weapon," he ordered.

"We'll never be able to fight that many," Segura protested.

"No, but we can slow them down. Take the horses into the gorge and wait for us around the corner."

Segura did as he was told while Daniel slipped the escopeta from its holster and gathered some leaves and dry twigs. The riders were visible now as he rubbed the flint and steel together till they caught fire. Mendoza had seen infantrymen who were able to load and fire a harquebus at two shots a minute even in the heat of battle, but he had also seen men set fire to their own powder and blow themselves up through their excessive haste or place the match cord too high or too low in the serpentine so that it missed the powder and failed to ignite. So far he had only seen Daniel fire off practice shots during the ride up from Valladolid. He was accurate enough, but not as fast as Martín, and Mendoza was not even sure that he could get off a shot before the horsemen reached them.

He noticed that Daniel's hand was trembling as he held the rope match against the tiny flame until it began to smolder and he carefully placed it in the serpentine before uncapping the powder bottle and tilting some powder into the firing pan and into the barrel. He glanced at the horsemen racing toward them across the open plain and unhooked the ramrod and dropped a ball into the barrel and pushed it down. The riders were now close enough to make out their faces and the color of their clothes as Daniel leaned the carbine against a rock and rested the stock against his shoulder.

"Steady, now," Mendoza murmured. "Don't rush it."

Daniel peered down the barrel and carefully cocked the serpentine, checking the alignment with the flash pan. The horsemen did not appear to have seen them, and they were still riding hard toward the gorge when he pressed the trigger and the serpentine snapped downward and brought the smoldering cord onto the powder. The gun jerked backward with a loud explosion and emitted a cloud of smoke, and one of the horsemen let go of the reins and seemed to raise his arms to the sky in a gesture of supplication or protest before falling backward and over to one side.

"Well done!" Mendoza congratulated him.

Daniel was already reloading, and his hands were no longer

shaking as the horsemen fanned out now behind the dead bandit's horse. They had clearly not expected to be shot at, and one of them fired a pistol in their direction, even though they were out of range. Another was waving his arms and shouting out instructions.

"Get the one in the leather hat," Mendoza said. "He's the leader."

Daniel squeezed the trigger, and once again the gun leaped and exploded in his arms. The leader's horse now buckled beneath him and tottered to one side, throwing him to the ground, and they watched him scramble around on all fours to shelter behind the fallen body. The other riders were also seeking cover, and the leader was signaling toward both sides of the valley.

"They're going to try to get around us," Mendoza said. "We need to go."

They ran back to where Segura was waiting with the horses and climbed into the saddles, guiding the animals as fast as they could across the rock-strewn floor. The gorge was not especially deep, but the steep, near-vertical walls cast them almost completely in shadow. Mendoza fully expected to hear voices or horses behind him at any moment, but apart from their own animals the gorge was silent and the bandits still did not seem to have realized that they were no longer at the entrance. After a few minutes, the path began to rise up in a gradual slope toward a lighter patch that indicated the end of the gorge.

They had nearly reached it when he heard the movement above him and looked up to see the rock falling out of the blue sky. There was just time to swivel his horse before it crashed to the ground right in front of him. The boulder was as large as a man's head, and he drew his pistol and looked up at the faceless silhouettes peering down from both sides of the canyon. There were many more than six of them, and they were throwing rocks and stones and shooting arrows, and now another line of men appeared at the exit to the gorge and began moving toward them on foot. Daniel was just behind him, and Segura was holding one hand to his head in an instinctive attempt to protect himself.

"Move!" Mendoza yelled.

Daniel leaned forward to spur his horse, and then suddenly he straightened up in the saddle and slumped forward, so that Mendoza saw the crossbow arrow protruding from the side of his neck. The militiaman was still holding on to the reins and trying to remain in the saddle, but his horse was wheeling around and around in confusion. Segura had not yet moved at all. Mendoza shouted at him to go forward as the stones and arrows continued to fall around them and the pistol shots ricocheted off the rocks. But the mayor seemed paralyzed.

It was not until Mendoza grabbed his horse's reins that the mayor appeared to rouse himself from his trance and dig his heels into his horse's flanks. Ventura's stallion now showed its mettle, sprinting from a standing start toward the line of men at the exit, some of whom were crouching down to fire pistols and crossbows. Still holding the reins of Segura's horse, Mendoza bent forward to present a smaller target. He heard a pistol ball whiz past his face and braced himself for the shot or arrow that would send him tumbling to the ground to his death as he grasped the reins with one hand and fired at a masked man who was rushing toward Segura with a sword raised above his head.

Mendoza tossed the smoking pistol away as the bandit fell to the ground, and he drew his sword, steering the horse toward the open space where the man had been standing. Some of the bandits were surrounding him, pulling at his legs and the horse's bridle as he slashed out wildly. He felt the blade connect with bone and heard someone howl, but hands continued to tug at his legs. And then suddenly the horse broke loose and he was riding alongside Segura and there was no one blocking their path.

Daniel was not with them, and it wasn't until they achieved a safe distance that Mendoza reined the horse in. He just had time to see Daniel's riderless horse racing toward the woods and the men on the ground hacking at his prone body before the horsemen came charging out of the gorge toward them. Once again he flicked the reins and dug his heels in. Mendoza was confident that Ventura's stallion could outrun their pursuers, but Segura's horse was lagging and looked exhausted. They continued to ride hard across the Jaca plain toward the Huesca road until they reached a pine forest where their pursuers disappeared from view.

"Go into the trees and hide yourself," Mendoza ordered. "I'll get them to follow me. As soon as we're out of sight, go back down to Jaca. Go and see Corregidor Calvo. Tell him to call out the militia and come to Belamar immediately with as many men as he can muster."

"What makes you think you'll get there yourself?" Segura asked.

"On this horse I have a chance. But you don't."

Segura nodded and rode off the path into the forest. Mendoza waited a little farther up the path till the first riders appeared behind him and then urged the stallion forward. As he had hoped, his pursuers continued to follow him. Without Segura to keep an eye on, he was able to give the horse its head, and he felt its power and strength as he galloped at full tilt through the forest and up the Huesca road and alongside the Gállego River, till he reached the footbridge that led into Cardona. Ignoring the toll keeper's cry of protest, he sprinted across it without pausing to pay and continued on until he reached the Belamar Valley. He did not slow down until he saw the familiar houses and church tower jutting out above the distant promontory at the end of the valley, and for the first time since coming to Aragon he actually felt glad to be back in Belamar de la Sierra.

BY THE TIME HE REACHED the brow of the hill, Ventura, Necker and a group of armed Moriscos were already running toward him from the main entrance, and his pursuers were visible riding away in the distance. They had barely congratulated him on his return when he told them that Daniel was dead. One of the Moriscos asked if Dr. Segura had been killed, too, and he and his companions looked visibly relieved when Mendoza told them that Segura had gone to Jaca. He got down from his horse and told Ventura and Necker about the pursuit and ambush as they walked to the main square. Gabriel looked equally relieved to see him, and Mendoza told him to take his horse to the stable and prepare him a bath. Martín immediately noticed his friend's absence and looked stunned and distraught when Mendoza told him what had happened.

"You're sure he's dead, sir?" he asked.

"I'm certain," Mendoza replied. "I'm sorry, Constable. He died bravely, doing his duty."

Martín nodded and followed Mendoza, Necker and Ventura into the village hall. The three men sat and stood around the hot, stuffy room and listened grimly as Mendoza told them about Péris, Jean Sánchez and the ambush in the gorge.

"Special Constable Azcona was killed in His Majesty's service," he said. "And it is our task to destroy the criminal conspiracy that has killed him and so many others. First, we must arrest Jean Sánchez. Second, it will be necessary to speak to Baron Vallcarca."

Necker immediately offered to go to Cardona to arrest the bailiff, and Martín volunteered to go with him, but Mendoza shook his head. "Sánchez won't want to return to Cardona now that he knows I'm back and the roads aren't safe. We need assistance from Calvo."

"Suppose Segura hasn't gotten through?" Ventura said.

"Then we'll send someone else," Mendoza replied. "And if Calvo can't send me the men I need, then I'll raise my own militia to go search for Sánchez. I need to know how many men in Belamar would be prepared to do this. I need men with weapons and the ability to use them."

Necker and Martín both agreed to go find out. When they had gone, Ventura told him about the murders of the charcoal burners and his decision to increase the number of sentries and place a lookout in the church tower.

"You did well, cousin," he said. "But that boy should not have gone up there by himself."

"Don't be too hard on him, Bernardo. He just wanted to impress the girl. You know what young men are like."

Mendoza looked past him as Juana and her elder brother, Agustín, appeared in the doorway, looking grim and anxious. Agustín demanded to know where their father was, and Mendoza assured them that he had thrown their pursuers off Segura's track and that their father was almost certainly in Jaca now.

"What if he isn't?" Juana asked coldly.

"Your father knew the risks and accepted them."

"He had no choice!"

"There was no other way to resolve this investigation," Mendoza insisted. "And if I don't resolve it, then your family and your village will pay the price. Your father knew that. That's why he came with me. He saved my life, and I did what I could to save his."

Juana glared back at him, and the two young people left the room in high dudgeon. Mendoza returned to the dispensary, where Gabriel was pouring water into the metal tub.

"What were you doing in the forest?" he said furiously. "Didn't I tell you never to leave the village alone?"

"I'm sorry, sir. I don't know why I did it."

"Being brave isn't the same thing as being stupid, boy! And if you ever disobey my orders again, I'll send you back to Valladolid, is that clear?"

"Yes, sir."

By the time the bath was ready, he felt calmer, and he sat naked in the tub while Gabriel scrubbed his back and arms and washed his hair. Afterward he changed into a clean shirt and felt as if he had returned once again to the civilized world. Gabriel still looked downcast and morose, and Mendoza gave him an exasperated smile.

"Come, Amadis," he said more gently. "Let's go and get some supper."

At the tavern Necker told them that he had found twenty men willing to form a militia, but only fifteen mules and horses. After supper Mendoza returned to the dispensary, where he lay on top of the bed wearing only his hose, with his shirt off. It was a hot and windless night, but he quickly fell into an unusual and not unpleasant dream, in which Elena was straddling him wearing nothing but a carnival mask, when he heard Necker calling him and woke to find the German standing in the doorway with a torch.

"Something's happened, sir. You'd better come."

Mendoza quickly pulled on his boots and followed Necker out into the street and down to the *lavadero*, where Ventura and a group of Moriscos were gathered near the smoldering brazier by the wash-house, peering down the road into the darkness.

"We have visitors, Bernardo."

"What time is it?"

"Just gone one o'clock."

Mendoza peered out toward the crest of the hill, where he was barely able to make out the shapes of four men on horseback.

"Is that you, Licenciado Mendoza?" called a voice out of the darkness. "You forgot something!"

"Son of a whore, it's the Catalan!" whispered Ventura. One of the horsemen came forward a few yards and then tossed a heavy object onto the dirt road. The four men turned away and vanished into the night, and Mendoza heard them riding off as Ventura and the Morisco sentries rushed forward to pick up the object. His cousin returned holding a bag that Mendoza knew contained a human head. His first thought was that it might belong to Segura, until Ventura held up the bloodstained head by the hair, and in the light of the torch he felt almost relieved when he recognized the eyeless face of militia-man and special constable Daniel Azcona.

CHAPTER TWENTY

MERCADER LISTENED CAREFULLY AS THE *fiscal* Ramírez read out the new indictments. From time to time, he interrupted to add something or remove or change words or phrases that he did not like. But such interventions were only adornments. The case against the Belamar Moriscos was overwhelming. On numerous occasions the defendant Pedro Navarro had witnessed the mayor and doctor Pedro Segura summon the demon in his surgery or in private homes while treating patients. Segura had also left inscriptions from the Koran in the rooms of sick patients in order to cure them. He had refused to tell the priest that his patients were dying so that they would not receive the last sacrament. He had used his visits as a doctor as an opportunity to preach the teachings of the false prophet Muhammad and had written and distributed Aljamiado books to disseminate his evil teachings. He had performed the banned ritual of circumcision and had married couples from Belamar according to the Moorish custom.

In addition, the aforementioned Segura had incited the Moriscos of Belamar and other Morisco places to revolt. He had conspired with the three Moriscos—Navarro, Péris and Royo—to acquire weapons and gunpowder from Navarre, which he had stockpiled in Belamar. He had rejoiced in the deaths of Fray Juan Panalles, the priest of Belamar, and the three Quintana brothers, the prosecutor went on, and had very likely been involved in them.

"I don't like that," Mercader interrupted. "Change 'very likely' to 'certainly.'"

Ramírez crossed out the offending words. The accused Segura's daughters had also assisted their father in his damned heretical practices, he went on. Juana Segura had helped her father write Arabic books. She was also a *curandera*—a folk healer who used sorcery in the course of her profession. Like her father, she consorted with the devil while collecting herbs and remedies in the forest, and the apprentice Juan Royo had observed her dancing naked and copulating with the horned beast. Segura's eldest daughter, Susana, was also guilty of heretical practices. The carpenter Pedro Navarro had seen her naked in a tub in her father's house, washing herself in preparation for prayer. Another witness had seen her perform the full-body *guadoc* in the Countess of Cardona's own house and observed her regularly offering the prayers of her damned sect.

There were ten other names on the list, all of whom confirmed the many reports that the Zaragoza Inquisition had already compiled over the years. These charges, Prosecutor Ramírez concluded, were only the most visible manifestation of the conspiracy that had been allowed to fester in Belamar, which now threatened the Inquisition, the Church and the peace and security of His Majesty's realms.

"Excellent work, Prosecutor Ramírez." Mercader turned to his secretary. "I want this rewritten, copied and ready to send by the end of the day. Send copies to the inquisitor-general and also directly to the king."

The two men bowed and left the room. Mercader remained sitting at his desk, admiring the interlocking geometrical shapes painted onto the wooden ceiling panels. Ramírez had done his work well. The charges were certainly serious enough to get Segura burned, and probably his daughters, too. Their interrogations would lead to other arrests, and it was only a matter of time before the heretic countess herself was brought to the Aljafería. When that happened, the Supreme Council and the king himself would know that Mercader was the man who had finally subdued the haughty Aragonese. He was still immersed in these pleasant thoughts when there was a knock on the door and his secretary reentered.

"Your Excellency. Familiar Pachuca has come from Huesca. He has a message from Commissioner Herrero."

"Send him in."

Mercader had not been expecting to see Diego Pachuca. Though Pachuca worked for the Inquisition, he was an unsettling presence, and Mercader was not always certain if his capacity for violence and cruelty was always directed toward God's service or even whether it was on the right side of sanity. Pachuca came into the room, his long arms dangling toward his knees, with the heavy, loping stride that made Mercader think of a wolf. He was wearing his usual green, bearing the white emblem of the Cross of Dominic, but his cape and boots were covered with dust and his sour face was unusually animated.

"Your Excellency, I have news from Commissioner Herrero."

"Oh?"

Pachuca bared his lips in an unpleasant gap-toothed yellow smile. "I think that Your Excellency would do well to leave for Huesca," he said. "As soon as possible."

Mercader did not appreciate being told what to do by his subordinates, and he was irritated by the faintly triumphant smirk on the lowly *familiar's* face.

"And why is that?" he asked.

"Commissioner Herrero wishes me to inform you that he has arrested Pedro Segura."

ON THE MORNING AFTER HIS RETURN, Mendoza summoned his men to the village hall and gave them new instructions. From now on, no one was to leave the village for any reason until further notice, even to work the fields, without authorization. Firewood, water and forage would be collected by organized teams with an armed escort, and all animals were to remain inside Belamar. Sentries and street patrols were to keep their braziers and torches burning throughout the night in order to deter any potential intruders and see that the streets were well lit.

These orders were proclaimed by the *pregonero* and only added to the collective mood of expectation, fear and dread in the village as the suppressed tensions and anxieties of the last month now found their outlet in the groups of neighbors who stood outside their homes seeking solace in numbers, listening to the latest rumors and sightings of bandits who could be seen moving across the fields or looking down on the village from the overhanging cliff as though they no longer even felt the need to hide themselves.

Mendoza spent most of the day ensuring that his orders were complied with. He was standing by the village wall looking over the ravine when he heard a trumpet sound from the tower. He immediately went to the *lavadero*, where Necker, Martín and a group of Moriscos were watching a man riding a mule who was being pursued across the valley floor by a larger group of riders, some of whom were shooting at him. The pursuers were gaining ground, and Mendoza ordered Martín to prepare to fire. The militiaman quickly ignited a fuse from the burning brazier and loaded the escopeta.

"Come with me," Mendoza said. Martín, Ventura and the Moriscos followed him to the crest of the hill, till he had a clear view of the lone rider and his pursuers.

"Aim behind him," Mendoza said. "Keep firing until I tell you to stop."

"But, sir, they're out of range."

"Hombre, I don't care if you hit anyone, just shoot!"

Martín fired twice. As Mendoza had hoped, the horsemen immediately slowed down, and the realization that they were being fired upon made them reluctant to come closer, so that their quarry was able to regain lost ground. The militiaman fired two more shots before the horsemen turned back, and the rider raced into town. The Moriscos clustered around him as he nearly fell from the saddle.

"It's Galindo, the miller's son!" one of the Moriscos cried.

Mendoza pushed his way through them. "Where've you come from, Galindo?" he asked.

"From Las Palomas, señor," Galindo replied hoarsely. "I was visiting my sister when they came to the village and attacked it."

"Who attacked it? Give the man some water!"

One of the Moriscos poured from a pitcher into a clay cup, and the miller's son drank it gratefully. "Bandits and mountain men," he said. "The *montañeses* are killing any Moriscos they find and looting their homes. Many houses have been burned. Many people in Las Palomas are dead. My sister and her children escaped to Cardona, but her husband was killed. They say the Inquisition has arrested Dr. Segura, sir. And now the Old Christians are going to destroy Belamar."

"Segura has been arrested?" Mendoza asked. "How? Where?"

"I don't know, sir. But they say he's in Huesca. And Inquisitor Mercader is coming to take him to Zaragoza for trial. Sir, you have to leave Belamar. Everyone must leave or you'll be killed. Cardona is on fire! There are hundreds of them coming. It's like an army!"

"You're a brave man, Galindo," Mendoza said. "Go and see your family now."

He gazed back down the road. He did not know how Segura had been arrested, but it was now clear that no help would be forthcoming. And as improbable as it seemed, Mendoza realized that his investigation was temporarily suspended and that for the time being he and his companions must prepare for war.

"Do you know me, Dr. Segura?"

Segura stared back at the thin little man who was sitting on the opposite side of the table watching him with a faint and almost playful smile that seemed at odds with the sorrowful expression on the statue of Christ in his thorns that was hanging from the wall directly behind him. He knew Commissioner Herrero, who was standing next to the table and wearing a cassock, with his hands folded just below his waist, his tonsured head illuminated by a shaft of light that descended from the high window like a halo. He knew Diego Pachuca the *familiar*, who had accompanied Herrero to Belamar the last time arrests were carried out there. But he did not recognize the little man with the face like a hatchet, and he did not understand how he had come to find himself sitting in an Inquisition jail with his hands chained behind his back, because his memory of the last two days was still hazy.

He knew that he'd done everything Mendoza had suggested and that it had worked out well. He concealed himself in the woods and watched the bandits ride past toward the Huesca road. He then threaded his way through the forest toward Jaca, taking care to avoid the road, and made his way directly to Corregidor Calvo's office. He told the corregidor about Péris and Sánchez and the bandits who had killed the king's special constable and tried to kill the *licenciado* himself during their return from France. He passed on Mendoza's request to call up the militia, and Calvo promised to send out messengers that same day.

At that point he was eager to return to his family, but Calvo insisted that the roads were not safe and that he would do better to return to Belamar with the militia the following day. This was sensible advice, and the corregidor had kindly given him money to pay for food and accommodation at the pilgrims' inn. He remembered eating supper at a local tavern and stepping out into the darkened street to return to the inn, which was only a few minutes away. He remembered how his legs seemed suddenly to turn to water and the street began to roll beneath his feet.

He remembered thinking that he must have been ill or eaten

something that did not agree with him, as he held on to the wall to keep himself upright. But soon the walls, too, seemed to be shifting, and he felt himself falling, and there was nothing he could do about it. That was the last he'd seen of Jaca. Sometime later he found himself lying in a cart, covered with straw, his hands and feet tied, a gag around his mouth and a bag over his head. He remembered struggling to free himself, and then someone hit him hard on the head with a stick and he passed out again.

It was not until they untied his feet and dragged him from the cart that he returned to consciousness, but even then they had to hold him up, because his legs were too weak to carry him. They took off the gag and removed the bag, and he saw Pachuca and the warden for the first time and knew that he was in the hands of the Inquisition. He wanted to ask them questions, but his tongue would not even form the words as they dragged him down the stone steps and along a torchlit corridor where they unlocked a heavy door and chained him to the wall of a cell that smelled of urine and dank straw.

That was two days ago. And since then he had not seen anyone except the jailer, who brought him food twice a day and did not speak to him. He had spent his time in darkness, unable to stand or even lie down properly or do anything except kick out at the rats that scuttled around his feet and pray to Allah to suppress the terror that threatened to turn to hysteria. From time to time, he fell into something like sleep, until the cold, the discomfort or the rats woke him. In his worst moments, he felt as though God had abandoned him, and he did not know why. And it was only now, on the afternoon of his third day in captivity, that Pachuca and the warden had come to his cell and chained him up and brought him back up the stairs, to face the pale official with the thin-lipped smile.

"I don't know you," Segura said finally. "But I think you are Inquisitor Mercader of the Inquisition of Aragon."

"'His Excellency Inquisitor Mercader' to you, Morisco," Herrero corrected him.

"Well, you may not know me, but I know a great deal about you," Mercader said. "In fact, I have been looking forward to this meeting for a very long time."

"I have no idea why."

"I think you do," Mercader insisted. "And there will be an opportunity for us to talk about that. But it will save me a great deal of trouble if you confess."

"Confess to what?"

"Come now, Moor. I'm not someone to play games with. Tell me what I want to know and you may also be able to do something for your children before you leave this earth."

Segura looked at him with alarm. "What have my children got to do with this?"

"Tomorrow I will go to Cardona," Mercader replied calmly. "I will arrest the countess and your daughters Susana and Juana, and your two eldest sons. I shall read out the Edict of Grace that your protectors tried to prevent. And then I will cleanse the stain upon the kingdom and remove every trace of your damned sect from Belamar. But if you confess freely to all your crimes, I promise you that your children will not be put to the fire."

"Before God I have committed no crime!"

"You dare to mention your God in my presence, Moor?"

"There is not my God or your God," Segura insisted. "Only the same God who judges us all, with a different name."

Mercader looked at him with disgust. "You damned heretic. Do you think that we don't know what happens when His Majesty's back is turned? Did you really expect that we would allow you to remain in our lands and continue to foul our Church forever? Our Christian martyrs were prepared to die for their faith, but you Moriscos only lie and dissemble for yours, while you dream of some Redeemer who will come and save you. But no longer. We will wipe you out. Every one of you. Till one day there will be no trace of Moor in Spain and no stink of the whoremongering prophet that your ancestors enforced on us."

"You tell me about force?" Segura exclaimed.

"I do," Mercader said. "And I promise you that the next time you see your children, Dr. Segura, it will be at the auto in Zaragoza. You will be gagged so that you will not be able to speak to them or say good-bye to them. And then you will burn. There is nothing you can do to prevent that. But you can at least save your children. Confess and you have my word that I will be merciful. If you don't, I will make certain that they burn before you do. And that will be the last thing you ever see."

Segura stared back at the cold, hateful eyes. "I will confess only to Allah. Not to the Christian bloodhounds who insult his Prophet."

The warden raised the baton and brought it down hard across Segura's collarbone, hard enough to hurt him yet not to break it. But Mercader was almost smiling as he ordered the prisoner to be returned to his cell, because he and Segura knew that the mayor had already begun to make the confession that would soon be extracted from him.

From what the miller's son had told them, Mendoza guessed that they had at least one day before they were attacked. He immediately dispatched the town crier to summon the population to the main square and sent his men around the village to spread the same message. Within an hour of the *pregonero*'s call, the square was so tightly packed that some people were forced to climb onto the overlooking roofs while others crowded into any available windows and balconies. Others clogged the surrounding streets, where excited children who had not grasped the reasons for the congregation ran around laughing and shouting excitedly, as if they were celebrating a village festival.

Some of the Moriscos were carrying bundles of their possessions and were clearly poised to take flight, and as soon as Mendoza appeared in the upstairs window of the town hall, the crowd fell silent. Until that moment he had not really thought about what he was going to say, and as he looked out at the anxious, expectant faces, he remembered the speech that Tacitus had placed in the mouth of the Caledonian chieftain Calgacus and of Cortés telling his soldiers to burn their ships.

"People of Belamar!" he shouted. "Tomorrow you will be attacked by men who want to destroy you! These men are your enemies, and they are also the enemies of your mistress and of His Majesty. They have already shown that they will kill without mercy. You all know what happened to the del Río family. Now they have destroyed Las Palomas, and they will destroy Belamar if you allow them to enter it."

For a few moments, it was impossible to continue, as the Moriscos began shouting at him and also at one another. Mendoza raised his arms and demanded quiet.

"All of you know that I came to this village as a representative of the king's justice," he went on. "And I have found myself in a village without justice, where men who disgraced the Church have exploited and oppressed you. I know you have no reason to trust me. Some of you may know that Dr. Segura has been arrested by the Inquisition. I assure you that I had nothing to do with this. And let me tell you now that I speak to you as a former soldier in the king's armies. There is no escape from what is about to happen. Belamar is already surrounded. The roads are cut off. Try to run and they will hunt you down in the mountains and kill you, and you will also make it easier for them to kill those who are left behind. No one can help us. Your survival depends on your willingness to fight for your families and your homes and to remain calm and obey my orders."

The crowd was absolutely silent now as Mendoza explained how the village was to be defended. A barricade was to be erected in front of the main entrance by the end of the day, and additional barricades were to be established farther back on the streets and in any available entrance to the town, using carts, church benches or whatever else was available. Stones, bricks and anything that could be thrown were to be carried onto rooftops and the wall overlooking the ravine, and firing positions were to be selected as soon as they knew how many guns and crossbows were available.

The village hall was to serve as a field hospital, and he needed volunteers to gather water and mattresses, plus shirts and cloth that could be used for bandages. All men who were able to fight were to get their weapons, return to the main square and report to Constable Necker and Sergeant Ventura. Women and the elderly were to take shelter in the church. The neighbors in every ten houses were to form work details and assign a foreman to direct them. Work on the village's defenses was to continue throughout the night.

As soon as he had finished, the square erupted into noisy chaos.

Ventura congratulated Mendoza as he withdrew from the balcony and went downstairs, where he was surprised to find Juana Segura waiting for him.

"I will take charge of the hospital," she said. "And I'll bring volunteers to help me."

"Are you sure you can do this?" he asked. "This is war."

"I've seen blood before, and my father has shown me what to do," Juana replied. "Without him I'm the best-qualified person in the village."

"Thank you."

"I'm not doing it for you," she said coldly, and turned to walk away.

WITHIN MINUTES the first volunteers began to assemble in the square with their weapons. Half an hour later, more than a hundred men of various ages had presented themselves to their two commanders. Some carried lances, some swords, and there was a sprinkling of pistols, hunting rifles, escopetas and harquebuses. But the majority were armed with stakes, or homemade bills or halberds made from farming tools, or pikes with knives tied to long sticks, or with axes and clubs. It was not the most impressive arsenal, Mendoza thought, and it certainly did not bear out the reports that the Moriscos of Belamar were stockpiling weapons and gunpowder, unless they were intent on committing collective suicide.

Throughout the afternoon more Moriscos began to trickle into the village with tales of burning, killing and destruction. Ventura and Necker formed the volunteers into separate groups and details and gave them at least the semblance of a command structure, with designated runners who knew their officers by sight and a mobile group of fighters able to move to where the defenses were weakest. Alongside the fighting groups, men, women and even young children gathered stones, bricks and roof tiles. One detail set to work dismantling the ruined house near the mill, to use its bricks and rotting beams for barricades. Others piled carts, beds and household furniture, dug shallow trenches and sharpened stakes to make primitive chevaux-de-frise.

Even old men and women carried stones in baskets or in their skirts down to the old medieval walls or brought food and water to their fathers and brothers. Some of them also brought food to Mendoza and his men without being asked. Mendoza was struck by the transformation that had taken place since the day he and his team first arrived. Having once feared them, the Moriscos now appeared to accept them as their defenders and fellow fighters. Necker had acquired an entourage of children who followed him everywhere and competed with one another to carry out his orders or run an errand for him, while many of the Moriscos now called Mendoza's men by their first names.

The Moriscos continued to work purposefully and resolutely into the evening with a cheerful confidence that Mendoza had often seen in soldiers on the eve of battle, who had convinced themselves that others, not themselves, would die and who knew that their chance of victory was dependent on one another. The response of the other Old Christians was more mixed. Those with Morisco wives and husbands immediately joined in the defense of the village, and so did some of the Old Christian families without Morisco connections. One Old Christian shepherd told Mendoza that his Morisca wife was more

Christian than he was and that he would rather die with her than leave her. Two Old Christian millers approached him and said that the village was home to all of them and that all of them should fight for it.

The baker Romero was noticeably absent from these efforts. Shortly after Mendoza's speech, he closed his shop, until Mendoza ordered him to open it and make extra bread throughout the day to add to the village's food supply. When he refused, Mendoza threatened to arrest him and told him that the bread would be distributed free if an attack took place.

The baker was furious and was only partly mollified when Mendoza told him that he would not have to pay for the flour from the mill. From time to time, Mendoza saw him scowling in the doorway of his shop with his arms crossed, sometimes with his wife beside him. In the late afternoon, Mendoza and Gabriel were standing outside the village hall watching Juana and her female volunteers tearing and cutting shirts, skirts and sheets into bandages when they spotted Romero and his wife coming toward them, followed by a small group of frightened-looking Old Christians.

"Licenciado Mendoza, we wish to speak with you in private," the baker announced pompously.

"You can speak to me here," Mendoza replied.

"We wish to leave Belamar in the morning," he said. "This is not our fight."

The other Old Christians nodded and murmured in assent, and Mendoza looked at them in disgust.

"This is not your fight?" he repeated. "Isn't this your *pueblo*?" He gestured toward the Moriscos who were hurrying back and forth across the square carrying bricks and furniture. "Are these not your neighbors?"

"They are Moriscos, Licenciado," Romero said. "It is not right that we should be forced to take part in this battle and that our families should be in danger. Our blood is clean."

"Enough!" barked Mendoza. "So you feel closer to these bandits and murderers than you do to the town where your own children were born? Why do you live here? What do you think will happen when this is over, that you will just return to your homes as if nothing happened? No, I won't make you fight, but you will not leave. And you will work alongside your neighbors to prepare the town, or I will lock you up."

"You have no right to do this!" Romero exclaimed.

"I have all the right I need. Now, go and get to work before I change my mind and lock you all up."

Gabriel and Juana exchanged complicit smiles as Romero and his wife withdrew to their shop and the other Old Christians left the square, looking chastened. Mendoza was not amused. Tomorrow he knew that some of those who were working to defend the village would be killed, and if the whole lot of them did not fight well, they would all die, and he and his men would die with them. If that happened, then there would be nothing left of Belamar, and the king and his ministers would never know what Mendoza now knew for certain: that everything that had taken place in Cardona since the murder of the priest and possibly even before it had been nothing more than a piece of theater or a game of chess in which the Moriscos, the bandits, the mountain men and their victims were only pawns being moved by unseen hands for purposes that would always be hidden, unless he survived to report them.

. . .

MERCADER HAD ORDERED the curtains on the left side of the carriage drawn because the sunlight irritated his skin condition. From the opposite window, he watched the mountains and valleys tediously unfold as the carriage bumped its way up the dusty road toward Vallcarca. The inquisitor did not like mountains. He disliked their extremes of heat and cold, their steep ascents and descents and the bone-crunching roads that turned into muddy swamps whenever it rained. Centuries ago these mountains had provided a refuge for monks fleeing the infidel invaders. Now they sealed off God's chosen people from their heretic enemies.

True civilization was not found in such places but down on the plains, in cities like Zaragoza, Madrid or Seville. And of all the cities he had ever seen, none was more beautiful or more civilized than Rome. As he stared out the window, he pictured the palazzos, villas and churches, the noble ruins and tree-covered hills, the wide streets and paved squares that he'd first seen when his father had taken him there at the age of twelve. Ever since then he had dreamed of inhabiting one of those palazzos. Or he might have one built himself, according to a design that would reflect his power and status, with comfortable rooms, and white marble corridors, and paintings by the finest Italian artists that he would personally commission, a palace that would remind the world of his presence long after he had departed it.

Compared with what Rome had to offer, even the grandest towns and cities in the Pyrenees were like pale imitations of something better, and even their most illustrious residents seemed to have modeled their thoughts, clothing and furniture on those of the inhabitants of the cities below them. Such places were to be endured rather than enjoyed, but Mercader had to endure them if he was to obtain his red cap and his palace by the Tiber, because the road to Rome led through filthy mountain inns and provincial cities like Huesca and Jaca that reeked of dung and echoed with the sounds of the barnyard, where second-rate officials like Corregidor Calvo and Commissioner Herrero grazed out their lives in obscurity.

Such men lacked the ambition or the talent to rise further, but for him the mountains of Aragon were stepping-stones to the Vatican, and now, as he sat bumping and rocking in the carriage with Herrero and the notary Esquivel, the pains in his backside were worth enduring, because he could not allow Herrero to take credit for Segura's arrest and for the other momentous events that were about to unfold.

That glory belonged to him alone. He had brought with him letters from Inquisitor-General Valdés and Bishop Santos giving him permission to conduct a full inquisitorial investigation into the Morisco heresy at Belamar. He also had verbal assurances from Herrero that the Baron of Vallcarca would provide him with an armed escort when he went to Belamar to read out the Edict of Grace and throughout the investigation. Vallcarca had even promised him the use of his own prisons until he was ready to transport his prisoners back to Zaragoza.

This was not strictly orthodox, but the baron's men would not actually make arrests and would only assist the Inquisition in doing so, just as they had done with the Moriscos Navarro and Royo. This assistance was now essential, since Mercader's own escort of ten men was only slightly larger than the one they had brought from Zaragoza, and that might not be enough to deter the countess and her bailiff. Both Herrero and Vallcarca had assured him that the road to

Vallcarca was safe and that ten men would be sufficient to take them to the *señorio*, where many more would be waiting.

"I trust that the monastery is more comfortable than this," he said as a bump in the road jarred his spine yet again.

"It's one of the oldest in Vallcarca, Excellency," Herrero replied.

Mercader looked dubious. Age did not guarantee comfort as far as monasteries were concerned, and an anchorite's bed was not what he required at the end of such a journey, when a feather mattress and silk sheets would do much better.

"And where does Mendoza stay?"

"I believe he's staying at Dr. Segura's dispensary, sir."

"Well, he's going to have a lot more room now."

Herrero and Esquivel smiled politely at this rare example of humor from the inquisitor, and Mercader wondered how Mendoza would react to his arrival. He doubted that the man would be pleased, but he would not dare oppose the investigation when he saw the inquisitor-general's letter. They followed the road through a wide river valley broken by patches of forest and occasional villages, and Mercader was on the point of dozing off when there was a shot from just outside the carriage, followed by a series of sharp hissing noises.

He heard a heavy thump on the carriage roof, the gargled cry, the agitated neighing of horses and the unmistakable sound of sharp objects cutting flesh before the carriage came to an abrupt halt. Both the notary and Herrero looked frightened as the door opened and Diego Pachuca appeared. For a moment Mercader felt almost comforted at the sight of his *familiar*'s blood-spattered face and the bloody knife in his hand, but then his relief turned to horror as Pachuca reached past him and thrust the blade almost up to the hilt into Esquivel's chest.

"For the love of God, man, what are you doing?" Mercader cried.

Esquivel made a horrible gurgling sound as he straightened up slightly, as if he were about to get out of the carriage, before sitting back lifeless, his eyes still open and his head lolling to one side. Herrero tried to open the other door, but as he did so, another shot rang out, and he fell back onto the seat holding his face. Mercader stared in horror at the bloodstained hole where Herrero's eye had been when Pachuca grabbed his collar with his thick, hairy fingers and pulled him closer, till their faces were almost touching, then sank the knife into his stomach.

The inquisitor doubled over with pain and shock. He felt the *familiar*'s stubble brushing against his face and caught a faint smell of wine on his breath before Pachuca dragged him from the carriage, held him upright with one hand and slashed him across the throat in a deft horizontal stroke. As Mercader fell to the ground, he had time to see the green-and-black-clad bodies lying around him and the men on horseback and on foot with pistols, swords and crossbows whom he did not know.

To his astonishment Mercader realized that he was dying, and he wished that he could have lived a little longer, just long enough to ask Pachuca why he was killing him. But he did not even have the strength to cry out as Pachuca and one of his companions lifted him up by his hands and feet. The inquisitor caught a last glimpse of the blue Spanish sky and wondered what he had done to incur God's wrath, and then he felt himself sinking down into the cold waters, and he knew that he would never make it to Rome.

CHAPTER TWENTY-ONE

ENDOZA WOKE WITH A DRY MOUTH AND A tightness in his stomach that he hadn't felt since Lepanto. He had slept in his clothes, and he stepped barefoot across the darkened room and pushed back the shutters. The sun was not yet visible, but the gray sky was already tinged with purple as he heard the cock crow. It seemed incredible to think that this might be the beginning of his last day on earth. Lepanto had been his last battle, and he had not expected to fight another, let alone against Christians in his own country.

The prospect of his own death did not frighten him; he'd been in danger too many times for that. But he felt sorry that he had placed Gabriel at risk. He felt sorry for Daniel, who had died because of him. His decision to visit Péris had also brought about the wood-carver's death, and though he felt little sympathy for Péris himself, the distraught expression on his widow's face had reminded Mendoza that he was responsible for that man's death, too. And now it seemed that Segura would burn at the stake, thanks to him.

All this filled Mendoza with a mixture of guilt and frustration, because for the time being at least it was not possible to take action against Vallcarca, Mercader and the other men who were seemingly prepared to set all of Cardona on fire in order to achieve their aims. And if things went badly today, then he would have failed completely, and all the deaths that had already taken place would have no meaning.

He put on his boots and buttoned his doublet before going to wake Gabriel, who was still snoring peacefully, his mouth open.

"Wake up, boy," he said gently.

Gabriel opened his eyes and immediately sat up like a startled deer. "Has it begun, sir?"

"Not yet. Get dressed."

Mendoza returned to his room, buckled on his sword and clipped a pistol to his belt. He was filling his pockets with ammunition and dangled a powder bottle from a strap around his shoulder when Gabriel came in, wearing the sword that Mendoza still could not get used to seeing on him.

"Ready?" he asked.

"Yes, sir."

They went downstairs and out into the street. Outside the village hall, small groups of armed men were standing around talking quietly while women came and went carrying trays laden with bread, cakes, buns and pitchers of water. Inside, they found Juana Segura with two Morisca volunteers and four stretcher-bearers, eating from a tray heaped high with curd patties. Her father's desk was piled with bandages, medicine bottles, ointments and a bowl containing a poultice mixture. A sword and a wooden lance were leaning against the wall behind it. Another table was lined with bowls of water, and there were mattresses and a pile of straw on the floor, in addition to two planks to be used as stretchers.

Gabriel visibly brightened at the sight of Juana, and she looked no less pleased to see him as she invited them to eat an empanada. Mendoza was not hungry, but he accepted one in an attempt to reduce the nervous agitation in his stomach. Gabriel also took one, and Mendoza noticed that his hand was trembling slightly, when Necker appeared in the doorway.

"Good morning, sir."

"Is everything in order, Constable?"

"As much as it can be," Necker replied. "Sir, can I have a word in private?"

The pie was surprisingly tasty, and Mendoza took another one and followed the German outside.

"Sir, I have to report that I observed some of the Moriscos at the cemetery praying this morning," Necker said in a low voice, looking around him warily.

"And? It's what men do before battle."

"Sir, I don't believe they were Christian prayers. They were bowing, not kneeling."

"I see. Have you prayed this morning, Constable?"

"Yes, sir."

"Then let us hope your prayers have been heard. And for the time being, let us not concern ourselves with whom these Moriscos pray to, as long as their prayers help them to fight better."

In that moment the lookout in the church tower let out three blasts. Outside, some of the Moriscos were pointing at the ridge above the ravine, where a line of moving men could be seen like a row of ants carrying large pins.

"Return to your position, Constable," Mendoza said. He hurried away from the square with Gabriel trailing along behind him. As soon as they were out of sight, he stopped and said, "I want you to go to the church."

Gabriel looked aghast. "But, sir, the church is for women and children."

"And I am holding you responsible for them," Mendoza said. "I made a promise to Magdalena that you would come back alive, and I intend to keep it. Go to the church and stay there. Those are my orders."

Gabriel continued to look so abject and humiliated that Mendoza reached out and tweaked his ear affectionately. "God bless you, boy. And know that whatever happens today, I will always hold you in the highest esteem."

Mendoza turned back down the main street, past the ramshackle inner barricade where a group of Moriscos were waiting with a collection of steel and wooden weapons.

"Courage, señores," he said. "Remember you are fighting for your homes today."

The Moriscos nodded, but some of them were no older than Gabriel, and their fear was obvious. Ventura presented a very different spectacle. He was sitting calmly on the edge of the *lavadero* while Martín and a group of about twenty armed Moriscos looked down at the valley, where a large mass of men was moving slowly along the road toward the village. His cousin appeared relaxed and at ease, as he always did on these occasions, and some of the Moriscos were clearly mystified and fascinated by his calm demeanor.

"There you are, cousin," he said. "I was beginning to think you were going to sleep through this."

"I tried." Mendoza glanced at the two intertwined tree trunks and a cluster of stakes jutting upward in front of a shallow trench that had been constructed just inside the entrance to the town. "I see you've been busy."

"It won't keep them out, but it may slow them down."

Mendoza studied the advancing column below. At first sight it looked like a single prickly mass, but as it drew closer, he saw that there were gaps and bulges in their formation that suggested an armed mob rather than a disciplined army.

"How many do you think there are?" he asked.

"A hundred. Maybe a hundred and fifty."

"There might be the same numbers coming down from the ridge. It looks like they're going to come along the road and the ravine."

"The wall and the cemetery are well defended," Ventura said. "The other entrances are all blocked. They're too narrow for that many to get through anyway."

"How many guns do we have?"

"Five harquebuses and three hunting rifles, two escopetas and about twenty pistols, but plenty of wood and steel and men who want to fight." Ventura grinned at the watching Moriscos. "Are you ready to fight, brothers?"

"Yes!" the Moriscos chorused back.

"I asked if you'll fight!" Ventura roared.

This time the response was more aggressive and visceral.

"Then I'll fight with you!" Ventura raised his sword high. Mendoza noticed that his wounded arm remained stiffly by his side, and he suspected that his cousin had aggravated his wound during the night's preparations. The Moriscos now took up their positions in a line behind the trench, and Martín and two harquebusiers crouched down near the barricade. Behind them they heard the sound of shooting coming from the direction of the ravine. Some of the Moriscos peered around nervously, and Ventura told them to keep looking downward as the bandits and *montañeses* drew closer. The front ranks were mounted on horses, mules and donkeys, and some horsemen were riding back and forth on either side of the columns in an attempt to coordinate their movements and keep them in some kind of order.

Soon the front of the column reached the point where the road began to climb upward, and the horsemen disappeared. They appeared a few minutes later at the brow of the hill, followed by a churning sea of armed fighters wearing an assortment of head scarves, morions, leather doublets and metal breastplates. Some wore white tunics with red crosses. Others were barefoot and wore clothes made from animal skins. They continued to swarm over the hill, spilling off the road and brandishing their weapons as they yelled insults and threats.

"Morisco dogs!"

"Heretics!"

"Murderers!"

One of the horsemen raised his sword above his head, and the noise immediately subsided.

"For Spain and Saint James!" he yelled. The ragged army of bandits, shepherds and would-be Crusaders echoed back the refrain that Mendoza himself had shouted in very different circumstances, and then the sword fell downward. With a great roar, the soldiers and horsemen came charging toward them.

Martín fired three times, his companion fired twice, and five bodies fell before the first wave of men and horses crashed into the cheval-de-frise. Ventura and the Moriscos surged forward, stabbing, slashing and jabbing at them with the swords and stakes while others fired crossbows down from the roofs of the outlying buildings. For the first time in thirteen years, Mendoza heard the sounds of battle as the street echoed with the crack of pistol shots, clashing swords, the wild neighing of horses and the grunts and curses of fighting men.

The Moriscos fought with furious desperation as the horsemen fired at them and the bandits and *montañeses* swarmed over the barricade. Mendoza saw one Morisco die from a pistol shot and another from a sword thrust to the throat, while yet another let out a terrible scream as a halberd swept down and nearly cleaved his arm at the shoulder. One bandit was pulled down onto a stake. Others screamed as they fell under the horses' hooves or were trampled by their companions. Despite the Moriscos' tenacious resistance, their line of defense began to bulge almost immediately from the sheer weight of numbers as the foot soldiers clambered over the barricades while the horsemen fired with pistols down at the defenders.

Within minutes it was difficult to determine where one side ended and another began as the bandits pushed their way in through the slender gap between the washroom and the opposite wall. Mendoza stood at the *lavadero* with Necker's spare pistol and calmly shot one of the horsemen. He quickly reloaded, but there was no time to fire another shot as the Moriscos dropped back and the bandits poured through the gap. He clipped the pistol onto his belt and ran out into the street with his sword in one hand and his stick in the other, pushing and shoving the Moriscos and shouting at them to turn and face the enemy and line up their weapons in a semblance of order as the bandits dragged the barricades and the horses pushed their way in through the narrow funnel, and the crush of bodies continued to push them inexorably backward.

OVER BY THE VILLAGE WALL, a very different battle was unfolding as the bandits and *montañeses* scrambled up the path and terraces, taking shelter behind the olive and apple trees or ducking beneath the terraces as the Moriscos fired pistols and crossbows and hurled rocks and stones down upon them. Necker raced back and forth between the cemetery and the lower wall, encouraging, cajoling and bullying the defenders and pointing out targets and gaps to be filled. He had positioned his two harquebusiers and five pistoleers at the point where the cemetery wall curved up and overlooked the terraces, so that they could fire at a downward angle into them.

From this distance it was difficult to miss, but there were so many attackers swarming up the terraces that they kept on coming even as their dead and wounded comrades fell in front of them. Some of them were carrying ladders, and others took up positions behind the trees and fired back at the Moriscos, forcing them to duck behind the walls. The shooting was also coming from behind them. One woman was shot down as she ran toward the wall from the cemetery, and Necker saw the harquebusiers firing at them from the cliff overlooking the town.

The Moriscos were beginning to leave their positions to seek cover from the crossfire, so that the bandits were able to get close enough to the walls to use their ladders. Others cupped their hands and hoisted each other up till they began spilling over the walls, pushing the defenders back toward the road and driving Necker and his men back into the cemetery. Necker ordered one of the harquebusiers to take up a position in the church tower and fire at the cliff.

Farther up the road, Gabriel and a group of Moriscos watched anxiously as the harquebusier came running at them in a low crouch and ran into the church. Gabriel still felt afraid as he watched the bandits fighting their way up the road toward him, but he knew that he would not run and that he would stay and fight for those who were inside the church, even if he died in the process. From where he was standing, he could see that the fighting in the cemetery was savage as the Moriscos and bandits closed on one another among the tombstones with knives and swords, in some cases writhing on the ground with their hands on each other's throats, pummeling each other like drunkards in a tavern brawl, till men fell dying or wounded among the already dead, and still the bandits continued to clamber over the wall.

Gabriel watched all this as he stiffened himself for the fight he knew would come. He was promising himself that he would do nothing to make his guardian ashamed of him when he heard the shot from directly above him. He looked up and saw the smoking harquebus pointing from the church tower toward the cliff, and a body tumbled down from the rock face into the town. Other shots quickly followed, and the firing from the cliff became more sporadic. Some of it was now directed against the church tower, pinging off the bell with a deep metallic gong, but the harquebusier continued to fire steadily back.

Still the bandits continued to pour up the hill. All over the road between the church and the old wall, men were fighting with swords and stabbing and hacking at each other with halberds, lances and billhooks. Necker and the Moriscos had fallen back now to protect the church, and Gabriel felt comforted and emboldened by the imposing presence of the German nearby as a group of bandits surged up the road, yelling and waving their weapons. Now the battle engulfed them, and there was no longer any time to think about what might happen as instinct took over and he jabbed his sword in the vague direction of the faces and bodies.

He felt the blade penetrate soft flesh and heard someone cry out in pain. Beside him a Morisco raised his hand to his neck, where a halberd blade had cut him. Gabriel saw the blood gushing from the wound, and the sight of the man's wild, staring eyes filled him with terror and also with fury. He was no longer conscious of anything but the fighting raging around him as he stabbed and slashed at the men who wanted to kill him and whom he wanted only to kill. For a few minutes, the two sides seemed evenly matched and neither was able to gain ground, and then the mobile fighters whom Ventura had withheld as reinforcements joined the Morisco ranks, and they began to push the bandits back down the road.

Suddenly the bandit line broke and the attackers began to run down toward the wall, and Necker and the Moriscos charged forward, letting out fierce, incoherent cries. Gabriel heard himself yelling, too, as he ran forward waving his bloodstained sword. It was only then that he noticed that one of the bandits had not run down the road but had managed to get around the church and was struggling to open the door. Without even thinking he ran toward the man. The bandit turned and raised his sword, but he had no time to bring it down before Gabriel thrust his sword into his stomach, all his weight behind it, and pinned him up against the wooden door.

· · ·

IN THE NARROW FUNNEL between the *lavadero* and the main square, the attackers were also gaining ground as more men and horses poured in through the main entrance. Mendoza had withdrawn to the second barricade and watched as Ventura and his men were driven slowly back. His cousin was at the front as always, despite his wounded arm, and as Mendoza watched the fighting, it occurred to him for the first time that Ventura's courage was not simply the result of an indifference to death and that perhaps there was a part of him that actually wanted to die.

Soon the fighting engulfed them, too, and Ventura and his men joined them at the barricade. Now the young men Mendoza had seen nervously standing at the barricade less than an hour before found themselves at the front line and stabbed and chopped with their homemade weapons as the bandits and *montañeses* hurled themselves against them. Once again the barricade was breached, and again the distinctions between attackers and defenders broke down as the two sides dissolved into a fluid melee. Some of the attackers crashed through the Morisco defense and ran toward the main square, only to be turned back by Morisco reserves freed by the battle at the church.

The entire street from the main square to the *lavadero* had now become a battlefield that echoed with the sounds of screams, curses, shots and clashing swords. Ventura and Necker were still trying to form the Moriscos into compact lines, but all semblance of military discipline had fallen apart on both sides as men and women hurled tiles, pots and pieces of furniture down on them from the upper windows and the bandits shot at them with their crossbows and pistols.

Although the horses helped push the Moriscos back, the narrow street and the crush of bodies made it difficult for them to maneuver and exposed their riders to attack from the ground and also from the rooms and rooftops above them. Some of the Morisca women who had not taken shelter in the church now joined their men, just as they had in Granada, and charged at the bandits with kitchen knives, chair legs and frying pans. After more than an hour of this, exhaustion forced a temporary respite, and bandits and Moriscos ducked into doorways or sheltered behind the remains of barricades and dead horses to pause for breath and curse one another. But then the fighting resumed once again, and the bandits continued to push them back toward the village hall.

Mendoza's sword arm was aching, and he shouted at the Moriscos to hold their positions as they fell back toward the main square. At the far end of the street near the *lavadero*, Ventura pointed out the Catalan, who was waving his silver mace and urging his men onward. He yelled at Martín to try to shoot him, but the constant forward movement of men and horses made it impossible for him even to load his weapon, let alone fire it.

Whether it was the Catalan's galvanizing influence or the realization that they were within reach of the Plaza Mayor, the bandits and *montañeses* now seemed to sense that victory was at hand, and some of them formed themselves into something resembling a phalanx and pushed forward in a close, compact mass. Most of the fighting was taking place on the main street or spilling out into the surrounding streets and alleyways, but some of the bandits with firearms fought or broke their way into the houses and took up firing positions in the upper windows and balconies.

Mendoza had taken shelter in an open doorway, and he managed to shout at Martín to go inside and fire back. Within a few minutes, the militiaman was exchanging shots with the bandits on the other side of the street. Mendoza was still standing just inside the doorway when he heard a shot from his side of the street and a Morisco collapsed right in front of him. Leaning out, he saw a bandit firing a harquebus down from a first-floor window only two houses away from where he was standing. The bandit was out of the line of fire of Martín and his companions, and he seemed able to pick out his targets at will as he calmly fired at the Moriscos and reloaded.

Mendoza fired at him with his pistol, but a moment later the harquebusier leaned out and fired again, and another Morisco fell, holding his arm. Mendoza edged his way along the wall past the mass of fighting men and slipped into the half-open doorway. Inside the house it was cool and dark, and the noises of the battle were slightly muffled as he paused to reload his pistol and made his way up the wooden stairs, which despite his caution creaked loudly with each step. He hoped that the noise in the street would conceal his presence from the sharpshooter upstairs, and when he reached the first floor, he was surprised to see that the balcony was empty.

For a moment he thought that the bandit might have been shot, but there was no sign of his body. He peered around the corner and immediately ducked back as he saw the flash in the darkened bedroom doorway, and the ball smashed into the wall behind him. He stepped into the room and fired at the doorway, but now the bandit was rushing toward him holding the harquebus by the barrel with both hands and swinging it like a club. The butt caught Mendoza a painful blow on the left shoulder, pushing him back onto the stairs. He drew his sword, but it was difficult to get within striking distance as the bandit jabbed the butt repeatedly at his face.

Mendoza retreated step by step as the bandit thrust the gun at him in an attempt to keep him at a distance. One blow caught him on the chin so that he stepped back and nearly lost his footing. Sensing victory, the bandit dropped the gun, pulled a dagger from behind his belt and hurled himself forward. In the same moment, Mendoza bent down, holding his sword with both hands, and thrust it into the center of the bandit's stomach just below the rib cage. The weight of the bandit's body knocked Mendoza over and sent him tumbling backward to the next floor.

He scrambled to his feet and extricated the sword, pausing to load his pistol once again. Downstairs the Moriscos had been pushed even farther back, and the street immediately in front of him was filled with bandits and *montañeses*. No sooner had he opened the door than some of the bandits came rushing toward him. He slammed the door, bolted it shut and dragged a table in front of it, but it was already beginning to give from the force of bodies as he dropped his stick and stood waiting in the cool darkness with his sword and pistol for the end that now seemed inevitable. He did not feel afraid, but disappointed at the thought that he would have to leave the world so soon. He hoped that Gabriel and the others would die quickly as he prepared to make his attackers pay as high a price for his life as possible.

The door was about to break when he heard two blasts on a trumpet coming from the direction of the *lavadero*. To his surprise, the banging on the door immediately stopped and the noise outside in the street began to recede. He waited a few moments before opening the door. There were now more horsemen than ever in the main entrance, but the Catalan was no longer visible among them, and Ventura and the Moriscos had regained the ground they'd lost.

As he watched the battle unfolding near the *lavadero*, Mendoza realized to his amazement that the bandits were also being attacked from behind and that they were trying to retreat. Within minutes he was back at the main entrance to the village, where an astonishing scene was unfolding. All across the hilltop, bandits were trying to fight their way past the mounted pistoleers and swordsmen wearing red sashes around their waists, who were coming up from the valley below on foot and on horseback. Others tried to avoid the road altogether and jumped down the rocks even as they were being shot at. Some of the bandits and *montañeses* threw down their weapons and begged for mercy from the oncoming horsemen and the advancing Moriscos, and not all of them received it.

As the Moriscos pushed forward to the crest of the hill, they saw bandits riding or running through the ravine and up into the woods in an attempt to escape their pursuers. At last the battle began to ebb, and Mendoza and Ventura gave orders to round up the prisoners. Men, women and children were pouring out of the town now, and they cheered wildly as another horseman came riding up the hill toward them with an upright and almost stately gait, and Mendoza recognized the familiar pennant bearing the lion and shield of the House of Cardona.

CHAPTER TWENTY-TWO

HE VULTURES WERE ALREADY HOVERING over the village as Mendoza made his way back through the main street, past the bodies of men and horses and the wreckage of the barricades. Juana Segura's orderlies were beginning to carry the wounded on planks to the village hall while men and women wept or hugged each other or sat on the street looking dazed and exhausted and astonished to find themselves still alive. In that moment Mendoza was concerned with only one person, and he felt a sick feeling in his stomach when he reached the church to find the door half open and streaked with blood and an unknown body lying on the floor next to it.

Gabriel was not there, but Necker was standing nearby watching the men, women and children who were coming out to inspect the aftermath of the battle that most of them had only heard. His two-handled sword was sheathed, but the splashes of red on his face made it clear that he had used it.

"You held them, Constable."

"We did, sir. And your scrivener fought well."

Mendoza nodded approvingly. "Do you know where he is?"

"In the village hall."

"Good work, Constable. Keep your defenses in place. They may try again."

Mendoza felt positively exultant now as he walked to the main square, which was filling up with wounded men. The stretcher-bearers were bringing in another groaning body on a plank to the village hall, which looked more like a butcher shop. The floor was covered in blood, and the wounded were lying on mattresses or piles of straw or sitting propped against the walls waiting to be treated, while Juana Segura and her assistants stitched, washed and bandaged wounds and hurried back and forth carrying pans of water. Despite the carnage, he suppressed a smile at the sight of his page kneeling over a man who was lying stretched out on a mattress while Segura's daughter prodded with a knife at a bleeding gash in his shoulder. The Morisco was clearly in agony, and Gabriel was leaning his weight against his chest and shoulder in an attempt to hold him down.

"Are you all right, boy?"

"I am, sir." Gabriel looked up and smiled grimly as the man writhed around beneath him. "You're bleeding."

It was only then that Mendoza was conscious of his aching jaw and the blood trickling down his chin. "It's nothing," he said as Juana Segura pressed the point of the knife deeper. "I'll see you later."

Outside, some wounded bandits had also been brought under

guard to the village hall and were waiting outside to be treated. Their guards stood watching as some of the Morisca women insulted and even spit on them. Mendoza ordered the women to leave them alone and walked down past the bodies and the broken barricades to the main entrance, where Ventura's Moriscos and the countess's militiamen were guarding a group of prisoners.

"What shall we do with this rabble, Bernardo?" asked Ventura.

"For now they can carry out the dead. Take the Moriscos to the rectory. You'll have to give up your bedroom and stay with us. We'll take them to the ravine and burn them later."

Mendoza looked down at the valley, where a carriage was coming toward them accompanied by a mounted escort. A few minutes later, it drew up in front of them and the Countess of Cardona stepped off with the help of one of her servants, followed by Susana Segura. She was wearing a long black cloak and a scarlet surcoat embroidered with golden thread, and a white muslin veil hung down over her immaculately braided hair. Mendoza had not seen her since their meeting at Las Palomas, and she looked steely and determined, like a warrior-queen, as she glanced around with a sad, desolate expression at the human and animal corpses and armed men.

"Long live the Countess of Cardona!" one of the Moriscos shouted.

"Long live!" The Moriscos and militia raised their weapons. The countess acknowledged them with a vague nod and smiled at Mendoza. "I'm happy to see you alive, Licenciado."

"And I am glad to see you, my lady," Mendoza replied. "We were very much in need of assistance."

"Is Dr. Segura's family well?"

"They are, my lady."

Susana glanced up at the sky and silently mumbled a prayer. The countess also looked visibly relieved. "Go to your sister," she ordered Susana. "Licenciado, will you join me in my carriage?"

"I'm not sure if it's safe for you to be out here, Countess. There may be sharpshooters."

"Perhaps," she said. "But what I have to tell you cannot wait."

A SERVANT HELD THE DOOR OPEN for the countess and Mendoza and shut the door behind them. "Did you find Vicente Péris?" she asked.

"We did, my lady, but he was murdered. And whoever was responsible also tried to kill us."

"And did you know that Inquisitor Mercader has been murdered? And Commissioner Herrero also?"

Mendoza stared at her in astonishment. "When did this happen?"

"Two days ago. They were murdered on the road from Huesca. They were on their way to Cardona to make arrests. The rumors say that Moriscos from Belamar killed them, but I know who is responsible. My bailiff Jean Sánchez and the Baron of Vallcarca. They are the ones behind everything that has happened here."

Mendoza still did not trust the countess enough to tell her that he had already begun to reach similar conclusions himself, and he listened impassively as she told him about her father-in-law's visit and Vallcarca's attempt to use Mercader's impending investigation to make her marry his son.

"And what makes you so certain that your bailiff was in France?" he asked her.

"He left a message saying that he was visiting his father in Lérida on the day of Espinosa's visit. I sent a servant to bring him back. He found Sánchez's father in rude health, and the old man hadn't seen his son in months."

"Did you have any reason to mistrust him?"

"None," she replied. "It was because I trusted him that I sent my servant to bring him back. Jean's mother was my wet nurse. He was my childhood playmate. I treated him as a member of my own family. I let him run my estates. I made him the most powerful man in Cardona. I wanted him to come back to the estates because I depended on him."

"And you have no idea why he would have turned against you?"

"None. But I'm convinced that he followed you to Béarn."

Mendoza told her what Péris had revealed to Segura and of his belief that Sánchez had killed Péris to conceal his role in luring the three alleged rapists into the hands of the Inquisition.

"Then he must have been working for Vallcarca," the countess said, "because it was the baron's militia that arrested Navarro and his apprentice. And there's something else you ought to know. I believe that Sánchez killed my husband on Vallcarca's orders."

Mendoza raised his eyebrows. This was not a possibility that he had even thought about. "May I know how you reached such conclusions?" he asked.

"Vallcarca told me that I could not defy him after what had happened to my husband! What is that, if not an admission of guilt? And it all makes sense now. Jean was with Miguel on the day he died. He was wounded himself during the attack, with a sword cut to the arm. I used to think he tried to save Miguel. Now I think it was just another deception."

Mendoza nodded and said nothing. Her allegations were certainly possible, but Péris was dead, which meant that there was no one who could testify that Sánchez had been responsible for luring him to Vallcarca. And without the bailiff, there was only the countess's own account of her conversation with Vallcarca to implicate the baron in her husband's murder or the death of Péris or in anything else.

"Well, surely you have enough cause to arrest Vallcarca?" she asked. "Put him to the torment and make him confess!"

Mendoza was surprised by her vehemence, and he also sensed an element of fear behind it. "You say that Vallcarca was using Inquisitor Mercader to blackmail you," he said. "Did he say what offenses you would have been charged with?"

Once again she looked guarded. "Well, he didn't mention anything specific," she replied airily. "I assumed it was heresy or some other concoction."

"But if the two of them were in collusion, then why would Vallcarca kill Mercader?"

"I am a simple woman, Licenciado. I don't understand Vallcarca's machinations. But is it not obvious, after today, that this is a man who is unconstrained by the laws of God and man, who will kill any number of people he thinks necessary to achieve his aims?"

"Someone definitely fits that description," Mendoza admitted. "And I will certainly speak to Vallcarca again. But now, my lady, I think you should return to Cardona. It's not safe for you to be out here."

"Would you like my men to remain to protect the town?"

"I don't think we're going to be attacked again, but you could leave half of them for another day, just in case. And I would like you to take our prisoners. We haven't room for them here. I would also like you to send a messenger to Corregidor Calvo in Jaca. Tell him to send as many men as possible to Belamar as soon as he can. And make sure your messenger has an escort. Enough people have died these last few weeks."

"Very well. And now there is one thing I must ask of you. Dr. Segura is in the Inquisition jail in Huesca. Can you get him released? His family needs him. Belamar needs him."

"That is very difficult, my lady. I have no power to alter the course of an inquisitorial investigation. I don't even know the charges against him."

Just then they heard a sudden commotion outside. Mendoza looked out the window to see two of the countess's militiamen coming up the hill on horseback. One of them was trailing a rope attached to the hands of a prisoner who was walking with obvious difficulty, aided by one of his escorts, and as they came closer, Mendoza was astonished to see that the man at the end of the rope was none other than the bailiff, Jean Sánchez.

MENDOZA GOT DOWN from the carriage and held out his hand to help the countess as the militiamen brought the bailiff over toward them. The haughty official who had once tried to expel him from Cardona was dragging his right leg. His knee was oozing blood through his torn hose. His clothes, face and hair were covered in blood and dust as he stared sullenly at the ground in front of him.

"We found him trying to crawl out of the ravine, my lady," one of the militiamen explained. "He can't walk by himself."

The countess was looking at Sánchez with an expression that was simultaneously sad, reproachful and astonished. "Why, Jean?" she asked. "Was it the money? Didn't I give you enough?"

"I don't have to explain anything to you," Sánchez said bitterly.

"But you will explain yourself to me, villain," said Mendoza, "when I take you to Jaca. This one is my prisoner, my lady."

"Take him," the countess replied. "I never want to see him again."

Mendoza said good-bye to her and accompanied the militiamen and their prisoner back to the village hall while she returned to her carriage. They had almost reached the main square when they saw Susana walking toward them. At the sight of Sánchez, her face hardened.

"What have you done to my father?" she asked.

Sánchez stared at her coldly. "Go to hell, you damned whore," he said.

Susana appeared momentarily disconcerted, and then her anger returned and she smacked the bailiff hard across the face. Sánchez merely shrugged and looked away as Mendoza nodded to the militiamen to take him away. Juana Segura greeted him with equal contempt and refused Mendoza's request to treat his wounded knee until he reminded her that he would not be able to interrogate Sánchez or put him on trial if he died. She cleaned and bandaged the wound, and Mendoza told the militiamen to chain him up in the stable beneath the dispensary. He ordered them to leave and stood in the doorway looking down at the sullen prisoner, who was leaning against a wooden post among the milling goats and sheep.

"You know, I don't normally like to put prisoners to the torment unless I have to," Mendoza said. "But unless you talk to me here, you and I are going to have a very painful conversation when we get to Jaca."

Sánchez gave a faint smirk. "We'll see," he said.

Even though the bailiff could barely walk, Mendoza ordered Martín, Gabriel and Necker to take turns guarding the locked stable door. The rest of the day was spent clearing away the bodies. By nightfall there were fifty bandits and *montañeses* piled up outside the town and forty Moriscos stretched out in the church. Mendoza insisted that sentries remain on alert throughout the night and assigned a special detail to keep a brazier lit near the stack of bandit corpses to keep the animals and vultures away from them. It was not until the early hours that he finally retired to his room and quietly thanked God for allowing him to live before he closed his eyes and slept.

THE NEXT MORNING the Moriscos began to dig graves in the cemetery while others carried the corpses outside the main entrance down into the ravine in carts to be burned. Throughout the day the buzzards and vultures continued to circle hopefully over the village as the smell of burning flesh wafted up from the ravine. There was not enough space for individual graves, and Mendoza told them to dig deeper holes so that the graves could be shared. The men performed these tasks with quiet determination as the women and children continued to distribute food and water. Some of the water was taken to the church, where Segura's sons prepared the bodies. Mendoza deliberately stayed away from it and ordered his own men to do the same so that they would not have to observe what the brothers might be doing.

Sánchez spent the day, as he had spent the night, locked in the back room in chains with Segura's sheep and goats. He spoke only once, when he asked Necker for permission to use the privy. In the evening Mendoza and Gabriel brought him bread, cheese and water from the tavern. They found Necker slumped on the stone bench in front of the fire with his head resting on his chest, and the embarrassed constable apologized profusely as he unlocked the stable door. Sánchez was still sitting in the gloom among the goats and sheep and the horses on the other side of the wooden corral. He did not even look up when Gabriel laid the tray at his feet while Necker unlocked his chains. He ate his meal in silence, and then Gabriel took the tray back. Mendoza sent the exhausted constable to bed and sat down in the alcove.

"When will we question him?" Gabriel asked.

"Tomorrow perhaps," he replied distractedly. He was still wondering why Sánchez had called Susana a whore when he noticed the frown that told him that another question from Gabriel was imminent.

"What is it, boy?" he asked wearily.

"Sir, why did you take me from the orphanage? Was it your decision or your mother's?"

"It was mine. But do we have to talk about this now?"

"Sir, am I a Morisco?"

Mendoza was silent, and he knew from the expression on Gabriel's face that his silence had already answered the boy's question.

"Sir, you know I have always looked up to you and respected you," Gabriel said. "But I have just fought in a battle. I have shed blood. I might have died, and I could still die. Surely this is as good a time as any other to tell me whatever it is that you have not told me."

Mendoza looked at his page. In that moment Gabriel seemed older and wiser than his seventeen years, and Mendoza knew that he was right. This was not a subject he had ever wanted to talk about, but after everything his page had been through, it seemed suddenly impossible to avoid.

"No, you are not Morisco," he said finally. "But your parents were."

For the first time, Mendoza told his page about his service in Granada with the army of the king's half brother, Don Juan of Austria, about the siege of Galera in the Alpujarras and the house-to-house fighting that took place when the Christian troops breached its defenses, about the Morisca woman he killed outside her house and the toddler he found among the heap of corpses inside it. He described how he had pulled the child away from his dead mother and carried him crying out of the burning house, but he could not bring himself to say that the child he rescued was covered in blood that might have been his mother's, because there were some details that he could not speak aloud, not only for his page's sake but for his own. Nevertheless Gabriel looked increasingly distraught as Mendoza continued.

"So you killed my mother?" he asked incredulously.

Mendoza shook his head. "No, boy, I did not. Your mother was killed by a cannon shot. When I entered that house, everybody but you was dead. The woman I killed was too old to be your mother. But if I hadn't killed her, she would certainly have killed me. The Moriscos of Galera were the bravest fighters I ever met—the women as much as the men. We treated them the same. I ordered her to surrender, but she wouldn't. I don't know who she was, but I do know that if I hadn't pulled you out, you would have died, too. Or you would have been sold into slavery, like all the other survivors."

"And why didn't you sell me?"

"Because . . ." Mendoza hesitated as his page continued to look at him with the same pained expression. It was a question he had often asked himself and never really been able to answer. "Because I don't like slavery, and I felt responsible for you. Perhaps I wanted to perform some act of kindness in the midst of so much evil. I don't know why, boy. I just acted that way, and once I started, I couldn't stop."

"And you never thought to tell me this?" Gabriel asked in an indignant, critical tone that Mendoza had never heard before.

"What good would it have done? So that you could know that your parents were killed in a war? So you could be a Morisco? You've seen here what that means. Be angry if you want to, but it was war. Sometimes in wartime you do things you would never do in other situations. Maybe you can begin to realize that after today."

Gabriel continued to stare at Mendoza as though he had just turned into another person in front of his eyes.

"Did Magda know about this?" he asked.

"No. Only my mother and my cousin. And I told them not to tell you. Well, now you've asked me and I have told you," Mendoza said. "Go get some sleep, boy. In the morning things might look a little different."

After Gabriel had gone, Mendoza continued to gaze into the fire, wondering if he'd done the right thing. Just before midnight Martín and Ventura came in together, and the militiaman took over Mendoza's shift while he and his cousin went upstairs. The faint light from Gabriel's doorway told him that his page was still awake, and he was tempted to see if he was all right, but he was too tired for any more conversation or reflection. No sooner had he extinguished the candle and lain down on top of the bed in his tunic and hose than he felt himself drifting off to sleep.

HE WOKE UP to hear the sound of footsteps on the stairs. It was only the faintest of creaks, but the obvious caution immediately aroused his attention, because his own men never took that kind of care. He sat up in the dark room and carefully unsheathed his sword as the door slowly opened. He waited until he saw the forearm and the glint of metal and then leaped from the bed and slammed the door shut. The intruder dropped the dagger with a grunt of pain. Before he could pick it up, Mendoza threw the door open and thrust his own sword into the crouching back, and the man crumpled to the floor.

Mendoza just had time to make out three other figures looming like phantoms in the gloom when Gabriel's door opened and his page appeared in the doorway.

"Get back inside!" Mendoza rushed forward and shoved him violently into the room. In the same moment, one of the three men grabbed his shoulder. He twisted around to his left as the knife stabbed point-first into the doorframe just behind him and grabbed the attacker's wrist as he withdrew it, but now the man gripped his throat with his other hand. His assailant was short and heavy, with powerful, thick wrists and muscular arms that smelled of sweat and animal dung, and his blackened face made him look more like a monster or an animal than a human being. Mendoza fell back into Gabriel's room, holding the knife hand up as the heavy body pinned him to the floor and winded him.

The other hand was squeezing Mendoza's windpipe as though he were trying to tear it out of his throat, and he felt himself choking. Behind him he heard curses, grunts and the sound of violent struggle, but he could no longer breathe, and still the knife was bearing down inexorably toward his face. Just when he thought he might black out, his attacker reared up and collapsed on top of him. He looked up to see Gabriel pushing a sword with both hands into the man's back as a pistol shot exploded like a thunderclap in the little hallway.

Necker pulled Mendoza to his feet, and he saw Ventura standing just behind him with a pistol in his hand. There were four corpses on the landing and the stairs, and Ventura now led the way past them and down to the ground floor. Goats and sheep were milling around in confusion before the still-smoldering fire, and the red glow illuminated Martín's body lying in the half-open doorway that led out onto the street. Mendoza turned him over and examined the wounds in his chest and throat as a group of militiamen and armed Moriscos appeared holding torches.

"He must have opened the door for them," Ventura said.

Necker made the sign of the cross. It was only then that Mendoza realized that the animals had escaped from the stable. He grabbed one of the torches and rushed over to the open door. Sánchez was sitting on the floor in the same position in which he had last seen him, seemingly oblivious to the horses that were kicking and stamping in the corral alongside him, and it was not until Mendoza bent over him that he saw the dark wound in Sánchez's throat. Outside, the militiamen and Moriscos were dragging the bodies into the street. All of them were barefoot, bare-chested and dressed in the same dark hose, their faces, arms and upper bodies smeared with charcoal. Mendoza passed his torch across them and gazed down upon the heavy, hairy-looking body who had nearly strangled him.

"I've seen that man before, in Zaragoza and Vallcarca. He's an Inquisition *familiar.*"

"His name is Pachuca." Segura's eldest son, Agustín, appeared in the street just behind them. "A real brute."

"The Inquisition did this?" asked Ventura in amazement.

Mendoza shook his head. "Someone else sent him. He killed the bailiff, and he would have killed me if Gabriel hadn't stopped him.

We need to find out how they got in." He looked back at Gabriel, who was standing in a daze near the fire in his blood-spattered nightshirt as the goats and sheep milled around him. Mendoza ordered him to get his boots. The village was wide awake now, and groups of Moriscos were walking around with weapons and torches in expectation of another attack as Mendoza and his men went into the streets to inspect the main entrance and the medieval wall. The sentries were still in place, their braziers still lit, and none of them had heard or seen anything unusual apart from the single shot in the dispensary.

Mendoza doubted that Pachuca and his men could have slipped past them without being seen, but there was no obvious point where they might have entered the village. Most of the houses were built so close together that they made a natural wall, and there was only a narrow, rocky ledge beneath them, which did not allow any room to mount a ladder that could have reached the high windows.

"Did anyone come into the town during the day?" he asked Ventura as they stood next to the cemetery looking over the wall.

"Only the Moriscos who buried the bodies and collected firewood."

"Doesn't it seem strange to you that I arrested Sánchez only yesterday, yet Pachuca knew exactly where he was? And he also knew where I was. Who went to chop wood? Was it only Moriscos?"

"No, there were some Old Christians, too. Romero took his children to help him. They brought back a cartload of wood. He said he needed it for his oven."

At the mention of the baker, Mendoza walked away from the church to the edge of the old wall and glanced back up at the row of houses on the main square overlooking the valley. All of them had the same high windows and the same narrow edge beneath them, but he noticed that one of the windows had a metal crossbar in front of it.

"That house with the bar. Isn't that the bakery?"

Agustín Segura said that it was.

"Come with me, señores," Mendoza said. "I think I know how this was done."

They followed him to the bakery, where he banged loudly on the door until Romero's wife appeared in a nightgown and shawl, holding a candle in her hand, and peered out at them with an expression of abject terror.

"Where's your husband, señora?"

"He's in bed," she quavered. "He's not well. What do you want?"

Mendoza pushed past her and went up the little staircase leading from the shop into the house, with his men following behind him. He had just reached the first floor when Romero appeared in the doorway of his bedroom in his nightshirt.

"What are you doing in my house?" he demanded in a voice that sounded more fearful than defiant. Mendoza walked over to the window, gripped the bar with both hands and shook it before leaning out to look down.

"Where's the rope?"

"What rope?" Romero replied in a tremulous and slightly hysterical voice.

"The one that you brought back from the woods today to let Pachuca in."

"I don't know anything about that!" the baker insisted.

"Really? Then what's this?" Mendoza took the torch from Ventura and held up Romero's left hand in front of him. "Charcoal. And these look like charcoal footprints on the floor."

"I was cleaning the oven."

"In your nightshirt with no shoes on? When your wife said you weren't feeling well? Get your clothes on. You're under arrest. Tomorrow we'll search the house and take a look down below. I think we'll find the rope soon enough."

"I work for the Inquisition!" Romero protested. "You can't arrest me!"

"Constable Necker, please keep an eye on the prisoner while he dresses."

Romero's three children were peering out of the adjoining doorway now, and his wife shooed them back into their room.

"Shame on you, Licenciado Mendoza, depriving three children of their father!" cried Romero's wife.

"You should have thought about that when you allowed your husband to bring in assassins to try to kill me, señora," Mendoza replied. "And you should hold your tongue unless you want to join him."

Señora Romero hastily retreated into her children's room. She did not even come out when they led her husband back to the dispensary, where Segura and some of the Moriscos had lined up the six bodies in the street.

"Take a good look, baker," Mendoza said. "This is your handiwork."

"The bailiff is still inside, sir," Agustín Segura said. "We didn't have the key to his chains."

"Leave him where he is." Mendoza glared at Romero. "He can keep our new guest company."

CHAPTER TWENTY-THREE

HE COUNTRY HOUSE AT ACECA WAS ONLY A short ride from Madrid, and from his vantage point on the banks of the Tagus the Marquis of Villareal watched the royal hunt unfold. He heard the sounds of trumpets, dogs and beating drums coming through the trees, and he could see the royal carriages that were drawn up in a semicircle in a wide clearing between the forest and the river. Immediately behind him the rowboats and sailing ships were lined up along the bank, waiting to take the king and his entourage back downriver to Aranjuez later that day, their sails, flags and ornate canopies rippling gently in the light summer breeze. To the west, beyond the hunters and woods, he saw the great house where Philip and his family had spent the last two days.

Although the woodlands fell within the boundaries of the Royal Forest of Aranjuez, the hunt had been organized by the majordomo at Aceca, who stood waiting anxiously a short distance away from the king's own carriage to see the results of his meticulous preparations. There were forty carriages altogether, with those of the king, his sister María the Holy Roman empress, and his three children at the center; followed by the members of their respective households; the gentleman of the king's bedchamber; the infante Philip's tutor; the maidservants and bodyguards of the empress; the servants and maidservants of the two princesses; and assorted bodyguards, pages, cupbearers, coachmen, dwarves and fools.

Standing on foot around the carriages were various soldiers, hunters and gamekeepers whose task was to prevent the animals from slipping through the gaps and keep the royal family equipped with a constant flow of weapons, arrows and ammunition. Only members of the family were permitted to shoot, but the entire party waited with tense excitement as the noise of dogs and beaters grew louder and flocks of startled birds flew up out of the trees. The king was sitting next to Catalina, with one pistol pointed toward the forest and another waiting on the seat beside him while his daughter leaned out of the window with the stock of the light hunting rifle pressed against her cheek. In the adjoining carriage, her older sister, the infanta Isabel, was also resting against a light hunting rifle with a long, thin barrel and a beautifully carved fishhook stock, while her sickly six-year-old brother, Philip, sat opposite her with the king's sister and his tutor, who attempted to ensure that the boy fired his little crossbow at the forest and not at the waiting servants.

There were few activities that King Philip enjoyed more than hunting with his family, and the knowledge that this would be the last summer that Catalina hunted at Aceca gave this particular hunt a bittersweet poignancy. In less than six months, the court would set out for Aragon, and before the following spring Catalina would already be in Savoy. Philip regarded both events with almost equal dread, and he tried not to think about them now as the first terrified animals burst through the clearing and ran toward them.

Catalina fired first and missed, and her servant immediately handed her a pistol while another reloaded the rifle. The other members of the family fired off their guns and crossbows until the forest echoed with shots, horses' hooves and barking dogs as the gamesmen tried to cut off the animals' headlong flight. By the time the fusillade was over, the clearing was scattered with dead and wounded beasts. In total two boar, three deer and thirteen rabbits had been killed, and the gamesmen and beaters now gathered up the carcasses as the royal party withdrew to the boats to eat a picnic lunch.

As was his custom, the king remained alone in his carriage a short distance away and opened his document bag. A servant brought him a quill, ink and his portable desk, and once again he began to work through the interminable flow of letters, council minutes, reports and ciphered dispatches that poured in from every corner of his empire. There had been a time, at the beginning of his reign, when he'd been able to keep up with the paperwork and even derive some satisfaction from it. Now it constantly threatened to overwhelm him, flowing into every spare moment of the day in such quantities that he could not keep up even if he replicated himself ten times over. He saw himself as Tantalus of Tartarus, perpetually reaching for fruit that was always out of reach, or Sisyphus, pushing a rock that continually rolled back a little farther despite his efforts.

It was true that his rock was only made of paper, but there were times when his gout made the task of administration no less grueling and exhausting, regardless of whether he wrote sitting or standing.

After forty minutes he was feeling about ready for lunch when Secretary Vázquez told him that the Marquis of Villareal was waiting to see him on a matter of urgency. It was only then that Philip noticed the marquis lurking by the boats with the large entourage that he took with him everywhere. The sight did not please him. The only business Villareal could have brought with him was the business of Aragon, which was never good, and the fact that the man had come all the way from Madrid to see him suggested that it was likely to be even worse than usual.

These suspicions were immediately confirmed when Villareal approached his carriage and bowed before him.

"Your Majesty, I apologize for this intrusion, but I have received grave news from Cardona, which I believe requires an immediate response."

Philip said nothing and listened solemnly as the counselor informed him that Inquisitor Mercader of the Zaragoza Inquisition, together with Commissioner Herrero of the Huesca Inquisition and seven members of their party, had been murdered by the Moriscos of Belamar de la Sierra and members of the Countess of Cardona's militia.

"But this is an outrage," he said.

"Indeed, sire. Corregidor Calvo believes that they were murdered on the orders of the Morisco who calls himself the Redeemer, in revenge for the arrest of the mayor of Belamar, the Morisco Dr. Segura. And now the *montañeses* have taken matters into their own hands and attacked Belamar. Corregidor Calvo believes that Licenciado Mendoza and his men have been killed. He has asked Your Majesty to send troops immediately to Cardona to restore order and prevent further bloodshed. I have the corregidor's report here."

He handed Philip the letter and stood by as the king scanned it quickly. Philip's face, as always, showed no emotion, but his somber expression and long silence made it clear that the letter had not been without impact.

"This is . . . unacceptable," he said finally.

"It is. And I believe—and Your Majesty's ministers also believe—that we must act with all the urgency that this matter requires. We must send troops and place Cardona in the royal domain. The authority of the Inquisition and the Crown must be restored. If this is not done, the disorder will certainly spread. It may not be possible for Your Majesty and the court to travel safely to Aragon in January. It may even be necessary to postpone the wedding in March."

Philip considered this for a moment. "And what makes you think that the lords will accept the measures you propose?"

"Your Majesty, the Aragonese Cortes will not oppose a royal intervention so close to the infanta's wedding. They will accept whatever is necessary to restore order in Cardona, and they will not oppose His Majesty's claims in the absence of any obvious heir, because dividing her estates up would cause too much conflict between the lords. Most would prefer to see the countess's estates managed by the Crown. Any objections can be addressed by Your Majesty in person when you visit Aragon next year. Sire, I cannot emphasize enough the gravity of the situation, but I also believe that if we act quickly, we can turn it to the Crown's advantage."

"How many troops do you think will be necessary to achieve this?"

"The corregidor believes that two thousand will be sufficient."

Philip stared out the window for a long time at the servants carrying trays to the canopies on the boats while Villareal remained as motionless as a statue. It was impossible to know what the king was thinking or even if he was thinking at all, but the marquis knew that it was now incumbent upon him to remain absolutely still and silent, even if the Prudent King said nothing for the next hour.

"Very well," said Philip finally. "Let the Council of Castile muster the necessary troops and have them ready. But they are not to leave Madrid until I give the order. I wish to consult the viceroy first."

Villareal bowed obediently, and the king turned away without a word and prepared to dictate a letter to his secretary. It was not quite the outcome the marquis had wanted, but he saw no reason that Sástago should oppose his recommendations. As he walked back to his waiting servants, he told himself that it had been worth making the journey and that considering the way things were done in Spain, the business of Aragon was going as well as it could.

IN THE MORNING Necker went out onto the ledge beneath the baker's house and retrieved the rope that Romero had dropped there. Ventura and Mendoza brought it with them when they opened the stable door and found Romero standing near the window with his hands tied behind his back, as if seeking solace in the daylight from the bloodied corpse that was still sitting peacefully among the goats behind him. He was trembling despite the heat, and his fat moon face was dripping with sweat. Mendoza looked at him without sympathy. "Good morning, Señor Romero. I trust you slept well?"

Romero glanced down at Sánchez's corpse with terror and revulsion. "How could I sleep, with him lying there?" he asked.

"I'm sorry that he disturbed you," Mendoza said. "But you have more pressing things to think about. After all, you actively colluded with his assassins. And the same men also killed my special constable, and they also tried to kill one of His Majesty's judges. I have hanged men for much less than that, and I will hang you unless you can give me any reason to save your worthless life."

Romero stared at the rope in Ventura's hands. "Why have you brought that?"

"It's the rope that your assassins used to enter your house and which you untied before we got there," Mendoza replied as Ventura dangled it over a beam. "But it has other uses."

"It's not my fault!" the baker wailed. "Pachuca swore he'd kill my children if I didn't do what he said."

"How did he tell you?"

"He sent a messenger two nights ago. The messenger woke me up and told me to go into the woods yesterday afternoon and gather as much wood as possible. Pachuca was waiting for me and gave me the rope. He said I had to be ready to lower it when he asked for it. I didn't know they were going to try to kill you!"

"What did you think they were going to do—sing to us? You didn't have to go to the woods to meet him. All you had to do was cross the street and tell me, but you didn't do that. Why did they kill Sánchez? Who sent them?"

"I don't know! I swear on the most holy sacraments! All I ever did was report on the Moriscos."

"Or make things up," Mendoza suggested.

"Panalles did the same! And just because I didn't see things happen doesn't mean they didn't happen. But I didn't murder anyone! Look at these hands, Your Honor, they're only good for making bread!"

Mendoza looked at the baker's face but not his hands. "Strange. I actually think you're telling the truth. Clearly as novel an experience for you as it is for me to hear it."

"Can I go home now?" Romero asked hopefully.

"You aren't going anywhere. And I'm going to take you to Zaragoza and charge you with conspiracy to murder. We'll see if the Inquisition wants to intervene on your behalf. But I will take the bailiff away. I can see you're beginning to tire of his company."

Necker summoned the Morisco stretcher-bearers to carry the bailiff's body down to the ravine. No sooner had they left the dispensary than the trumpet in the church tower sounded once again. Mendoza and Gabriel immediately went down to the main entrance, where Ventura and the Morisco sentries were watching a line of mounted men moving rapidly across the valley floor toward them. It was not until the first riders appeared above the hill that Mendoza recognized the corpulent figure of Pelagio Calvo, and he realized that the countess had finally gotten a messenger through to Jaca.

MENDOZA HAD NOT SEEN CALVO since the massacre at the del Río farm, and the corregidor looked a little more like the man he remembered from Lepanto. He was wearing a helmet and a leather doublet, and a pistol was protruding from his belt in addition to the sword that hung from his waist. His stubbly face was grim as he surveyed the remnants of the barricade and chevaux-de-frise and got down from his horse.

"Christ, Bernardo," he said. "I heard you had a bit of a fight, but I didn't expect this."

"Nor did we," Mendoza replied. "But we held them."

"Well, I'm glad to see you alive," Calvo said. "I only heard about this yesterday from the countess's messenger. I brought all the men I could find. Vargas will be here later this morning with reinforcements. I just wanted to get here quickly in case you were attacked again."

"So you never saw Segura? Or the messenger I sent to you from France last week?"

"No." Calvo looked at him in surprise. "Why would I have seen Segura? And what in the name of all the devils in hell were you doing in France?"

Calvo had brought only fifteen men, Mendoza observed, but they were well armed and they looked as though they knew how to use their weapons. Some of them looked very tough indeed.

"Leave your men here," he said. "We have a lot to talk about."

The corregidor gave the order and accompanied Mendoza back to the village. He looked shocked and angry as Mendoza described the battle and the number of casualties and showed him the wounded who were still lying in the village hall.

"I warned you about this, Bernardo," he said as they stood by the medieval wall, watching the Moriscos digging graves. "And you should know that I've written to the king and the viceroy to ask for military assistance. I've asked His Majesty to place Cardona directly under the jurisdiction of the Crown and use his armies to occupy the *señorio*. I told him that we are now in a state of rebellion and that this Redeemer must be stopped if the wedding is to take place."

"You had no authority to write to the king on these matters without consulting me first," Mendoza snapped. "The Redeemer is a fiction. Everything about him is fake. Only the murders are real. But this has nothing to do with Moors and Christians. We are facing a criminal conspiracy, not a rebellion, and I do not need soldiers to deal with it!"

Calvo looked chastened and confused now, and Mendoza proceeded to tell him about Péris's murder, the countess's allegations against Vallcarca and the death of Sánchez.

"I'm sorry, Bernardo," he said. "But this doesn't make any sense. If Sánchez was working for Vallcarca and the baron was using the Inquisition to try to put pressure on the countess, then who killed Mercader and Herrero? And who ordered Pachuca to kill Sánchez last night?"

"Pachuca must have been working for Vallcarca," Mendoza replied. "Maybe the baron was worried that Sánchez would talk about him. But there's more than one game being played here, and there are many different players. One thing I'm certain of: Belamar is not the prize. This has always been about the countess."

"Then we must arrest Vallcarca!"

"With fifteen men? You'll need more than that."

"Not today we won't. He's in Huesca shafting one of his mistresses in his hunting lodge. He won't have much of an escort. We could snatch him before he even knows what hit him. Damn it, Bernardo, there's no better time! If he goes back to Vallcarca, we'll never get him out of there."

Mendoza agreed that the plan was worth trying. While Calvo returned to the main entrance, he briefly consulted with Ventura as Gabriel saddled his horse. His page was still looking downcast. It was impossible to know whether it was Martín's death or the previous night's revelations that had upset him more, but there was no time to ask as he and Necker rode out to the top of the hill, where Calvo was already waiting with his men.

. . .

THEY HAD BEEN RIDING HARD for nearly an hour along the familiar path through the valleys toward the Gállego River when Calvo turned his horse away along a narrower path that led up a steep, forested slope.

"Aren't we going to the bridge?" Mendoza asked.

"This way is quicker!" Calvo shouted back. "It leads directly to the hunting lodge."

The path entered a shallow gorge, and they followed the left bank through thick woods and rocks until it began to descend once again and the two sides began to converge. After a few minutes, they reached a small clearing, which gave way to a natural funnel formed by pine trees and rocks, at which point Calvo raised his hand.

"What is it?" Mendoza asked. "Why have we stopped?"

Calvo had his back to him and turned around with his flintlock pistol pointed directly at Mendoza's chest. "Unbuckle your sword and give me your pistol, Bernardo. You too, Constable."

Necker's hand was poised on the hilt of his sword, but Mendoza shook his head and they dropped their weapons to the ground.

"Get down from your horses," Calvo ordered. Mendoza and Necker dismounted, and Calvo did the same, keeping the pistol leveled at Mendoza's chest as his men encircled them with swords and pistols drawn.

"They're not militia, are they?" Mendoza asked, watching some of them climb down from their horses.

"No, they're not. Now, put your hands on your heads."

One of Calvo's men took their horses, and they followed the corregidor through the forest until the path gave out onto a small enclosed valley with a large cave in the rock face to the left of it. Directly in front of them stood a roofless stone hut no bigger than a sheep barn that had a pile of stones lying around its base, which appeared to be a former hermitage. A small fire was still giving off smoke in front of the cave, and sitting beside it were three men, who stood up as they approached and stared at them with hard, sullen expressions. Mendoza noticed that two of the men had bloodied tunics and another had a bandage tied around his head, and he knew that they had gotten their wounds at Belamar. As they drew nearer, he noticed a large wooden cross that had been lashed together with rope lying on the ground near the ruins.

"Where's Lupercio?" Calvo asked.

"Gone to look for pilgrims," said one of the bandits.

"Now?"

"He said you're not to kill the judge till he returns."

Calvo scowled and told the bandits to tie them up. Two of the guards bound their hands behind their backs with twine, and Calvo ordered them to be taken over to the hermitage, where Calvo gestured toward the outside wall.

"Sit down," he commanded. Mendoza and Necker lowered themselves awkwardly to the ground and leaned against the wall as Calvo squatted in front of them with the pistol resting on his thigh. He was smiling faintly, and he no longer seemed clumsy and incompetent, but icily efficient.

"Don't look so surprised, Bernardo. We can't let you leave Cardona. If you did that, a great deal of very hard work would be ruined."

"Whose work? Vallcarca's?"

Calvo smiled again. "You were always the clever one, Bernardo, but you're only seeing part of the picture. You were right about the baron. He wants Cardona, and he thought he could use the Inquisition to persuade the countess to marry Rodrigo. He got Lupe and Sánchez to kill Panalles. He had Péris and the Moriscos framed. All that was well done, but he wasn't the only player."

"The Catalan?"

"Lupe?" Calvo looked scornful. "He couldn't organize something like this. He worked for the baron, but he also worked for someone even bigger. Just like you and me, Bernardo."

"Villareal?" Mendoza asked incredulously. "He was behind this?"

Calvo chuckled happily. "It's fair to say that the marquis is not a great admirer of the Baron of Vallcarca. In fact he loathes even the air that man breathes. So he wasn't going to let one of the richest *señorios* in Aragon fall into Vallcarca's hands, not if he could get it for the Crown. But even the king of Castile can't just send royal troops into Aragon for no reason. Vallcarca's efforts were enough for the Inquisition, but they weren't enough to make the king pay attention. His Majesty is very indecisive. Villareal needed something more serious, like a Morisco rebellion. Even a holy war."

"So the Redeemer was his idea?"

"Initially. Lupe came up with the detail. The Quintana brothers. The Arabic on walls. The crucifixions and desecrations. Villareal called it 'sparkle.' He was always telling me, 'More sparkle. I need more sparkle.' So Lupe and I provided it."

"Is that why you murdered Mercader? For sparkle?"

"A dead inquisitor creates a lot of heat."

"And del Río? Was that sparkle, too?"

Calvo shook his head. "That was Vallcarca's work. His son even took part in it. The baron simply wanted to cover his tracks after Ventura found out about Franquelo and the horses. And then he got Lupe to take care of Pepe. Of course, this served our purposes, too, so Lupe did it his own way and made it look as though the Old Christians were taking revenge. Villareal wanted a war. To do that we needed a lot of dead people, and we needed a good judge to come here and record it all. A judge with a reputation for rigor and thoroughness. As you said, there are many players in this, and some of them didn't realize that they were only pieces—like you."

"And Sánchez."

Calvo nodded. "Sánchez was working for Vallcarca, till we paid him more."

"And you? What do you get out of this?"

"Money, Bernardo! Much more than a provincial corregidor can ever get. When the Crown takes over Cardona, Villareal will be the administrator, and he will see to it that I receive the rewards I should have received for all the years I spent in His Majesty's service, and Cornelia will be able to live in the manner to which she wants to be accustomed. Think about it: I'll be the man who saved Aragon for the infanta's wedding. That's worth at least a baronetcy and a palace."

Mendoza looked at his old friend in disgust. "Christ's blood, Pelagio. What kind of thing have you become? Do you think if you put your wife in a palace, it will stop you being a cuckold?"

Calvo's smile abruptly faded. "Steady, Bernardo. Lupe is very angry with you after what happened in Belamar. You've broken up his band, and he intends to crucify you. I was going to ask him to kill you first—for old times' sake. Otherwise you'll die on the cross with your eyes wide open."

"You're still missing certain fundamental points here, just as you always did. Ventura won't believe your story. He saw us leave together."

"Ventura and your page will never leave Cardona alive," Calvo said. "I'll make sure of that when I bring them to see you on the cross. Your depositions will be destroyed, and as for your letters . . . well, I've read them all, and I know what to say and what to leave out when I send my own reports. In Madrid they still think that the Redeemer exists and that the Moriscos killed two Inquisition officials. Without you no one can tell them any different. Now they'll think that the Redeemer and his men killed the king's special justice, Alcalde Mendoza. And who is going to believe anything to the contrary after everything that has happened? And then His Majesty will send the soldiers to the Morisco lands and the Crown of Castile will take possession of Cardona."

"May you burn in hell, you son of a whore," Mendoza said.

"Come now, Bernardo. There's no hell. That's just a story the priests tell to terrify children. This is the only world there is, and the only men who prosper in it are the ones with the cojones to take what they can find. Ah, here he is."

Mendoza and Necker looked at the path they had just taken as the Catalan came riding out of the forest accompanied by another half a dozen men. He had already seen them, and he smiled as he reined in his horse. He was a big man, almost as tall as Necker, but slimmer and wirier, with a thin mustache and leather riding boots that came up just above the knees, plus a wide feathered hat that suggested he had once been an army officer.

"So you did it, Calvo," he said, getting down from his horse. "You're a difficult man to kill, Licenciado Mendoza. You should have died at Belamar. Even Pachuca couldn't kill you, but I assure you that

I will. I'm going to break your knees first. Then I'll work my way down your shins. Do you think that will hurt? I do. I think you'll beg me to stop, but I won't."

Just then all of them heard a shot, followed by another. The bandits jumped to their feet and stared at the path with their backs to the hermitage while the men who were still on horseback turned back onto it. Calvo and the Catalan also turned away as the shots continued. The corregidor was just getting to his feet when Mendoza swung his legs sideways and tripped him up. Before Calvo was able to get up, Mendoza had locked his legs around his neck, and now he squeezed them tight, dragging him back into the open doorway.

"Get his sword!" he hissed.

The Catalan had seen them now and was calmly walking toward them, still holding his horse by the reins as Necker turned his back and unsheathed the corregidor's sword till the blade was exposed just enough to slice through the twine on his wrists. He scrambled to his feet and cut Mendoza loose. Mendoza picked up his pistol as Necker rushed toward the Catalan with Calvo's sword and ducked as the silver mace came swinging around from the left in a wide arc. Necker crouched and slashed sideways from the right toward the Catalan's waist, cutting him across his left thigh. The Catalan grimaced and took another swing, which connected with Necker's shoulder and knocked the sword from his hand. He was just about to land another blow when he saw Mendoza standing in the doorway with the pistol pointed at him.

"Drop it," Mendoza ordered. "And put your hands up."

The Catalan lowered the weapon as the Moriscos and the Cardona militiamen came pouring out of the trees and charged the bandits. Mendoza glanced toward them, and as he did so, the Catalan flicked his arm upward and sent the mace sailing toward his head. Mendoza ducked and fired as it crashed into the wall behind him. The Catalan clutched his stomach with one hand and then, with gritted teeth, leaped toward his horse. Within seconds he was back in the saddle and riding slumped forward out of the camp as the little valley echoed with the clash of steel and pistol shots.

"Are you all right, Constable?" Mendoza asked.

"I think my arm is broken, sir," Necker replied. "Should I pursue him?"

Mendoza shook his head. "No, Constable. With one arm, even you won't catch him. Let him bleed."

Within minutes it was over and the bandits who had not been killed had surrendered to the Moriscos, who herded them into a group near the fire.

"You left it late," Mendoza said as Ventura came riding toward them.

"You could show some gratitude, cousin." Ventura looked down at Calvo, who was sitting dejectedly on the ground, and then back at Mendoza. "So you were right, cousin. Congratulations."

"How did you know?" Calvo asked.

Mendoza bent to pick up the mace. It was a remarkable weapon, unlike anything he had ever seen, with a head made from two eagles' beaks and lions' heads with additional beaks protruding from their open jaws.

"A man who writes letters to the king telling him things I know to be false? Who undermines my investigation without consulting me and then comes to save me with only fifteen men? Such a man is worthy of suspicion, even if he is an old friend. And as for not seeing Segura . . . well, it's just a little odd that the man I sent to Jaca ends up in the hands of the Inquisition and you say you didn't even see him."

Calvo said nothing as Mendoza ordered one of the militiamen to tie his hands.

"Are we taking them back to Belamar?" Ventura asked.

"No. To Jaca."

"Bernardo, please." Calvo regarded him imploringly. "Don't take me to Jaca. Just finish me here."

Mendoza looked at him contemptuously. "Do not address me by my first name. You will die, but not here. You will go on trial like any other common criminal, and the whole world will know your crimes. And then you will find out if there really is a hell."

CHAPTER TWENTY-FOUR

HEY REACHED JACA IN THE MIDAFTERNOON and rode slowly along the Calle Mayor, past the shops and workshops and the market traders, priests and pedestrians, some of whom stopped and stared incredulously at the familiar figure of the corregidor and the other eight prisoners roped together on foot to a mule. They were just passing Calvo's office when the constable who had accompanied them on their arrival from Zaragoza to Jaca more than a month earlier came out to meet them, accompanied by two of his officers, and stared in astonishment at the sight of the prisoners and his former superior.

"Constable Vargas," Mendoza said. "Weren't you out raising the militia?"

"No, sir." The *alguacil* stared at Calvo, who did not look at him. "I wasn't told to. Sir, may I ask what is going on?"

"Corregidor Calvo and these men are under arrest for

banditry, murder and treason," Mendoza replied calmly. "I'm taking them to the cathedral jail. His Majesty would appreciate your cooperation."

"Of course, sir."

The three constables joined them now as they escorted the prisoners to the cathedral jail. Two ragged beggars who were seated outside the cathedral door came toward him, and one of them brandished the stump of his arm and said "Lepanto!" before Vargas shooed him away. A moment later the warden came out to meet them in a rough brown gown and sandals. He gaped at his former superior as Mendoza repeated the charges against the nine prisoners.

"But, Your Mercy, this is Corregidor Calvo."

"I'm aware of that," said Mendoza. "And I want him to have his own cell. I warn you that if anything happens to him, I will hold you personally responsible."

"No one has his own cell here, sir," the warden protested. "There's no room."

"Then he will share with the others."

"Bernardo," Calvo said suddenly. "Could I have a word?"

"I told you not to address me by my first name," Mendoza said icily.

"Your Honor. Please may I speak to you in private?"

"You can use my office, sir." The warden gestured toward a little room by the entrance. Mendoza ushered Calvo inside and shut the door behind him. He sat down at a grimy table, on which the warden had left a half-eaten bowl of bean stew, a mug of beer and a crust of bread.

"Well?" he said.

"I beg you, Bernardo—Your Honor. I know I'll hang for this.

But please put me under house arrest until you're ready to take me to Zaragoza, for old times' sake. You knew my father."

"I did. And I know what he would have thought of you."

"I give you my word of honor I won't try to escape."

"You dare talk of honor!"

Calvo nodded. "All right. Forget the past, then. What if I offered you something in return? What if I told you I know where Segura is?"

"Dr. Segura is in the Inquisition jail in Huesca. And there's nothing that you or I can do to get him out of there."

"He's not in Huesca," Calvo said. "He's in the seigneurial jail in Vallcarca."

"How do you know this?"

"Because Lupe and Pachuca took him there. We wanted to make sure Mercader came to Vallcarca personally. So Pachuca took him to the baron's jail and the baron informed Herrero. Mercader and Herrero were going to bring him back to Zaragoza with the other prisoners from Belamar."

Mendoza looked at him contemptuously. "Very well. You can stay at your house. But neither you nor your wife will be allowed to leave, and you will receive no visitors."

"Thank you, Your Honor."

"It wasn't only the money, was it?" Mendoza said suddenly. "Was it Vallcarca who cuckolded you, or was it his son?"

Calvo was momentarily taken aback, and his face was bitter and filled with self-loathing as he stared down at the floor. "His son—among others."

Mendoza led Calvo out into the passageway, where Necker, his arm in a sling, was talking to Vargas. "The prisoner is to remain under house arrest," Mendoza said. "His wife can remain with him, but neither they nor their servants can leave or receive visitors. Constable Vargas, I expect you to ensure that the house is well guarded and that these orders are observed. Constable Necker will assist you until I return in two days' time. Please take care of his food and accommodation."

Outside, Ventura and the Moriscos were still waiting with the horses, and Mendoza told Ventura to bring Calvo's horse with them. They rode alongside Necker and Vargas, who escorted the corregidor on foot till they reached his house, where they found his wife standing in the doorway, accompanied by two servants.

"Licenciado Mendoza!" she called in a shrill, sharp voice. "I trust you have good cause to arrest the man who saved your life?"

Mendoza looked at the hard, flintlike eyes, the creamy white skin and the voluptuous figure that had undone his old friend so comprehensively. "Oh, I have most excellent cause, madam."

He nodded at Vargas and Necker, who ushered Calvo into the house and blocked his wife's path, and then he turned and rode away.

On reaching the Huesca road, Mendoza sent the Moriscos and the militiamen back to Belamar, and he and Ventura continued the journey to Vallcarca with Calvo's horse in tow. It took nearly two hours to reach the *señorio* and another half hour before they passed the gibbet, where the corpse he had seen nearly two weeks earlier had now been reduced to a skeleton.

Mendoza was not entirely convinced of the wisdom of entering Vallcarca, and the sight of the gallows did nothing to reassure him. He wondered whether he should have kept his escort, but a large group of armed men riding through the *señorio* would have invited unwelcome attention from the baron's militia. Their absence did not necessarily improve his chances of survival. It was possible that Vallcarca or his son had returned from Huesca. The baron had already tried to kill Mendoza once, and it was unlikely that he would allow either of them to leave the *señorio* alive if their presence was discovered.

By the time they reached Vallcarca, it was nearly dark, and Mendoza was relieved to see there was no sign of life from the palace. As they rode into the main street beneath it, he saw members of Vallcarca's militia walking among the stream of carts, horses, cows and pedestrians that flowed past them. One or two stared in their direction with mild curiosity, but none seemed to recognize them or show any further interest. Mendoza asked for the seigneurial prison and was directed just around the corner from the cathedral to the magistrate's court. He left Ventura with the horses and went inside and down the stairs until he came upon a heavy wooden door with a metal grille. He knocked on the door, and a moment later a red face with a walrus mustache and a beard appeared in the little hatch.

"Yes?"

"I am Licenciado Mendoza, criminal judge at the Royal Chancery of Valladolid," Mendoza said in his most pompous and imperious voice. "I'm here to transfer the Morisco Pedro Segura to His Majesty's custody."

"Segura is a prisoner of the Inquisition," the warden replied.

"Inquisitor Mercader has been murdered, and this Morisco is wanted in connection with the crime!" Mendoza insisted.

The warden showed no sign of emotion. "Even so you'll need the baron's authorization first."

"I have spoken to the baron. And I have a warrant for the prisoner's arrest!" Mendoza held up his letter bearing the royal seal.

"And you are obstructing His Majesty's officials in the course of their duty!"

The warden looked suddenly confused and had clearly never been faced with a dilemma like this.

"All right, all right," he grumbled. "There's no need to take that tone with me. I only work here. Wait there."

Mendoza waited impatiently in the little corridor till he heard the sound of footsteps and clanking chains. A few moments later, the door opened and the warden appeared, with one arm around the shoulder of the disheveled-looking Juan Segura. Segura's arms and feet were chained, and he looked smaller, frailer and older than when Mendoza had last seen him. His face was bruised and covered with dirt, and his white hair and beard were flecked with straw as he stared at Mendoza in confusion.

"You have to sign the ledger," the warden said, bending to unlock Segura's chains. "Name, date and position."

Mendoza stepped into the dark entrance hall and leaned over the table, where a candle was burning near an ancient-looking ledger that seemed as if it could have been there since the fourteenth century. He dipped the quill into the ink bowl and quickly wrote the required information.

"It seems to be in order," the warden murmured. "But I still think we should check with the magistrate first."

"I don't have time for this"—Mendoza sighed impatiently—"and I don't think the baron will take kindly to you sticking your nose into matters that are not your concern. Here's a little token of His Majesty's appreciation."

Mendoza dropped a coin into the warden's hand and led Segura toward the stairs. The mayor walked stiffly and with obvious difficulty, and when they reached the street, he stood looking around him with a dazed expression at the people moving back and forth in the fading light.

"But this is Vallcarca," he said wonderingly. "I thought I was in Huesca."

"I thought so, too," Mendoza muttered.

"But Herrero and Mercader were here. I spoke to them."

"And now they're both dead, and we have to leave."

Segura looked even more confused now as he mounted his horse and they rode slowly back along the street the way they'd come. As soon as they turned the corner, Mendoza picked up speed, and they did not slow down until they had nearly reached the town of Cardona. Segura listened in silence as Mendoza told him about the murders of the two inquisitional officials, the battle at Belamar and the other events that had taken place in his absence.

"So it seems you were right," Mendoza said in conclusion. "The rapists in Vallcarca were not Moriscos. And it was Sánchez who killed Péris and tried to kill us."

"On Corregidor Calvo's orders?"

Mendoza shook his head. "I don't think so. Sánchez was working for Vallcarca, but he was also working for the Marquis of Villareal. It's clear from what Péris told us that he was part of the baron's plot to bring the Inquisition to Belamar. Of course, Vallcarca couldn't allow us to come from France and report this. But Calvo was working for Villareal. That's why he kidnapped you and handed you over to Pachuca. You were bait—to attract Mercader to Vallcarca so that he could be killed."

"So who in the name of all the devils killed Sánchez the other night?" Ventura asked.

"Pachuca was Villareal's man. But Calvo or the Catalan must have given the order."

Segura shook his head and sighed. "So we Moriscos were merely pawns in a rich man's game?"

"In part. Mercader certainly didn't see it that way. He was a pawn, too. But your children are alive, and your daughter Juana has done you proud."

"Praise be to God. But why did you come to get me, Licenciado? If Vallcarca had discovered you, it could have gone badly for you."

"I made a promise to your daughter."

"Well, I thank you."

Mendoza said nothing. The Belamar Valley was bathed in a silvery light and looked calm and peaceful, as though a great storm had passed through it as they rode beneath the starry sky toward the village. Outside the main entrance, the sentries stirred uneasily at the party's approach, and their wariness turned to wild exultation when they recognized Segura. Within a few minutes, the new arrivals were surrounded by an entourage of men and women who came to touch Segura's legs and shake his hand. Some of them danced and others clapped their hands in rhythm while children ran along excitedly beside them, shouting that the doctor had come home. By the time they reached the main square, Segura's children had already come out to meet them. Mendoza watched as he embraced his sons and kissed his daughters one by one, and then Juana came over toward Mendoza. She no longer looked angry or hostile, and her wet cheeks shone in the moonlight.

"Thank you, Licenciado Mendoza," she said.

Mendoza nodded. Gabriel was watching quietly from the shadows, and he waited till she had returned to her family before coming forward to greet his guardian.

"Everything all right, boy?" Mendoza asked stiffly.

"Yes, sir. So you were right about Corregidor Calvo. I'm glad Sergeant Ventura was able to get there in time."

"So am I," he said. "And now there is nothing more to keep us here."

CHAPTER TWENTY-FIVE

THE NEXT DAY BELAMAR FINALLY BEGAN TO bury its dead. Father García had already come from Cardona to conduct a purification ritual in the church, and that morning he held yet another funeral Mass for all the village's dead. The countess attended, accompanied by Susana, and Gabriel stood near the back of the packed church with Ventura and Mendoza and watched as the Moriscos attempted to join in the prayers and hymns that many of them hardly knew.

He wondered how many of them really believed that Jesus would return to judge the living and the dead and whether the dead were being buried as Moors or Christians. He wondered whether all countries were like Spain, where nothing was what it seemed to be on the surface and men and women hid who they really were and what they really felt or thought. He wondered if the king was aware of the corruption and injustice that pervaded his kingdoms. And most of all, he wondered what kind of future awaited him in a country that he no longer belonged to. Now their business in Belamar was done, and the next day they would begin the journey back to Zaragoza and Castile, and he would return to his old life, except that his life could never be the same as it was, because he was no longer the person he thought he was.

In the past he had never understood why the boys at the *colegio* who bullied and taunted him had called him Moor. Magda told him that it was because he was cleverer than they were and because of his black hair and darker skin. She had reassured him that Spaniards had dark skin, too, and that he was as much a Christian as they were—and a better Christian, because he turned the other cheek. But now he realized that they'd sensed what he had not even begun to suspect until he came to Belamar.

These thoughts oppressed him as he followed the mourners down to the cemetery. The entire population of Belamar had turned out for the occasion, and there were tears and lamentations as the keeners wailed and moaned and tore at their shawls and waved their arms at the sky. Men, women and children wept openly as the bodies of their friends and relatives were laid carefully into the ground wrapped in white shrouds before the graves were partially filled and other bodies were laid on top of them.

At last the list of names came to an end, and Mendoza called Gabriel over as he went to speak to the countess. She was standing at the edge of the cemetery with Segura, Susana and Juana, and she had obviously been crying herself.

"I understand that you are leaving us tomorrow, Licenciado," she said.

"We are, my lady," Mendoza replied. "And before I leave, I would like to take down a formal deposition from you."

"Now?" she asked.

"If I'm to consider the allegations you have made against Vallcarca and your father-in-law, I need a written statement."

"Very well, then." The countess accompanied them to Segura's study and sat at the table opposite Mendoza while Gabriel took up his position behind his *escritorio*. She calmly repeated what she had already told him about her previous meetings with Vallcarca and her father-in-law as Gabriel wrote the conversation down. Afterward Mendoza looked her statement over. "Thank you for your time, my lady," he said, "but there's one thing I am still not clear about. Why was Vallcarca so convinced that the Inquisition would arrest you? Was there anything he knew, or thought he knew, that could have been used against you?"

"There was nothing." Her face showed no sign of emotion as she returned his gaze. "Nothing that you yourself don't already know."

"Very well. Then I must ask for your cooperation in another matter regarding the prisoners you took from Belamar."

"Rest assured that my courts will punish them with the severity their crimes warrant, Licenciado."

"I don't doubt it," Mendoza replied, "but the bandits and the *montañeses* are only pawns. The men who directed them must also face justice. I would like your magistrates to offer amnesty to anyone who can give them any information about these men—and to send any such information to me in Zaragoza." Mendoza handed her a rolled sheet of paper. "And I want this read out in all the towns and villages of Cardona so that the offer of amnesty can be extended throughout the *señorio*. Otherwise there will never be peace in Cardona. I would also like an escort of twenty men to take my prisoners from Jaca to Zaragoza in three days' time."

"So you mean to arrest Vallcarca?"

"Among others."

"It will be done as you ask, Licenciado. I ask for just one exception—my father-in-law."

"But if Espinosa was acting on behalf of Vallcarca, then he was also criminally responsible."

"My father-in-law is a greedy fool, but he is not a murderer. I would like the opportunity to punish him in my own way."

"Very well, then. As you wish."

"And surely the carpenter Navarro and his apprentice can be released now?"

"There is nothing I can do for them, my lady. That is a matter for the Inquisition. But the two Moriscos were not innocent. They were ready to join the Redeemer."

"But they weren't guilty of rape," she protested.

Mendoza nodded. "Indeed. And I shall inform the Inquisition in Zaragoza of my findings and see if it may be possible to obtain clemency or at least a remission of sentence for them."

"Then perhaps we will know peace—if His Majesty can be persuaded that we are not all heretics."

The limpid blue eyes stared at him calmly, but Mendoza sensed the anxiety behind them. She really did have the face of an angel, he thought. It was difficult to gaze on such loveliness and believe that it was capable of deception. Yet she had lied again and again, just as Segura and the Moriscos had lied, and if he failed to report what he knew, then he would be complicit in the lies they'd told. In that moment he thought of his Morisco childhood friends, many years ago, when they had played games of Moors and Christians at the Alhambra palace and taken turns on each side. He thought of Galera and Lepanto and the other battles he'd fought in. He thought of the Lutheran nun on the Inquisition pyre and all the other persecutions of men and women who only wanted to worship their own gods in their own way, and it seemed to him that the countess's lies were necessary, that they were honorable and even benevolent, in comparison with the lies of Vallcarca, Calvo and Villareal.

"That is a matter for the Church and the Inquisition, my lady," he said. "My investigation in Belamar is concluded, and I do not propose to advise His Majesty on matters outside my jurisdiction."

The countess looked visibly relieved. "Then I have one other favor to ask you."

"And what is that?"

"I intend to appeal directly to His Majesty to change the Cardona statutes so that my daughter, Carolina, can inherit my estates."

Mendoza looked at her in surprise. "Forgive my impertinence, my lady. But do you yourself not intend to marry?"

"I have . . . other plans. My lawyers inform me that the king is sometimes prepared to grant such exceptions and allow the inheritance to be passed down through the female line in special circumstances. Particularly when the petitioners have done him great service. I believe that I have served His Majesty well these last few days."

"You have indeed, my lady. Without your intervention we would all have been killed and the War of Cardona would only be just beginning."

"Then it would be of great assistance to my appeal if you could mention this in your report to His Majesty."

"Of course."

"Then I thank you. And I and the people of Belamar will always be grateful to you—and also to your companions."

SHE SMILED BENIGNLY AT GABRIEL, who ushered her downstairs to where Susana was waiting. The four of them accompanied the countess to her carriage in the main square, and Gabriel stood next to Mendoza and bowed as she looked out the window and waved to them. Afterward he drifted over to the medieval wall and looked disconsolately over the terraces that had only recently been strewn with the dead. He was still sitting there when Ventura came and sat beside him.

"You're looking very down in the mouth, boy," he said. "I hear that my cousin told you about Galera."

"He did."

"And that's why you're walking around looking as if a dog just ate your supper?"

"How should I feel, now that I'm the child of Saracens? Happy?"

"Why not?" Ventura laughed. "It doesn't matter what you were. It's what you are now that counts. And anyway, being the son of Moriscos from Galera is nothing to be ashamed of. They were brave men and women who fought for their homes and families—just as the Moriscos here did."

"They were heretics."

Ventura pulled a face. "Let me tell you something, boy. When I was a child, I saw my father—your guardian's uncle—wear a sanbenito because someone said he was a Jew. He had to wear it for three months, every time he went out into the street. He mostly stopped going out at all, but the shame was on his face even when he was in the house. The shame didn't come from him—others put it there. That damn rag still hangs in the church to remind me that I share in his sin. But you know what? I don't care if he was a Jew or not a Jew. I don't care if a man is a converso or a Marrano or a Morisco or a Saracen, and you shouldn't either. Because the only thing that matters in this life is that men behave with honor. And your guardian is an honorable man. Anyone else would have left you in that house to die. But he brought you up and educated you as if you were his own son. He gave you a life, and tomorrow you will be going back to it."

"To spend the rest of my life pretending."

"Everybody pretends, boy. This is Spain! Priests pretend to be holy. Women pretend to be virtuous. Jews and Moors pretend to be Christians, and men without a drop of blue blood in their veins buy titles and pretend to be nobles so that they can pay no taxes and have other men bow and scrape to them. So stop feeling sorry for yourself. And I believe there's someone you need to say good-bye to."

He nodded in the direction of the church, and Gabriel looked around just in time to see Juana turn away. He had not talked to her properly since the battle. Even when they worked together in the hospital they hardly spoke, and since then he'd been busy writing letters and proclamations. Now the realization that he would never see her again added to his gloom. He continued to sit by the wall after Ventura had gone, his mind swarming with gallant and heartfelt words, before he finally mustered up the courage to go look for her.

He found her in the village hall, scrubbing the floor with the women who had helped her, while the stretcher-bearers carried out the straw and mattresses. He immediately offered to help them, and before anyone could say yes or no, he took the bucket from Juana's hand and went down to the *lavadero* to fill it. For the next hour, he emptied buckets of bloodied water over the terraces and went to the *lavadero* to bring replacements. By early evening the cleaning was completed and he had still not said a word to her and she had not tried to speak to him. He no longer had any reason to be there, and he went back to the dispensary in a mournful mood to wait for supper in his room.

Mendoza's room was empty, and Gabriel lay on his own bed staring at the ceiling. He had not been there long when he heard a faint knock on the door. He hadn't even heard anyone coming up the stairs, and he opened the door to find Juana standing barefoot with an empty bucket in her hand, looking at him accusingly.

"So, scrivener, you were going to leave me without saying good-bye?"

"No, I wasn't, I—"

Before he could finish, she reached out and pulled him toward her and kissed him on the lips for a long time with her eyes closed. There was no need for gallant words now as he squeezed her to him and rested his hands on her slim hips. All the fear and death of the last few weeks were gone now, and his heart soared as he held the slight, eager body of the first girl he'd ever felt anything for tightly in his arms, and then he heard the sound of his guardian's stick on the stair, and she pulled away from him and extricated herself.

"Good-bye, scrivener," she said. "And don't forget me."

"Never," he whispered hoarsely as she turned and walked away.

IN THE MORNING Segura and his children came out to watch them leave. Ventura brought Romero out into the main square on the baker's own horse, and Mendoza was surprised and clearly moved to find that a large crowd of Moriscos had gathered to say good-bye to them.

"We didn't need a send-off," he said gruffly.

"I didn't ask them, Don Bernardo," the mayor replied. "You will always have friends here."

"Thank you," said Mendoza. "And I wish the people of Belamar better times—and a better priest."

"We all hope for that." Segura smiled and held his hand in a tight grip. "And may God go with you, Licenciado Mendoza."

He shook Ventura's and Gabriel's hands and muttered the same benediction. Beatriz choked back a sob as Ventura doffed his hat in an extravagant bow and mounted his horse. Juana met Gabriel's eyes only briefly and then hurried away from the square with her hand over her mouth as the crowd broke into a round of spontaneous applause, and the men rode down the street where they had fought for their lives only a few days before.

The Moriscos came out of their houses now or stood in their windows or on balconies to clap and cheer as they went past. Mendoza stared straight ahead, but Gabriel could tell that he was moved, and his own throat and chest were fit to burst with sadness and pride. The crowd followed them out of the main entrance and cheered as they descended the hill into the valley, where some of the peasants in the fields stopped to wave them on.

"What will happen to them now?" asked Gabriel when he was finally able to speak.

"The same thing that happens to all Moriscos," Mendoza replied. "They will be forgotten for a while, but sooner or later the Inquisition will come here again."

At the footbridge they paid the toll keeper for the last time and paused to look back on the valley once again, and then they turned the corner and descended toward the Jaca plain, as the sun rose higher into a sky that looked like polished blue stone. On arriving in Jaca, they took Romero to the cathedral jail. Mendoza told Ventura to wait for the countess's militia to bring the prisoners and went with Gabriel to take Calvo's deposition. They found Necker and one of Vargas's constables standing outside the closed door in almost the same positions they'd left them in.

"Everything in order, Necker?"

"Yes, sir. No one has been in or out, as you said, sir. Señora Calvo has asked to be let out. I said no."

"And the corregidor?"

"Not a sign of him, sir. But I have heard them arguing."

"I'm sure you have." He knocked on the door, and a servant answered it almost immediately. "We're here to speak to your master." Mendoza stepped inside without waiting for a reply while Gabriel followed close behind with his *escritorio* dangling from his shoulder. In the same moment, Señora Calvo appeared in the kitchen doorway on the other side of the courtyard, looking bored and petulant.

"How long must I stay here?" she asked.

"For as long as I say so, madam. Where is your husband?"

"In his room. He's been in there since yesterday morning. Feeling sorry for himself, no doubt. What I don't understand is why *I* have to stay here with him."

Mendoza felt himself about to say something that he knew he would regret.

"Which door?" he said tersely.

"The second one on the left."

He went upstairs, tapping his stick angrily on the marble floor, and knocked on Calvo's door. There was no answer.

"Calvo?"

He knocked more loudly, and there was still no response. He pushed on the handle, but the door was locked. "Calvo? Open the door, man!"

Downstairs in the courtyard, Señora Calvo and the servants were looking up at him, and Necker and the constable had also been attracted by the noise.

"It's bolted from the inside," Señora Calvo said. "The fool has probably drunk himself into a stupor."

Mendoza pushed against the door with his shoulder, but it remained solidly shut.

"I need someone to break it down!" he shouted.

Vargas's constable hurried away, and Necker came upstairs and tried without success to break open the door with his good shoulder. Ten minutes later the constable returned carrying a large blacksmith's hammer.

"And who's going to pay for the door if you smash it?" Cornelia Calvo complained.

Mendoza ignored her. After a few blows of the hammer, the wood around the lock began to splinter, and suddenly the door flew open. The constable stood back, and Mendoza stepped inside the darkened room. Even before he drew back the curtains, he could smell the familiar aroma that he had smelled so often in the last few weeks. Calvo was lying sprawled across the bed in his white shirt and hose, and the sheets around him were soaked with blood from his slashed wrists. The blood had also spread onto the floor, where it formed a pool around the knife that had fallen from his hand. The corregidor's grizzled face was as white as marble and in death he looked calm and serene, as if some burden he'd been carrying had now been lifted from him. On a table by the window, a sheaf of papers had been piled neatly next to an inkwell and quill.

Behind him Mendoza heard Cornelia Calvo let out a strange sound that was somewhere between a howl of pain and an exclamation of disgust or frustration as he read the short note addressed to him on top of the pile:

> *My dear Bernardo,*
>
> *Please forgive me if I call you by your first name out of respect for our friendship. You were right, of course. I should have died at Lepanto. Had I done so, I would have left this world as a hero and a martyr. Didn't the pope promise absolution for the sins of all those killed in the battle? Yet we survived, and in the years that followed, I discovered things about myself that I did not realize then I was capable of. You know I always admired you, Bernardo. You were the one with the high ideals, with all your beautiful schemes to help the poor and make the land fertile and your quaint belief in justice. But this country is not beautiful or just. And now I must leave this world covered in shame and dishonor, and I cannot stand to let you or anyone else judge me even in the short time I have to remain in it.*
>
> *So I have decided to break my word and betray you once again and make my own escape. But before that happens, I have something to give you, as a token of our*

friendship. You will find here my full confession regarding everything I have done, with all the facts that I have already told you and the details you need to know about this dirty business. I also include Villareal's letters to me in the hope that they will be of interest to you.

And now my journey is about to end. I do not ask your forgiveness, but I ask you from time to time to remember me how I once was, rather than the man you knew more recently, though it may be you will prefer not to think of me at all.

Your friend,
Pelagio

Mendoza gazed out the window at the sunlit street and remembered the young man with a bright smile and thick dark hair, arm wrestling for money in a tavern and smiling grimly while Mendoza and the other students cheered him on and chanted, "Cal-vo, Calvo!" He remembered shouted arguments about moral philosophy, student brawls when he and Calvo had staggered home to their lodgings arm in arm and battered and bloodied like soldiers, crawling through the rushes to watch the poor women bathing naked in the Tormes River. He remembered a distant Christmas when he and Calvo and their friends had drunkenly sung carols in the Plaza Mayor in Salamanca and how Calvo had performed a drunken galliard when the city watch ordered him to go home.

Most of all he remembered the brave young warrior who had fought the Saracens at Lepanto thirteen years earlier, a Spanish warrior whose strong arm had swept Mendoza off the deck and lowered him to safety and given him life. As long as he lived, he would never be able to connect those memories to the fat little man who'd been ready to see him crucified and who now lay on his own bed in his own blood. Only God could know the reasons for that transformation, but he promised himself that he would prove his old friend wrong and see that justice *was* done.

Behind him Necker, Gabriel and the constable were standing just inside the room, and as he gathered up the papers, he heard Cornelia Calvo's footsteps fading away in the corridor.

"Should we remove the body, sir?" asked the constable.

"No. Leave him here. And no one is to speak of this until I say so. Boy, give me your *escritorio*."

Gabriel looked at him curiously as he went out into the corridor carrying the *escritorio* and intercepted Cornelia Calvo on the stairs.

"Where are you going, señora?" Mendoza asked.

"To grieve for my husband," she said coldly.

"Perhaps if you had cared for him more when he was alive, he would not be dead. Come with me."

She did not protest as he ushered her across the courtyard past the terrified-looking servants and into the kitchen, where he closed the door behind them.

"Sit down," he ordered. "Can you write?"

"Of course I can write," she said.

"When you arranged to see Rodrigo Vallcarca, did you write or use your servants to communicate with him?"

"How dare you? I never—" Her white cheeks were flushed now. "I have no idea what you are referring to."

Mendoza leaned over the table so that his face was only a few feet away from hers. "Do not lie to me, señora. As far as I'm concerned, you are partly responsible for that corpse upstairs. I don't have Calvo, but I will charge you with complicity in his crimes unless you cooperate with me."

"I knew nothing about his business!"

"Maybe, maybe not. But as the investigating judge, I assure you that I can see to it that you go to the galleys for at least five years. Do you think you could survive that, madam?"

Señora Calvo stared back at him and shook her head.

"Nor do I," Mendoza said. "And if you want to avoid it, then you're going to have to help me."

"How?"

Mendoza smiled humorlessly. "You are going to write a love letter."

CHAPTER TWENTY-SIX

ODRIGO VALLCARCA WAS NOT THE TYPE OF man to think ahead, but even he knew better than to tell his father that Corregidor Calvo had been arrested and taken to Zaragoza. To do that would have required him to ride out to the hunting lodge, and it would also risk depriving himself of the night of pleasure that now lay ahead of him. Instead he waited until his family had retired to their rooms and then walked quickly through the rows of eucalyptus trees and out beyond the front gate to the little copse where his servant was waiting with his horse already saddled. He rode on alone, because servants were not required to be present for an occasion like this, and now the prospect of a night with Cornelia Calvo in her husband's own bed made his flesh ache and filled him with a craving that grew sharper as the trees and mountains flashed past him.

He saw her lying naked beneath him, and the thought of

her wrapping her thighs around him was enough to make him squeeze the horse more tightly with his own. Even now when he put his fingers to his nose, he could still smell the perfume from her letter, in which she had called him her darling, her lover, her young bull, and told him that her bed was empty and her lips were moist. She had never sounded so passionate and so eager, and as he urged his horse on through the moonlit night and felt the warm wind blowing in his face and hair, he promised himself that she would walk with difficulty the next morning.

On reaching the outskirts of the city, he slowed down and rode through the darkened streets to the stables near the pilgrims' inn, where he left his horse and continued on foot. Soon the corregidor's house appeared before him. He quickened his pace at the sight of the faint glimmer of light from the upstairs bedroom and imagined her white skin against the sheets in the canopy bed. On reaching the front door, he glanced around him and turned the handle. As she had promised, it was unlocked, and he slipped inside like a thief. No sooner had he shut the door behind him than he felt the barrel of a pistol against the back of his head and heard a voice saying, "Put your hands up and keep perfectly still."

Vallcarca did as he was told while a hand slowly drew his sword from its sheath.

"Is this a robbery?" he asked. "If so—"

"Shut up until you're spoken to."

Vallcarca heard movements from one of the other rooms now. For a moment he thought that Calvo had lured him into a trap as two men emerged from a doorway on the other side of the courtyard. One of them was carrying a torch, and as they came closer, he saw the judge who had humiliated him in front of his servants, accompanied by one of Calvo's *alguaciles*.

"Mendoza?" he exclaimed. "Why, that bitch from hell!"

"That's no way to talk about a lady," Mendoza said. "Bring him in."

Still holding the pistol pressed against Vallcarca's temple, Ventura prodded him forward in the back with his own sword and directed him toward the open doorway. Inside, Mendoza sat down at a table, where a younger man was already waiting by an *escritorio*. Ventura gestured to him to sit down.

"Rodrigo Vallcarca, you are under arrest," Mendoza said.

"What the hell for?"

"For the murders of the priest Father Panalles, Gonzalo del Río and his family and the *alguacil* Franquelo. I am also charging you with the murders of the Count of Cardona, Inquisitor Mercader and Commissioner Herrero and all the members of their party, in addition to rape, banditry and other offenses against His Majesty's peace."

"What?" Vallcarca stared back at Mendoza with an expression of stupefied incomprehension. "But this is nonsense."

"I have signed confessions from the bailiff Sánchez and the Morisco Vicente Péris and from three of the bandits who took part in the murders of the del Río family. I have enough proof to hang you ten times over."

"You've got Sánchez?" Vallcarca's face fell. "When? How?"

"Never mind how. Their statements prove beyond any doubt that you are the man who organized and directed these crimes, and before you hang, you will confess to every one of them."

Vallcarca bit his lip and looked around him with a bewildered and trapped expression. In the flickering light of the candle, the judge's face had a slightly hellish glow and his black eyes were devoid of pity or mercy.

"Damn it, Mendoza," Vallcarca protested. "It wasn't me. Sánchez is just trying to save his own skin! I swear on my mother's milk I didn't order any of this! I just did what I was told!"

"That's what Sánchez said," Mendoza replied. "Except that he said he took orders from you."

"It's not true! Sánchez killed Cardona on my father's orders! It was my father who sent him to kill you in France! It was nothing to do with me."

"Isn't it?" Mendoza nodded at Gabriel, who picked up his quill and dipped it in the inkwell. "In that case, if you want to save yourself, I advise you to start telling me why."

BARON VALLCARCA AWOKE in his hunting lodge to hear the startled flutter of birds just outside the window. Lying in the darkness with the woman sleeping beside him, he heard the unmistakable sound of horses' hooves from somewhere in the distance. The sound was so faint that he thought he might have imagined it, and he slipped out of bed and peered through a gap in the curtain. It was not yet daylight, and there was no sign of life from either inside or outside the house. Even the servants had not yet gotten up to start the fires and prepare the guns.

He was tempted to go back to sleep a little longer, but he felt the same tingling sensation at the back of his neck that had once saved him from Huguenot sentries or assassins during the wars in France, and he had learned never to ignore it. The woman stirred vaguely but did not wake up as he put on a shirt and unsheathed the sword that was hanging from the chair before walking barefoot into the dark hallway. As he descended the stairs, he thought once again that he heard movement from outside. He padded over to the window and looked down over the yard, but it seemed silent and empty. Finally he drew back the latch and opened the door. It was only then, as he stepped onto the wooden veranda, that he saw the man in the morion helmet standing directly in front of him with an escopeta pointed at his head.

"Drop your weapon," the man commanded.

Vallcarca took an instinctive step backward as other shapes began to move toward him in the darkness, and he reached for the door handle.

"One more move and your brains will be all over that door," said the man with the escopeta. "Dead or alive, it makes no difference."

Vallcarca dropped the sword. All around the yard, men were advancing cautiously toward the house now in a semicircle, bearing pistols, swords and escopetas, and one of them was walking more slowly, tapping a stick on the ground.

"I wouldn't try it, Baron. The house is surrounded. And it would not bother me at all if my men were to shoot you like a dog."

"Mendoza," Vallcarca said disgustedly as one of the men stepped onto the veranda and held a sword against his throat. "What brings you here so early?"

"I'm arresting you in the name of the king for murder, blackmail and other crimes against the public peace."

"Well, can I at least get dressed first?"

Mendoza shook his head. "Your servants can bring what you need to Zaragoza."

"Zaragoza! Damn it, Mendoza! I'm Vallcarca, not some peasant! At least let me get my boots on!"

"Take him."

Vallcarca clenched his fists and looked momentarily inclined to resist until the point of Ventura's sword dissuaded him. One of the constables tied his hands, and Ventura prodded him forward with the sword. Some of the servants had come out onto the veranda now and watched as their master was led barefoot and tied up through the yard. Mendoza ordered them to go back inside, and he followed Vallcarca out along the road to where the horses and carriage were waiting. Ventura pushed the baron into the carriage, and Mendoza and his cousin sat down opposite their prisoner as they rode back toward the Huesca road.

"I don't know where you got these allegations from, Mendoza," Vallcarca said furiously. "But neither you nor the corregidor will ever see me hang."

"Corregidor Calvo is dead," Mendoza replied calmly. "But your son has been very cooperative."

"What are you talking about?" Vallcarca looked suddenly less certain. "My son's at my father-in-law's house."

"Not anymore," Mendoza said.

They stopped at the turnoff to Huesca and waited until the countess's militia escort appeared, together with the carts carrying the prisoners they had taken from the Catalan's band. As the cortege came closer, Vallcarca saw his son sitting in one of the carts with his legs and feet bound together. He glared at him incredulously, but Rodrigo looked away as if he had not seen him. Mendoza gave the order to move out, and they began to wind their way back down to the scorched white plain as the sun came up and flooded the arid hills with dazzling, luminous light. They were not long past Huesca when they came across a group of travelers who were coming in the opposite direction in a procession of horses, mules and carts. One of them was a sweating priest in a black soutane, perched uncomfortably on a mule and leading a donkey carrying a large bundle.

"God be with you, brothers," he said, glancing nervously at the prisoners and their armed escorts. "How is the road ahead?"

"Very quiet," Necker replied.

The priest and the other travelers looked relieved.

"May I inquire where you are going?" Mendoza asked.

"To Belamar de la Sierra," the priest replied gloomily. "It's a Morisco village. Do you know it?"

"I do, Father," Mendoza said. "As a matter of fact, we have just come from there."

"I understand there have been some problems in the village," the priest said.

"There were, Father." Mendoza smiled as the carriage moved away. "But I think you'll find that things are much calmer now."

THE ARRIVAL OF such a large contingent of prisoners caused great excitement in Zaragoza, where rumors of what had taken place in Cardona had already begun to circulate through the city. As they rode along the crowded Corso, pedestrians, shopkeepers and artisans stared curiously at the wild beasts from the mountains who had murdered two inquisitors. The more daring bystanders ran up to the carts and attempted to hit the prisoners before Ventura beat them off. By the time they reached the city jail, a large crowd was following them, and some of Mendoza's men were obliged to push them back as the prisoners were led inside.

The prisoners were still being processed when the viceroy arrived, accompanied by his servants. Mendoza had already written to Sástago to inform him of his imminent arrival, and the viceroy congratulated Mendoza on a successful conclusion to his investigation. When Mendoza replied that the investigation would not be concluded until his prisoners had been tried and convicted, the viceroy looked suddenly anxious. He nevertheless invited Mendoza, Ventura, Gabriel and Necker to stay at his house once again, while Vargas's men and the Moriscos made their way back up to the mountains.

After a fine lunch of roasted peacock and almond sauce, the reasons for the viceroy's anxiety became clear when Mendoza gave him a detailed account of the investigation and everything that had taken place since they'd last met.

"My God, Mendoza," Sástago said. "I told you your investigation would be difficult, but I didn't expect anything like this. This is real villainy. The king was preparing to send troops to put down the rebellion. There was even talk that the wedding might have to be called off."

"There is no need for that, Your Grace. This is a conspiracy, not a rebellion. I know the names of the men responsible. And I intend to make sure that they pay the price for their crimes—from the highest to the lowest."

"Was Mercader aware of this?"

"No. Pachuca was Villareal's man. Mercader believed what he wanted to believe. He wanted heresy, and Vallcarca was only interested in Cardona. He had the countess's husband killed so that he could get her to marry his son. When that failed, he tried to get an Inquisition investigation in Belamar so that she would turn to him. If she was arrested, that was all right, too, because then Espinosa would have become her daughter's guardian and he would have married *her* off to Rodrigo. It was a good plan, but Villareal wasn't going to let it happen. He bought off the baron's men and used them for his own purposes."

"Which were?"

"Cardona. Villareal wanted the *señorio* for himself. He wanted to persuade the king to send troops to occupy Cardona, partly because he didn't want Vallcarca to get it and also because he expected to be rewarded for his efforts. And why not? He was Aragonese. He was already directly involved in this affair from the beginning. As treasurer of the Council of Aragon, he would have been the logical choice as Crown administrator for Cardona once law and order had been restored. Of course, that would not have taken long, because he was responsible for organizing the mayhem in the first place!"

"A clever plan," Sástago agreed. "And a diabolical one. But who is this Catalan?"

"His name is Lupercio Borrell. He's a bandit. He was in the baron's employ, but he was also Villareal's man. That's all I know about him."

At the mention of the name, Sástago looked even more anxious. "He's not just a bandit, Don Bernardo."

"You know him?"

"I know of him. Borrell was a spy for our cause in France during the Wars of Religion. The Crown paid him, but he reported directly to Villareal here in Zaragoza. And there's something else you should know. Some years ago one of Villareal's daughters was impregnated by Rodrigo Vallcarca. Some say she was seduced. Others said she was raped. Either way the young lady had the baby before Villareal sent her into a convent. Of course he was angry with her—she ruined a very lucrative marriage. But the marquis was even angrier with Vallcarca. Naturally it was all hushed up. It didn't seem relevant—until now."

"So it wasn't just money," Mendoza said. "Honor was involved—if you consider that murdering innocent people and stirring up treason and rebellion in order to take revenge on your enemies is an honorable thing to do."

"But a man who will do such things will not allow himself to be ruined. Be careful, Licenciado. Villareal has the ear of the king. He is also a grandee."

"And his rank will not protect him from His Majesty's justice," Mendoza said firmly.

The viceroy said that he had just received a letter from Villareal's secretary asking why he hadn't had any communication from Licenciado Mendoza or Corregidor Calvo in nearly two weeks and requesting further information on the situation in Cardona. The letter had also suggested that Mendoza was not competent and might have lost control of the investigation.

Mendoza looked unperturbed. "The marquis will never receive any letters from me," he said. "From now on I will communicate the results of my investigation only to His Majesty."

Sástago frowned once again. Whatever happened to Villareal, he said, neither Vallcarca nor his son nor any of the other prisoners could be tried by a Castilian judge, and Mendoza would not be able to take any of his prisoners to Castile. Diplomacy and the infanta's wedding demanded that these norms be respected. He had nevertheless arranged a compromise with the justiciar of Aragon, in which the prisoners would be tried by an Aragonese judge and Mendoza would be able to advise and give evidence but not to pass sentence.

Mendoza was not entirely surprised by this. The following day he and the viceroy met with the justiciar of Aragon, Juan de Luna, who said that Mendoza would be required to hand over all his depositions to the trial judge. Mendoza politely refused and said that Castilian law did not allow him to hand over documentation that he had acquired in the course of an investigation. Both Sástago and the justiciar looked worried now, and after some discussion Mendoza agreed to allow his Aragonese counterparts to read and even copy his depositions in his presence or the presence of his scribe but not to hand them over.

He also managed to extract certain commitments in exchange for his cooperation. Rodrigo Vallcarca was not to be sentenced to death on condition that he testify against his father. Any prisoners or bandits who provided information on the conspiracy against Cardona would receive a similar commutation of sentence, and the Countess of Cardona's father-in-law, the Marquis of Espinosa, was to be banished from the *señorio* in perpetuity.

That same day Mendoza dictated a letter to Gabriel that was addressed for the first time directly to the king, in which he detailed his case against Villareal. Gabriel spent the rest of the afternoon copying out Calvo's confession, and the following day Mendoza included the original in the letter that he sent to the king. He also went to the Aljafería and asked to see Mercader's colleague Orellana, a dour-looking monk who was now the sole inquisitor for Aragon pending Mercader's replacement. The conversation did not get off on a good footing, as Orellana informed Mendoza that the baker Romero was an employee of the Inquisition and as such could be tried only by the Holy Office.

"I am aware of this, Your Excellency," Mendoza replied. "And it was my intention to hand the prisoner over to your jurisdiction as soon as I arrived in Zaragoza. Unfortunately, the justiciar has now assumed responsibility for all my prisoners."

"Well, this is always the problem in this kingdom," Orellana complained. "The Aragonese are intransigent."

Mendoza agreed that they were and said that such intransigence had not helped his own investigation. Orellana listened with more interest now as Mendoza explained the purpose of his visit. He did not presume to ask the Holy Office what the Moriscos had been accused of, he said, but he did know that they had originally been arrested on charges of rape and that these charges were false. His own investigation had revealed that the two sisters had been attacked not by the Moriscos but by men acting on the orders of the Baron of Vallcarca, as part of a criminal conspiracy against the Countess of Cardona in which Inquisitor Mercader had become unwittingly involved.

Orellana had clearly not been aware of any of this. "So the baron ordered the murder of the priest?" he asked.

"Indeed. It was carried out by the bailiff Sánchez, a bandit named Lupercio Borrell and Constable Franquelo. The bailiff was also an accomplice in the murder of the Count of Cardona two years ago."

"And the three brothers?"

"They were also killed by Borrell and his band, as part of a criminal conspiracy undertaken by Corregidor Calvo under the direct orders of the Marquis of Villareal. The bailiff Sánchez was also part of the same conspiracy, and so was the Inquisition *familiar* Pachuca.

Corregidor Calvo and the bandit Borrell were also responsible for the murders of Inquisitor Mercader and Commissioner Herrero."

Orellana was staring at him with a mixture of incomprehension and astonishment. "And you have proof of this?" he asked.

"I do, Excellency. I have a full confession from the corregidor. I would be happy to pass on a copy to the Holy Office."

Orellana thanked him for his cooperation and sat back in his chair with a worried expression. It was not the purpose of the Inquisition, he said, to punish the innocent, and he promised to reconsider the verdicts against the Moriscos and take this information into account. Mendoza left feeling satisfied that this was the best he was likely to get and confident that Villareal's name would now be passed on to Orellana's superiors. The following week he gave evidence to the new investigating judge, Argensola, for the first time. His testimony lasted two days, and the judge's questioning assuaged many of his doubts about the willingness of the Aragonese to carry the investigation to its conclusion. The next week Vallcarca was subjected to the torment, and after four days of torture Argensola informed Sástago that Vallcarca had confessed to all the charges against him.

MENDOZA WAS NOT REQUIRED to play any part in these proceedings, but he was unwilling to leave Zaragoza until justice had been served. He and his men stayed at Sástago's palace. They slept in comfortable beds and ate fine meals every day. The ache in his leg had finally subsided now that he was no longer obliged to ride a horse each day, and he had time to visit churches, cathedrals and bookshops and make sketches of the city from the other side of the Ebro.

Despite these pleasures he was eager to return to Valladolid, and he was anxious at the lack of any response to his letter to the king. Gabriel and Necker were equally keen to return to Castile, and Ventura was also becoming bored and restless.

Over the next month, the judicial process moved surprisingly quickly. In two large trials the bandits received a range of sentences that included service in the galleys and in penal colonies and the amputation of hands and feet. Five weeks after their arrival, Vallcarca and his son were sentenced by Judge Argensola in the criminal court at the Audience of Aragon in the palace of the Counts of Luna. Mendoza, Gabriel, Ventura, and Necker were all present at the trial. Rodrigo Vallcarca received eight years on the king's oars, and Vallcarca was given a death sentence. The baron looked older and less imposing than when Mendoza had last seen him, and his bull-like presence was notably reduced by the impact of the torture. He did not even make eye contact with his son. When the sentence was read out he merely smiled faintly and looked across the gallery at Mendoza.

On the night of June 12, Mendoza visited Vallcarca in his cell to bring him wine, sweets and biscuits. The baron had just made his last confession, and Mendoza found him sitting on the edge of a cot that seemed too small for him, wearing a white shirt with a prison blanket wrapped around his broad shoulders. He exuded an air of gloomy resignation and sat at the table to share the food and drink.

"So, Mendoza," he said. "You've come to savor your triumph?"

"To pay my respects, Baron."

"Baron!" Vallcarca pulled a sour expression. "Well, that doesn't matter now, does it? But I have made my confession, and the priest says there is hope for me."

Mendoza doubted it, and he poured the wine in silence. Vallcarca raised his glass in one of his large hands and drank it down in a single gulp. "I thank you for bringing sweet wine to a dead man, Licenciado. Did you know that William of Orange has been assassinated?"

"I did."

"And do you think His Most Catholic Majesty is responsible?"

"I have no idea."

Vallcarca laughed. "You see, Licenciado. Even princes must sometimes behave like common highwaymen. What choice did I have?"

"Everyone has a choice," Mendoza said. "The warden says that Rodrigo wants to see you, to ask for forgiveness."

"He can go to hell." Vallcarca poured himself another glass. "Maybe I'll meet him there. Then we can talk. Let him ask the *priest* to forgive him."

"There's one thing about this affair that I still don't understand," Mendoza said. "Why did Sánchez betray his mistress? Was it only for money?"

The baron looked at him with a faintly amused smile. "No one does anything just for money, Licenciado. The bailiff was jealous."

"Jealous of whom? The countess has no plans to marry."

Vallcarca's smile widened. "Who said anything about the countess? And I'm not talking about a man."

Mendoza looked at him uncomprehendingly, and then he remembered the hateful expression on the bailiff's face when he spoke to Susana and the insult he'd directed at her, and he realized that what the countess had been concealing from him had been in front of his eyes the whole time.

"Sánchez was in love with Segura's daughter?" he asked.

"Correct!" Vallcarca said. "And the countess was the reason he couldn't have her. There was his wife, of course, but you don't let things like *that* get in the way, do you? And you know what love can do when it turns rancid. Or maybe you don't, Licenciado?"

Mendoza felt momentarily angry with the countess for having deceived him, but the emotion quickly subsided as he looked at the smirk on Vallcarca's face.

"Does Segura know about this?" he asked.

"That pious old Moor? How do you think he'd feel if he knew his daughter was a sodomite?"

"But I suppose you used it against her?"

Vallcarca shrugged. "I tried, Licenciado. And thanks to you I failed. And now I would like you to leave. I need a little more time to prepare to meet my Maker."

THE FOLLOWING MORNING Vallcarca was decapitated in the market square. Gabriel did not want to see the execution, and Mendoza, Ventura and Necker joined the procession of dignitaries as Judge Argensola led the prisoner from the prison to the place of execution, where a large crowd had gathered to watch. Vallcarca dispensed with his guards and walked slowly and deliberately toward the execution block with his arms tied behind him, in an open tunic with his chest puffed out and a calm, unruffled expression. He loudly repented his sins to the waiting monks, glanced up at the drifting clouds and then laid his head on the block.

A moment later the ax came down and the bearded head fell to the ground. The executioner proceeded to carve the body into the four pieces that were to be displayed on the outskirts of the city. Finally the crowd began to disperse, and the Inquisitor Orellana came over to Mendoza and told him that the Morisco carpenter Navarro would not be burned but sentenced to the galleys instead. His apprentice would be set free, and their families would not lose their property. Vargas was also among the spectators and told him that the Catalan Lupercio Borrell had been found hanging from a tree near the Puerto de Somport with a sign around his neck that read BANDIT. Some said he'd been killed by *montañeses* who had heard Mendoza's proclamation accusing him of the murders of the Quintana brothers. Others said he had been killed by his own men.

Mendoza's work was done, and he told the viceroy that he and his men would be returning to Castile the following morning. That night he and Ventura ate supper at the viceroy's house for the last time, and the viceroy invited Necker and Gabriel to join them. The next morning Mendoza ate breakfast with the old viceroy and thanked him for his hospitality and assistance.

"Not at all, Licenciado," the viceroy replied. "Aragon and the king should thank you and your men for putting an end to this villainy. Now we can all look forward to the infanta's marriage next year. And I have just been informed that a new corregidor has been appointed in Jaca and that he will shortly be passing through Zaragoza."

"And the king of Navarre is now heir to the French throne," Mendoza said. "And he may have to become a Catholic. So perhaps the Béarnese will lose interest in Spain."

"Perhaps," Sástago said. "But I must warn you, Mendoza. Villareal sent a messenger to me personally this morning. The marquis is furious that you don't answer his letters. I would say he is also rather concerned."

"He has good reason to be," Mendoza said.

"I hope you know what you're doing, Licenciado Mendoza," the viceroy said. "There's one other thing I wanted to ask you. I was talking to Judge Argensola after the execution, and he told me that during Vallcarca's interrogation the baron said that the countess was a *bujarrona*. He said that she and her maidservant were having . . . intimate relations." The viceroy pulled a face on uttering these words, as though he had just tasted a bitter lemon. "Did you ever have reason to suspect such a thing?"

Mendoza showed no sign of surprise or emotion. "I did not, Your Grace. And this sounds to me like another attempt by a desperate man trying to escape judgment."

"That's what I thought." The viceroy looked pleased. "Well, maybe now that all these villains are out of the way, she'll find herself a good man. She has to if she wants to preserve the House of Cardona."

"She does, Your Grace," Mendoza agreed. "And I have no doubt that she will find one."

CHAPTER TWENTY-SEVEN

THE COUNTESS SAT WATCHING CAROLINA scatter bread crumbs along the edge of the patio while Susana walked along beside her. From the roof and the high wall and the branches of the lemon tree, a few sparrows fluttered down and began to peck at them as Susana raised her finger to her lips to indicate to Carolina that she should remain silent. The countess and Susana smiled at each other, in a way that they were able to do only when they were removed from the scrutiny of the outside world. One day that might change, the countess thought, when Carolina grew older and learned that certain forms of love were sinful and forbidden, but for now the immediate threat that had been hanging over them had been removed.

She knew that this security was fragile and that the threat would never disappear completely. There was always the possibility that one day she or Susana would be discovered, that some other Sánchez or Vallcarca might emerge to denounce or blackmail her, that some new inquisitor would take the place of Mercader. But more than ever it seemed a risk worth taking, and now, at last, she had found a way to reduce it. She had the letters of approval from Sister Margarita and Bishop Santos. That same morning she had discussed with Father García the final arrangements for Sunday's service and approved the message that was to be proclaimed by the *pregonero* over the coming days.

She knew that what she proposed to do was sinful. To renounce the flesh in public when she had no intention of renouncing it in private was not an act that could please God. But there were so many things she would do to please him that she was convinced that God would forgive her, and there was no other way that she, Susana and Carolina could remain together in this world and preserve the House of Cardona. One day she would convince her Morisco vassals that the Son of God had been born of a virgin. She would convince them to believe in the Holy Trinity and the Resurrection. She would bring those souls to Christ one by one, through patience and persuasion, till there would no longer be any distinction between Old Christians and New Christians. And one day, if God willed it, she would make her last confession in her own bed and not in an inquisitorial jail, surrounded by her daughter, her grandchildren and the woman she loved most of all.

She smiled at the thought as Tomás came out onto the patio and told her that the Count of Espinosa had arrived. For the first time in her life, she felt relieved to see her father-in-law. Because Espinosa was the one remaining issue she had not resolved, and since he had fled to Toledo, it had begun to seem increasingly unlikely that she could resolve it. She had sent two messengers in an attempt to coax him back, and now he had returned in search of the one thing that always attracted him. She promised herself that he would not leave unless she got exactly what she wanted.

She waited a few more minutes before going out to the drawing room. The last time she'd seen him there, Espinosa had been unctuous, hypocritical and menacing. Now he oozed fake humility and fake repentance as he got up and tried to kiss her.

"Isabel," he said. "I'm sorry."

She walked straight past him without offering her cheek and sat down in the same seat where she had greeted him less than two months before.

"Of course you're sorry," she said, looking at him coldly. "Because your master is now dead and your plot has collapsed."

"I didn't know anyone would be killed!" he protested. "I only wanted to protect Cardona."

"You wished to protect yourself, sir."

"You judge me too harshly. You were being stubborn. Marrying Vallcarca was our best option."

"*Your* best option. And please stop pretending that this had anything to do with my welfare. You demean yourself, sir. You would have seen me in the Aljafería!"

"I thought that you'd agree to marry Rodrigo first."

"You lie to me as you lie to yourself. You are a villain, sir, and I could *never* judge you too harshly!"

Espinosa stiffened, and the haughtiness returned, curdling his bony, cadaverous features into a contemptuous scowl. "And is that why you asked me here? So that you could tell me that? You could have said it in a letter."

"There are some things that cannot be said in letters. I summoned you here because you are fond of business propositions. Well, I have one to make to you. I will give you three thousand ducats toward your debts. In return you will renounce your family's claims to Cardona. You will agree never to return to these estates or have any contact with my daughter or any member of my family. You will agree to all this in the presence of a notary."

Espinosa looked unimpressed. "That's a lot to ask for three thousand ducats. It won't even cover half of what I owe."

"To guarantee this arrangement," the countess went on, "you will sign a full confession in the presence of witnesses admitting that you and Vallcarca tried to blackmail me. You will state that any imputations of bad character or impious behavior attributed to me were inventions concocted by the two of you. In the event of any violation of this agreement, copies of this confession will be sent to the justiciar, to His Majesty and also to Licenciado Mendoza."

Espinosa looked incredulous now. "And what makes you think I would be stupid enough to agree to something like that?"

"Because you are now in Cardona, and if you refuse, I shall have you arrested and placed in the seigneurial jail. My own courts will interrogate you and try you and find you guilty. And I assure you, you will hang."

"Hang the father of your own husband? Come now, Isabel. That's not you at all."

The countess was sitting demurely with her hands folded on her lap. "You have no idea what I am capable of, sir. Licenciado Mendoza knows everything about you. It is only because of me that you have not been arrested already. You have no more choices. You will do as I say or you will die in Cardona."

Espinosa's clawlike hands were wrestling with each other, and he stared back at her with a mixture of helpless anger and self-pity. "You would blackmail an old man?"

The countess's face was expressionless as she got to her feet.

"I would, sir," she said coldly. "You came back here for money. And I advise you to accept what I am offering. You may wait here while I summon the notary. If you even attempt to leave this room, you will be arrested. Would you like Esteban to bring you some lunch after your journey?"

"I've lost my appetite," he replied.

"I'm sorry to hear that." The Countess of Cardona smiled benignly, and with a faint swishing of her velvet gown she walked out the door and shut it quietly behind her.

ON THE WAY BACK TO VALLADOLID, their mood was very different from that on the outward journey. This time there were no ribald anecdotes, no tales of old wars and battles, no cursing and laughter. All of them were conscious of the two companions whom they'd left in the mountains, though no one spoke about them. Conversation was sparse and mostly perfunctory. Even Gabriel, who had spoken to everyone and never stopped asking questions on the journey up from Castile, now spent much of the day riding alone, immersed in his own thoughts.

Ventura was also subdued, and Mendoza sensed that he was sinking into one of the brooding moods that often overcame him when there were no wars, adventures or affairs of the heart to distract and excite him. His cousin became noticeably more morose the closer they drew to Valladolid. On the final day, they reached the Esgueva River, and everybody's spirits seemed to lift at the sight of the city walls except Ventura's, who appeared even gloomier as Necker began talking almost animatedly about how much he was looking forward to seeing his wife and children again.

"And what will you do, cousin?" Mendoza asked.

"I don't know. See how things are in Madrid. Perhaps I'll go back to Flanders."

"Why don't you stay with us till you make up your mind?"

Gabriel urged him to accept the invitation, and Mendoza was pleased to observe that his page seemed almost cheerful. He waited until they reached the outskirts of the city before riding alongside the young man.

"There's something I've been meaning to say to you," Mendoza said awkwardly.

"Sir?"

"There are many men in Valladolid or Madrid who would like a page or a secretary. I could arrange it for you with an excellent recommendation, especially after what you've done."

Gabriel looked at him in surprise. "Why would I want to do that, sir?"

"I thought perhaps you might feel different . . . after what I told you."

"I thank you for the offer, sir. But I want to go home."

"I'm glad to hear it—"

Mendoza was about to call him "boy," but suddenly it seemed no longer appropriate. Gabriel smiled at him, and Mendoza smiled, too, and as they entered the familiar streets once again, he realized that in some way he did not fully understand, the little boy he'd saved at Galera had also rescued him and enabled him to preserve the humanity that the War of Granada had very nearly taken away from him.

Without Gabriel he, too, might have lost his bearings, like his cousin, and spent his life chasing danger or ended up as bitter and resentful as the old friend who had once plucked him from the deck of an infidel ship.

"Bernardo," his cousin asked him now, "do you remember when the abbot told me I should go into the world to do some good?"

"Of course."

"Do you think we did some good in Aragon?"

Mendoza smiled. "I believe we did," he said.

ONCE AGAIN THEY RODE into the Plaza Mayor, past the Royal Chancellery, and the lawyers swarming like black bees, and the notaries with their brown leather bags and sheaves of papers, along the cobbled streets until they saw his house, and Mendoza could not remember a time when he'd ever been so happy to see it. The three of them unloaded their bags and weapons, and Mendoza knocked loudly while Necker took the horses to the stables. A few minutes later, Magdalena appeared in the doorway and clapped her hands to her cheeks at the sight of them.

"*¡Dios mío!*" She made the sign of the cross and looked gratefully up toward the sky. "Thank you, Lord!"

Tears were rolling down her cheeks now as the little housekeeper embraced Gabriel and pressed her head against his chest and pulled his face down toward her to kiss him. Gabriel bit his lip and stared resolutely at the door behind her in an effort to contain his own tears.

"I told you I'd bring him back alive," Mendoza said.

"I prayed every day for all of you! Every day!"

Mendoza told her that Ventura would be staying with them for a while, and she hugged him and Ventura, too. He had thought that he would give his report to Judge Saravia that day, but it was getting late and he was in no mood to see him. Nor was he ready yet to see Martín's wife and Daniel's fiancée and tell them what had happened. Magda gave him his letters, including one that she said had arrived only two days before from Aragon. He recognized Sástago's handwriting and went to his bedroom and looked at his books, his pictures and the vihuela resting against the wall. It was still in tune, and he played a few notes and then laid it back down, because he was not yet ready for music.

Instead he sat at his table near the window and opened Sástago's letter. It was only a short note, thanking him once again for his work in the investigation. The viceroy informed him that he had written to the king to praise Mendoza for his efforts in bringing peace and tranquillity to Aragon and uncovering the scandalous and unpleasant events that had threatened the royal wedding. The letter also brought surprising news from Cardona. In the week of his departure from Aragon, the countess had declared her intention to become a *beata*—a holy woman—and had pledged to build a new monastery and convent in the Cardona estates. The archbishop of Zaragoza had approved this decision, and her new status was to be publicly proclaimed in a ceremony at the church in Cardona attended by Archbishop Santos and leading members of the Aragonese clergy.

Though the countess would not go into a convent or lose her title, she had taken vows of celibacy and pledged to dedicate the rest of her life to pious works. The legal status of her estates was not yet clear, the viceroy said, but she was believed to be seeking a special dispensation from His Majesty to allow the Cardona inheritance to pass directly to her daughter, Carolina. Even more surprising, her father-in-law had signed documents renouncing the Espinosa family's claims to her estates. All this was known even in Zaragoza, because the countess had made sure of it. A lot of men would be disappointed by this decision, the viceroy said, including some he knew, but what the world had lost, the church had certainly gained.

Mendoza smiled. He imagined the countess kneeling in front of the altar and the wounded blue eyes gazing up toward the cross as she pledged herself to Christ in front of a packed church. He had no doubt that the congregation would have been impressed by her piety, because the Countess of Cardona was a very pious and very convincing woman, who was cleverer than any of them thought, and she was willing to take great risks to protect those she loved. And whether or not her secrets were ever revealed, he promised himself that it would not be due to him.

THE MARQUIS OF VILLAREAL looked out the window as his carriage climbed up the hill from the Manzanares River alongside the old defensive walls toward the broad plateau where the great stone façade of the Royal Alcázar loomed over the capital. The road was busy, and some of the travelers paused to admire the gleaming silver-and-walnut carriage with its team of six horses and its fifteen-man escort. Villareal stared stoically past them toward the four conical towers and the rows of symmetrical windows, where his gaze rested anxiously on the Golden Tower that housed the royal apartments.

For years his life and career had revolved around the Royal Palace. Within its walls he had made love and money, friends, allies and enemies, and he had continued the inexorable ascent that would one day take him into the royal household. There had been times when things had not always gone as they should, but he'd never felt that his position within the court or the government was under any real threat. Even his rivals understood that he was one of the king's most trusted ministers, and until very recently Villareal had believed that, too. But now he could not shake off the feeling that the world he had once belonged to was slowly and invisibly pulling away from him and that there was nothing he could do to prevent it.

It was six weeks since he'd last received a report from Alcalde Mendoza and a month since he'd received the letter announcing that all the judge's future reports would be sent directly to the king. Since then his secretary had written four letters to Zaragoza demanding an explanation, without receiving an answer. He had even sent a letter and a messenger to the viceroy's house, but Mendoza had refused to speak to him.

It was obvious that Mendoza had now become his enemy. As the carriage approached the central gate, he reminded himself that Calvo was dead, and so were Sánchez and the Catalan. Whatever Mendoza knew, or thought he knew, and whatever he'd told the king, there was no one left alive who was able to testify against Villareal. Yet he had written to the king two weeks ago to recommend a replacement for Corregidor Calvo and to demand Mendoza's recall and still had not received a reply.

That silence was far more troubling than Mendoza's, and he tried to suppress his anxiety as the carriage entered the courtyard and came to a halt alongside the patio where the Council of Aragon had its chambers. A servant opened the door, and he stepped down onto the cobblestones and glanced around at the familiar crowd of hawkers, food vendors, courtiers, lords and ladies, servants, pages, officials and petitioning soldiers who filled the vast space. He nodded at the courtiers and officials who required acknowledgment, and they nodded back or bowed and fluttered their fans. All this was how it should be, and it was not until he saw Secretary Vázquez standing outside the doorway of the Council of Aragon that his stomach tightened and the anxiety flared up once again.

"Good morning, Secretary Vázquez."

"Excellency." The secretary did not bow or return the smile. "His Majesty wishes to see you."

"Of course," Villareal replied. "Shall I attend His Majesty after the council meeting or later today?"

"The king wishes to see you now."

Villareal nodded obediently and followed the secretary up to the first floor, past the rows of paintings and past more officials and courtiers, some of whom, he was now certain, were looking at him differently. The secretary left him in the reception room, and he glanced absently at the rows of paintings by Titian, Antonis Mor, Tintoretto and Bassano and other artists whose names he'd forgotten. Normally he liked to arrive early to his meetings with the king in order to admire them, but now he paced up and down until he came to a halt in front of the triptych by the Flemish painter Bosch, one of the king's favorites.

The central panel showed a peaceful, bucolic scene of peasants enjoying themselves around a giant hay wagon while Jesus looked down from a cloud above them. Some were singing, dancing and playing musical instruments. Others were preparing and eating food against a background of green hills. In the third panel, an army of demons and half-men/half-animals were storming a town with siege ladders and burning, raping, killing and looting while the corpses of naked men and women littered the ground all around them.

The juxtaposition disturbed him, and he did not understand the painter's intentions. He was still staring at the painting when Secretary Vázquez emerged through a door and summoned him inside. The king was in his study, dressed in his usual black, and did not look up as he entered the room.

"We have received an unusual request from the Countess of Cardona," he said. "She wishes to change the status of the Cardona inheritance so that her estates can be passed on to her daughter. I am minded to do as she asks, given that it now appears she was not what she seemed to be. And this judge of yours speaks very highly of her."

Villareal bowed slightly. "As Your Majesty wishes."

"He speaks less highly of you, Counselor," the king went on. "In fact, we have lately received a troubling letter from Zaragoza in which Alcalde Mendoza has made some very serious accusations."

Villareal had the peculiar sensation that the floor was moving beneath his feet. He would have liked to sit down, but he received no such invitation as Secretary Vázquez read out the contents of Mendoza's letter in an emotionless monotone.

"Your Majesty, I categorically deny these scurrilous and groundless accusations, and I defy Judge Mendoza to produce any evidence to support them," he said emphatically when Vázquez had finished.

Philip nodded at his secretary, who presented him with the copy of Calvo's confession, and the two men watched in silence while Villareal read it.

"Sire, this document has no legal value. It is the last testament of a man who is about to kill himself and has clearly lost his senses. I have never had the relationship with the corregidor that he describes."

"And yet he insists that you did. And Judge Mendoza has also sent us letters that you sent to him in which you refer to 'our business in Cardona' and a man called Lupe?"

"I was referring to the corregidor's investigation, sire. And the name refers to the bandit Lupercio Borrell, whom I wanted Calvo to arrest."

"Señor Borrell was also in our employ at one time, was he not? When he assisted the Catholic cause in France?"

"That is correct, Your Majesty."

"And he performed some valuable services on our behalf?"

"He did, Majesty. But he has since become a criminal and a bandit, and it was my understanding that he was working for Baron Vallcarca."

"I see." The gray eyes continued to look at him with the same terrifying disdain. "And what did you mean by 'sparkle'?"

"'Sparkle,' Your Majesty?"

"You asked the corregidor for more sparkle—on more than one occasion."

"I wanted the corregidor to pursue his investigations with more vigor." Villareal was conscious that his forehead was sweating, and he resisted the urge to wipe it. "I believe that Alcalde Mendoza has misinterpreted my language and my intentions."

"Yet you yourself have told me that this judge is of good reputation. And now you say that he is incompetent and reckless and you have asked me to recall him."

"I have since discovered that his reputation was inflated. It has been obvious for some time that he has been out of his depth in this investigation."

The king nodded. "Perhaps," he said icily. "But Grand Inquisitor Quiroga has written to us praising Judge Mendoza for his cooperation, and he has mentioned your name in connection with the murders of his officials."

It seemed to Villareal that a howling, cold wind was blowing through the room. He felt dizzy and light-headed and wished that he could sink into the floor and vanish.

"Sire, this is a conspiracy to blacken my name. You know that I have always served you well."

"Indeed. But now your services are no longer required. You are no longer my counselor, and you are no longer welcome at court. You may return to your estates, but you will no longer travel anywhere with more than four servants."

"Your Majesty—"

Philip smiled. It was an odd, disturbing smile without a trace of warmth, humor or understanding, a smile that told Villareal the conversation was now over and so was his career. He bowed deeply and left the room, and as the door closed behind him, he knew that he would never be coming back.

ON SUNDAY, Mendoza went to church early and lit two candles, one for Daniel and one for Martín, and waited for the congregants to arrive. He was pleased to see Elena among them, and he was even happier to see that she was without her husband. After all this time, he was not confident that she might still have any interest in him, but as soon as he saw her lips part with pleasure beneath the veil, he knew that he had no need to worry. When the service was over, he went outside and waited for an opportunity to speak to her and suppressed his impatience when he saw Saravia waddling toward him.

"There you are, Mendoza," the judge said, looking at him suspiciously. "I heard you were back, but you didn't come to see me."

"I arrived late yesterday afternoon, Your Worship. I intended to report to you first thing tomorrow."

"Did you? And did you know that the king was preparing to send three thousand troops to Cardona and he has now reversed his decision? Did you know the Marquis of Villareal has been dismissed from his post and expelled from the court? No one seems to know why, but they're saying he will be lucky to escape criminal charges."

"I was unaware of that, sir."

"Well, you can give me a full report tomorrow."

Mendoza promised that he would, and as the judge wandered off to speak to a group of lawyers, he saw Elena with the corner of his eye, gracefully maneuvering her way through the crowd toward him with her maidservant, like the figurehead of a ship.

"Licenciado Mendoza!" she said. "You have descended from the mountains. Have you brought the stone tablets with you?"

"Unfortunately, I was unable to find them, Doña Elena." He bowed. "I returned yesterday."

"But was your mission successful?"

"As much as could be expected."

"Well, your return is fortuitous," she said, fluttering her fan. "On Wednesday we are having some entertainment at my house. There will be music, poetry and dancing. Will you come and play the vihuela for us?"

"Duty permitting, madam," he said with the faintest of smiles.

"I hope it does," she said, lowering her voice. "Because my vihuela needs tuning, and no fingers have touched its strings in your absence."

Mendoza nodded gravely and said that he would he happy to make them sing again. He watched her leave and then moved lightly across the vast square, tapping his stick, with his black cloak trailing behind, scanning the arches and nooks and crannies in search of vice and crime as the cathedral bells rang out in celebration and the fragment of an old poem flashed through his head—"Do not be late, for I am dying, jailer / Do not be late, for I am dying"—and another voice answered back, in time with the bells, *Not yet, not yet.*

ACKNOWLEDGMENTS

I would like to thank Jonathan Ferguson and Henry Yallop, from the Royal Armouries Museum in Leeds, for sharing their knowledge and expertise regarding sixteenth-century weaponry. I also wish to extend a special thank-you to my agent, George Lucas, who saw the potential of this book at a very early stage and carefully nurtured it through to publication. Without his encouragement and support, it can truly be said that it would not have been written.